The Crazy Corner
Horrible Stories

The Crazy Corner
Horrible Stories

by
Jean Richepin

translated, annotated and introduced by
Brian Stableford

A Black Coat Press Book

ISBN 978-1-61227-142-2. First Printing. January 2013. Published by Black Coat Press, an imprint of Hollywood Comics.com, LLC, P.O. Box 17270, Encino, CA 91416. All rights reserved.
The stories and characters depicted in this novel are entirely fictional.
Printed in the United States of America.

TABLE OF CONTENTS

Introduction

Les Coin des fous, histoires horribles by Jean Richepin (1849-1926), here translated as *The Crazy Corner: Horrible Stories*, was originally published in Paris by Ernest Flammarion in 1921. It was the author's fourth collection of short stories, but a long gap separated it from the third, *Cauchemars*, published by Charpentier & Fasquelle in 1892. The stories included in *Le Coin des fous*, however, began publication immediately after the earlier collection, and the latest of them dates from 1900.

I have also translated the contents of *Cauchemars* in this collection, as "Nightmares," with the exception of one story, which I have reproduced in a slightly abridged, but otherwise unchanged, version from Richepin's fifth collection, *Contes sans morale*, issued by Flammarion in 1922 as a companion collection to *Le Coin des fous*. I have translated six stories from the latter collection here, under the heading "Tales without Morals," for purposes of comparison, but have not included another story that is a slightly modified version of the story entitled "Pft! Pft!" in *Cauchemars*. I have also added one further item from the author's collection of dramatic pieces *Théâtre chimérique*, published by Charpentier in 1896, under the heading "Chimerical Theater."[1]

As the reader of the present collection will observe, the skeletons of two of the other stories in *Cauchemars* also served as frameworks for stories in *Coin des fous*, although the flesh set on the skeletons in question is considerably transfigured. The transfiguration of earlier materials reflects a significant shift in the Parisian marketplace for short fiction that took place in the 1890s, when the daily newspaper *Le Journal* was founded as a aspirant rival to the well-established Republican paper *Le Matin*. Both papers used feuilleton fiction as a means of attracting readers, attempting to reproduce the circulation wars associated with the first big boom in feuilleton fiction in the 1840s, when Eugène Sue and Alexandre Dumas' serials competed for reader loyalty in *Le Journal des Débats* and *Le Siècle*.

Le Journal attempted to position itself upmarket of *Le Matin*, and of the other two major Parisian dailies of the period, *Le Petit Parisien* and *Le Petit Journal*, especially in literary terms, and instead of concentrating on the long action/adventure serials favored by its chief rival, its first editor, Fernand Xau, concentrated on short fiction, showcasing such writers as Octave Mirbeau and Alphonse Allais. When Xau was replaced in 1899 by Henri Letellier, the new editor followed the same policy, making more use thereafter of Jean Richepin and Edmond Haraucourt. *Le Matin* continued to rely heavily on longer serials, especially those written by its staff reporter Gaston Leroux and the prolific Jean de La Hire and Paul d'Ivoi, although it did introduce an occasional short-story section entitled *Les Mille et un matins*, while *Le Journal* began publishing more serials, poaching Leroux as well as using writers from its own stable.

The significance of this development was not simply that it broadened the Parisian market for short fiction, but that it put new pressure on the kinds of fiction written for that market because of the unusually narrow slot it offered, somewhere between 1400 and 1700 words. Alphonse Allais' wry humor was easily adaptable to that format, but Octave Mirbeau and other writers who followed in Mirbeau's footsteps in *Le Jour-*

nal developed a much blacker kind of comedy, in a genre for which the Comte de Villiers de l'Isle-Adam had provided the most widely-used label via the title of his collection *Contes cruels* (1883)[2], although it had originated in the 1830s in the short fiction of Jules Janin and Petrus Borel's *Champavert* (1831). It was in this genre that Richepin had already been working in most of his short fiction, and he adapted to the more restrictive format with considerable alacrity—including, as has been observed, adapting some of the stories he had already written. In *Le Coin des fous* he preferred the label *histoires horribles* to *contes cruels*, because "the horrible" was his particular specialty.

While Mirbeau and others celebrated the ironic cruelty of fate in a relatively slick and sophisticated fashion, Richepin developed an uncompromising ghoulishness that had much in common with the contemporary developments in drama developed and showcased at Le Théâtre du Grand-Guignol, which opened in 1897. Of all the late 19th century writers of *contes cruels*, Richepin was the cruelest when it came to the treatment of his characters, not so much in the nasty fates to which they were often delivered—which are typical of the entire genre—but in the merciless way in which he describes and characterizes them. This is why his stories were more horrible than horrific; they do not attempt to frighten their readers, as some horror stories do, but to evoke a reaction in a different part the spectrum of horror, closer to indigo than red in metaphorical terms.

Le Coin des fous also illustrates the fact that there was a partial rehabilitation of supernatural *contes cruels*, at least for a while, in the 1890s, closely associated with the rise in the *fin-de-siècle* period of the overlapping Decadent and Symbolist Movements. Some writers associated with those movements eschewed the supernatural, including Mirbeau, who also

---

[2] Available in Black Coat Press editions as *The Scaffold* (ISBN 978-1-932983-01-2) and *The Vampire Soul* (ISBN 978-1-932983-02-9).

had strong Naturalist sympathies, and Richepin—who was also ambiguous in his affiliation—had originally placed himself in that camp, but the sheer stress of turning out stories of brief dimension in quantity made supernatural twists very tempting. Even with that addition to his range however, the whole spectrum of the stories translated in this collection show the author wrestling continually with the problem of finding appropriate endings for his sketchy exercises in grotesquerie, sometimes to the extent that he attempts to make a virtue out of refusing to provide an ending.

In this connection, it is worth observing that the stories were written in a period when the underlying theory and method of short story writing were undergoing a significant transition. The traditional "tale," which achieves brevity by exploiting the synoptic prerogatives of a manifest teller, was in the process of giving ground to a mode of story-telling that attempted to borrow the immediacy of novelistic technique without the detail and length previously deemed necessary to achieve and cement that immediacy: the "slice of life" story. That method of short story writing reduces the narrative distance between a teller and reader by employing a passive narrative voice situated much closer to the protagonist's stream of consciousness, and substituting brief impressionistic references for elaborate description. Its development was primarily associated in France with Guy de Maupassant, but it was also favored by Mirbeau. Richepin remains something of a traditionalist in this regard, but the pressure of the new fashion is evident in the manner in which he deploys and characterizes first-person narrators, and abbreviates the reportage through which their accounts are usually filtered. If he shuns the solution that has since become orthodox, he is nevertheless grappling with the problem in his own fashion.

Richepin was luckier that many writers who produced stories for *Le Journal*'s slot, in contriving to have them reprinted in book form, albeit belatedly, although his contemporary Edmond Haraucourt did manage to publish two volumes of short stories including *contes cruels* in his own particular vein, and most of Villiers' and Mirbeau's work was reprinted reasonably promptly. In general, book publishers preferred longer and meatier works even in story collections—the reader will observe that *Cauchemars* includes an original novella alongside its shorter pieces in order to bulk them out. Many stories of the brief length favored by *Le Journal* and the *Mille et un matins* series are, in fact, calculatedly trivial, and even the finest exponents of the form do not always escape triviality, but it is nevertheless an interesting format, both in terms of the extreme pressure it puts on narrative method and in terms of the crucial role it played in the evolution of the *conte cruel*. Richepin was one of the most distinctive exponents of the form, and one of the most striking, as this showcase will hopefully serve to illustrate.

The translation of *Coin des fous* was taken from the Bibliothèque Nationale's copy of the Flammarion edition, as reproduced on its website *gallica*, but that copy is defective and is missing four pages; I am indebted to Jean-Marc Lofficier for obtaining and supplying the missing text. The translations from *Cauchemars* and *Contes sans morales* were also taken from the *gallica* versions, while the translation of the story from *Théâtre Chimérique* was taken from the version reproduced on archive.org. Where I have been able to ascertain dates and places of original publication I have added them to the titles of the stories as footnotes.

Brian Stableford

THE CRAZY CORNER

To Max and Alex Fischer,[3]
in memory of our "extralucid" evening,
I dedicate this book affectionately.
J.R.

---

[3] The brothers Max[ime] (1880-1957) and Alex[andre] (1881-1935) Fischer wrote mostly humorous fiction in collaboration from 1900 until Alex's death; they were the literary directors of the Ernest Flammarion imprint for many years, from 1904 onwards.

Lilith[4]

The first time the two young men had witnessed the strange scene they had not suspected anything strange, and they had scarcely taken any notice of it.

After having left their poor mansard by its sole skylight, they had installed themselves in the broad guttering of the roof in order to smoke a pipe in the tranquility of the mild late autumn evening, and they were only thinking about savoring their relaxation while breathing the fresh air rising from the large trees in the solitary garden. Their legs hanging down among the highest leaves, at the very top of the bare wall, devoid of any opening, which served as the background of the garden, they did not even think of looking to see whether anything was happening beneath them. They had, therefore, seen the strange scene, that first time, almost unconsciously, and had no suspicion of anything strange therein.

It had been almost the same the second time, and that occasion had not excited them even more, although they had experienced a slight surprise on seeing exactly the same scene reproduced at exactly the same time.

So what, though? One reflection, was there anything surprising in the fact that the old man behaved for a second time in an identical fashion in identical circumstances? Undoubtedly, hazard alone was the cause of the scenes of the other evening and this one seemed to be the same one, scrupulously repeated. It was a coincidence, of course—no more.

The scene, moreover offered nothing in itself that was not quite simple and quite natural, did it? It was the banal action of an old man making a tour of his garden before going to bed, and calling to someone to come out—his wife, his servant or his dog—and calling in that particular voice because he had

---

[4] *Le Gaulois*, 11 November 1895.

15

that particular voice, and at precisely the same time because that happened to be the time, and that was all!

But the two young men had been forced to astonishment, and to judge the scene positively strange, when, thereafter, their attention awakened and their curiosity on the alert, they were convinced that the repetition of the actions and gestures could not be attributed to hazard, that the old man's conduct was habitual and deliberate, and that the slightest details seemed to have been regulated once and for all, minutely and, one could easily believe, ritually.

Every evening, whatever the weather, even on rainy evenings when the two young men allowed themselves to be soaked in their gutter rather than not see it, the same bizarre ceremony had taken place.

Just at the moment when the last vibrations of the nearby clock were sounding a quarter to midnight, the two battens of the French windows of the pavilion opened, and the old man appeared, clad in a long overcoat, bare-headed, carrying above his head a little muted lantern with a thin and pale beam of light.

He leaned to the left, then to the right, and then forwards, with slow movements that had initially appeared to the two young men to be the attitudes of someone leaning forward in order to see better into the shadows, but which now represented themselves as manifest salutations, like those of a priest to an idol.

The old man then took three large strides forward, and two small ones back—and repeated that combination of steps three times, once in each direction in which he had bowed.

Having arrived thus at the entrance to a cypress arbor, which formed a dense labyrinth in the middle of his garden, he swiftly blew out his lantern, and then, in a plaintive, whistling, emphatic voice, which was low but nevertheless carried a long way, he called into the darkness of the labyrinth: "Lilith! Lilith! Lilith!"

What did he do in the labyrinth? How long did he stay there? By what exit did he emerge to go back to his pavilion? That was what the young men were never able to determine.

The old man probably came back by means of a path that ran along the left hand all of the garden, garnished with a bower of virgin vines, which circled around the pavilion in such a way that he could get back in through a door located on the other side—but that was only a supposition, because no furtive human footsteps were audible on the gravel of that pathway, and his extinct lantern did not permit any divination of where he went.

The only thing of which the two young men were certain was that he stayed in the labyrinth for at least a quarter of an hour. When the clock sounded the first stroke of midnight, the old man's voice could be heard there, now as if coming from underground, doubtless because of the thickness of the cypresses—and that voice was no longer appealing, but seemed thankful, and said only once, with a profound sigh of ecstasy: "Lilith!"

The two young men were "apprentice great men"—that was what they called themselves, those poor, ambitious adolescents hungry for power and glory, of the sort that reading Balzac could still create forty years ago. They had made their poverty communal in that Montrouge mansard, where they each took turns to serve the other as cook and housekeeper, and where they had both promised to be Orestes and Pylades, Nisus and Euryale, Pierre and Jaffier.[5]

They said to one another: "We'll discover the old man's secret of. Perhaps it will be the commencement of our fortune."

---

[5] The first two pairs of exemplary friends derive from Classical mythology; the third is from Thomas Otway's play *Venice Preserv'd* (1682), but the latter is surely included because of its citation by the schemer Vautrin in Honoré de Balzac's *Le Père Goriot* (1835).

With prudence and cunning, they asked around the neighborhood. They learned that the old man have lived there for a long time, looked after by his aged wife, his granddaughter and a maidservant. Yes, looked after—for he was, it seemed, a little crazy. The granddaughter hardly ever went out. Only the old woman was occasionally seen outside; she went to the market herself. They were *rentiers*, owners of the pavilion and the garden. The old man had been "some kind of a teacher." In spite of the fellow's craziness, they were "well-thought-of in the neighborhood."

Armed with a name and the "some kind of teacher" the two young men set out in quest of further information. They did, indeed, find traces of the old man at the Collège de France. Briefly, a long time ago, he had taught a course there on Assyriology. He had published two pamphlets on Chaldean magic. Those publications had got him sacked, as a lunatic.

At the Bibliothèque Nationale, the two young men asked for the pamphlets, tried to understand them, and were obliged to give up. The sentences therein were bristling with occult formulae and shibboleth terms, and thus written either, indeed, by a madman, or with the design of constructing an indecipherable cryptogram They could not discern anything therein but the name of Lilith, repeated to the point of saturation.

They admitted to one another that it was necessary to seek the commencement of their fortune elsewhere than in the old man's seemingly-vain secret.

Well, they were wrong, and the absurd imagination to which their reading of Balzac had driven them was right. They learned that only a few days ago, and I saw them both become singularly pensive when they were informed of it, and go pale with bitter regret.

It was at one of those dinners whose foundation is also due to a Balzacian idea, at which people of the same generation, all of whom emerged together from the Parisian battle and all of whom have more-or-less hollowed their niche in life, meet up for years on end, three or four times every winter.

The two young men are participants in one such dinner, but only figure there, alas, in minor parts. The former apprentice great men have not become great men. One of them is simply a government official; the other, a good advocate, is the head of a legal firm that does not handle major cases. In the Parisian battle in which they hoped to play Napoléon, they are survivors, no more. They gladly put the blame on destiny, saying: "We didn't have a lucky break."

They were talking about an old comrade who had had all the luck: honorary positions, lucrative positions, renown, power, fortune, happiness—he lacked nothing, as was repeated enviously.

"One could easily believe," someone said, "that he's a sorcerer who has a talisman. I'd think so, if we weren't in the 19th century."

"We've hit the nail on the head," replied Z***. "I can affirm, personally, that our former comrade is indeed a sorcerer in possession of a talisman." And, as people laughed, he added: "He's the heir of the last priest of Lilith, and he possesses a fragment of black stone."

Z*** then told us the story of an old scholar, an Assyriologist and mage, who had been reputed to be mad, and whose granddaughter had been espoused by our comrade.

Everyone knows that Z*** is one of our best straight-faced humorists, and that he loves to play tricks even on his closest friends, but as he does so wittily, with inventions of the most brilliant fantasy, people listen without resentment and even thank him for putting one over on them. Everyone therefore savored his pretended revelations, his air of mystery and the rich imagination he deployed in reviving the fantastic old man, the last priest of Lilith and possessor of the fragment of black stone that is the ultimate *open sesame* of her supreme worshipers.

Among all those charmed and attentive guests, however, two drank in his words open-mouthed, wide-eyed and pale-faced, racked by dolorous tics. They were the two former apprentice great men, who were tormented by a retrospective and impotent avarice, and the certainty that it was not a fanciful tale, that the comrade who had had all the luck owed it to a real and authentic talisman, that they might have been the esteemed and triumphant Jasons, but that they had lacked the faith necessary to obtain it.

And I, who had once been the confidant of their singular and vain adventure, now saw again, in the troubled mirror of their dilated pupils, behind the veil of suppressed tears that filled them like a tragic fog, the strange scene that they had described to me forty years before, with disdainfully skeptical smiles, of the old man making his three salutes to the idol of shadow, executing his magical march toward the labyrinth and calling into the depths of ancient darkness to the ancient goddess who was thought to be abolished but perhaps lives on, still omnipotent:

"Lilith! Lilith! Lilith!"

A Legacy[6]

I'll be damned if I had ever expected to be the legatee one day, however small the inheritance might be, of old Doctor Amable Cherpillard!

Undoubtedly he had once been a comrade in the Latin Quarter, and then a colleague, of my father's—but not, however, his friend! Of that I was certain; their relationship, long-standing though it was, had never been intimate at any time. As for me, personally, I had hardly had any contact with him, even in the distant days when I went every year to spend my summer vacations with my parents in Wimeurs-les-Eppes. I had known him then, above all, by reputation, and as some sort of poor imbecile to whom I had never manifested any great sympathy. Finally, in the course of the last twenty years, no longer going back there after the death of my parents, I had completely lost sight of him.

There was, therefore, no plausible reason for the fellow to have thought of putting me in his will, and even less for him to have thought of doing so in such a singular and romantic manner. It was, however, necessary for me you yield to the evidence. The notary's letter was there, in front of my bewildered eyes. It informed me that Doctor Amable Cherpillard had left me…a sealed letter, which would be put into my own hands, on the express condition that I would, after having read it, burn it in the presence of the said notary.

However little attraction the posthumous confidence of a man of no significance at all could promise me, my curiosity was excited by it even so, so alluring is the romantic—and I took the train.

During the journey I reproached myself a thousand times for allowing myself to be hooked by such a bait, as all the de-

---

[6] *Le Journal*, 13 June 1899.

tails I had once heard about the character and life of the old doctor gradually came back to me. They reconstituted a physiognomy truly devoid of interest. What more was I about to learn about the old imbecile? It would surely not be worth the trip!

To begin with, I recalled, in vivid colors, the face of Amable Cherpillaud, on the day when I had seen it for the first time—the day of his marriage—forty years ago. Oh, the sad, ridiculous, ingrate face, more lamentable than ever in such circumstances, even more lamentably sad, ridiculous and ingrate!

Amable Cherpillaud was then about fifty years-old, but fifty years pickled in provincial ennui, in the consciousness of a dull and animal ugliness, in the routine of a life devoid of thought, action and ambition. A poor little country doctor, who had, until then, lived on a hazardous clientele, he had just come into an inheritance that permitted him to live henceforth in the renunciation of a profession that he did not like—and the bitter bile of all his past frustrations was plainly legible on his thin face, simultaneously sullen and proud, along with the base joy of now being envied.

That was all that could be read there, though; nothing else. Beneath those two hints of green and red, which were manifestly temporary, was the everyday pallor that would resume its neutral, uniform, bleak grayness—the emblem of an irremediable and essential imbecility.

And yet, a true joy, a joy of passion, ought to have flourished there that day, on that stupid face, and transfigured it, since the doctor, thanks to his money, was marrying the most beautiful girl in the neighborhood—but he did not even seem to be smitten with the radiant Madeleine Grimblet, blossoming in the glory of her seventeen florid years, so pale and so pink beneath her curly hair, like clusters of black grapes, so "well set," as they say out there, with her young still-virginal grace and her hips, already rounded, and her curvaceous womanly bosom, ripe for love.

No, he seemed to be marrying her solely to put one over on all those who desired her—and that visible sentiment rendered him even uglier beside such splendor: a thin and dried up old man, a half-plucked cockerel, a scarecrow with hare's-tail side-whiskers, a long vulpine nose, narrow and wrinkled eyes, a turkey's neck, slack, lobeless ears, an interminably stupid upper lip, a curt and fugitive chin, and pale lips giving him a mouth like the slot of a money-box.

And I had always seen him, after that, getting even uglier with age, while his wife became ever more lovely, and became the beautiful Madame Cherpillaud—no longer merely the most beautiful daughter of the locality but, as current fashion puts it, the queen of the region.

And as current fashion also puts it, what was then said was that Madame Cherpillaud, utterly devoted as she was, and very devoted, played the old imbecile for a fool. Oh, without the slightest scandal, of course, as these things are done in the provinces. Wearing the trousers and manipulating the simpleton ostentatiously, she indulged the fantasies of a fiery temperament at home—or so the secret chronicle said. Cherpillaud being unable to satisfy her, the task fell, it appears, to the gardener.

Thus, at least, with a great reinforcement of laughter, said the Brantômes[7] of Wimeurs-les-Eppes. They even added that the gardeners succumbed to the task, one after another, no matter well-chosen and well cared-for they were—and I had a very clear memory, in fact, of always seeing some new strapping lad in the doctor's service on each of my trips out there: some thickset and robust rustic, of whom I heard it said later that he had soon perished and had "gone the way of consumption."

---

[7] Pierre de Bourdeilles, Abbé et Seigneur de Brantôme (1535-1614) was a memorialist whose anecdotal accounts of "great captains" and "gallant ladies" are generally reckoned to be more amusing that accurate.

In the same way, the memory came to mind of having heard drunks, on evenings of celebration, singing a lewd and mocking popular song at the doctor's expense, of which I shall only cite one verse, because the others—especially the last—risk too much honesty.

Do you know what I eat
When I eat at home?
I'm forced to eat oatmeal.
Poor folk, that's not good.
I have lots of good white bread.
It's white and soft;
But it's for our wife
And her va-a-let.
Tra la la la la, my wife's for others.
Tra la la la la, my wife's not for me.

And I also recalled that Amable Cherpillaud did not flinch under the insult, imperturbably retaining his complexion of a neutral, uniform, bleak grayness—the emblem of an irremediable and essential imbecility.

In truth, he gave the impression of either being a consenting individual, as was repeated, to his shame, or of knowing absolutely nothing at all, as his air of perfect stupidity might have caused one to believe.

Other details were revived in my memory, but they added very little to the fellow's physiognomy. Those I got from my father. In his estimation, Cherpillaud was a very paltry scientific intelligence, who had only scraped through his doctorate and had never worked thereafter, clinging to the old methods of fifty years before, bleeding his patients with leeches—and who, in sum, had sinned most of all, as a physician and as a man, by virtue of an absolute stupidity combined with the most crippling weakness.

It was with these memories and notions regarding the doctor that I arrived at Wimeurs-les-Eppes, entirely regretting the journey that a vain curiosity had caused me to undertake, and convinced that the poor imbecile's legacy could not possibly be anything interesting, in spite of its romantic form.

The notary handed the sealed letter to me ceremoniously, in front of a large log fire that was blazing as if it were conscious of having soon to fulfill a legal duty. That fire and the ministerial officer had a majesty that obliged me an equal majesty in breaking the five large seals of red wax. I thought that we—the fire, the notary and myself—formed a consummate grotesque.

To make myself slightly less self-conscious, I risked a timid joke about the beautiful Madame Cherpillard and the gardeners, knowing that the notary had once been one of the filthiest Brantômes of Wimeurs-les-Eppes.

The notary interrupted me, croaking as gravely as a crow: "Madame Cherpillaud died six months ago, of cancer."

I swallowed my saliva, and started quietly reading the piece of paper, which said:

For you, Parisian spirit who must despise provincials in general, and, in particular, the poor imbecile that I appear to be, these few notes are written.

I loved Madeleine profoundly and I could not do without her—her body, I mean.

I am faithful to the doctrines of Cabanis,[8] absolutely materialistic and atheistic. I do not believe in remorse.

Nevertheless, without anyone being aware of it, I kept up to date with the doctrine of Pasteur. I believe in microbes.

For ten years, my wife, convinced of my omnipotence, was completely and delightfully submissive to me.

I want her to die with me and therefore she will, my wishes in that regard having already been executed.

---

[8] The physician Georges Cabanis (1757-1808) published a famous *Traité du physique et moral de l'homme* in 1802, which caused something of a sensation in espousing the doctrines cited.

I do not know whether tuberculosis and cancer will ever be cured, but I know perfectly well how to induce them.

Acquaint yourself with the story of my life, if you do not know it, and conclude, young man, by telling yourself, like Balzac, that great eccentrics and great criminals are only to be found in the provinces.

I threw the piece of paper in the fire, put on my hat, and ran swiftly to catch the train to go back to Paris, where the eccentrics and the criminals do, indeed, have less opportunity to become great, occupied as they are, like everyone else, in an incessant battle, amid turbulent hosts of boors.

The Clock[9]

With a grave and slightly cracked voice, melancholy in its timbre in the calm evening air that it rent with an abrupt sob, the first stroke of seven rang out from the bell-tower of the Hôtel de Ville.

Like soldiers on parade, whose automatic gesture is triggered by a command, all the pedestrians in the Mall came to a halt, reached for their fob-pockets, took out their watches, checked the time on the dials of the watches, put them back into their fob-pockets, shaking their heads sadly, and raised their arms to the heavens.

Then, with a voice as melancholy in its timbre as that of the bell-tower, almost with sobs like the ones continuing to rend the calm evening air, they said to one another, in tearful groups:

"I make it five to seven myself."

"Me, five past seven."

"Me, two minutes past seven."

"Me, three minutes to seven."

"Me, one minute to."

"Me, half a minute past."

But none—absolutely none—showed exactly seven.

And as an old man appeared in the Mall at that moment, heading toward the Église des Génovéfains,[10] all gazes bombarded that old man with reproaches, which were no less indignant for being silent, some even going so far as to manifest

---

[9] *Le Journal*, 14 March 1900.

[10] Genovefa is the Latin form of the French Geneviève, the name of a legendary saint widely revered for having saved Paris from Attila's Huns by fervent prayer, and became the guiding light of an order of canons and nuns that spread throughout France in the 17th century.

not merely indignation but scorn, and some, even a veritable horror.

The old man, however, did not present, either in his gait or in his physiognomy, anything seemingly capable of inspiring such a violent, undisguised and unanimously vengeful antipathy.

He was dressed in the most decent fashion, which denoted the most respectable of bourgeois individuals. His shoes were coarse, but well-polished. His trousers, a little too short, were not frayed. His jacket, a little too long, only gave a little more majesty to his tall stature. Besides which, age had not curved that stature, which the old man held upright with the special pride that is the prerogative of a clear conscience.

His clean-shaven face, pale beneath long white hair, was not content, as they say, to respire honesty; it positively transpired it—and the two most luminous droplets of that venerable transpiration were the old man's eyes: two eyes of pure diamond, In which shone, simultaneously, a mystical exaltation, a child-like candor, a patriarchal serenity and a heroic valor.

What secret reasons, then, could have led all those pedestrians in the Mall—and, by their mute intermediary, the entire town—to manifest toward the old man so much indignation, and so much scorn, not to say horror.

That is what you will begin to understand, or at least to suspect, when you know that the old man was the only clockmaker in the little town, that all the church clocks, pendulum clocks and pocket watches in the town were regulated by him, that they had always kept time admirably for more than thirty years, and that he was presently neglecting them.

But why was he neglecting them at present? Through what breach had his disrupted professional honorability fled? How had that pure gold been transmuted into vulgar lead? Ah, that's a long story! Listen, instead, to the reflections of the people.

"Look, he's going to spend the night at the Église des Génovéfains again."

"He'll be there until tomorrow morning with his folly."

"Then, naturally, during the day, he can't do any more."

"And he resets watches any old how.

"And he goes to sleep over the pendulum clocks, instead of watching over them as before."

"He doesn't even bother with the Hôtel de Ville clock anymore."

"He doesn't care about anything but the old crock over there."

"And I ask you, what's the point? He's mad—completely mad."

"Obviously, since the cleverest haven't been able to make head nor tail of it."

"He'll come off worse than that, mark my words."

"The clientele comes first, doesn't it? Like me..."

"Me too, of course! Just let another clockmaker set up in business here, and we'll see, once and for all."

"One's coming from Saint-Jean, I've been told."

"So much the worse for Père Bringard. He'll die of starvation."

"Unless he dies of old age before then..."

"That might be the best thing for him. There's danger over there."

"Oh, not only danger from machines, you know!"

"Yes, yes, I know—even more so from legends."

"Exactly. Is it true or isn't it? Still, our forefathers were no more stupid than we are, eh? Well, they believed, and firmly, that one couldn't touch it without it bringing you bad luck."

"Which doesn't prevent the old madman from running off yet again, to spend all night flirting with his old vagabond witch of a clock."

For it is, in fact, a matter of a clock. At the Église des Génovéfains there is an ancient clock, one of those fabricated in the Middle Ages by patient workmen who consecrated their entire lives to it, multiplying its cogwheels, its pulleys, its weights and its counterweights in order that, at the hours of the Angelus, one would hear it sing interminable and cheerful carillons, while from its face, opening like a tabernacle, the Holy Virgin would emerge, to whom the Angel Gabriel bowed, and before whom filed in slow procession the holy apostles, six for the morning Angelus and six for the evening Angelus, and all twelve for the midday Angelus.

Now, for many years, if not forever, the ancient clock of the Église des Génovéfains had been broken down—and there were, indeed, legends about that: like the one asserting that the master clockmaker who had constructed it had only completed the task with the aid of the Devil; and the one claiming that, after a certain number of revolutions, the Devil had stopped the clock; and the one declaring that the secret of it had been lost forever, and that misfortune befell anyone who tried to recover that secret—and a whole string of stories embroidered on that subject by the popular imagination.

Today, of course, hardly anyone believed any longer in those legends and stories. A few people still talked about them, but only to laugh at them. But Père Bringard, personally, did not laugh at them. And, by dint of thinking about them, after thirty years of long meditation, he had ended up believing in them.

In particular he believed this: that the soul of the master clockmaker of old had been a captive of the Devil since the day the clock stopped working, and that the poor soul in question would be liberated when the clock worked again. And, mostly thanks to that charitable hope, and also a little because of his pride as a clockmaker, he had harnessed himself to the task of repairing the clock, putting all his patient ingenuity into the task, and all his faith.

To the very few friends who remained to him, and who took pity on his madness, and tried to cure him of it, he replied confidently: "I'll get there. I've already done this and that. One more exact weight to find, of a particular metal, and the clock will work, you'll see."

Meanwhile, he spent all his time and his nights on it, and neglected all the clocks and watches in the town, and became an object of indignation, of scorn, and even of horror—but he had not been cured, and had redoubled his efforts toward his chimera, wanting to attain it before dying, and thinking every day that he was a little closer to the point of attaining it, and passing through the hostile groups, repeating like a chorus: "Tonight I'll surely be finished. It will be tomorrow, at midday. Tomorrow, at midday, the clock will work. Tomorrow, at midday. Tomorrow, at midday."

But the days went by without the clock working—and now, urchins followed Père Bringard through the streets, yapping: "Hoo! Hoo! Have you made it work, the Delusion? Tomorrow, at midday. Tomorrow, at midday."

And yet, one fine day, at midday, from the belfry of the Génovéfiens, the carillon rang out, *ding ding dong*, singing its joyful song, while from the face of the clock, opening like a tabernacle, the Holy Virgin emerged, to whom the Angel Gabriel bowed, and before whom filed in slow procession the twelve apostles.

A miracle! A miracle!

People ran from all over town. They searched for Père Bringard to give him an ovation. They cried that he was the glory of the region. They waxed ecstatic before the resuscitated clock. Miscreants were weeping with joy.

But Père Bringard could no longer hear anything, or see anything. From one of the chains of the clock, in the guise of a weight—liberating the soul of the master clockmaker of old by finally making his beloved work—the old man had hanged himself.

The Parrot[11]

"Don't forget, Monsieur," the bric-à-brac merchant continued, "that the parrot is part of the lot. Exactly—the parrot! Including the perch, of course."

As I shrugged my shoulders again, he went on, listing the objects and pointing them out with his finger, after a smack of the lips that attempted to incite my admiration. "A considerable lot, Monsieur, one might say! Plenty to satisfy a collector. The herbal! The collection of seashells! The album of mineralogy! The six volumes of unpublished writings! And finally the parrot, along with its perch!"

"Don't go on!" I replied. "Once again, I wouldn't know what to do with it all."

"What!" he exclaimed, with a well-feigned expression of astonishment. "Not even the parrot?"

"Especially the parrot."

"Oh," he said, "that's a pity, a real pity. Such a curious animal, so rare! What a specimen! And the only one of its kind, one may say! For myself, Monsieur, believe it or not, but I've never seen one like it in my entire life."

"Well, me neither, obviously!"

It was, in fact, the most extraordinary parrot, not only that my eyes had ever encountered, but that my imagination would ever have been able to dream up, so old, ugly, thin, bald, scrawny, featherless, bleak, dull, colorless, misshapen, pitiful, wretched, shabby, dilapidated, lamentable, implausible, asthmatic, phantasmal, emaciated and problematic was it.

But for a sort of cough that shook it from time to time, it might have been stuffed: an exceedingly old stuffed bird, worm-eaten, from which, at every cough, a little sepulchral dust fell and blew away.

---

[11] *Le Gaulois*, 2 February 1896.

One of its eyes, too, which a fit of asthma had caused it to open slightly, retained some semblance of life. A vague spark then lit up therein, in a pupil the color of frosted glass. The other eye, staved in and dried up, was nothing but a black hole.

Between coughs, its immobility remained absolute. The specter became a mummy again.

"It will definitely be dead by tonight," I told the bric-à-brac seller.

"Oh no, Monsieur!" he replied. "It's been like that for years and years, to my knowledge. At any rate, for the last fifteen years that it's been with me, I've never seen it any different. Its late master assured me that he had always seen it the same way—and the poor fellow died virtually a centenarian. So judge for yourself! It was him, the dead man, from which all this rubbish came, bought at auction after his death. A considerable lot, isn't it, Monsieur?"

And the tradesman began once again to list the items, terminating this time with: "Twenty-five francs the lot! Yes, Monsieur, I'll let you have the lot for twenty-five francs. And I mean the whole lot, including the parrot and its perch."

In reality, among all that rubbish, as he put it, I could not find much to interest me. The herbal, the shell collection and the mineralogy album were wretched second-hand gods composed of disparate pieces and fragments. By the funereal and dust-covered parrot, I was positively horrified. The only thing that interested me slightly—very slightly—was the stack of manuscripts. And even them...

Personally, certainly not—but I had thought that perhaps they would be of some interest for one of my friends, the dyed-in-the-wool Basque Vincent Ytzirgayn.

There were five thick wads tied up with string and an enormous open satchel. Now, in riffling through pages taken at hazard from the satchel, I had realized that their subject-matter was dear to Vincent Ytzirgayn's heart—to wit, Basque linguistics and ethnography. The handwriting was an almost indecipherable scribble, but the satchel doubtless only contained notes and rough drafts. On the other hand, the five thick parcels seemed to be a fair copy of the finished work. On the red paper covers, carefully inscribed in well-rounded characters were the significant titles: *Roots, Nouns, Verbs, Prefixes and Suffices* and *Agglutination.*

Was it a question of an original work, or merely a second-hand accumulation? I didn't know the Basque language well enough to decide—but Ytzirgayn knew it well, and in any case, I was sure that it would give him pleasure to see that voluminous file for investigation.

I pointed to the papers with a casual and disdainful gesture and said to the dealer: "How much do you want just for that?"

"Aha!" he exclaimed. "So you're a collector of manuscripts—and a connoisseur, that's obvious! Very precious and very rare manuscripts, Monsieur! The dead man held them in very high esteem. He spent his entire life writing them. He said..."

"How much do you want for them?" I interjected, annoyed by the patter that he was about to resume.

The haste that I displayed to conclude the bargain doubtless seemed to the cunning salesman to be the manifestation of a violent desire that he could exploit. "I can't break up the lot, Monsieur," he replied. "It's twenty-five francs for the lot. That's my final price—and very fair!" And he seemed to me to combine his cunning with a facetious irony in adding: "Including the parrot, and its perch, of course."

But not at all—truly, it wasn't irony. I was obliged to admit that when, having received the twenty-five francs, on which he was not prepared to offer any discount, he went on: "You're not taking it, then, the parrot?"

"No!" I replied, impatiently. "How many times do I have to tell you? Neither the parrot, nor the herbal, nor the..."

"Oh," he said, "I don't care about the rest. It isn't worth the trouble, I agree. But that, Monsieur—the parrot—I assure you that you ought to take."

While wrapping up the five wads and the satchel in a large piece of yellow paper, which he folded and refolded in order to make the task last longer, the tradesman continued: "It's old and ugly, I don't deny—but its old age is a curiosity. Oh, just think that it might be hundreds of years old, that animal! Exactly—several hundred years! Its late master claimed, it seems..."

"You're annoying me with your parrot. I don't want it. I wouldn't want it if you paid me to take it. There—is that understood?"

And I completed the wrapping myself, in order to save time—but the bric-à-brac dealer grabbed me by the arm and said: "Hold on, Monsieur. Take it, with its perch, and I'll give you back five francs."

"Aha!" I cried. "So it's an embarrassment to you, that parrot?"

"No, no," he said, utterly crestfallen.

"Then why are you so determined to foist it on me?"

"Because...because you have a face that reminds me of a client I once had—a collector! And I wanted you to profit from...a good opportunity."

I burst out laughing and fled, after hurling at him, by way of farewell: "Well, keep it for yourself, my man—including its perch, of course."

The last letter that my friend Vincent Ytzirgayn had written to me was postmarked Madeira. He had gone to study the autochthonous population, in which, he claimed, subsisted—or ought to subsist—a residue of the ancient Atlantean race. That race is also, in his estimation, represented by certain American peoples and by the Basques. He had extremely curious hypotheses and theories in that regard, which would probably make scholars smile, but enchant poets like fairy tales.

It was to Madeira that I sent the five wads of paper bound with string and the satchel full of notes, not without having cast an eye over them myself. But I confess that I had rapidly been put off by the damnable scribble of the handwriting, which was truly too indecipherable.

Two months later, I received by way of reply the following telegram:

Was on mountain excursion. Why is parrot not with papers? Parrot indispensable. Where is it? Am returning.

I was away from Paris at the time myself. By the time that the telegram took to be transmitted to me, in a letter that took nearly a week to catch up with me, and I had returned to Paris. I found that my friend Vincent Ytzirgayn had got the before me, and that he had been waiting for me at my house for two days, mad with impatience.

The first thing he said—his first exclamation—on seeing me, was: "Where's the parrot?" Then, without even giving me time to reply. He went on: "Oh, my friend, what a find! What luck! Can you imagine that these papers are a mine of arguments for my theory! Certain proof! The author has established the connections I've been seeking between the linguistic and ethnological branches of America and Europe. The old language of Atlantis, the mother tongue, which was thought to be dead, still lives. The manuscripts are proof of it—but I'll explain that on the way. Where's the parrot to which the manuscripts make reference? Where it is? Let's go search for it? I need it."

In the cab, he cleared up my confusion by explaining his urgency. The author of the manuscripts had obtained the parrot from a sailor who had brought it back from Mexico with tablets in Aztec. The tablets, once read, affirmed the genealogy of the bird, a descendant of the bird-priests, custodians of the sacred language.

"The language of Atlantis, my dear chap—yes, the dead language of Atlantis. And it talks, it talks, that three-hundred-year-old parrot, child and grandchild of similar parrots. It talks, I tell you. Where is it?"[12]

---

[12] This story-idea was not original to Richepin, having been previously deployed by Paul Vibert in a story reprinted in *Pour lire en automobile* (1901; tr. as *The Mysterious Fluid*). Vibert, however, acknowledges that he appropriated the idea

We had arrived at the bric-à-brac dealer's. In the shop window, I saw the perch.

"Where's the bird?" I demanded, anxiously, gripped by my friend's fever.

"The parrot, Monsieur?" replied the dealer. "Well, it ate five sous' worth of cooked meat a day, that parrot, and every night it chattered away as if the Devil had got hold of it."

"That's why you wanted to stick me with it, eh?"

"Damn it, yes—I can tell you that now, Monsieur. And that's why, in the end, I killed it."

"Killed it!" cried Vincent Ytzirgayn. "You killed it!"

I thought that he was about to seize the tradesman by the throat. I had to grab him around the wait to stop him.

"Murderer!" he shouted. Then, he sobbed: "The sacred parrot! The descendant of the bird-priests! The last of the Atlanteans!"

I calmed him down as best I could. The shopkeeper made signs to me behind his back indicating that the poor fellow was doubtless mad. I replied mutely, with my gaze, that I couldn't deny it.

"And did it say anything as it died?" asked Vincent Ytzirgaym, finally, having calmed down a little, but with his eyes full of tears.

"Yes, Monsieur."

"Do you remember the words it pronounced?"

"It only pronounced one, Monsieur."

"What was it?"

"Quawk!"

---

for a story series contained in that collection from the title of Richepin's first collection, *Les Morts bizarres* and refers to Richepin as a neighbor, so the reproduction of the theme probably had the original user's blessing.

The Two Portraits[13]

It is well-known that Orientals do not like having their picture taken. They have the superstition of believing that it is necessary to take a little of the model's soul to animate the image, and that the portrait thus becomes a double of the sitter, surviving him and still subject to the adventures, dangers, sufferings and passions of terrestrial existence.

Perhaps, after all, it is not a superstition, and there is something real in that chimerical belief. The artifice of nature, Bossuet[14] says, is inexplicable; that of art is no less so. Anything is possible. Who knows?

An Oriental sage would certainly not be astonished by the following astonishing story. He would find it not merely plausible but quite simple. What would astonish him is that anyone would find it astonishing. For myself, while reluctant to share the bizarre opinion of Orientals regarding the survival of portraits, I confess that the story seems rather strange to me. I shall tell it, in any case, without trying to clarify its mystery, and without exaggeration, leaving scientific and skeptical minds the care of deciding whether it really does contain a mystery of singular magic, or only the appearance of one.

One day, in a boutique that I often visit, as a window-shopper rather than a customer, feasting my eyes on old paintings, precious prints, rare books, trinkets, items of furniture, curiosities, *objets d'art* and old fabrics, I noticed two rather fine portraits, which attracted my attention precisely because of their lifelike intensity.

Certainly, they were not badly painted, doubtless the work of some accomplished portrait-painter of the English

---

[13] *Le Journal*, 5 December 1898.

[14] The celebrated orator, historian and critic Jacques-Bénigne Bossuet (1627-1704).

school that flourished at the beginning of this century, but they did not bear, in their composition, the hallmark of a master, even an obscure master having produced therein two unknown masterpieces. One sensed in them the sage and sure work of an honest pupil devoid of genius, and nothing more. In sum, therefore, as paintings, from a purely artistic point of view, they were of no great value.

They must, however, have borne an extraordinary resemblance to their models. That was appreciable right away, without it being necessary to have seen the models in question—and it is in that respect that the Orientals' notion became imposing. Evidently, to animate the effigies to that extent, it had been necessary to remove a little of their souls to the effigies, and it was the souls in question that continued to illuminate the eyes of the two portraits so ardently, so splendidly and with such marvelous life.

That soul, moreover, in each work, was quite special and characteristic. It was a hateful soul. Nevertheless, the hatred gleamed differently in the two gazes, and the artist had been able to render that difference with a force and clarity of expression that permitted the *present* sentiments of the two individuals to be read in full, without any hesitation or possible uncertainty.

I say "present" deliberately, for the sentiments with which that man and that woman had palpitated when their images had been reproduced were certainly still palpitating therein today.

The man had a canine visage, broad and clean-shaven, heavy chops that were retracted on one side of a prominent tooth in the form of a fang, a short and leathery neck, a triple chin lifted up by the collar of a military uniform, and the red complexion of a butcher—and the ferocity of that entire bestial face was summarized, concentrated in and darted by the small, sharp, cruel, slightly squinting eyes with brown-green irises, almost the color of bile, and jaundiced and bloodshot sclerotics.

39

The woman, extremely pretty, with a "keepsake" head[15] with vaporous blonde curls, sweetened by slim child-like features and a creamy skin streaked with strawberry pink, had exceptionally large pale blue eyes, evoking the idea of a profound and mortally cold lake whose waters would drink you slowly, envelop you in a shroud of paralysis and freeze you like hemlock.

And the hatred of the man, violent, brutal, murderous, congested and explosive, burst forth furiously toward the woman. And the hatred of the woman, patient, sly, venomous, livid and muted, extended its languid and atrocious serpentine coils toward the man.

I asked the shopkeeper the price of the two paintings. He gave me a long speech about the English school, the perfect conservation of the canvases and the authenticity of the portraits, which had come directly from the Mansfield gallery and represented two members of that illustrious family, Lord and Lady Mansfield, made famous by a certain court case that had generated a lot of noise in London in 1828. Finally, after pouring so much sauce in order that I might swallow his fish, he served it to me for an exorbitant price that I could not afford—and I left the two portraits with him, continuing to look at one another with those eyes, whose hatred as still alive and still *present*.

Finding myself in England a few months later, I remembered the two portraits, the memory of which haunted me by virtue of the strange gazes, and I was curious to discover what might have lay behind Lord and Lady Mansfield's tragic hatred, so tenacious that it was not yet extinct although they must have died a long time ago.

---

[15] "Keepsakes"—the term is in English in the original—were ornate 19th century gift-books produced as annuals, many of which had colored frontispieces representing a pretty girl, of the sort also frequently found in the miniature paintings enclosed in lockets.

One of my friends, a great ferreter through libraries, with a particular fondness for famous trials, informed me right away. He was very familiar with the 1828 court case that had once caused a scandal in London.

"Oh, not because of the crime itself," he told me, "which was quite banal, but solely because of the rank occupied in the gentry by the criminals." And he told me the story of Lord and Lady Mansfield, which did not seem as banal to me as he had implied. For, if the circumstances were, indeed, no different from those customary in those kinds of crime of passion, I understood, personally, how exalted and wild the sentiments must have been in the perpetration of those crimes. I knew it because of the eyes of the two portraits, which had remained so prodigiously and terrible alive in my memory, as they were on the canvas, and would be for all eternity.

Lady Mansfield had deceived her husband. He had found out about it. He had killed the lover with his fists, had been acquitted of murder of the grounds of legitimate self-defense by means of "natural weapons," and had then continued to keep his wife, in order to martyrize her. Six years later, he had died, leaving her his entire fortune, which was colossal. The heirs had then accused Lady Mansfield of having poisoned the Lord, after having drawn up a forged will. She had been convicted, and had hanged herself in prison. Such was the famous case that had generated a lot of noise in London in 1828.

On my return to Paris, I hastened to the shop, not having decided to buy the two portraits in spite of their price—which really was too dear for my meager purse—but thirsty to see those gazes again, in which still-living hatreds gleamed so frenetically.

"Alas," the shopkeeper told me, "you should have bought them. They would be in your home, whereas they are now lost—lost to me, to you and to the world. Two such beautiful specimens of the English school, which..."

I cut short his retrospective sales patter and asked him hastily what he meant. He explained to me, while showing me the two canvases. During a rearrangement that he had been

41

obliged to make, a clumsy blunder had been committed and there had been a collapse, one result of which was that a bottle of sulfuric acid had broken over the face of the man, which was no longer anything but a black blur, while the other portrait had fallen on to a wrought iron chandelier, whose points had gouged out the woman's eyes.

"What bad luck!" moaned the shopkeeper. "Would you believe it? What an unfortunate accident—one might have thought it had been purposive!"

And I thought, privately: *Perhaps it was.*

The Enemy[16]

The name engraved on the visiting-card did not strike any chord in my memory. On the other hand, the few lines traced after the name in question immediately and irresistibly rendered me sympathetic to the unknown visitor.

Those lines, in fact, revealed on graphological analysis, without the slightest possible hesitation, a noble, dolorous and desperate soul. Without a doubt, the man who had written those lines was not lying in affirming that he had come to ask for mental assistance in a matter of life and death.

To refuse such a request, made by such a soul, appeared to me to be a veritable crime against humanity. Even if the visitor might be a madman, which was not suggested by his handwriting, I had an imperious duty to see him.

I therefore received him, not without a tragic presentiment—with which moreover, my anxious and quivering curiosity was in harmony.

The graphological analysis of the card had not deceived me with respect to the man. At the sight of him, when he came in, I recognized the noble, dolorous and desperate soul that I had read in advance. His gaze said so even more than his handwriting. It fully displayed a soul that had arrived at the most elevated peaks of philosophy, descended into the most profound gulfs of dolor, and had been driven into the final cul-de-sac of despair by the most frightful desperation.

"Monsieur," the man said to me, abruptly, "don't take me for a madman. I'm not prey to delusions of persecution. When I have told you what it is of which I am the victim, you will be forced to recognize that I really am being persecuted and that I have the most abominable enemy that anyone has ever suffered."

---

[16] *Le Journal,* 21 June 1900.

In spite of the assurance he gave so energetically regarding the solidity of his mental state, and in spite of the assurance given to me by the fact that his handwriting showed no symptoms of dementia, I confess that I concluded immediately that it was a case of insanity of exactly the kind he rejected—which is to say, delusions of persecution.

How likely did it seem, in fact, that a man like that might really be persecuted by an enemy, without being able to find a means of freeing himself therefrom? His bearing, his jewelry and the expensive automobile parked outside my door indicated a wealth permitting him to face up to pecuniary persecutions, and proved that he had, at least, not fallen victim to those.

His rectitude, the virile pride of his visage, the decisiveness of his gestures and his voice, and the flame of valor illuminated in the depths of his eyes, in spite of their sadness, scarcely denoted a coward, and implied instead, on the contrary, a hearty fellow incapable of tolerating an insult without exacting a prompt and sure vengeance. Finally, he had something indefinable about him, suggestive of a man fortunate in love, naturally endowed to cause more suffering than he endured. Besides which, he had not specified that his enemy was female, so I could not think in terms of a woman having poisoned his life irredeemably.

Conclusion: the enemy of whom he complained must be a purely imaginary enemy, like those forged by unfortunate individuals prey to delusions of persecution.

All of that I had thought very rapidly; he had doubtless read it in my eyes, for he replied in this way: "No, Monsieur, don't be deceived. The enemy who has reduced me to despair is not an imaginary enemy. He is well and truly human, made of flesh and blood—a man like you and me."

"But in sum," I said, "what has he done to you?"

"What has he done to me?" he cried. "Oh, if you only knew! It's atrocious. It's Hell. It's a perpetual Hell. It's a Hell that follows me everywhere, always."

He had taken his head in his hands and shook it violently, as if to make all the fires of that Hell spill out.

"Come on," I said gently. "Calm, down a little, I beg you, and be precise. I still don't know the nature of this supreme mental assistance for which you've come to ask me, as indicated on your card. If I'm to give you that assistance, I need at least to know of what it consists—and firstly, in consequence, what this terrible enemy has done to you."

The man had got a grip on himself again and stopped sobbing. He was now grinding his teeth and chewing on angry words.

"Well, for example," he said, "When I have written verses, he sends them to me with all their faults underlined in pencil, and very exactly."

"Bah!" I interjected. "There's nothing very cruel about that, and if you only have grievances like that against your enemy..."

"When I love a woman," he continued, "and am beloved, he renders her odious to me, and renders me detestable to her."

"How does he do that?"

"That's his secret."

"What is it?"

"I have no idea. All I know is that he achieves his objectives, the torturer—that, thanks to him, my purest loves always end up in dirty waters."

He started sobbing again. Afterwards, he resumed grinding his teeth again, angrily.

"But if I told you everything he dares to do to me," he continued, "you wouldn't believe me. Can you imagine—and this will show you how far his audacity as a tormenter goes—that I cannot eat a dish that pleases me without him spitting in it!"

Decidedly, and without a shadow of a doubt, he was insane. He understood that I thought so, and said, sadly: "I can see that you take me for a madman, alas! And given that, it's futile to ask you for the supreme mental assistance for which I've come to you in search."

With an impatience that I could no longer hide, I replied: "My God, Monsieur, either you have a deranged mind, I which case I can do nothing for you, not being an alienist, or you have all your faculties, in which case, if your enemy, instead of being imaginary, is quite real, you're the worst of cowards for allowing..."

He did not let me finish my sentence. A glimmer of joy appeared in his bleak gaze. He cried: "Yes, am I not? Yes, that's it: the worst of cowards! In my place, you'd have defended yourself from that enemy?"

"Indeed!" I said.

"But how?" he asked.

"It doesn't matter how," I replied. There's dueling. There's the courts. That's a matter of taste. In theory, there's even murder..."

He rubbed his hands, pressed mine and thanked me, striding back and forth, repeating: "Yes, yes—that's the only solution. I'll kill him. I'll kill him." Suddenly, with a loud cry, he concluded: "It's settled. I'll kill him."

And he went out like a gust of wind.

He's certainly demented, I thought, going back to work and forgetting the wasted half-hour.

Who would have thought that in that half-hour I had, on the contrary, perhaps seen the bedrock of pure wisdom?

That same evening, in fact, in the same handwriting, displaying a noble, dolorous and desperate soul, I received the following note:

I have killed my enemy. I have killed the *enemy. I beg you to come and see, and recognize the fact.*

I went there.

The man had committed suicide, by shooting himself in the heart.

A Duel of Souls[17]

It was a subject of universal astonishment in the legal world when Lionel de Vargnes left the magistracy, by means of an abrupt and inexplicable resignation. He was, in fact, as people said, bound for the most brilliant future. He was the last offspring of a family in which father and son had been magistrates for generations, and which has given the *noblesse de robe* one of its finest paragons. He was predestined, by atavism, to follow that career, and no other. He loved it passionately. Having handed in his resignation, he found himself without a goal, without a reason to live, incapable of interesting himself in anything whatsoever.

It seems to me, he said to himself, employing a forceful term from the *patois* of his native Picardy, *that quitting the magistracy has* desouled *me*.

And if anyone asked him thereafter why he had quit the magistracy he replied: "Because staying there would have desouled me even more." But he did not explain why, and thus his conduct remained an enigma to which no one knew the key.

That key, however, without looking for it, someone ended up finding. How? It doesn't matter. By way of what channel has it reached the present text? The secret is undisclosed. The essential thing is that this is the key.

One day, at the very outset of his career as an examining magistrate, Lionel de Vargnes received the following anonymous letter:

Monsieur, you and I are the last representatives of two enemy families, in conflict for several generations. Yours has furnished illustrious magistrates; mine criminals no less illus-

---

[17] *Le Journal*, 29 March 1897.

trious. Naturally, it is yours that has always triumphed in this duel, since you are the Benjamins of Destiny, the descendants of the just Abel, whom God loves, while we are the descendants of Cain the accursed, whom God detests. But I have resolved that this must end, and to avenge all my ancestors upon you, by inflicting upon you a torture of remorse such as none of my ancestors, condemned by yours, has ever known. I shall make you send an innocent to the executioner. I could have only told you afterwards, but I have the pride of believing myself strong enough to warn you in advance. My victory will be all the more spectacular, my revenge more complete and my enjoyment more profound. Now, Monsieur, en garde!

This letter appeared to Lionel de Vargnes to be the work of a madman, and he paid scant attention to it at first. Some time afterwards, however, he could not help remembering it, having been led, during a case he was examining, to conclude against a man whom he was subsequently obliged to recognize as not guilty.

The unfortunate man struggled vainly against a web of hostile evidence, so well-woven for his damnation that Lionel de Vargfnes had been forced to say to himself, in the final analysis: *It's truly believable that hazard was not working alone in giving him all the appearances of guilt, and that an ingenious scoundrel planned things cleverly to deceive the law.*

A trivial point, a small oversight in the plan, had fortunately saved the poor devil; Lionel de Vargnes' subtlety had done the rest. To prove the man's innocence to himself, the examining magistrate had deployed all the resources of a veritable inductive genius. He had finally succeeded—but not in finding the real guilty party, who had remained unknown. In closing the case, Lionel de Vargnes had involuntarily remembered the madman's strange letter. Then he had shrugged his shoulders ad thought: *Bah! A bizarre coincidence, nothing more! Why should I worry about it?*

He did worry, about it though, regardless. From that moment on, it became impossible for him to forget the letter. His memory was haunted by it. He could not embark upon an examination of any importance without feeling an imperious need—to which he yielded—to recover the letter conserved in his files and reread it. He found it, moreover, a singular tonic to keep his faculties as an examining magistrate ever alert. Chimerical or not, that frightful threat of a possible error rendered him much more meticulous in perspicacious in his scrupulous work. At the same time, he found therein a sharper charm, the delights of an incessant and terrible danger, and the sensuality of risk.

Sometimes, he smiled at what he called childishness. Often, too, in order to excuse himself in his own eyes, he said to himself: *After all, perhaps it's that to which I owe being such a good examining magistrate.*

But it happened more often still that he shivered at this obsessive thought: *But what if it's true? What if the madman wasn't a madman? What if the frightful thing were to be realized?*

For Lionel de Vargnes had the soul of a great magistrate, one of those souls that considers the function of a judge as a sacred function, and the idea of a judiciary error was as abominable to him as the idea of sacrilege to a convinced priest.

There is hardly anyone except the gourmets of criminal cases who remembers the Grivadas affair. The wider public did not take any great interest in it, being the impassioned by the elections. The newspapers were overflowing with political matters. That story of poisoning passed almost unnoticed, in short articles far from front page. It had had, however, what was required to delight those who gladly sweetened their morning coffee with judiciary news.

It was a matter of a mysterious and complicated drama, which had a widow and two children for victims, a physician for a hero, a life insurance policy for a motive, which is a slightly hackneyed cliché, but also—which is entirely original—the employment of a culture medium as a poison. In

49

brief, it was the entry of bacteriology into the annals of criminality.

The physician, moreover, defended himself stubbornly, and protested his innocence, fortified by a perfectly honorable prior existence. On the other hand, everything combined to accuse him, including the devoted but exclusive and seemingly jealous care he had lavished on the widow and the two children. It was established with the support of irrefutable evidence that he had, under the pretext of curing them of one illness, slowly and cleverly intoxicated them with another. The remedies and treatments of the first had been the vehicles of the infectious microbes of the second. The traces of that deliberate infection had been found, neglected by design until the moment when its incurability was absolute. The entire scientific procedure had been reconstituted, along with the entire moral framework of the crime, truly horrible in its novelty.

How? By the investigation, of course! The sagacious, marvelous, miraculous investigation carried out by the extraordinary examining magistrate, the only man skillful enough to have thwarted such a clever scoundrel.

That examining magistrate was Lionel de Vargnes.

The case was about to go to the court of assizes, and the result was not in doubt for anyone at the Palais; the physician would be found guilty. To all the evidence accumulated against him, nothing was opposed except his protest of innocence. To the irrefutable conclusions of Lionel de Vargnes, there was no possible response but: "I'm the victim of an infernal fatality. The facts are there, incomprehensible to me—and yet, I'm innocent."

Momentarily, in confrontation with such obstinacy, which had a tone of sincerity, Lionel de Vargnes had had his habitual scruple, and remembered the madman's letter. But no! There was no reason to hesitate, to have the shadow of a doubt. That the physician was guilty, Lionel de Vargnes, the Christian with the great soul of a magistrate, would have sworn that he believed. He had, therefore, without a tremor in his fingertips, signed the document sending the case to the court of assizes. It was as if he were signing the death warrant.

Two days later the physician was found dead in his bed. By a prodigious effort of will, he had retracted his tongue into the depths of his throat, thus producing the complete occlusion of the respiratory pathways, and asphyxia. A letter addressed to the examining magistrate—which had, in consequence, had to be written and sealed under the gaze of his guard—affirmed, with the authority of his imminent death, *in extremis*, his innocence, and repeated solemnly that he was the victim of an infernal and incomprehensible fatality.

The newspapers reported that strange suicide the following day in a small corner of the "Court News," and that the Grivadas affair would not have its denouement in the court of assizes, the guilty man having passed judgment on himself. And everyone, in fact, including Lionel de Vargnes, remained convinced of his guilt—but in Lionel de Vargnes' case, not for long. For that same day, he received, in the same handwriting as before, these lines:

Monsieur, for the second time I have just failed to avenge my ancestors. The first time, you defended yourself well. This time, hazard has served you. The third time will be good for me. Soon, you will deliver the Innocent to the executioner! I wish it; it will happen.

Well, no, said Lionel de Vargnes to himself, it won't happen. *Whether the man is a madman or not, he frightens me.*

And Lionel de Vargnes handed in his resignation.

The Painter of Eyes[18]

That Jacob van Hechtvaëre the Elder was a great painter it is impossible not to proclaim, to shout out, when one sees his self-portrait.

Unfortunately for his glory, the opportunity to do that was not given to very many people, and a cruel, tenacious, implacable ill luck has determined that for two centuries, there was never anyone among the rare privileged individuals able to proclaim it with the necessary authority and reverberation.

The portrait, in fact, was bequeathed in 1692 to the convent of *Provendistes Grises*[19] of Waëgtmeux-en-Thiérache by the master's daughter, with the proviso that it should be kept veiled and only unveiled once a year, at Toussaint, during the mass for the dead. The nuns, the local curé serving the chapel of the *Provendistes Grises* and a few of the faithful led by a particular devotion to travel the three leagues of poor road that led to the convent, situated in the woods, were therefore the entire public, insufficient as a donor of renown, to whom the admirable and magical portrait of Jacob van Hechtvaëre the Elder had been shown for two centuries, for one hour per year.

Of his other paintings, some could be seen in the museums of Gand and Valenciennes , the library of Audenarde and a few Belgian churches—but there was nothing of genius among them. They were the work of an honest craftsman painter, who knew is trade but nothing more, of whom there were many in the Flemish school of that era. It required a fine connoisseur, a veritable expert, to find any personal touch

---

[18] *Le Gaulois*, 5 December 1895.

[19] This canonical order is fictitious, and the term *provendiste* does not appear to exist in French, presumably having been improvised by the author as an *ad hoc* equivalent of the English *prebendary*.

therein that distinguish him slightly from another of that ilk—his nephew Jacob van Hechtvaëre the Younger, for example, with whom the most skillful often confused him.

But what a unique masterpiece his self-portrait was, what an incomparable marvel! Magical—yes, really magical! Or rather, supernaturally magical! The words are not excessive; they are merely accurate. And everyone would doubtless agree with them if they understood the reasons for the singular bequest made by the master's daughter to the convent of the *Provendistes Grises*, and everyone would admit that Jacob van Hechtvaëre the Elder could not have been other than a great painter if they were able to read the story of his portrait—the strange story that follows.

For many years, Jacob van Hechtvaëre, or, as he was called in Waëgtmeux-en-Thiérache, the town of his birth, Master Jacob, had been exercising his profession as a painter and living on it honorably and happily. Doing "anything appropriate to his estate"—portraits, still lives, landscapes, religious and historical subjects, allegories and decorations—he did not refuse any work, nor ask too high a price. At the same time, he was a teacher at the École Municipale des Arts et Métiers de Waëgtmeux-en-Thiérache, and therefore seemed not to have anything to desire, since he found in his trade both consideration and profit.

His habits, his manners and his mode of dress fully confirmed this appearance. Calm and regular, a conscientious worker, a good father whose household flourished with an amiable wife and three beautiful children, a hearty eater and drinker, with a broad smile, he led an enviable existence. He got up early, breakfasted lightly in order to have a free hand, harnessed himself to his task until three o'clock in the afternoon and then dined copiously, having the rest of the day to digest at his leisure and take a well-earned rest. He took it at the inn, while refilling his pipe over and over again and drinking six large tankards of pale, sparkling and foamy beer, while he chatted slowly about his arts with his friends and pupils. At nine o'clock in the evening he went home for a light supper before finally enjoying a tranquil sleep. And the next day, when he woke up, he began again doing exactly what he had done the day before.

However, Master Jacob, in spite of appearing so very fortunate, was not happy in the depths of his soul. An honest artist, passionate about his art, he judged himself mediocre and suffered in consequence—but no one around him could have suspected it. His admirers, friends and pupils attributed to his modest bonhomie the confessions he let slip, generally after the sixth tankard, when he said things like:

"Bonsoir, then! There's another day wasted!"

"Oh, if I were sure of making a masterpiece by ceasing to see you, with what joy I would leave you forever!"

"I shall try to dream that I am a great painter, to console me for not being one."

And the few enemies that he had, because of his prosperity, took that as a pretext for insinuating that his modesty was false, and that his bonhomie hid an abominable vanity, capable of anything to obtain satisfaction. The most malevolent among them cited, in support of this insulting opinion, a comment that often recurred in Master Jacob's laments—a perfectly inoffensive comment that his friends, quite rightly, saw as nothing but a joke.

"To make a masterpiece," Master Jacob gladly repeated, "one must sell one's soul to the Devil,"

It is quite certain that he said that without malice, without thinking that anyone might take him at his word. How could anyone doubt it, when they looked at the man's honest and kindly eyes, his broad expansive face, and his smiling thick-lipped mouth, in which the pale beer foamed like milk on the lips of an innocent at the teat? Not to mention that Master Jacob fulfilled his religious duties very devotedly, never missing mass and taking communion at all the great festivals.

In truth, then, it would have been necessary to have a diabolical mind oneself to imagine that Master Jacob was serious in talking about making a pact with the Devil. And the proof that he did not mean it seriously is that one day, his nephew, Jacob van Hechtvaëre the Younger, who was a joker, said to him: "And if the Devil came to propose the bargain, what the Devil would you reply, Uncle?"

"Well," Jacob van Hechtvaëre the Elder, who also liked to laugh, gaily replied, "I'd tell him what I told you when you ask me if you can paint."

And what he replied in that case was a small coarse word by which the people of Waëgtmeux-en-Thiérache, although reckoned as Flemings in the estimation of certain historians, nevertheless prove that they are truly French.

On the evening of Mardi Gras in 1681, a little after nine o'clock, as Master Jacob as emptying his fifth tankard, and had just repeated his favorite comment, while refilling his pipe for the eleventh time, a stranger came into the inn. No one knew him. Everyone, in subsequent conversation, agreed in saying that he looked like a Spaniard. He was wearing a crimson velvet mask, a broad-rimmed hat on top of a red bonnet, a vast and long scarlet cape draping his entire body and leather boots, one of which, by virtue of being much rounder, more flattened and fuller than the other, visible denoted a club-foot.

As if the unknown man were known in the locality, he sat down in a familiar fashion with Master Jacob's group, poured himself a tankard from their pot and said to the painter, point-blank: "What you lack in order to make a masterpiece, Master Jacob, is knowing how to paint the eyes."

Although everyone had celebrated Mardi Gras to excess and were thus indulgent to the masked man, who also seemed to be celebrating it, they had no desire to laugh, Master Jacob less than anyone. In fact, a mortal pallor suddenly discolored his face, which had been very red because he eaten and drunk more than usual that day. And it seemed to him that his heart stopped in his breast, so accurately had the stranger's words struck him in the sore wound of his secret suffering.

"You're right," he replied, with ashamed humility, "You're absolutely right, Messire—I can't paint eyes."

"Would you like me to teach you to paint them?" the stranger asked.

"Yes, yes, certainly!" cried Master Jacob, a trifle terrified, but simultaneously enthused by such a proposal.

"Well then," said the man, "come with me."

They tried to stop Master Jacob from following him, but he, ordinarily so placid, swore, blaspheming the name of the Lord, that he would break the skull of anyone who even tried to stop him.

And he went out into the night with the stranger.

The next day, his curious friends interrogated him about the adventure.

"Well," he said, "we all had our heads upside-down because of Mardi Gras, including me and the stranger. I lost him in the crowd. It was a bad joke. Let's not talk about it anymore."

But it was soon evident that he had not stopped thinking about it, and that something must have happened between him and the man, by virtue of which his entire life was turned upside down. He had lost his contented appearance. He no longer came to the inn every evening. When he did come, he scarcely smoked or drank. After a certain time he no longer came at all. Now, he never went out of the house. He remained shut up in his studio. Even his wife and children never saw him. He finally took his mania for reclusion so far as to refuse to attend mass one Sunday. From that day on he no longer went to church. He did not take communion at Easter that year.

The curé, who was one of his old friends, came to see him, was almost obliged to break down the door in order to get into the studio, and asked him mildly about the reasons for his unreasonable conduct.

"You'll know them," Master Jacob replied, "when I've finished my masterpiece."

"And what is this masterpiece to which you're sacrificing your salvation?" asked the priest.

"I don't think I'm sacrificing my salvation to it," Master Jacob replied. "I've taken my precautions in that regard."

"Pay attention," the priest went on. "You seem to me to want to cheat the Evil One. He's the Evil One. He's the one who will cheat you. You won't get the better of the bargain."

Sadly and proudly, Master Jacob retorted: "So much the worse, then. But at least I'll have been, for once in my life, a good painter."

A month later, Master Jacob was found to have died suddenly in front of the finished masterpiece. It was his self-portrait: the marvelous, magical and supernatural portrait that was left in 1692 to the convent of the *Provendistes Grises* of Waëgtmeux-en-Thiérache by the abbess Claire van Hechtwaëre, the Master's daughter.

A piece of parchment was attached to the corner of the painting, on which Master Jacob had written these words:

The Devil has informed me as to the secret of painting eyes. That secret consists of decanting the life from the models one wishes to represent and fixing that life on the canvas. In doing that, one slowly kills the people whose portraits one paints. I did not wish to kill anyone but myself. Only being able to conquer genius in becoming homicidal, I have preferred only to commit suicide. I hope that divine mercy will count that preference in remission of my crime. I beg that my prideful sacrilege be punished by refusing me the posthumous glory to which my masterpiece has the right. It is sufficient for me to know that I have made this masterpiece. I commend my soul to the prayers, in case the Evil One does not leave me the time...

Death had struck the poor man in mid-sentence.

And that is why, every year, at the convent of the *Provendistes Grises* of Waëgtmeux-en-Thiérache, unveiled for an hour on the day of Toussaint, attendance at the mass for the dead is allowed to the marvelous, magical and supernatural portrait of the great unknown artist—to whom is restored here, for the first time, the entire name with which he signed his unique masterpiece: Master Jacob van Hechtwaëre, the Painter of Eyes.

The Mirror[20]

The old man in whose shop the old mirror was offered for sale had nothing strange about him to distinguish him from so many other old men in whose shops old mirrors are offered for sale.

Like almost all his fellows, he had a hooked nose clad with spectacles, gray wisps of hair under a rabbit-skin cap, a long, dirty and jaundiced beard and a strong German accent.

The old mirror, on the other hand, did not resemble the many old mirrors that so many old men sell.

To begin with, it was not framed, contrary to the custom of all those old mirrors about which the old men say to you, guilefully: "The frame is ebony."[21]

This old mirror had for its only rim the overlap of the sheet of lead on which the glass was set. That sheet of lead was, moreover, quite thick, and as the glass too was thick, the mirror was extremely heavy.

That absence of a frame might have had for compensation the beauty or the dimension of the glass, of which the old man would not have failed to make the most. In truth, he could not, the mirror being scarcely thirty centimeters square and the glass, although thick and very smooth, not having an agreeable tint. One might have thought it composed of green, stagnant, marshy water. That did not tempt self-reflection; it gave you a face worthy of the Morgue.

Like all his fellows, however, the sly old man knew the craft of salesmanship. So he showed, for preference, the back of the mirror, extolling the weight and quality of the lead

---

[20] *Le Journal*, 29 June 1899.

[21] The shopkeeper's speech is represented by a calculatedly horrible eye-dialect supposedly representative of his thick German accent, but I have made no attempt to duplicate it.

sheet, and taking particular care to point out a square of paper stuck in one of the corners.

"Very interesting, due to its rarity, for a collector."

And indeed, the piece of paper intrigued and tempted the young man in the process of examining it in a singular manner. The young man had recognized, at the first glance, Gothic characters of a very ancient form, inscribed in very fine handwriting, tracing lines of unequal length, which were probably verse.

"A German song!" said the old man. "A pretty song!"

"In High German, then," said the young man, "for I know modern German, and I can't make head nor tail of this."

The old man took a greasy wallet out of his pocket, opened it, sorted through the papers it contained, separated out one page and held it out to him, saying: "I have the translation and I'll sell it with the mirror." But he held it so as only to be seen at a distance, and did not confide it to the young man, who was already reaching out for it.

"Hold on," the old man continued. "It's thirty francs for the mirror, with the lead and the translation. Thirty francs the lot. An opportunity, a nice opportunity, for a collector, very nice."

The young man paid the thirty francs and carried away the mirror, whose weight occupied both his hands alternately, preventing him from reading the translation immediately, which had been put into an envelope by the old man.

Having arrived home, the young man put the mirror down, propped up against a pile of heavy books on his worktable, and curiously set about reading the translation of the Gothic poem. This is what it said, in bizarre French, probably word for word:

Under the glaucous water of the mortal pool where prisoner I am, dead alive,
The wrath of the enchanter by his enchantments has enchanted me.

And I weep here, Undine sealed in the web that is my coffin.

Until the day when the clairvoyant and handsome Prince I shall see.

In the clear and limpid running water of the river of his homeland;

With me he plunges, the clairvoyant and handsome Prince, beautifully enlaced,

And the river of his homeland to the enchantments of the enchanter will put an end.

And end too to all the sufferings suffered by the clairvoyant and handsome Prince.

An end too to this poem, which so many have read without reading well (pay attention, you!)

An end too to the song that here I weep, silently, Undine fixed, alas!

Under the glaucous water of the mortal pool where prisoner I am, dead alive.

As he finished the final line, the young man looked into the mirror, and saw the face of a drowned man—but that did not astonish him at all; he had had that vision already in the old man's shop, and knowing full well that it was necessary to attribute it to the green tint of the glass and nothing else.

What did astonish him was the pleasure he obtained from seeing himself thus, with the face of a drowned man, and the very long time that he remained in that contemplation, from which he could not tear away his eyes or his mind, delighting therein.

And what astonished him even more, and yet did not astonish him at all, but seemed, on the contrary, to be the most natural thing in the world, was that he soon ceased to distinguish his own face in the mirror, discerning nothing there but a vague green, marshy stagnation—and then he saw, little by little, designed in the floating, melting, scarcely-perceptible features of an apparition on the brink of vanishing, a new face.

It was the face of the Undine. She had water-weed for hair, softly serpentine. Her pupils darted a pale glaucous fire, in which all the gray-green of the ambient water was concentrated, She was weeping—and, at the same time, a furtive smile wandered over her wan lips.

And all of that was very distant, very alien, very deep, gently and infinitely.

Where was that distance? Where was that alien place? Deep in what? He did not think of asking himself that. He looked. He saw. He was fascinated. He fell prey to it, gently and infinitely.

"What a singular hallucination!" he said, abruptly coming round.

A hallucination, of course! He could not doubt it. A perfectly explicable hallucination, moreover, he thought. The reading of the poem, the gaze fixed for a long time upon the mirror, the kind of hypnotism that the fixity in question produced, the particular tint of the glass, was more than was required to take account, rationally and scientifically, of the optical illusion succeeding a reverie and amalgamating with it an appearance of reality.

For now, in the mirror, it was certainly himself that was contemplating—with the face of a drowned man, undoubtedly because of the green tint that...but himself, certainly, and no longer the Undine, the imaginary Undine!

He smiled at his slight absence of mind. After which, sadly, he said to himself: *It's a pity, even so, that it was only a hallucination. It's a pity, too, not to believe in that sort of legend. To be the clairvoyant Prince who delivers her would be so fine! Simply having the idea that one might be him would be so delightful! But now, now...to have such an idea it would be necessary to be mad, absolutely mad!*

Then, more sadly still, with a veritable despair: *They aren't to be pitied, the mad! They're enviable. Oh yes!*

He reread the translation of the poem. He learned it by heart. He repeated it to himself while staring at himself in the mirror. He gave himself the hallucination again. Again the

Undine appeared to him. She was always weeping and smiling.

From day to day, her features became more precise. Now, she was no longer content to smile and weep silently. In a very low, very vague voice, like the murmur of a subterranean stream, she said: "You are the clairvoyant Prince, since you have seen me, since you see me."

Every time, before vanishing, in a melancholy fashion, she added: "Why can't you believe them, these truths that you so wickedly call legends? Why don't you love me—me, who loves you?"

And one day, his friends found the young man on a slab in the Morgue. Mariners had fished up his cadaver, retained underwater for rather a long time by the weight of a sheet of lead, which he was clutching in his arms against his breast, gently and infinitely.

Undoubtedly, in rolling over stones in the river, the mirror had cracked and broken. Only a single piece of it remained between the overlapping edges of the lead sheet. The glass was in the river.

Doubtless, too, the water had detached the piece of paper stuck to one of its corners, on which the poem in Gothic letters had been inscribed.

All of it can be explained, as you see, quite naturally, by the madness of the young man.

But perhaps, too, the Undine has been liberated by him, and they are living happily, forever, in a magical palace of azure and emerald.

Are you quite certain of the contrary? Quite certain? Perfectly certain?

I'm not.

Fezzan[22]

From his innumerable voyages, all undertaken solely for his own satisfaction, our friend Henry de Brès has brought back the most curious photographs and the most interesting memories there could be. If he wrote the latter down and illustrated them with the former, he could make money and a reputation therefrom, but he's rich, extremely slothful when it comes to writing, and hasn't the slightest desire for notoriety. He is therefore content only to let a few intimate friends riffle through his albums and his memory. I profit from that as much as I can.

The other day, therefore, while soliciting his obliging commentaries with avid questions, I was looking at the recent views, skies, landscapes, costumes, scenes and portraits with which he has further enriched his treasure during a long exploration of the ancient deserts of Libya, south of Tripoli, beyond Murzuk, in the mysterious Fezzan.

I suddenly came across two singular figures, which gave me, simultaneously, a sense of strangeness and an irresistible desire to laugh.

Imagine, in fact, two exactly similar individuals, completely black and completely naked, with the bodies of desiccated mummies, grimacing faces, their hands covering their sexual parts in a grotesque gesture of modesty, without it being possible, thanks to that gesture, to discern whether they were a couple, or even whether the two individuals had any sex at all.

The idea arose instead that they were two phantoms, two neuter ghosts, the phantoms and ghosts of two simian animals with vaguely human silhouettes, androgynous by nature, but

---

[22] *Le Journal*, 14 April 1900.

androgynes aborted in a double eunuchism, and simultaneously shriveled by all the most intense wrinkles of decrepitude.

Half-horrified and half-guffawing, I couldn't help exclaiming: "Oh, what monsters! Oh, what ridiculous pair of monsters!"

Then, intrigued, I enquired: "But what are they, in sum? Negroes? Negresses? Apes? Devils?"

It was with a soft and distant smile, full of melancholy regret and tender recognition, that Henry de Brès replied, with his eyes upraised to the heavens: "Angels."

I could clearly see, by the expression on his face, that he wasn't making fun of me—and I thought I understood, too, that my horror and my hilarity, with regard to those two individuals, had caused him pain. I offered my apologies, pleading my ignorance regarding their history—an ignorance that only asked to be educated; and my questions on that subject could not have been more pressing.

"I'll satisfy your curiosity, my dear friend," said Henry de Brès, "but I confess that it won't be without a certain chagrin, for it's always sad to remember a paradise, and talk about it, when one has lost it irredeemably. Now, a paradise on earth, I have known in reality, and those two beings, those two ridiculous monsters, were, I repeat, its angels. And that lost paradise I shall never find again, since its two angels are dead."

His gaze was slightly veiled. A mist of furtive tears had risen in his pale eyes. He added: "And it's my fault, alas, that they're dead!"

He rolled and then lit a cigarette of gilded Chébli tobacco and extracted from it a few large puffs of blue smoke, which enveloped him like a cloud of dreams, and said:

"I stayed for quite a long time, as you know, in the Fezzan—but what you don't know is that I very nearly died there. I caught a fever of slow consumption, the character of which is to wear you away, so to speak, to the very fiber, the weft of the muscular tissue. I had become a bag of bones in a loose skin. A doctor from the oasis of Khufra, who was my friend, saved me by confiding me to the care of those two old negresses, two twin sisters, who were the custodian of a particular science capable of rebuilding muscles: witches and cantatrices, he affirmed—in reality, masseuses. But what masseuses!"

At this point, with voluptuous eyes, Henry de Brès contemplated their portrait, as if, in contemplating them, he was experiencing once again a past enjoyment. Frissons ran over his cheeks like a breeze over a watery surface, and flecks of saliva pearled in the corners of his lips, while he said:

"Nothing can give you an idea of the infinite, profound, ecstatic, divine caress that the palms of their hands and the tips of their fingers paraded over my skin, caused to penetrate into my fibers, sinking smoothly to the marrow of my bones. Beneath that caress, I felt my dead flesh being reborn, swelling as if my tissues were putting forth buds, gushing with sap, enlivening my blood. It was paradise. I tell you—paradise on earth, paradise!"

He seemed to be there, as before. He had the expression of delight that one has when one is enraptured in an amorous embrace. He became languid therein, silently.

"And consider," he continued, that each session of that exquisite treatment lasted at least a hour, that there was scarcely an interval of ten minutes between sessions, that they commenced at daybreak and ended with the glimmer of the first stars—or, to put it better, that they lasted perpetually, as in an eternity of enjoyment. Oh, the paradise, the beautiful paradise, the unforgettable paradise of my two angels!

He fell silent for a second time, reliving through the smoke of the Chébli his former hours of ecstasy, while I contemplated at length in my turn the portraits of the two negresses, so old, so monstrous, so phantasmal, so strange, so monstrous, so ghostly, not understanding by what enchantment they could have so intoxicated that solidly rational man.

I risked a comment on that subject, making allusion to what the doctor had said, who affirmed that they were witches.

Henry de Brès replied. "They did, in fact, sing, each taking the role in turn, in a voice both shrill and distant, like the drone of a fly mingled with the sound of subterranean water. It was in a language that I didn't know, infantile, guttural and chirping, punctuated at intervals by clicking sounds like little kisses—and those kisses I seemed to feel raining down on me, and the chirping tickled me at the tips of their light fingers, and the subterranean water ran in their sweat, scented with musk, and the fly was droning beneath the palms of their hands against my skin. Oh, the paradise!"

Abruptly, Henry de Brès got to his feet, his eyes almost haggard.

"Would you believe," he cried, "that I was mad enough, one day, to love them, those two witches? Yes, yes, it's the truth. Angels of my paradise, as such I saw them, transfigured and radiant. Life and strength had returned to me, through them. And then, one day, overcome by lust, I took one of them in my arms and sought her lips. Which one? I no longer know. Even looking at that photograph, taken a few hours before, I can't tell. They resembled one another so closely! Not only in the face, but also in the soul and the heart, alas. In brief, what more can I tell you? They both loved me, the unfortunate women. Yes, both of them. And so, and so..."

He began to weep. I no longer understood any of it. I imagined that bizarre scene in which, as in the photograph, horror disputed with the comical: that scene of my friend Henry de Brès, so handsome, so elegant, coupling with that monster, that decrepit ape.

"An then," he concluded, suddenly, "they rushed at one another, in a rage of bestial jealousy, and they strangled one another, then and there, in my honor. Poor angels!

In my turn, I blew out a few puffs of blue smoke, which enveloped me in a cloud, and we remained silent, in a nightmare mist.

The Other Eyes[23]

"Beware, young man," Abbé Garuby piped, softly. "You're wrong, I tell you, to want to attempt this redoubtable experiment. You'll expose yourself to sure and dolorous disillusionment. You'll see strange, monstrous things, to drive you mad, irredeemably mad, when having closed your carnal eyes, I have opened what I call *the other eyes* for you."

"Have no fear," the young man replied, arrogantly. "My reason is solid; I'll answer for it. It has resisted the reading of all metaphysics. As for my heart, it's more solid still, if that's possible. It's absolutely safe from disillusionment, since it has no illusions whatsoever. You have, therefore, every freedom, and without the slightest scruple, to open for me what you call *the other eyes*."

"Consider," said the Abbé Garuby, slowly, "that the other eyes will permit you to look into the very souls of others."

"That's precisely what I'm avid to do," the young man replied, "if only to establish, conclusively, *de visu*, whether people really have souls."

"It really is *de visu*," said Abbé Garuby, smiling, "that you will establish it. I mean that the soul will appear to you as a form. But once again, believe me, the experiment is redoubtable—for that form is generally hideous. Now, let us suppose that you look, with the other eyes, at the soul of someone who is dear to you—your mother's, for example..."

"I have the good fortune," the young man interjected, "the inestimable good fortune, of being a foundling."

"In that case," Abbé Garuby continued, complacently, "let us say, if you wish, the soul of your mistress."

"A mistress, me!" the young man exclaimed, disdainfully. "I'm a virgin."

---

[23] *Le Journal*, 21 December 1899.

"Aha!" said Abbé Garuby, rubbing his hands. "You're stronger than I would have thought. Well, simply imagine that the other eyes reveal to you the soul of your best friend."

"Between the best and the worst," the young man declared, resolutely, "I don't know what the difference is, since I have no friends at all."

"In that case," Abbé Garuby proclaimed, raising astonished eyebrows, "you are, I confess, truly strong, and probably in a fit state to brave the redoubtable experiment. I shall therefore not refuse any longer to submit you to it, and I am at your disposal."

"My word!" said the young man, with mocking irony. "I confess in my turn that I find you very strong, and much stronger than I would have thought. For I won't conceal from you, mysterious and terrible Abbé, that I thought that, if you were refusing to open my other eyes, it was primarily for fear of letting me see, naked and in all its hideousness, your own soul."

"In which you are mistaken, young man," retorted Abbé Garuby with profound unction. My own soul is, in fact, not one of those that can be seen, even with the other eyes. It is situated in infinite space, and even to perceive its scintillation requires a telescope that you do not possess, strong as you are. But let's leave my soul there, I beg you, and occupy ourselves, without further ado, in opening your other eyes."

So saying, Abbé Garuby had suddenly ignited in his usually dull gaze the pale and flamboyant phosphorescence that created there, when the occasion required, a magnetic nucleus of irresistible hypnotic effluvia. At the same time, he had imposed his icy hands on the young man's cranium, digging into his temples two thumbs that seemed to be drilling into his brain. And a moment later—a moment of fulgurant brevity—the young man sensed his carnal eyes closing, and the other eyes opening within him.

And then, before him, visible to those other eyes, the form of a soul surged forth: a form duly established *de visu*, as the Abbé had promised him; a strange and monstrous form, so hideous that the unfortunate nearly fell backwards in a faint of disgust and terror.

The form of that soul was, in fact, nothing but an ulcer compounded out of an innumerable conglomerate of ulcers, agglutinated with and engendered by one another, all copulating with one another in abominable and purulent leprous fungal growths, which seethed like clumps of vipers, sweating venoms, viruses, pus, putrescence, noxiousness: a living, pullulating death, all horrors blossoming in an apotheosis of horror. And in all those nightmarish figures, which really were established *de visu* as being the form of that soul, the other eyes also saw the symbolic significance; for every one of those ulcers, facets of the total ulcer, was a vice in action or in potential; and all the vices were there, with all their various nuances and combinations, multiplying endlessly in the prism of the infernal spectrum whose seven essential colors are the seven deadly sins.

Terrified, his heart in upheaval, his head crazed, trying in vain to close within him the other eyes that nothing could any longer close, the young wan wondered who had delivered that vision to him, and thought, while his teeth chattered: *It's Abbé Garuby's doing, for sure. But what is he trying to do?*

Then, abruptly, the idea went through his mind, anguishing, atrocious, even more terrifying than his terror: *But no, no, Abbé Garuby wouldn't do that—for the soul that my other eyes see, that soul whose form appears to me, established* de visu, *that soul of an unimaginable hideousness, is his soul, his own soul, Abbé Garuby's own.*

Suddenly, recovering his strength, drawing himself upright in his pride, feeling exalted to the point of heroism, the young man cried: "Terrible soul, hideous soul, soul of Abbé Garuby, it's not in infinite space that you are situated, and there is no need of a magical telescope to perceive the scintillation of your accursed star. I see you. It's you who are here, before my other eyes—but I no longer want to see you. I want you to deliver me from the horror of seeing you. You, your hideousness, the terror and disgust you inspire in me, and your ulcers, and your form with its facets of vices, and the blossoming of your abominations in the prism of the seven deadly sins, and you, finally, soul and body, you, mysterious, terrible and infamous Abbé Garuby, I shall annihilate you, being unable to annihilate my other eyes, I shall annihilate you, monster, monster, monster, filthy monster!"

In the young man's hand, between his fingers, which clenched upon it, the shaft of a weapon had been placed. Who had placed the shaft of that hatchet in the palm of his hand? He had no idea. He did not even think of trying to find out. His fingers clenched on the shaft. The hatchet was brandished. Already, it was whirling in the air, whistling, shining, fulgurant.

And while, from a corner of the room, Abbé Garuby watched that spectacle of dementia with his customary dull gaze, rubbing his hands together and sniggering silently, the bewildered young man, grim and heroic, his carnal eyes opened wide and stupidly terrified, contemplated the broken shards of the mirror in which his other eyes had seen, a moment before, the form of his own soul.

The Gaze[24]

Before that closed door, the alienist had passed at a rapid pace, while turning his head distractedly, as if he were determinedly thinking about something else. But I was not deceived by it; the abrupt decisiveness of his movement led me to understand that he did not want me to talk about *that one*. So I said to him: "What about that one? Is he not interesting, then?"

Embarrassed, he replied: "No, not very. A banal case. Delusions of grandeur. General paralysis[25] in the second phase. Nothing particularly odd."

His embarrassment reeked of deception. I only put all the more insistence into the manifestation of my keen desire to see the madman in question.

"All right!" aid the alienist. "But be content to look, without going into his room. In fact, he has sudden fits of furious insanity, during which he's dangerous."

And, making the least possible noise, he opened the peephole pierced in the door.

The man was standing up, motionless, his arms wide, his fingers splayed, in an ecstatic pose. I could only see his back, but I deduced that ecstasy from the rigidity of his body, and I imagined his contemplative eyes fixed on a point on which the attention of his entire being was concentrated. It was the blackest point of the darkest corner of the room, and yet, my

---

[24] *Le Journal*, 18 July 1900.

[25] "General paralysis [or paresis] of the insane" was identified as a psychiatric disorder in the early 19th century, but was eventually recognized as a neurological condition resulting from infection by syphilis. That suggestion was first made in 1857 but not proven until 1913, so Richepin was probably aware of it but not entirely certain.

contemplative gaze being attached there too, that black point soon appeared to me to be vaguely luminous, as if the gaze of the madman were reflected there. I made that observation to the alienist in a whisper.

My voice, although very subdued, awoke the ecstatic from his ecstasy. He turned toward us. He had a handsome face, gentle and noble, the high forehead of a thinker, the sinuous mouth of an eloquent man, the ardent eyes of a poet. He did not seem exalted by dementia at all, but caressed by a dream. He attracted amity. It was with sadness, not with anger, that he murmured, looking at the alienist:

"When will you return what you have taken from me, thief?"

With a dry and irritated click, the alienist closed the peephole again. Then he drew me along the corridor, saying in a detached tone: "Delusions of persecution are always concomitant with delusions of grandeur. A banal case, I repeat! General paralysis in the second phase!"

"That's odd," I replied. "It interests me, this banal case. Is that because of the man's face, which is extremely sympathetic to me? Undoubtedly. But I'd like to know the story of that madman. Why don't you want to tell it to me? Why?"

"Oh," said the alienist, "if you're that determined, I'll tell you. I don't have any reason not to tell you."

He was still lying. I sensed quite clearly that he was yielding to the almost menacing suspicion of my demand, and that it was, in sum, very disagreeable to him to yield to it. Thus, it was in a sullen fashion that he told me the story, standing in his office, without even having invited me to sit down in order to listen to it. He was, evidently, in great haste to be done with it.

Even as he told it to me, however, the story nevertheless seemed exciting. The man's dementia had, in fact, manifested itself via the empery of a gaze. One day, in an antique dealer's shop, the man had bought a portrait from the previous century—a portrait of a sea-captain—and his madness had been born from the gaze of that portrait. In the eyes from which that gaze emanated, the lines formed by the concentric circles of the iris and the pupil, by the streaks of light and shadow, and by the elliptical curves of the sclerotic, constituted a very special geometrical design, it seemed, by means of which the madman claimed to be able to obtain the exact determination of a point...

At that juncture, in spite of his desire to speak dryly, the alienist could not help giving way to a sort of emotion, which made his voice tremulous and his gestures feverish.

"That point," he said, "would be the location, in Brazil, of an ancient city made entirely of gold, now buried underground." Becoming calm again, he added: "You know that that idea is one of the most frequent in delusions of grandeur. A city made entirely of gold—it's absurd!"

"It's that, then," I said, "that city made entirely of gold, that he reproaches you for having stolen from him?"

"It's the gaze, most of all," the alienist replied, swiftly

"I don't understand," I said.

He had replied more rapidly than he would have wished. He was obliged to explain to me what he had let slip.

"Well, yes," he continued. "The gaze of the portrait, the gaze of those eyes with the strange geometrical design—the gaze that is, to him alone, revelatory in some way—for the eyes a greenish yellow color, in which it seems that the very soul of gold resides."

Again the alienist's voice trembled, and his hands shook. In his eyes too, that soul of gold appeared. The gleam that sprang forth from them at that moment reminded me, I don't know why, of what I had seen a little while before in the black point that seemed to be reflecting the madman's eyes.

"But how, then, have you stolen that gaze?" I asked.

In a steady and mechanical voice he replied: "By lacerating the portrait."

"Perhaps you were wrong to do that," I said. "If the eyes in the portrait had such an intensity of gaze, if the very soul of gold, as you put it, was alive in that gaze, such a portrait was a masterpiece of sorts, and, by lacerating it, you've committed a veritable artistic crime."

Violently, he cried: "The crime would have been to allow the subsistence in that portrait of that gaze, that frightful tempter of a gaze. For there was something in that gaze, believe me, that could trouble not only the already-enfeebled brain of a man afflicted with general paralysis, but even a sound and solid mind. I swear to you that once the geometrical design of the eyes had been observed—and it was real—the empery of that gaze became so powerful..."

He stopped speaking. He was utterly pale. One might have thought that he no longer perceived my presence—that he was elsewhere, that he was seeing in this imagination, that gaze.

Abruptly, the shrill and precipitate sound of an electric bell woke him up. At the same time, a warder came in search of him, for an inmate prey to a crisis. Without taking the time so say goodbye to me, still half-hypnotized, the alienist went out, leaving me alone in his office, the door of which remained open.

I was suffering an internal disturbance that made me feel ill.

I felt as if I were drawn toward a pile of papers held down on the table by a paperweight. The paperweight, a bronze representing a Chinese monster, seemed to be challenging me to liberate those papers. I knocked it over. I scattered the pages that it held captive. I cast my eyes over them furtively.

They were covered in geometric designs, equations and calculations. I recognized the alienist's handwriting.

I continued scattering the sheets. I dispersed them feverishly throughout the room. Something that had surely been buried beneath the pile forced me to do that. I finally reached that something.

I thought I was about to faint. In front of me, a fragment of a painting, cut out of a canvas with scissors, showed me a pair of eyes: the eyes of the portrait that the alienist said that he had lacerated, the eyes darting that famous gaze—the gaze in which, indeed, the very soul of gold was alive.

He had certainly robbed the madman; he had robbed him of that gaze, in the contemplation of which he too, the alienist, was in the process of losing his reason.

Oh, that gaze, that gaze, that gaze!

And I ran away, in a storm of fear, from that gaze, which I had only seen, myself, for the duration of a lightning-flash, no more—and of which, nevertheless, I can never think without saying to myself:

Who can tell whether the madman was really mad?

The Red Casket[26]

This is why I[27] stole Count Boris Zagoureff's famous red casket, how I stole it without stealing it, how I thought at first that I had been stolen while stealing it, and how I had not in fact been stolen while not stealing it.

Among so many fine and beautiful thefts, the perfect and fruitful execution of which made me justly famous, this one is certainly one of the most curious, and does me the most honor. I do not know whether that opinion will be shared by others, but it's mine, and I know what I'm talking about.

The first time that hazard put me in the presence of the famous red casket, I was absolutely unaware that it was famous. It was, therefore, my instinct alone that caused me to twitch at the sight of it and say to myself: *You shall be mine.*

Take note that an ordinary thief would not have given that famous red casket a second glance, especially in the circumstances in which I encountered it.

To begin with, in fact, the casket could not provoke the idea that it contained jewels or valuables, something akin to a portable safe. It did not have the square, massive, armored form of containers of that sort. It was oval, clad in soft leather, without a metal lock, simply closed like an enormous purse by a string knotted with a double bow.

In the second place, even if, beneath that appearance, there had been a container of precious things, what the devil would have that lanky Russian count, threadbare all the way to the weave, with his red hat and his starveling face—a ruined

---

[26] *Le Journal*, 11 August 1900.

[27] The author adds a footnote identifying this story as an extract from "the unpublished memoirs of the burglar Murzet," although its original publication was subtitled "Mémoires de Flamboche."

gambler risking the occasional meager silver coin at baccarat in the casino—have put into it? Even supposing that the red casket had once contained jewels or valuables, the jewels and valuables must have made their exit from it a long time ago in order to gad about on the green baize.

So, as you can see, for an ordinary thief, the red casket had nothing particularly attractive about it.

But I flatter myself with the thought that I am no ordinary thief.

Now, the first time that hazard put me in the presence of the famous red casket, I noticed two things that were significant to me, which were that Count Boris called the bag-like thing "my casket," and that he carried it like a heavy object.

I concluded from that that he attached some value to it, and that there was something in the so-called casket other than dirty socks or spare detachable collars.

And that is why I twitched immediately and said to myself: *You shall be mine.*

That same day, I began to gather information about my man and his red casket. It was only then that the quality the red casket had of being famous was revealed to me. No one, in fact, mentioned Count Boris Zagoureff to me without immediately adding: "Oh yes—with his famous red casket!"

No one, however, could inform me as to the contents of the famous red casket. To tell the truth, no one was curious about it—except that a few gamblers gave me this tip: "The count's an eccentric and a lunatic, who must have a collection of moonstones in it, in which he has faith as fetishes. They're good, his fetishes! The poor fool loses everything he has, when he has anything to lose!"

The explanation was plausible, but scarcely satisfactory. I scented something better than that. I wasn't at all discouraged.

I made the acquaintance of the count. It wasn't very difficult—a matter of a few games of cards, which, it goes without saying, I let him win.

What I gained from them was finding out what value he attached to the famous red casket, by observing that he was never apart from it, that he always had it suspended from his left wrist by the drawstring, even while holding and playing his cards.

As for talking to him about it, you can be sure that I never made such an error. He did not seem like a man to unclench his teeth upon a secret. Gradually, I became his quotidian comrade, without a word or a glance on my part enabling him to suspect my passion for the red casket.

For it had become, on my part, a veritable passion, devouring and irresistible. To have the red casket was necessary to my life. I have these utterly crazy itches for property. That's why I'm a thief, moreover, far more than out of self-interest. But let's pass on! I'm not here to analyze my psychology. Nor do I want to sing my praises and brag about having devised, in order to carry out the theft of the famous red casket, some new and miraculous method.

No, my genius was limited, on this occasion, to seducing and conquering the count, of becoming an indispensable and ever-present friend, with whom he could not do without—to the point that he eventually invited me to stay with him. In that, yes, I was very adept, very clever. It took me six weeks, but I got there, and still without the slightest allusion to the famous red casket, which I gave the appearance of considering, quite naturally, as an integral part of the arm from which it was suspended.

As for the theft itself, I carried it out by having recourse to the classic and banal method of a soporific potion.

Oh, it's not artful, I admit—but it's extremely reliable, and convenient. The essential thing is to make use of it at exactly the right moment, with the motto: *Not too little, not too much.*

I had measured out the requisite dose into one of the innumerable cups of tea that the count and I drank every night. The anticipated effect was produced with clockwork regularity. To undo the knot of the drawstring that attached the famous red casket to the count's wrist was no more than child's play for me—and yet, as I did that, my fingers were trembling. Is that stupid! Me, who has nerves of steel! But there's no denying it; this time, my fingers were trembling.

I was afraid. Of what? Of him, who was asleep? Surely not. What, then?

And I no longer wanted to carry away the red casket. I wanted to open it, there, and look at the contents, there, near to where I had stolen it. Theft has these mysterious and delicious sadisms. That, too, is why I'm a thief. But once again, let's pass on. Perhaps I'll analyze myself some day. Not now!

When the knot was undone, and the casket—or, rather, the bag—was open, the first thing I saw was hair. Oh, admirable! Unique! Golden.

I plunged my hand into it. I pulled it toward me. A head appeared: a woman's head, marvelously beautiful in spite of the closed eyes, the skin greasy and faded by embalming.

In that dead face, one thing seemed to be alive: the mouth, whose parted lips allowed a glimpse of sparkling teeth; the mouth, which was smiling; the mouth, which bore a perfectly fresh tint of rose.

I was no longer afraid. My fingers were no longer trembling. I uttered a burst of interior laughter as I thought: *Good God! I'm stolen!*

Then I uttered another, as I said to myself: *Good God! No, I won't be stolen!*

And before putting the head back into the famous red casket, before retying the knots of the drawstring, before putting everything back in order, as if nothing had happened, I deposited a long kiss on the sparkling teeth, and bit the rosy mouth.

In a White Dress[28]

Smiling and affable in his hirsute patriarchal beard, but with occasional mocking little gleams behind the crystal lenses of his gold-rimmed spectacles, the old philosopher of the editorial staff had listened religiously, without interruption or comment, to all the amorous stories recounted by the young men, particularly by the handsome Paul de Ruexens, a shareholder in the newspaper, the incontestable and uncontested *arbiter elegantiarum* of the group.

"Well of course," he exclaimed, all of a sudden, "you're all lady-killers, that's obvious." Then, addressing Paul de Ruezens: "You especially, it goes without saying." And, warming up, his voice almost oratorical and his gesture that of priest elevating a monstrance, he continued admiringly: "You, as everyone knows, whether in society or the demi-monde, have only to express a desire, or even simply to appear desirous, without actually being so, to be the great conqueror."

Then with a seductive trill of the organ at first, and afterwards with a savant brutality whose rudeness was all the more flattering: "Believe that I congratulate you with all my heart, for that must be infinitely agreeable—but permit me not to be unduly astonished, for the thing is explicable by a host of reasons, physiological and psychological, moral and immoral. There is, to begin with, your physique."

With the chin that he naturally bore aloft raised even higher by this gross compliment delivered to his face, Paul de Ruexens swelled up, blossoming in his authentic Belgian beauty, with his pale pink flesh, his red tightly-curled hair and large eyes of a profound azure, in which the warm sun of the Spanish conquest seemed to linger. In all sincerity, and even without self-interested cajolery toward a shareholder, one

---

[28] *Le Journal*, 18 April 1900.

could proclaim that he had all that it required to please women and to be the kind of Don Juan who, in any society whatsoever, as soon as he is one woman's lover, is desired by all the rest. And so the old philosopher of the editorial staff, beneath his apparent flattery, was only being truthful.

If the gentleman had accentuated his flattery, however, it was because he had subjected himself to restrictions for a long time, holding something back that had only been manifest thus far in the mocking little gleams behind the crystal lenses of his gold-rimmed spectacles, which finally burst forth, impatiently, in this abrupt and unexpected sally: "Which doesn't alter the fact that, in spite of all your trump cards, as a man beloved, I can beat you hands down."

Like his compliment of a few moments before, it was full in the face that he sent that to the handsome Paul de Ruexens, without any warning, at a stroke, in the manner of a slap.

Everyone, the shareholder first and foremost, took it as a joke, and welcomed it with a loud burst of laughter, finding it funny because it was so unexpected.

"Don't laugh," said the old philosopher. There's no reason. You see, I can't think about this beautiful story, more beautiful than all of yours, this exquisite and delightful story of love—pure, veritable and ingenuous love—without having a desire to weep."

And that as said in a grave tone, which caused all the laughter to die away respectfully, in spite of the habit they had of subjecting the old man to ridicule, and even though he lent himself to it at that moment more particularly than ever, for he had taken off his spectacles, laying bare the gross globes of his myopic eyes, which had been myopic for sixty years; and he was wiping his checkered handkerchief—an invalid's handkerchief—sometimes over those dull eyes and sometimes over the misted lenses of his spectacles, without anyone being able to tell, and seemingly unable to tell himself, whether the tears were in his eyes or in his spectacles.

While liking to amuse themselves at his expense, they knew that he was a good storyteller when he wanted to take the trouble, and they sensed that he was about to tell a story. They had only to fall silent for him to begin. They fell silent at a gesture from the shareholder, curious to know in what manner the fellow had been able, as a man beloved, to beat the handsome Ruexens hands down.

"It was about twenty years ago, the old philosopher began. "I was even less handsome than I am now, which is saying a lot. Today, my white beard and the gold of my spectacles give me a certain venerability, which has its charm. Then, I didn't even have that. My oxtail-colored complexion, an old rusty pince-nez, the wretched clothes of a poor schoolteacher advertising for private pupils at twenty sous apiece, a black and incorrigible poverty, an empty stomach and all pride obliterated, all gave me a special, magisterial, unique ugliness, which was, I must confess, veritably hideous and imperiously repulsive."

A slight murmur of approval granted the probable exactitude of this retrospective portrait. The old philosopher replied to it with a mocking bow, and continued:

"It was in that condition, however, that I had an opportunity to be loved, as none of you, I repeat, has ever been. What can I say? It's implausible, but that was the way it was. The wind of love blows where it pleases, doesn't it? It was, in any case, I hasten to declare, in order to render the implausibility less glaring, by a very young woman. Let's not mince words and spit it out: by a virtual child."

A few jokers risked an "Oh!" of feigned indignation. The old man joined in, *rinforzando*.

"Me too, damn it!" he went on. "I was startled when that gamine set her cap at me. Imagine a girl of about thirteen, not much more. But pretty, of course! A little satyress. And to think that for six months, it appears, I'd passed her every day without noticing her! She told me that. Yes, every morning, on my way to give baccalaureate lessons at a house in the Rue Monsieur-le-Prince, I stopped outside Père Meusiot's second-hand bookshop—and she lived opposite, a serving-girl in a kind of laundry. A servant, you hear, at that age! She told me all that in a single breath, calling me *tu*, into the bargain, and offering straight out to come and sleep with me. You can see here how I leapt backwards."

He did it again from memory, nearly knocking his chair over. Hilarity had resumed its rights; everyone laughed. He laughed too, especially in remembering the terror he had felt then, at the idea that some local pimp had sent the brat in the hope of blackmailing him afterwards. And he imitated the coarse voice in which he had sent her to the Devil, calling her a filthy little thing and threatening to call the police.

Immediately, he had stopped going past that end of the street—but a week later, the little mummer had buttonholed him at the other end and had said to him, weeping and sobbing: "I know why you don't want to. It's because you think I'm a slut, isn't it? Well, it's not true. Never, never, with anyone! And I love you, so there! I want you to take me."

And she went into extraordinary detail, according to the old philosopher. With what filthy words but what a naïve soul she explained all that, he described and commented on delightfully.

"Ha ha!" said someone. "One would think that you had regrets about it, you old lecher!"

"Yes," he replied, "I have regrets about it—but for her soul."

And again, no one had any desire to laugh, he said that so sadly.

"I was wrong to start this story," he added. "I can never finish it."

People protested. They begged him to finish. He let himself be persuaded. He had put his spectacles on a few moments before; he took them off again, in order to weep more comfortably—large, slow tears this time.

"How," he went on, "did she find out where I lived, and how, above all, had she been able to get in? I don't know. Still, one night, when I got home, I found her there, lying in my bed. She swore to me that if I didn't sleep with her, she would throw herself out of the window. At the same time, she leapt out of bed and threw herself into my arms. She was dressed in a white muslin dress. As I stammered some rapid questions, very anxious at seeing her so excited, she replied that she had dressed like that in order to get married, since we were going to be married, and that it was, moreover, a first communion dress, and that she had stolen from her employer, expressly in order to come to me like a little angel, since she was one. And a whole lot of other similar things, sweet, tender, poetic, inventive, gracious...and also that she was older than thirteen, so there! That she was over fifteen! Exactly! And that finally, from the fifth floor, where I lodged, to the courtyard, down below, she would surely kill herself, and immediately, if..."

The fellow really could not finish his story, he was sobbing so much.

"In brief," said Ruexens, with a coarse laugh, "what happened, man so beloved? Come on, tell."

The old philosopher put his spectacles on again, secured them on his nose, and darted through the crystal at the Belgian Don Juan a glance laden with scorn. Then, to everyone's great amazement, he replied, without reflection:

"You don't deserve to be told that story, Monsieur. You're a lady-killer, undoubtedly, Monsieur, but you don't know what love is."

Then after launching a long jet of saliva into his invalid's moustache, he added: "You'll never be anything but a pig, my lad."

The Goat-Kid[29]

In order not to perceive the sudden and profound impression, a real thunderbolt, that he produced upon the Countess Maroussia, it would have been necessary, in spite of his conceit, for Yves de Guirnec to have been utterly, as they say in his native Brittany, blind in all three eyes. The Countess had, in fact, made visible, without any inhibition and quite plainly, what she was experiencing. She was one of those Russian grand dames who, whether ingenuous or cynical, have the superb insolence of their sensations and sentiments.

It was, however, with a tranquility no less insolently superb that the Breton had received that ardent and mad mute declaration—and he could not have replied in a more brutal and more peremptory fashion by shouting "No" in the tone of a cavalry officer's command.

So, no sooner was the countess outside than there was a barrage of questions, wanting to know the inexplicable reason for such coldness. Still coldly, but giving as good as he got, Yves de Guirnec replied to them—and the more he replied, the less anyone understood.

"You didn't think she was pretty, then?"

"Indeed! Very pretty."

"Not seductive, even so."

"I beg your pardon! One could not be more seductive."

"You did notice her glances?"

"Addressed to me, yes."

"And her significant smiles?"

"Rather say provocative."

"In which she positively offered herself to you?"

"So I gathered."

---

[29] *Le Journal*, 4 May 1900.

"You know that she has an income of seven hundred thousand francs a year."

"So much the better for her."

"And that she's a widow."

"So much the worse for her."

"But in the end what do you have against her?"

"It's the first time we've met."

"Someone could have old you some story..."

"I did not know her name, her nationality."

"In brief, she displeased you?"

"Not in the least."

"But you wouldn't want her for a wife?"

"Oh no, of course not!"

"For a mistress, perhaps?"

"Nor that."

"What, then?"

"Then nothing."

"Breton dimwit, who digs his heels in for no reason!"

"Breton dimwit if you like, but for no reason? Stop there!"

"Oh, you have reasons?"

"Certainly."

"Well, what are they?"

"You wouldn't understand, good-for-nothing."

"Explain them anyway."

"If you insist!"

"Absolutely."

"Let's go, then."

And, in the great silence that descended, after having slowly lit a cigar, Yves de Guirnec, taking on an air of mystery, uttered these words in a fateful tone:

"It's because of a goat-kid."

There was an explosion of laughter, cries and protests. Some thought he had gone mad. Others thought they had gone mad themselves, or deaf. Had they heard correctly? What did it mean? What connection could there be between the Countess and a goat-kid? Was the serious Yves de Guirnec turning into a practical joker?

"You're much further forward, aren't you?" he continued. "And now, it's necessary for you to sit down in a circle, and be as good as gold, while I, poor thing, tell you a story, like a grandmother at bedtime. In a Parisian smoking-room at two o'clock in the morning, if that's not absurd! Anyway, you're the ones who wanted it."

A few of them didn't want it, and went back to dancing. Several remained, but gradually edged away toward the drawing-rooms—for Yves had set out, doubtless out of malice, to tell his story at length and, so to speak, Breton-fashion. He would never finish! Even I, curious as I am about stories, nodded off while listening to it.

"Once upon a time," he said, "there was a goat-kid that came every day to eat bread from the hand of a painter. And it was the prettiest goat-kid that one could ever see. So the painter loved the kid very much—very, very much."

There followed a interminable description of the kid, its deeds and feats, and all its delicacies—how it had eyes in retreat toward the temples, in which, when one looked a them in profile, once could see the pupil in the form of a crescent moon with points terminated by stars, whereas the other kids did not have those stars; and how, when the kid sniffed the urine of its mother-goat on the ground it raised its upper lip in the shape of a circumflex accent, whereas the other kids raised theirs in a simple arc; and how...

Doubtless those two details solicited my attention more particularly because of their eccentricity, for those I can remember—but they were mingled with many and various details that I no longer have in my memory. And I remember too that at a certain point in the tale—toward the middle, I think—those two characteristic details cropped up again.

The painter had bought the kid for which he had so much affection, and the kid had become a great she-devil of a nanny-goat, with which the painter no longer knew what to do. He had tried to return it to the goatherd, pointing out those two singular things, to which the old man had replied; "If the nanny has them, it's necessary to kill her, because nannies that have them bring bad luck to the herd."

But the painter had not wanted to kill the nanny-goat, which was his old and so pretty little kid. Besides, he did not believe what the goatherd said. The superstitions of simple people are so stupid! The painter was young then, and when one is young, one tends to make fun of rural sorcerers, doesn't one?

Finally, the painter, when he left the country, had made a gift of the goat to a poor man who already had two nanny-goats and a young billy-goat. That gave the poor man the beginnings of a herd. A year later, the painter came back to the locality, and learned that the poor man's herd had been wiped out by disease and that the poor man himself, while caring for the nanny-goat, had been killed by a thrust of her horn.

Then the painter had run into the old goatherd, and the goatherd said to him: "You see where it leads to, a kid that has the signs."

And the tale finished there, at about three o'clock in the morning. Yves lit a third cigar, and I was the only listener he had left.

"But after all, my dear friend," I said to him, "what about the Countess Maroussia?"

"I'm no longer the skeptical painter today," Yves de Guirnec replied, "that I was at twenty. I've become a true Breton again, believing in spells and signs. Now, I've seen Countess Maroussia's eye in profile, and I've observed her smile. She has the kid-goat's signs, that's all!" He added: "I seem stupid to you, eh?"

A Russian general who seemed to be asleep in my corner spared me the embarrassment of replying by abruptly interrupting our conversation, to which he had listened, and saying: "Messieurs, the Countess is the widow of her fifth husband—who died, like the other four, violently."

Booglottism[30]

Twelve hours, ten of which were night, to see Smyrna—
obviously, that wasn't much. But what can one do? The boat
was only stopping there for those twelve hours, from six in the
evening to six in the morning. Pierre Brignolles had neither
the time nor the money that he would have needed for a longer
stay, while waiting for another boat. Nor did he anticipate ever
having an opportunity to come back. He therefore took advantage, even so, of the opportunity that was offered, such as
it was, and went ashore, promising himself to do his best to
enjoy his brief and summary windfall as best he could.

It was the middle of June. He still had two hours of daylight. Then the darkness would be transparent, and almost as
luminous as day. In sum, he had the means to avoid boredom.

And, in fact, scarcely had he disembarked than Pierre
Brignolles avoided boredom. He had not taken thirty steps
along the quay, amid the porters and the guides who offered
their services in Turkish, Greek, Arabic, Maltese and in that
bizarre French-like language that resembles the gibberish of
Molière's mamamouchis,[31] and was still in the process of
fighting his way through them, when a enormous beardless
negro put a gold coin into his hand and whispered in his ear, in
bad English: "Come! Many others for you, out there, if you
come."

At the same time, the negro scattered the porters and
guides by means of a large leather courbache, with which he

---

[30] *Le Journal*, 12 September 1898. The title is an improvisa-
tion; there is no such word.

[31] A word invented by Molière to serve as a fake title acquired
by the eponymous protagonist of *Le Bourgeois gentilhomme*
(1670), which became generalized as a term for foolish aspira-
tion to nobility.

menaced them. The rabble formed a circle, but with cries and laughter that seemed to be mocking Pierre Brignolles. He did not understand any of it. Nevertheless, the very bizarreness of the thing appealed to him. In his turn, the threatened the mockers with a gesture signifying that he had a revolver in his pocket, and resolutely followed the negro.

What did that singular cicerone want? Why had he been given a gold coin and promised others? What was the "out there" to which he was going? Precisely because he understood it less and less, Pierre Brignolles reveled in it, as a lover of mystery, hazard and adventure.

The negro guided him through a labyrinth of back streets, marching ahead of him, without saying anything more now. They arrived thus at a little café with no one inside, and where they sat down while they were served two cups. Then the negro, still in bad English and still whispering in Brignolles' ear, said to him: "You French, no? Me see you French."

"Yes," the young man replied.

"You like lovely women? Me see you like them."

"Certainly," said Pierre, who did not detest them.

"You also like money, because you not rich," the other continued, winking. "Me see you not rich."

"Indeed," replied Pierre Brignolles, who, having paid for his passage, was returning to France with thirty-seven francs in his pocket, including the negro's gold piece. And, to emphasize his reply, he displayed everything that he possessed in that pocket, and simultaneously took out his revolver for a second time, as if he wanted to let it be understood that he did not have much but that he was ready to defend himself energetically if anyone tried to take it.

In fact, a suspicion had just been born within him regarding the negro's intentions, imagining that the latter might have brought him to this deserted café in this remote quarter in order to rob him. But the negro understood, smiled silently, put three more gold coins into his hand, and added: "Many others for you, out there."

"But where, out there?" Pierre Brignolles interrogated, summoning up what English he knew.

"Home of lovely woman," the negro replied. "Home of very lovely woman, who pay you much, if want with her, but not see anything."

The adventure and the mystery were becoming spicier. Pierre Brignolles was delighted. He did not experience scruples any more than fear. He stood up bravely, and replied: "Go. I follow you. I want."

And they resumed their journey through the labyrinth of back-streets, all the way to a sort of cul-de-sac forming a vault, under which it was almost pitch-dark. There, the negro opened a little low-set door, which introduced Pierre Brignolles into a cellar-like vestibule, this time totally black, then took him by the hand and led him along a seemingly-winding corridor to a much larger room—insofar as one could judge by the resonance of footsteps in the dense obscurity.

Having arrived in that place, the negro asked the young man whether he had any matches on him. Pierre replied in the affirmative and handed the box to the negro, who struck one.

By that abrupt light, Pierre Brignolles saw that he was in a round chamber, with no exit except on the side where the door to the corridor was, that in the middle of that, chamber cushions and carpets were heaped up, and that on that improvised bed lay a woman, stark naked, with a marvelous body, but whose head was hermetically enveloped by veils.

The match went out, and the negro said to Pierre Brignolles: "This is the very lovely lady you do with. Me know what time you boat leave tomorrow. Me come back to find you, take you to boat. You do tranquil, but you not see that face."

And how the Devil, even if he had wanted to, could Pierre Brignolles have seen the woman's face? The negro had gone out now, closing the door behind him, taking the box of matches with him.

My word! *Honni soit qui mal y pense!* Pierre Brignoles was twenty-four years old; the body of the unknown woman

91

had appeared to him to be splendid and young; the bed of carpets and cushions was profound; the closed chamber sweated sensuality; what had to happen happened.

It was an absolutely crazy night of love, but also a cruelly absurd night of love, for it passed without a single kiss being exchanged mouth to mouth between the two lovers. The woman had certainly taken off her veils, liberating the thick and silky tresses of her hair, but her face, which he was obliged not to see, he was also obliged not to touch. A kind of mask in leather and wood shielded it with an impenetrable visor, solely pierced by three holes, through which an ardent and delicious breath emerged. And like her face, the woman's voice remained a mystery. She did not speak. Sighs and hoarse gasps at certain moments—that was all. Not a single word!

Pierre Brignolles played his part. He was one of those instinctive individuals who know how to enjoy things without worrying too much about whys and wherefores. He did not even try to imagine the why and the wherefore. He had better things to do, and occupied himself with them alone—so much and so well that he slept like a log, dreamlessly, after that reality more beautiful than a dream.

"You go. Be time."

It was the negro, who woke him up, dressed him, led him back through the winding corridor and then through the little low-set door opening into the cul-de-sac, and then through the labyrinthine back-streets. Then there as the brightly-lit quay, swarming with the rabble who yapped and laughed all around them. The negro scattered them with his courbache. The boat's launch was waiting at the quay. Pierre Brignolles embarked upon it, and went back aboard, still bewildered, intoxicated by his night of love, dazzled by his mysterious adventure, and quickly returned to his cabin, where he plunged, fully dressed, into a brute sleep while the boat moved off.

At eleven o'clock, during the meal, Pierre Brignolles, in low spirits, was eating avidly when he heard the ship's doctor talking to his neighbors.

"Yes, it's a very strange case. The girl, it appears, has an admirable body. A totally beautiful Greek! But she's mute, and almost idiotic, it's said, because of that monstrosity. Imagine an enormous tongue, like that of an ox. At any rate, it's a case of what's known as booglottism. It's extremely..."

Pierre Brignolles raised his head. Mechanically, he put his hand into his pocket, which seemed heavy. He caused coins to clink that he was unaware of having. He blushed.

Then, ferociously, he resumed eating, saying to himself: *Bah! En voyage!*[32]

---

[32] The significance of this phrase is difficult to translate pedantically, but it has something in common with an Englishman saying "I'm on holiday!" or an American saying "What happens in Vegas stays in Vegas"—with Smyrna standing in for Las Vegas in this instance.

The Mask[33]

"Oh well," Harry Sloughby said to me, "All our imaginations are poor, compared with reality." He winked, and added, with a smile: "Even yours, Mister Merchant of the Imagination!"

And he reminded me, while mocking me with his humorous malice, of some of the more extravagant solutions that I had invented for that insoluble problem, so mysterious and captivating.

It was the question of the strange individual that we had then baptized "the Mask."

When I say that we knew him, it's a manner of speaking. In sum, we had only seen him, looked at him, contemplated him, and studied him, inasmuch as it was possible to study him—but no matter how far we were driven to indiscretion by our desire to know him, we did not really know him, that Unknowable.

His existence, in fact, did not permit penetration any more than his visage, which was and remained, always and everywhere, masked.

Harry Sloughby, who has, as they say, acquaintances with God and the Devil, had found the means of bribing one of the Mask's domestics and making him talk—yes, he had gone as far as that! And it wasn't easy to do, since the domestic was mute! Even that miracle had told us nothing.

The mute, who was Hindu into the bargain, knew no more than we did about his master. He had been in his service for a long time, but he knew nothing whatsoever about the man, not even his name—and he had only ever seen his face masked.

---

[33] *Le Journal*, 30 August 1899.

Did the Mask take his mask off when he was alone? One could assume so; to affirm it was not permissible. In order to sleep, the Mask shut himself in a bedroom containing a toilet and bathroom, and that room was sealed by an iron door like the door of a safe.

As we had followed the Mask many times, and Harry Sloughby had had him followed especially by his old friend O'Greenaddle, the detective, we had also discovered that the individuals visited prostitutes regularly. They had been interrogated. Their responses had always been similar.

"He's extremely generous. He only stays for a few minutes. He doesn't take his clothes off. He never takes his mask off."

As one can imagine, before anything else, Harry Sloughby had sought information from the Minster of Police, with whom he was on friendly terms. He had found nothing there but a copy of an official document, previously stamped in Calcutta, authorizing Mr. James Smith, merchant, to wear a mask on his face in England, as he wore one in India, by reason of the necessity not to cause scandal.

Harry Sloughby had given me an exact translation of that, and had, in addition, given me the English text, from which, with the aid of several dictionaries, I had not been able to extract any further meaning.

That the bizarre man was really named James Smith—which is to say, just like anyone else—we did not want to believe. That he was a merchant, we found grotesque. Merchant of what? Does a merchant have the idea of living in such an original manner? Get away!

All of that—the name, the title of merchant, all of it—had to be nothing but a mask!

Where our imaginations worked overtime, and doggedly, to the point of obsession, as you can guess, was on the final phrase of the document: "by reason of the necessity not to cause scandal"—and with reference to that matter, inventing the most extravagant stories: the face of a monster; elephantiasis; a wound; obscene tattoos—who could tell? It was there that I distinguished myself, it appears, by my extravagance, as Harry Sloughhby reminded me ironically at that moment.

"And to think," he repeated, smiling, "that all that, compared with the reality, was...how do you say it in French? Oh yes, I have it: *gnognotte*...in the end, nothing but wretched *gnognotte*: rubbish!"

Well, damn it," I exclaimed, tell me the real reason!"

"Splendid!" he said. "Admirable! Marvelous! Sublime!"

He took a fat wallet out of his pocket, and then took a piece of parchment out of the wallet, and handed it to me, saying, very gravely this time: "You can read it yourself, my friend. That's the best thing."

As I prepared to read, he took hold of my hand and continued: "But first, let me ask you something. In your opinion, ten years ago, how old would the Mask have been?"

"Between forty and forty-five, in my estimation," I replied.

"He was over sixty-eight," he said, "For he has just died, last week, almost an octogenarian—only eighteen months short."

"Damn!" I exclaimed. "he was extraordinarily well-preserved."

"He was," said Harry Sloughby, "until his very last day. And this is what was written to me in that regard by our friend Dr. Burpitt, who was summoned to the man's death-bed, at the express request of the dying man, and who was charged by him with carrying out what is stipulated in this parchment. Listen to what my friend Burpitt wrote to me."

Harry Sloughby had taken a letter from his wallet, in which I recognized the long, delicate handwriting of our old friend the doctor, and he translated what follows for me, first reading the doctor's own text, extraordinarily enthusiastic for a man ordinary so composed, so calm, so cold—in a word, so scientific:

"Imagine, my friend all that Greek mythology was able to express of the most noble and simultaneously the most seductive—which is to say, the majesty of Zeus combined with the grace of Aphrodite, and you will still scarcely have an idea of the truly unbearable emotion that then came to dazzle my gaze and make the entire lyre of my brain vibrate. My knees gave way beneath me, and it seemed that my very being was about to volatilize as if in a thunderclap. It was the revelation of Beauty."

"Oh!" I interjected. "Has our sage Burpitt gone mad? Or have you gone mad, my dear friend? What connection is there between the doctor's esthetic ecstasy and the Mask?"

"Read the parchment now," exclaimed Harry Sloughby. "Read—you'll understand. "Splendid, I tell you! Admirable! Marvelous! Sublime!"

I read; here, very nearly, is a translation of what I read:

This is my testament, which I bequeath to Doctor Burpitt.

After my death, Doctor Burpitt will be my heir, on condition that he obeys strictly all the instructions contained herein.

He will unmask my face and look at it, for as long as he wishes, and will thus be able to render testimony as to the reason that has caused me to live masked; but he will be the only one to render that testimony.

He will, in fact, after having contemplated me at his leisure, coat my face with quicklime and cover it again with its mask.

It was at the age of eighteen that I made the resolution to wear that mask; no one, since then has seen my face—no one at all!

I did not want anyone to see it, no one in the world being worthy of it, in our era of abominable ugliness.

For I was, I am, and always will be handsome; I am beautiful.

I am handsome with a fulgurant beauty, whose glare no one can endure without suffering, of which one would die if one felt it fully.

But such a death would be too pure and too heroic for my ignoble contemporaries, and I have refused to give them that divine enjoyment, even after my death, even in memory.

Doctor Burpitt is a noble soul, chilled by science, who will be able to see me without dying of it, and will be able to render testimony that I was neither vainglorious not insane, but a god.

I die happy, since I have had the solitary joy of being, in the course of the eternal becoming of things, one of the eternal effigies of the Beautiful.

The world will only have known my Mask. Perhaps that is still too much.

I am the symbol of life.

The Ugly Sisters[34]

"Why didn't I stay in Paris? Why didn't I seek, like the other comrades in the gang, to carve out my niche there? Because I felt that I would bury myself in that niche. Because I realized, one day that I had, and increasingly would have, a horror of Paris, because of its nauseating and crushing banality."

"What do you mean?"

"I mean that in Paris everyone is the same."

"While in the provinces..."

"Go on, go on, mock the provinces. Come out with one of your old clichés, Parisian nourished on ready-made ideas! Tell me that a province is a pond and that Paris is a sea, that one stagnates in a pond and sails on a sea, battles, discovers Americas, blah, blah, blah! But I can use rhetoric too if I wish. I can reply that in a pond there are flowers, frogs and many other things that you know nothing about—and then, into your tempestuous sea, throw flints or even diamonds! With the ebb and flow of its tides, it will reduce them to shingle, so there! But enough rhetoric. And sod your Paris!"

"Well, you're still the same old eccentric."

"And I'm not the only one here, thankfully. That's why I like it here. Do you know that here, in my poor pond, there are at least a dozen minds thinking for themselves, having ideas of their own—reasonable or extravagant, but their own? Can you name me as many in Paris?"

"It's an amusing paradox."

"But it's not a paradox. It's the truth, damn it! And I'm not the first to say so. Your beloved Balzac, who, I believe, knew it so well through its characters, says somewhere; 'there are no eccentrics but those in the provinces.' Eh?"

---

[34] *Le Journal*, 10 May 1900.

"Perhaps Balzac was right, after all, and the argument, on reflection, is sustainable."

"But it leaps to the eyes! And it couldn't be otherwise. Just think of the stuffiness of provincial life, of all the precautions that it's necessary to take there against an ever-threatening curiosity, of the secret and intensive cultivation that passion acquires there, of the great dung-heap of hypocrisy that nourishes vice there."

"Watch out! Rhetoric's lying in wait for you in your turn. That's just words."

"Oh, Monsieur wants facts! Monsieur will doubtless write a story—the story of not having wasted his time in the provinces. You need a flower, a frog from my meager pond! If the opportunity arises, you won't be sorry to have found the idea for a novel or short story here. Well, I'll give you one! I've often thought about it, but if I were a novelist, I wouldn't dare to write it. Perhaps you, a Parisian, will dare. Pay attention! Do you remember the Ugly Sisters?"

Of course I remembered them. How could I have forgotten them? They scared me so much, when I was small. And later, when I had begun to look at people and things while trying to understand them, they seemed to me, at first, so strange in appearance and then so particularly symbolic in their strangeness.

During my childhood, when I went to school in that small town, the two Ugly Sisters were already old ladies—or, at least, seemed so to me, although they were no more than fifty years old, or thereabouts, at that time. But they were so thin, so wrinkled and so decrepit that they gave me the impression of two witches of old.

Always together, always clad in black, furtively trotting along, the gaze of their little mousy eyes ferreting everywhere, they were the terror of the local brats because of their loud voices and the little gray moustaches shading the corners of their mouths. They probably delighted in inspiring that terror, for, when kids passed close by then grumbled loudly, darting glances like drills, and pulling faces in such a way as to make their wisps of hair bristle—and the children ran away, whimpering!

The Ugly Sisters were not, however, malevolent women. I found that out when I was older and came back, as a student on vacation, then as an apprentice man of letters putting himself out to grass in the quiet small town to which my parents had retired. I knew through them that the Ugly Sisters were simply religious old women, fairly well off, very generous to the poor, with no friends, who went walking a lot between church services, whose only fault was that they did not like children. Apart from that, one could scarcely reproach them for anything—except that they were not natives of the locality. They had come to live there at the age of forty, without anyone knowing why, for they had no relatives or acquaintances there.

As for their fashion of living without a maid, people generally approved of it. Did two women living alone, even when well off, have any reason not to do their own shopping, housework and cooking? If it pleased them, moreover, to dress themselves perpetually in mourning, what right had anyone to hold that against them, if that was their desire? No one could accuse them of avarice; they were so generous in giving alms!

And so, even in that gossip-ridden small town, they were unanimously esteemed; and, according to the local expression, when one had said "the Ugly Sisters," one had said everything there was to say.

In consequence of which, recently molded by reading "Un Coeur simple," I had imagined in their respect a beautiful and touching romance worth of Flaubert. I had even tried to write it. Then, wisely judging that Flaubert had written it himself, I had renounced making the acquaintance of the Ugly Sisters in order to study them—which, I must admit, they had prevented, by presenting to me, as if I were still a child, their shrill voices, their piercing gazes and their angry-cat moustaches.

Oh, yes, certainly I remembered them, and on hearing their name, immediately evoked their faces, with all that strangeness and symbolism. And I told my friend that I knew them, and believed that I had understood them.

"Right!" he said. "You've understood nothing at all, and you don't know anything. As for the story you wanted to write, it wouldn't have been as good as theirs, the true one, which I'll reveal to you, in substance. To begin with, know that the Ugly Sisters died, at the age of ninety-two, in a double suicide."

"At ninety-two?"

"Yes. Gassed themselves, like grisettes!"

"Those religious old women?"

"Oh, no more religious than you or me."

"What! Their devotion..."

"Play-acting. Like their entire life, moreover. And how they played it to perfection! Imagine that I, curious about them, spying on them, finding them mysterious, wanting to know their secret, lived in close proximity to them for half a century, in the same small town, without ever being able to suspect a thing! Oh, what a marvel! And you don't know why I adore provincial life!"

He had taken me by the arm, had put my hat on my head, had donned his own, and was dragging me through the streets, saying to me; "Yes, I've thought about it many times, their story. And I assure you that, Parisian as you are, you still won't write it, any more than anyone else will. And yet, what an admirable, prodigious, unique book it would make. You'll see."

"But where are you taking me?"

"To the cemetery, where their grave is, as the two of them wanted. Their will left a fortune to the hospice, on condition that their gravestone was set up there, with the inscription you're going to read."

We had reached the cemetery, and the gravestone, on which I read:

Here lie, after seventy years of a perfect union, Jules and Fernand, alias the Ugly Sisters.

The Double Soul[35]

"You see, Doctor," the young man concluded, "that my story, which I believe I have told you in an entirely reasonable fashion, is surely that of a madman—and that's why I've come to consult you about the case, to ask for the explanation of your expertise and the treatment of your care."

The last few words were accompanied by an elegant gesture and a gracious simple. The long and detailed story had been told all the way through in a calm voice, in measured, well-chosen and precise terms, with a sure method and a rare clarity of exposition. One would not have thought him a sick man talking about his own illness, but a scrupulous narrator explaining the condition of a third party, with no other concern than furnishing a clear and exact description.

The knowledge, experience and diagnostic genius that characterized Doctor Vincenod, and had legitimately won the celebrated alienist so much glory, had made him a man difficult to astonish and incapable of ever stopping short in anything concerning mental illness. This time, however, the celebrated alienist found himself nonplussed, caught napping, hesitant and in the dark.

He remained silent, not daring to make any reply, not knowing what to settle upon or compare, too completely entangled by all the details of the story to find a guiding thread therein, unable to reach a conclusion, lost in vain inductions, and visibly suffering, as a man accustomed to solid certainties, from being cast adrift in that fashion among murky and inconsistent hypotheses.

This is the story that the young man had told him: a veritable story of madness, narrated rationally.

---

[35] *Le Gaulois*, 22 December 1895.

The son of a Picard gentleman and an Englishwoman, the young man had spent his childhood and a part of his adolescence, until the age of sixteen, without experiencing anything out of the ordinary or having anything abnormal happen to him—without anything noteworthy at all, except that, every winter, the traveled to the south of France and Italy with his parents, who spent alternate months of the summer in England and Picardy, and that, in sum, his instruction and education, very complete and very careful in spite of that nomadic existence, had been provided solely by his father and his mother, both of whom were very distinguished intelligences.

At sixteen, he had lost his father, and on the day of his death, caused by a hunting accident in Corsica, to which he was a witness, it was as if he had ceased to exist himself. At least, he could not find any other expression to render the absolute vacuity of his memories, totally abolished from that day on, for a period of two years.

What had happened to him in the course of those two years? Not knowing that himself, nor had he had the resource of being informed by others. On reawakening to life—again, there was no other expression to render that sensation of reawakening—at the age of eighteen, he was also deprived of his mother, and had no idea when and how he had lost her. He found himself in Paris, in a hotel, where he was staying under the name of James Garfield, with no luggage, but with a wallet containing thirty thousand francs in French banknotes.

He had then gone to Picardy, put his affairs in order, and, above all, tried to reacquaint himself with himself. There, all that he had learned from the notary was that two years before his mother had come, furnished with all the necessary documents, to liquidate the succession in her own name and that of the son and heir whose guardian she was. Since then, no one had had any news of her.

Between the ages of eighteen and twenty he had traveled, living on his thirty thousand francs. At twenty, another eclipse similar to the first had ensued, and had similarly lasted for two years: another period in which he positively ceased to exist, conserving no memory of it, even the vaguest and most obscure.

Finally, a month ago, he had found himself, at the age of twenty-two, staying in the same hotel as before, under another English name—Harry Baskett, this time—again without any luggage, and again with a wallet containing thirty thousand francs in French banknotes.

Dr. Vincenod was still silent. The young man was still waiting for a response.

"Monsieur," the alienist said to him, finally, "I'm forced to confess that I don't understand it at all. This is a mystery which, it seems to me, does not concern science, but rather the police."

"The police wouldn't have any clue to follow," the young man put in. "I repeat that I have never, on waking up in Paris, had anything on me that could serve as a starting-point for any investigation. My clothes do not bear the name of a tailor. My pockets contain nothing except the wallet. Only my assumed name might imply that I've arrived from England—but that name, whether Garfield or Baskett, is quite common over there. I tried to take advantage of the unique and slender information furnished by the choice of an English name, but I was unable to get anything out of it. The police could do no more. I think that your science might be more useful to me. I must be—I certainly am—the victim of a mental illness. Which? That's what I implore you to discover. At least, what does the disturbance that strikes me periodically resemble? That's what your generosity, the love of your art and the very concern for our glory, oblige you to try to discover."

Dr. Vincenod was not easily manipulated, but, thus backed into a corner, he contented himself with answering: "The true glory of a serious physician is to affirm nothing when he is in doubt."

"Well, Doctor," the young man replied, "admit me to your sanitarium for treatment, study my case, make me an experimental subject, and try to change your doubt into affirmation."

"Yes," said the doctor. "I'll do that."

And the young man entered the alienist's establishment as a patient under observation.

He remained there for twenty-three months, without the doctor being able to observe anything odd—which irritated him. For, reluctant as he was to emit a hypothesis of which he was not sure, the alienist did have one, and believed it with all his conviction, and was enraged by his failure ever to find the shadow of a fact that might serve to justify it, or even put it to the proof. His most ingenious and subtlest investigations remained impotent.

He had concluded, but without any proof, that it was a case of multiple personality.

Suddenly, one evening, the proof began to emerge. In the middle of a conversation, the young man started speaking English. At the same time, he went pale; his eyes changed expression and he seemed prey to a crisis of somnambulism. It was only for a transient moment. He came back to himself, and continued the conversation in French. Interrogated by the doctor, he could not remember having spoken English; he had no consciousness of being absent from himself.

On that basis, the alienist concluded that his hypothesis was confirmed. Undoubtedly the duplication of personality manifested itself regularly, at two-year intervals; when the two years of one personality came to a end, the other was ready to come into play; between the two of them, one curious phenomenon was indispensable, a kind of mental trigger by which the first self yielded its place to the second.

Dr. Vincenod was delighted. It had been granted to him to witness that unique operation, to record the process, to establish the mechanism, and probably to study the underlying law.

The next morning, the young man had vanished. With a sureness, an ingenuity of precautions, a combination of audacity and cunning entirely typical of certain lunatics, he had put his warder to sleep, had put on his costume, having stripped him, and…was gone! A marvelous escape, leaving no trace.

The police, immediately alerted by the doctor, could not find any.

A month later, the *Psychic News* published an article by Professor Burpitt entitled "The Double Soul".

On reading it, Dr. Vincenod wept with fury. It was *his* case, which had been stolen.

The young man, after waking up in London in his other personality, had gone to consult the English alienist and had told him the whole story recounted here to Dr. Vincenod. Over there, he recalled nothing of his life until the age of sixteen, nor anything of the years elapsed between eighteen and twenty.

Nevertheless, the English professor, bolder or less conscientious than Dr. Vincenod, had not hesitated, himself, to reveal to the young man the mental monstrosity that had to be the key to the mystery. He had said to him:

"You have two souls."

Fearfully troubled by that observation, the young man had replied:

"Who can tell whether I don't have three? For between one and the other, each one animating me for two years, there has to be one that presides over my transformation, which causes me to disappear here and reappear there, taking its precautions so well that my two biennial souls cannot even perceive one another."

And he had left in despair.

The worst thing of all, and what brought Dr. Vincenod's fury to a peak, was that science would not profit from that marvelous case.

"But what a case, though!" he cried, with and admiration mingled with rage. "What a case! Just think that the young man might have a double cerebral organization! Just think that one might, by dissection..."

"Well, why not?"

"No longer any means, alas. If I might express myself thus, the poor fellow has blown his brains out!"[36]

---

[36] This punchline loses something vital in translation, because in English it is perfectly routine to refer to someone having "blown his brains out," whereas in French, the singular is conventional when one refers to someone having "*se faire sauter la cervelle,*" although the doctor deliberately uses the plural, *les cervelles,* here. The idea for the story presumably emerged from Richepin's awareness of that linguistic idiosyncrasy.

The Other Sense[37]

These are all the letters that my friend the philosopher Pierre Brûlast wrote to me—and, as you shall see, the only ones that will have been written—during the last five years of his life.

You will perhaps recall that in October 1891, at the École Libre des Science Morales, he personally announced his decision to leave Europe in order to submit himself to the education and discipline of a mysterious Tibetan mahatma, whose name alone was a secret not to be revealed. He hoped to bring back therefrom, he said, a new doctrine, destined to revolutionize psychology and metaphysics. He refused, moreover, to explain himself more fully on that score, and declared that his absence would last at least five years, the time required for the primary initiation. During that phase, he would limit himself to keeping a single friend up to date with his studies, to the extent that he would be allowed, who would keep the secret thereof until 1 January 1921.

I had the honor of being chosen as the custodian of these strange of these strange confidences. The fixed period has elapsed. I am publishing the letters, without comment. Will philosophers learn anything from them, or will they only be of interest to alienists? I do not think that I need to worry about that, and I am simply fulfilling my duty as a testamentary executor here.

December 94, aboard ship
My dear friend.

It is more than probable that the result of my research, after five years of primary initiation, will be of a nature to

---

[37] *Gil Blas*, 12 January 1892, reprinted in *Le Journal*, 9 May 1898.

make me seem like a lunatic. I therefore want to prove that before undertaking it, at least, I was in full and entire possession of my mental faculties. For that, I will briefly explain the reasons for my determination, and I assume that common sense—even the commonest—will not find them too extraordinarily strange.

It is not necessary to be a great scholar of physiology and psychology to admit that our pretended five senses are really one and the same sense. Weight, heat, light, electricity and magnetism serve as labels for the unique force that moves things. In the same way, sight, hearing, smell, taste and touch are merely, in sum, appearances and specializations of touch alone. In brief, humans are endowed with a single material sense, and no more than one.

But is it true that, as the ancient adage has it, there is nothing in the intellect that has not originated in sensation? That is what I do not believe, and that is what the greatest minds have not believed. It is sufficient, to convince the most hardened materialists of that, to recall in that regard, not merely occultist thinkers of every sort, but simply pure metaphysicians. The elite of humankind, apart from a few rare exceptions, has been convinced of the existence, outside of sensation, of a world with which communication is possible for us. Whether one categorizes it under the label of the infinite, the perfect, the absolute, the ideal, the unconscious or even the unknowable hardly matters. Unknowable, perhaps, but certainly not imperceptible—unless the elite of humankind is prey to mental alienation. Not being able to accept that conclusion, I therefore align myself with that elite in postulating an existent extrasensible world, conceivable to us and into which, in consequence, we have the right to penetrate.

Given that, I observe that we cannot, in fact, penetrate it through the intermediary of the senses—or, rather, the one unique sense that I have labeled the material sense, which is touch. It is precisely by virtue of having tried to apply that sensation to the world in question that we have come to deny that world or to declare it closed. From that stem the aberrations of metaphysics and the blindness of positivism.

Now, I claim, personally, that the world-outside-us must correspond to a sense within us other than the material sense. Otherwise, how could we have, even vaguely and confusedly, as we do, the suspicion that the world in question exists? Having that suspicion in the irrefutable proof that we have that sense. It seems to me that this logic is more down-to-earth than any argument to the contrary.

Now, another thing—and I am appealing here to the most elementary notions of medical practice, undoubted even by the weakest of medical students. Is it not true that the atrophy of one sense gives an advantage to the development of a neighboring sense, which, in a way, substitutes for the atrophied one? The best example is furnished by blind people which a keen sense of hearing, or a subtle delicate sense of touch.

I shall not go on; the observation is banal—but I take this consequence from it, on which I focus attention. If our sense of the extrasensible world is vague and confused, is it not because our material sense is over-exercised at its expense? And if, on the contrary, once could reduce the exercise of the material sense to its energetic minimum, almost to obliteration, would that not give a singular force, a miraculous intensity, to the other sense? To pose the problem, as one says in geometry, is to resolve it.

Well, I have posed it and I shall resolve it. Such is the objective of my absence. For it has been resolved before, but those who have resolved it have not said anything about it; they are yogis, ascetics and mahatmas. I shall learn their art of annihilating the material sense to the advantage of the extrasensible sense, and that art I shall divulge; and once the results of that knowledge have been acquired, I shall formularize them.

What I shall bring back, not merely to Europe but to the material world, is the key to the world-outside-us. And I can already announce to you the title of this new gospel; it will be called *An Exegetic, Theoretical and Practical Treatise on the Other Sense*. You can see, and you will be able to testify, that I am quite the opposite of a lunatic.

Yours, and in the firm hope of future reason,

Pierre Brûlast.

December 92,
Rhanga-Boddhi-Ngou
Dear friend,

After a year of patient effort under the guidance of the incomparable Master, I have the pleasure of informing you that I have reached the first step of the mystical LADDER. The aloes bursting into flower with the noise of a cannon-shot, the red blaze of the setting sun, the sharp spine of the cactus, the violent perfume of musk, the firebrand of the triple alcoholic extract distilled from rice by volcanic fermentation—such are the supreme sensations of which I retain an awareness that is already distant and fugitive. They seem to me to be perceived, out there, by a dying self.

On the other hand, the effluvia from on high envelop me more closely. I experience prickling sensations within my skull and, I don't know where, an awakening dawn by comparison with which the most flamboyant midday would be misty. I am not mistaken; from the dung-heap of the old sense, which is rotting, the new sense is germinating—but how badly these stupid images express what I want to say, what I have there. Finally!

Simply know, my friend, that I am going sagely mad. But even that does not say what I think. Is it really what I think? No, no—rather what I sense. For I sense it, there's no doubt about it. Through these smoky words, do you not sense it a little yourself. Break your eardrums, and you will hear.

Until next time, from the threshold of the first landing,

The ascensionist Pierre.

December 95, at the second stage.

Friend,

The Master will not consent to the revelation of the first three dozen moons that have vanished thus far. All that I can tell you, and under the seal of mahatmic secrecy, is that the progress has been slower in those two years, in the death-throes of the inferior sense. There have been rebellions, partial resurrections. A rose has tried to flower as before. A yellow has lit up. Wine, offered by a ruse, has sung its flattering song. The palms of the hands, joined in ecstasy, have had frissons of warm pulp. It has been necessary to employ stupefying lethifers. The other sense wept in anguish, a wailing infant that the recurrences of the atavistic material sense attempted to strangle in its swaddling-clothes of astral light. The Master, thankfully, has said the words to it that one does not speak, and has proceeded charitably to applications of gestures condensing the diffuse ether ready to dissolve. The ether has been solidified in a living point, pricking the nervous centers, killing the memories there, crucifying the avatars in the egg of hopes. The torture was sweet, unctuous, long drawn-out and miraculous for the new-born. The ordeal finally succeeded— but only three blank bodies out of five; one remained neutral, in gray; that least, alas, still manifests itself blackly. It was necessary to begin again with that one, procrastinate and postpone to a later session. Hence, no letter last year. But April has been more favorable, and here I am at the second stage, the panorama almost extinct down below, and upwards, a fresh rain of nebulous dew. A thousand regrets for being unable to reveal more. The Master leaves me the sweet consolation that I shall have the faculty of crying to the horizon from the third platform, in a year, one can believe. Be patient then, my good friend, as say the things propitiatory to your happy and soon-to-be-disincarnate,

Pierre, still swaddled in Pierre.[38]

---

[38] Pierre is, of course, French for "stone."

December 95, on the platform.

You without a name.

It is me, also without a name, who is *speaking*, but through him, the Master. He has, himself, though disincarnate, a possible reincarnation not subject to degeneration. *Not me!* So he is writing, collecting my furtive ultimate ideas on the wing, which are in non-being, *supposable*. Neither heard, nor seen, nor tasted, not scented, nor touched, but scarcely, that is what I am, *and rightly so*. Clear the rest, more and more, *like the night*. And all emerges therefrom. As for the promised horizon, *cling to the beyond*. Nothing to add. The other sense will create other words.

Yours,

The Being-quasi-non-Being

September 96, Earth

Dear friend,

I have finally come down to earth, and sufficient memory has come back to me to write you this final letter, proving to you that I am, as before my departure, in full and entire possession of my reasoning faculties. On the other hand, I have completely forgotten what I was able to confide to you in my previous letters, and I do not even know how many there were, or even whether I have, in reality, written them to you. Besides which, that hardly matters. The anomaly will be explained on my return, by my new quality of a disincarnate having the right to temporary reincarnation without degeneration. Don't be alarmed by only understanding half of that. You shall see how simple it is, in sum. Furthermore, I have no intention of instructing you here, by means of a few words. The main thing is for you to know that I am at the end of my experiment, sure of having succeeded, and ready to distribute the acquired and merited treasure. Now, of that, you have no suspicion. As I had so sagely foreseen, the atrophy of the material sense, having become complete and—save for licit and inconsequential reincarnation—definitive, as given complete liberty to the extrasensible sense. Deaf, blind, taste and smell dead, touch disperse into pure nothingness, I have a clear perception of everything that was confused and once seemed imperceptible to me. It only remains for me to establish the new language to express what I sense, so well, so keenly, so intensely, so prodigiously limpidly, with my extrasensible sense developed, as one says in mathematics, to the nth power. And such will be the object of the book to which I shall henceforth devote myself: a book which I beg you to advertise, in publishing the correspondence that I ought to have addressed to you since my departure. That correspondence can serve as a prolegomenon to the book in preparation, which still has for its explicit title: *An Exegetic, Theoretical and Practical Treatise on the Other Sense.*

Until my return among you, with the book.

Yours, with all my heart,

Pierre Brûlast.

No more than the first, that last letter, it is evident, is not the letter of a lunatic. It is the letter of a philosopher, albeit perhaps a slightly eccentric one. But what philosopher is not, as soon as he involves himself with metaphysics, especially if he amalgamates metaphysics with mysticism? There will not, however, be too many anxieties to conceive regarding our friend's reason, on reading those two letters. The others, certainly, are more worrying. But what is utterly despairing is that the latter is accompanied by a memorandum drafted by Dr. Samuel Blount, chief physician at the Blue House Sanitarium in Caclutta, of which a translation follows:

This letter was written by Pierre Brûlast a fortnight before the fit of insanity by which he has been afflicted. He is now in treatment here, afflicted with general paralysis, with a simulation of complete sensorial atrophy. The case is incurable.

Such are, published exactly, the documents relating to my friend, the philosopher Pierre Brûlast. I am publishing them, as I promised to do, without comment, but nevertheless with this simple reflection, which I cannot help myself venturing at hazard: it is sometimes very difficult to discern whether the patient or the alienist is the real madman.

The City of Gems[39]

"All right," said the doctor, "since you're so insistent. But don't forget that he's utterly mad, that his madness is contagious, and that he has already unhinged two..."

At a gesture by which he understood that I was wounded by his doubts relating to the solidity of my reason, he did not go on, and, summoning a warder, he instructed him to take me to room 27 and to leave me alone there with the patient, but to remain in the corridor, ready to intervene if I needed him.

"In case the conversation turns into an argument," he added, "which I advise you to avoid carefully, in the patient's own interests, given that contradiction might cause a fit of furious insanity."

The occupant of room 27 did not seem, however, so very terrible, and the doctor's prudence appeared to me to be an exaggerated precaution when I found myself facing the very short, very humble and very inoffensive old man to whom the warder introduced me, sating; "This Monsieur has come to talk to you, in order that he can write something in a newspaper."

On the way, before we reached the room, the warder had told me that that as the surest way of convincing the gentleman to speak freely.

He had said "the gentleman" and no word, in fact, could have been better chosen to characterize at a stroke that calm and mild septuagenarian with a pale but smiling face, with long white hair fluffed up over his ears, like Béranger's,[40] a

---

[39] *Le Gaulois*, 20 March 1896, reprinted in *Le Journal*, 23 May 1898 as "Adamantopolis."

[40] The poet and popular songwriter Pierre-Jean de Béranger (1780-1857) compensated for the baldness on the front and top of his head by letting the semicircle of hair that remained to

restful, almost somnolent attitude and ingenuous eyes in which the blue flower of an child-like-gaze blossomed.

A rapid spark, nevertheless, suddenly lit up in that child-like gaze, and my imagination saw then, instead of the blue flower, the pale blue gleam of burning sulfur. The gentleman's eyes darted a flash that dug into the depths of mine, with a piercing and discomfiting acuity.

"He's taking your measure," whispered the warder, "and I think your face reminds him of someone."

Abruptly, the sharp gleam softened, the spark went out, the blue flower blossomed again in the child-like gaze, and the old man said to me in a distant and seductive voice: "I'd be glad to talk to you, Monsieur. Sit down, I beg you, and get ready to listen to me."

And I remained alone with the madman, the warder having retired, closing the door, behind which I perceived his silent immobility, mounting guard.

"Monsieur," said the old man, after a rather long pause, "are you a mineralogist?"

"No, Monsieur," I replied.

"A chemist?"

"No."

"An Egyptologist, then?"

"Nor that—or, at least, very slightly."

"Too bad," he said, "for you're not best placed to listen to me. Your newspaper could have chosen someone better. Oh well! You seem to me to be intelligent, and I can make myself clear. I hope that, in spite of your incompetence, I can make myself comprehensible to you."

Immediately, and with considerable composure—without any fever of speech revealing the cerebral agitation of a madman riding his chimera, but, on the contrary, with every appearance of a lucid and well-ordered intelligence, like a pro-

---

him grow long, so that it covered his ears and the nape of his neck. His portrait was familiar, although he lived before the advent of photography.

fessor methodically expounding a science possessed in depth, and sufficiently master of his subject to reduce it to the scope of an ignoramus—he set about giving me a veritable lecture course in mineralogy and chemistry, in relation to the formation, analysis and synthesis of precious stones.

I had no difficulty following him, and only wondered where he was trying to get to, while he informed me as to the theory of the crystallization, the cleavage, the general and particular properties, the differences in polarization, the density and the composition by various oxides that characterize the various species of gems, especially diamond and corundum, the latter comprising the Oriental ruby, the emerald and the sapphire, and the principal deposits thereof found in metamorphic rocks and sedimentary strata, and how the mysterious labor of nature in their regard had been partly reproduced in laboratories by the modern chemistry so justly described as the chemistry of carbon.

Where he was trying to get to he finally manifested to me by this sudden question: "In brief, Monsieur, is one insane, I ask you, for believing and sustaining that humans can make gems?"

"No," I relied, "not in the least—for, according to the little I knew already, and especially after what you've just told me in such a clear fashion, I believe it as absolutely as you do."

He thanked me with a serene gesture, paused once again for rather a long time without saying a word, and then, in a slightly less composed voice than before, his speech more agitated and his lips slightly tremulous, he continued:

"Monsieur, it is against the absurd pride of that modern chemistry, against the monstrous aberration of progress, that I have been broken. Because Saint-Claire Deville and Caron have only been able to obtain corundums devoid of thickness, and because the rubies of Frémy and Freil are thin sheets and no one can get to the point of coagulating them in the form of hexagonal prisms, because Despretz has only reconstituted diamond in the state only perceptible under a microscope, they have concluded that where modern chemistry remains impotent until further notice, anterior humankind must have been even more impotent."[41]

"Pardon me," I said, "but I can't quite see..."

He interrupted me almost violently, darting the same sharp gaze at me as at the beginning of my visit.

"What is it you can't quite see?" he cried. "Do you, too, think that humanity has not already produced civilizations superior to ours? Do you not know, for example, that the ancient Egyptians were the custodians of a science bequeathed to some of their priests by earlier sages, who escaped the drowning of Atlantis?"

He had stood up, was speaking loudly and gesticulating broadly. A slight foam flecked the corners of his mouth. In the corridor, I heard the footsteps of the warder drawing nearer to the door.

"Monsieur," I said, in a very calm tone, "you're wrong to be annoyed with me; I'm in complete agreement with you."

He sat down again, fell silent and closed his eyes. The pause was much longer this time than on the two previous occasions. I thought that he had gone to sleep. He was extremely pale.

He reopened his eyes slowly, started to smile, and gestured to me to sit down close beside him. He held his cupped hand over his mouth, as if to whisper in my ear. I got ready to do as he wished.

"Listen to me carefully," he said, in a very low voice. "I see that you're worth to know everything. You shall know everything."

---

[41] The references are to the chemist Henry Sainte-Claire Deville (1818-1881), whose most significant publication on artificial gemstones, in 1858, was co-signed H. Caron; Edmond Frémy (1814-1894), who synthesized rubies during the 1870s in collaboration with an assistant named Freil and Auguste Verneuil; and César Despretz (1798-1863).

Moving aside slightly, he showed me with his gaze a voluminous heap of papers on which he had been sitting, and which I had mistaken for a dirty bundled-up pillow.

"In there," he said, "is the irrefutable proof of what I'm saying. I'll let you have it when the time comes. You'll see, to begin with, how I discovered that the Egyptians manufactured corundums and diamond. You'll read there the description of such stones, excavated by me at Thebes, and what determines, without any possible doubt, the certainty of their artificial origin."

His voice became that of a professor again, in order to speak to me knowledgeably and methodically about colored glasses analyzed by Klaproth,[42] to distinguish them from true rubies extracted from certain mummy-cases, and to inform me that the Egyptians had been perfectly familiar with, and had noted hieroglyphically, the table of the equivalents of the oxides entering into the composition of gems.

Then he resumed his mysterious one to add: "But that's nothing. What my papers will reveal to you that's more interesting, truly rare and miraculous, is the existence and location, in the heart of Africa, at a point whose exact longitude and latitude I've determined, of the City of Gems."

He continued in a whisper, now, in an almost-imperceptible murmur, which buzzed in my ear like one of those laments of which one hears spare fragments in a dream;

"Crypts, crypts! The night full of multicolored stars...handfuls to take...in order not to depreciate the precious stones, they buried them there! Centuries! Centuries! Too many...still! And large, so large, so enormous, since they had the time to work them in the crucible, like nature herself... The Regent, the Sancy, the Orloff, the Mogul, the Koh-i-Noor, small, very small, beside that one! Of, the sunbursts the star-pebbles! The light in flowers! Me, old, a prisoner, dying, won't see... The City of Gems! The City of Gems!"

---

[42] The German chemist Martin Heinrich Klaproth (1743-1817).

And for a long time, a long time, he chanted like that, sometimes expressing himself in those fragments of sentences whose meaning I grasped, sometimes replacing the words with a sort of inarticulate chirping, but without any vocal excitement, without any dementia prey to his frenzy, but rather with the melancholy of an exile remembering the lost homeland, lulling himself with his sadness, eventually putting it to sleep and putting himself to sleep...

For he ended up gradually falling into a somnolent bewilderment, from which he only awakened momentarily at increasingly long intervals, to babble vaguely the name of the City of Gems, reopening his ingenuous eyes, in which his childlike gaze became pale, like a dying blue flower.

"Well," said the doctor, when he saw me again. "Did he talk to you at length, and was it interesting?"

"Prodigiously."

"And troubled?"

"A little, I admit."

"Did he offer to let you read his papers?"

"Yes."

"Do you still want to see them? I can have the warder fetch them."

"No thanks. I'd rather remain under the impression of that strange and magical dream. His writings, since you affirm that he's mad, must be an incoherent farrago, which would break the charm wretchedly, and, all in all..."

"You're mistaken," the doctor put in. "I've read his papers myself, and they're truly astonishing in their clarity, and the force of their argument."

"But how?"

"Ah, you see, it's frightful how logical madmen sometimes are. Once one admits their point of departure, as soon as one refuses its absurdity, one is their prey. They lead you, they lead you!"

He took me by the arm and squeezed it forcefully.

"Look," he said, "even I, in spite of everything, with my life settled, my family, the fifty years of science that have put lead in my head, even I, at times have moments when I almost envy the fate of the two unhinged individuals who departed on his word for the heart of Africa, pilgrims heading for the City of Gems."

And in his cold alienist's eyes, suddenly and bizarrely illuminated, in his bright golden eyes that made the red of the obscure obsession he was confessing seem even brighter, I read an unexpected, disquieting, furtive, bitter, dolorous and almost criminal: *who knows?*

The Plague-Man[43]

I shall tell the story as simply as possible, without seeking, by an excessively artistic expression, to make the singular adventure seem even more singular. I shall furnish the precise details, the names and the dates, that authenticate the memory for me, and which, for others, will render sound testimony as to my veracity.

In spite of everything, I have no great hope of being believed. But what right do I have to be annoyed? Even I, to whom the thing happened, to whom my sure memory and solid reason certify the exactitude of the facts making up the web, when I reflect upon the adventure, no matter how convinced I am that I really lived through, have all the difficulty in the world persuading myself that it was not a dream.

That is why I am offering it as a story and not as a history, preferring, in sum, the renown of the extravagant storyteller to that of the fallacious historian.

Few people know the English artist Michael Joshua Hawks, but the rare initiates of his strange talent retain an eminent place for him in their artistic esteem that is equally rare. They think—and I am one of them—that his talent is actually genius, and that Hawks will become famous on the day he decides to publish his visionary work, especially his "Illuminations of Horror."

It is, in ink drawings heightened by color, on blocks of talc, a complete account, phase by phase, of the frightful developments of the plague. Already terrible when one looks at them in daylight, placed flat on sheets of paper, those designs seem animated by a phantasmal life when Hawks shows them

---

[43] *Le Gaulois*, 1 November 1895, reprinted in *Le Journal*, 1 May 1897 as "Le Yoghi."

to you in transparency, in the fulgurant glare of his lamp, which emits an abrupt jet of incandescent magnesium.

It is impossible then not to utter a scream of fright, which is immediately followed by a cry of admiration—to which Hawks usually replies: "It's not me who deserves admiration; I've copied nature exactly, and nothing more."

But that response only astonishes you more, because everyone knows, and he admits it himself with a mysterious smile, that he has never left London and could not, in consequence, have studied in nature those tragic scenes of plague, always represented in his drawings as happening in India. And if anyone objects, he contents himself with accentuating his smile, and adding: "Of course—and yet, what is out there, I have seen here, although that wasn't there, in truth."

People gladly forgive him these eccentricities because they admire him and, at the same time, they love him. For, apart from that childlike desire to mystify you, Hawks is a charming companion, entirely as if he were not a great artist.

Having had an opportunity to render him an important service, and his gratitude having rewarded me with an increase in his good graces, I thought I was able, one day, to reproach him for his petty defect. Our Parisian argot lightened the accusation, and I didn't hesitate to offer him my criticism in the form: "Why the Devil put on this hoaxer act with your friends?"

He took on a serious expression, doubtless believing that I had insulted him by thinking him a hoaxer, and replied, with a forceful handshake: "You're right. I don't have the right, at least with you, to give that appearance. I need to prove to you that I'm not." Then, sadly, he added: "You're the one who wanted it."

An hour later, we caught a cab at the end of the street, in which we arrived, after tortuous detours, in the vicinity of Brompton Hill Road. During the entire journey we remained silent, at Hawks' request. He seemed ill at ease, morally as well as physically. In addition, the weather was frightful. Rain and sleet were falling in a yellow fog. We were shivering perpetually and stifling.

Drink a mouthful of cordial," Hawks said to me as we got out of the cab. He handed me a silver flask. I swallowed a mouthful of a warm and bitter liquid.

After fifty yards or so covered on foot we went into a small dark tavern. The proprietor was a Hindu. Gawks said a few words to him in a low voice. Then we went up to the first floor, where the Hindu installed us in a dark room, solely furnished with a large divan and lit by a night-light with a frosted globe.

Hawks had brought a box containing his "Illuminations of Horror." He told me to look at the transparent blocks of talc for a long time in that wan light.

"Commit the images firmly to memory," he added, "in order to ascertain their exactitude by comparing them to the reality."

When I had finished, he said: "Check the time on your watch, and write it down, as well as today's date, in your notebook.

I did as I was told. It was twenty past four in the afternoon on 12 December 1894.

When I finished writing in my notebook, as I raised me head, there was a man in front of us, although I hadn't heard or seen him come in.

He was on his knees, seated or rather folded up, including his heels; his face was ecstatic, his body entirely naked. That body was ascetically thin, the bones sticking out beneath the desiccated skin. The face, drowned beneath an enormous avalanche of white hair, the wisps of which were mingled with those of an equally white and no less enormous beard, seemed completely reduced to two eyes, haggard dilated and staring.

Hawks pronounced a brief phrase in an imperious tone, in a foreign language, in which I only perceived the word *yogi*.

Abruptly, the yogi's gaze plunged into mine. At the same time, the hot and bitter taste of the liquor I had drunk a little while before rose into my mouth again, and I felt simultaneously as if I were intoxicated by that liquor and hypnotized by that gaze.

Nevertheless, I was neither in the sleep of drunkenness nor that of hypnosis, for I distinctly heard Hawks saying to me: "Look at the models that I used to draw my 'Illuminations of Horror' from nature. You can and ought to see them as I see them myself. It's out there, and not here, and yet it's copiable here, and it is."

And I was so far from sleep that I replied to Hawks, reasoning with perfect lucidity: "Yes, indeed, I see. Undoubtedly your cordial is based on hashish, and by that means, the images I studied just now on your blocks of talc are being amplified."

For I saw them live, positively, and I was in a cold sweat of quivering horror.

It was in a village of bamboo huts, under tall trees with plumes of palms or large, flat leaves, near an immense river cluttered with monstrous plants, whose banks melted into muddy marshes—and all that amid the flamboyance of a harsh sun pouring out a rain of diamonds.

In the huts, whose walls seemed to me to be transparent, lay men, women and children, prey to the hideous disease, all the stigmata of with were manifest: crimson anthrax illuminating ardent embers on the black, the shoulders, the armpits, the groin; gangrenous pustules hardening into brown scars; pale red tumors and petechiae; faces convulsed and racked by stupor; fuliginous tongues and lips—in sum, everything that called forth cries of fright and admiration before the terror so magisterially expressed in Hawks' brilliant, visionary and exact "Illuminations of Horror."

Yes, yes, what I *saw* really was what he had rendered. I could not doubt it. But I saw it, myself, through hashish or hypnosis, undoubtedly, and according to his drawings. But where and how, before making his drawings, had he found the primary material necessary to his visions of hashish or hypnosis?

I asked him that, almost furiously. He replied, almost coldly: "I repeat to you that it exists, out there. The yogi is making you see it at a distance. But it exists. He releases it at will, in order that I can copy it. Do you understand, now? Do you understand? This yogi is known as *the plague-man*."

Here, in my memories, so coherent up to that point, there is a gap. Surely, under the influence of the liquor or the hypnosis, I lost consciousness for a while. Not for very long, though, for I found myself getting out of a cab at Hawks' door, and saying to him, angrily: "Definitely, my friend, you're a great artist, but also a poor friend. Your habitual mystifications were, strictly speaking, excusable. This isn't, any longer. You're making a fool of me now—it's too much. Goodbye!"

He tried to reply. He wanted to take my hands, to take me into his house. I refused. If he had admitted that he had wanted to take the hoax to its conclusion, I would still have forgiven him, but he was obstinate in his denials; he continued to play me for a fool. That really is intolerable, isn't it? It made me indignant.

Six weeks later I received an issue of the *Indian News*, in a band on which the address had been written by Hawks, in which an article had been ringed in red pencil.

The article related that plague had suddenly broken out in the village of Pendjah-Sloe, in the wake of a tornado, which had emerged unexpectedly, without any meteorological preliminary, in the midst of a serene sky. It had been possible to circumscribe the epidemic and prevent its spread. It seemed to have been caused, inexplicably, by the tornado, itself inexplicable. The reporter ventured curious theories on that subject, regarding the mysterious correlation of certain epidemics with atmospheric cataclysms. He offered statistics in support, including the exact date and time at which the tornado had surged forth and the first manifestation of the scourge had appeared.

That date was 12 December 1894. The local time corresponded with a London time of four-twenty in the afternoon.

So what? Had the yogi simply been seeing at a distance, having made me share hi vision in what occultists call the *astral mirror*? Or was he even more than that? Was he the formidable mahatma of evil that Hawks called the Plague-Man?

I have never dared to reach a conclusion, and you ought to understand now why, when I reflect on that strange adventure, that however convinced I am of having lived it in reality, I have all the difficulty in the world persuading myself that it was not a dream.

The New Explosive[44]

Being almost incompetent in the particular matter in question, having been the only witness to the frightful experiment—in conditions, moreover, that I could not help but find strange and troubling—I am force to confess, honestly, that my testimony offers none of the guarantees necessary to scientific testimony.

I will say even more: this testimony, my own testimony, the testimony of my own eyes and ears, I am the first, when I think about it, to call into doubt.

And yet, I saw and I heard; I am sure, in any case, of having really seen and heard, and not in the course of a dream.

Of the fact that I wasn't dreaming, at least, palpable proof remains: the letter from my friend Harry Sloughby confirming the existence of the experimenter and my presence at the frightful experiment. While I am writing I have that letter in front of me, and I am rereading it in order convince myself that I wasn't dreaming.

This is what it says:

No, my dear chap, you won't see the thing again, at least not alone, for our man has left to prepare his great coup. He claims to be all set now to attempt it. In what location? That I don't know—but what does it matter? If he succeeds, as he hopes, we'll know soon enough when we go to the Devil. My only regret then will be not being able to laugh with you at the big joke.

Very cordially yours,

H. S.

---

[44] *Le Journal*, 29 August 1900.

Evidently, according to that letter, I witnessed the experiment. But was the experiment really as frightful as I recall? The joyful tone of my friend Harry Sloughby leaves me uncertain about that. How, if he believes in the consequences of the experiment that I narrated to him, can he treat it as a big joke? But isn't it, in the final analysis, me who made it into a big joke for him?

The last time we had met in London, six weeks earlier, we had had a long metaphysical and cosmogonic discussion in which, going from one thing to another, I had ended up saying to him: "The eternal evolution of matter[45] seems to us, for the moment, to be in a period of concentration—but the previous period, and, in consequence, the next, of diffusion, remains in potential. It would be sufficient for a shock to reawaken that dormant potential for the period of diffusion to recommence, and then..."

Abruptly, Harry Sloughby had interrupted me with these words, which I took to be a joke: "I know someone who's trying to produce that shock."

---

[45] The "evolution of matter" became a popular topic of discussion in France after the discovery of radium by Marie and Pierre Curie in 1898, although this story was written before Gustave Le Bon published his supposedly-definitive account of *L'Évolution de la matière* (1905). Richepin, however, is not referring to transformation by disintegration but to some kind of periodic inversion of the force of gravity, implying a cosmological model in which the universe expands and contracts alternately—an idea subsequently to be embraced (briefly) by Einstein as a reaction against the discovery of the expanding universe by astronomers, including Edwin Hubble. Richepin might have been prompted to come up with the idea by the work of Bernard Brunhes (1867-1910), who discovered the periodical reversal of the Earth's magnetic field, although he had great difficulty persuading his contemporaries of the truth of his deduction.

When I reproached him for a joke of such a vulgar kind in a conversation as elevated as ours, he added: "I'm not joking. I repeat that I know a man whose cosmogonic ideas are in precise accordance with yours, and who wants to apply them—that's all."

"But he's a lunatic," I replied.

"He is, indeed, reputed to be mad," my friend retorted. "He's even been locked up and treated as such. Thanks to my intervention, he's been released again. Since then, he's inherited a considerable fortune. He's taken advantage of it to try to apply his ideas. He's occupied in establishing a science that he called chemical cosmogony. Would you like me to put you in communication with him? If you like, he'll doubtless show you some curious things. He's never shown anything to me—he thinks that I'm a practical joker."

Presumably, I had what was necessary to please the man in question. Probably, it was the sincere and ardent enthusiasm for metaphysics that carried me away during our first conversation, with a kind of intoxication suddenly poured into me by the otherworldliness of his gaze.

The man's eyes, in fact—surely the eyes of a madman— had immediately given me the impression of those bottomless pits that are sounded, or rather imagined, between certain constellations, in the depths of which it is as if one sees the Absolute itself asleep.

I'm expressing as best I can, but really quite badly, what I experienced in plunging myself into his gaze. What I can also say, to translate my sensation to some extent, is that the gaze in question absorbed all the power of attention of which I was capable at that moment. What face and what body did the man have? How old was he? I didn't notice, and I have no memory of it.

What I do remember, apart from his gaze, is that we were alone, he and I, in a deserted park, and that he let me talk, entirely given over to the metaphysical drunkenness with which his gaze intoxicated me, and which he poured into me with that gaze, in some way, in increasingly copious draughts, *intoxicating* in the full sense of the English word.

What I also remember—for I ought to say everything—is that my friend Harry Sloughby, before introducing me to the man and abandoning me alone with him in that deserted park, had weighed me down with a sumptuous meal with bloody meat, strong drink and black cigars, under the pretext of rendering me, against the probable emotions I was about to have, particularly solid and "energetic."

Nevertheless, I hasten to add, when I went into that deserted park, it seemed to me that I was in full possession of my faculties.

What I don't remember at all, however, is the length of time during which the man allowed me to talk metaphysics beneath his gaze. All that I know is that I went into the deserted park at about two o'clock in the afternoon, and that I only recovered consciousness in bed at my friend Harry Sloughby's house, having slept for a long time, the following morning.

But I do retain the memory, clearly envisioned, with full consciousness of not having been dreaming, of the frightful experiment.

I had just explained, in lyrical terms, the anterior or forthcoming state of matter in the period of diffusion, and the possibility of a shock reawakening that period of centrifugism, potential within presently-centripetal matter, when the man, his gaze hypnotizing me, said:

"Perhaps I can produce that shock. I've found the necessary explosive. It's only a matter of fabricating the quantity necessary to blow up our astral system. I have enough of it already to blow up the Earth. I've made the calculations. You shall see."

In front of us, in the center of a clearing, a stone sphere as balanced on a pedestal. It was about two meters in diameter.

The man opened a little box, similar to a snuff-box, which seemed to me to be empty. He appeared to take something out of it. He put that imperceptible thing on the rim of a hole bored in the sphere, blew on it, and said:

"Now my grain of explosive is at the center of the sphere. The sphere stands for the terrestrial globe; the explosive is a dose sufficient to blow it up in a quarter of an hour. You shall see."

He started to run. Alarmed, I followed him. As we arrived at the château, out of breath, after running for a quarter of an hour, I heard a mighty detonation.

The man looked at me, with his gaze in which the Absolute was dormant, which I "saw" awaken in a flash. I was thunderstuck by it. I must have fainted. I don't remember any more.

I only came to, as I said, in the house of my friend Harry Sloughby the next morning, with a terrible headache, about which he said to me, smiling in his mocking manner, ever the practical joker: "Metaphysics after too good a dinner, my dear chap, makes your hair hurt."

I told him about the frightful experiment. He said: "You must have had more to drink at the old man's place?"

"Nothing," I replied, "absolutely nothing, except for his gaze."

"You're as mad as he is," he said. "Oh, these poets!"

Vexed, almost angry, I left him after that, six weeks ago. The other day, after a note from him inviting me to go hunting in Scotland, I asked him to arrange for me to visit the man again. You have seen his letter in reply.

And that's the story of the new explosive. You can conclude from it what you wish. For myself, I confess, if the man sends us all to the Devil very shortly, I shall think, like my friend Harry Sloughby, that it's a big joke.

NIGHTMARES

Pft! Pft![46]

Once upon a time, in a country that I cannot specify—for, in truth, the country is called by all names and the time is all of time—there was a woman, of whom I likewise cannot give you an exact description.

Everyone, in fact, saw her differently, and everyone was right, since they really saw her that way.

It is necessary to tell you, however, that she did not do anything in order to be judged in one fashion or another. She contented herself with being, in reality, what people believed her to be, not knowing herself what she was.

A few wise men insinuated that she was doubtless nothing; and others, wiser still, added that that was precisely the origin of her charm. They compared her to clouds, whose magic depends on the dreamer who contemplates them, and to the symphonies of the sea, in which one hears the music that one sings within oneself.

The said wise men were assuredly not particularly stupid in their comparisons, and yet, like all wise men, they were great fools—for that nothing, which they translated so disdain-

---

[46] *Gil Blas*, 11 June 1889, reprinted, in slightly revised form in *Le Journal*, 18 September 1897 as "Il y avait une fois..." [Once Upon a Time]; the revised version was reprinted in *Contes sans morale*.

fully as nothing, was also something. The proof of that is that they could not refrain from paying attention to it, and seeking an explanation for it.

Perhaps much wiser were the self-confessed fools who did not seek that explanation, and simply took the mysterious woman for what she was—or, at least, what they believed her to be, and who thus lived by means of her and within her.

Lived, yes, and also died, alas!—and died after having previously suffered the thousand deaths in detail that are known as disappointed desire, deceived faith, shattered hope, jealous love and betrayed love.

But why that *alas*? Are not those thousand deaths in detail life itself? With the consequence that the amorous hasten gladly to their suffering, and savor them, as if they had these poetic lines for a motto:

> Go on, take my life; it's yours: I yield it to you.
> Write what you please on that great white vellum.
> Tear, if you wish, all the pages from the book.
> Eat my flesh, drink my spirit, empty my stomach,
> But let us live! It is still living
> To see one's blood flow.

Furthermore, it ought to be observed, in the mysterious woman's defense, that she did not make them suffer in that way out of cruelty. She was no more wicked than anything else. She even had, on many occasions, fits of tenderness, of compassionate shame. She grieved sincerely for those she had rendered unhappy.

Many a time, she warned them, in all honesty, by saying to them: "You know that I don't love you."

To which they generally replied: "What does it matter? For myself, I adore you."

And truly, after that, what right had the men she deceived and tortured to complain?

To others, undoubtedly, she sighed, breathlessly: "I love you!"

Then she deceived them too—but then she had this excuse: "I was deceived myself. I thought I loved him. It isn't my fault. Oh, how I suffer from my error!"

And she said that so prettily, and with such good faith, that it was necessary, as a disinterested judge, to find in her favor.

Then again, she always ended up turning everything to laughter, even her own suffering, and that of others even more so. The foundation of her philosophy—for that nothing, in spite of the opinion of the wise men, had a philosophy—was that it was necessary not to attach any importance to anything whatsoever.

She did not have a hard heart, and did have a heart, since she occasionally wept—but once her back was turned, she no longer thought about her pain, shrugged her shoulders and "moved on," making a sound with a dainty movement of her lips: "Pft! Pft!"—so often that a wise man with a malicious tongue ended up nicknaming her "Madame Pft! Pft!"

She was not annoyed by that; on the contrary, she took it as a compliment. The nickname seemed to her to be amusing. After reflecting on it at her leisure—for that nothing reflected—she even judged it a convenient employment. Instead of seeking excuses for her conduct thereafter, instead of giving explanations to those who interrogated her as a sphinx, she simply replied to them: "Pft! Pft!"

Then the wise man with the malicious tongue said to himself, scratching his head and congratulating himself on his inventive genius: "Damn it! Might I, without suspecting it, have made a great discovery? Might I have found the key to the enigma?"

He thought so, and pursued the thought so far that he fell madly in love with the mysterious woman, whose mystery he imagined that he had elucidated.

To tell the truth, as he was a wise man and a scholar—which is to say, one of those proud individuals who are extremely skillful at fooling themselves—he did not want to admit that he was in love, and lulled himself with the idea that he was simply obsessive in his scientific duty.

"No," he repeated to himself, obligingly, "I haven't been seduced by that doll. I'm intent on studying her, that's all."

Now, neither more nor less than the vulgar, he set out to study her by paying court to her, by desiring her, and being avid for her; and, in sum, under the pretext of putting that soul in the crucible, he occupied himself naively in melting in his turn in the hollow of the bed where so many others had melted. No more and no less than so many others, he melted there, the poor wise man—and he learned nothing at all in melting there, the deplorable scholar.

He did not know himself whether he was loved. She could have told him, honestly, that he was not, as she had so honestly told others; but with him, because of his pretentions to divination and the cunning he affected, she amused herself a little by not being frank. When he questioned her, bewildered by passion, she riposted, smiling, looking away: "Pft! Pft!"

She deceived him—that goes without saying—but into that blow she put malice and cruelty, as one can easily believe. In fact, she provided him, as a fortunate rival, with a pure imbecile.

He would have been cowardly enough, that brave scholar, to have forgiven her, if she had consented to make him that confession. If necessary, he could have explained that depravity of taste scientifically, explained it to the point of excuse and absolution. Was it not a natural effect of contrast, that the woman might prefer a brute to an elite intelligence? He would have proved it magisterially, to give himself pleasure. But she did not even leave him that consolation. When he asked her, weeping, if he ought to believe in that rival, and when he proposed piteously to the guilty party to proclaim her innocent, she performed a pirouette, and murmured: "Pft! Pft!"

He knew then all the rage of jealousy and despair. He came to conceive the most criminal projects in consequence. He did not hide them, and threatened to render her responsible for them.

"Yes," he cried, "that rival to whom you have sacrificed me, I shall kill him."

She shook her head, to indicate that she did not believe in that sanguinary design, and then she added: "And anyway, even if you do: Pft! Pft!"

Transformed into a ferocious beast, the scholar showed himself to be more brutal than the beloved brute. He lay in ambush for him one evening, cut his throat, butchered the unfortunate fellow, ripped the heart from his breast and came to throw that horrible trophy, still beating, at the woman's feet.

This time, to be sure, she was a little frightened—but, a gleam of triumph having ignited in the murderer's eyes, she did not want to recognize that triumph. She stiffened herself against her terror, contemplated the hideous morsel of red flesh tranquilly, turned it over with the tip of her umbrella, and said, with a gracious moue: "Pft! Pft!"

"Oh, monster, monster!" cried the scholar. "I'll kill you too, then. Yes, I'll kill you. I want to know whether you have one—a heart—and, finally, what there is inside it. And I shall know. I want to. I want to."

His gaze was wild, his hand tremulous.

"What there is in my heart?" she replied, unemotionally. "I'll tell you what there is. Oh, it's quite simple, you know. There's this." And, blowing in his face, she threw at him yet again her mocking: "Pft! Pft!"

Then he completely lost his head. With his two hands, with clenched fingers, he gripped the woman's neck—the neck, so white and so delicate, that he adored—and he squeezed it pitilessly for a long, long time.

She did not have the strength to cry out. She scarcely struggled, like bird whose neck is being wrung—but in dying, her last breath exhaled a supreme response, for that imperceptible breath said once again: "Pft! Pft!"

"At last!" roared the scholar, when she as quite dead. "At last, you won't say it again, that *Pft! Pft!* You won't mock my love, or my science, again. And as I've studied you alive, I shall bravely study you dead."

And he set about dissecting her, conscientiously, hoping to observe the thing that she was, and he convinced himself that she really was that nothing, since he was unable to find anywhere within her the soul that he denied her.

And that made him glad.

To perpetuate that joy and maintain the ever-present testimony of his victory, the implacable scholar exercised his ingenuity. Or rather, without his being aware of it, the inconsolable lover had the fantastic idea of tanning the mysterious woman and giving her back to himself as a living form.

For he still loved her!

And he loved her more than ever, when he had reinflated that abominable pelt. In his adoring aberration, he still found her beautiful, and knelt before her, and asked her forgiveness.

What can madness not do?

Dazed and alienated, he came to desire once again that mannequin full of air—and in a rage of lust, he threw himself upon that horror to possess it.

And suddenly, as his amorous arms hugged that bladder frantically, as his teeth bit into it with hectic kisses, there was a rip, and through those monstrous lips, a long hiss escaped, stinging his face with the posthumous irony:

"Pft! Pft!"

An Adventure

Get away! cried Pierre Dufaille, shrugging his shoulders. Get away! What are you saying, that there are no more adventures? Simply say that there are no more adventurers! Yes, no one nowadays dares to trust himself to hazard. As soon as there is a hint of mystery, a sniff of danger somewhere, people baulk. But if one lets things happen, going forward blindly, bravely facing whatever comes, one finds adventures! And I myself, as you see me, who never looks for them, have well and truly encountered one in my life, and a spicy one, I can assure you.

I was in Florence, traveling, and traveling wisely. All that I permitted myself, by way of adventure, was listening now and again to the dishonest propositions by which foreigners are pursued in the Place de la Signoria, in the evening, by bold pimps with the heads of venerable priests. Those excellent fellows will generally take you to their homes, where the debauchery takes place in a very simple and almost patriarchal fashion. The least of haberdashers can take the risk without fear, with eyes closed.

One day, as I was contemplating Benvenuto's admirable Perseus for the twentieth time, in front of the Loggia de Lanzi, I suddenly felt my sleeve tugged by an insistent, almost imperious hand. On turning round, I found myself face to face with a lady of about fifty, who said to me, in a jabbering voice with a thick German accent: "You're French, aren't you, Monsieur?"[47]

"Indeed," I replied.

---

[47] As usual, Richepin renders the woman's speech in a tortuous eye-dialect, for which I have made no attempt to substitute.

"And," she added, "would you like to lie with a very pretty lady?"

This time, I laughed as I replied: "I should think so."

The serious manner and expression of the procuress, the strangeness of the thrust made in broad daylight and in the most baroque accent, were the funniest thing—but what was worse when the earnest German woman said to me: "Do you know how do what they do in Paris?"

"What do you mean, my good lady?" I asked her, bewildered. "What the Devil do they do in Paris that they don't do elsewhere?"

Without the slightest blush, as if she were repeating words that she didn't understand, she replied: "I mean French *obscenities*."

Honestly, what would you have answered in my place? You invest your self-respect where you can, don't you? Me, I replied brazenly: "Yes, Madame, all of them, without exception."

To tell the truth, less immodest than the woman, I blushed slightly—but not for long, because, immediately afterwards, I went pale when she replied: "I want to satisfy myself of that in person." She said it without any departure from her phlegm, which no longer seemed comical to me now, and made me more than a little anxious.

"What!" I exclaimed. "In person! You, Madame? Explain yourself."

If I had been slightly surprised thus far, I was utterly astonished by her explanation. My word, it was an adventure. It was turning into a romance. I couldn't believe my ears. This is what it was about. I'll spare you her gibberish.

She was a confidant and companion in the home of a lady of the highest society, who had a desire to be initiated into the most secret refinements of Parisian corruption, and who had done me the honor of choosing me for that task—except that, she wanted to be sure beforehand that I was worthy of the mission, and it was the paid companion who had been charged with checking me out.

A kind of preliminary exam, what! I was being cast in the role of little Florus,[48] if I might put it like that.

Of course, I thought, *she isn't as stupid as she seems to be, this gawky old German woman. She's telling me brazen fairy tales—it's a matter of putting one over on me.*

And, while laughing surreptitiously, I listened distractedly to what she added in order to make up my mind.

"My mistress is the prettiest lady one can imagine—a real beauty. A spring flower!"

"Forgive me," I said, "but even if your mistress really is a spring flower—excuse me for being sincere—that's absolutely not the case with you; and what she asks for herself, it might not be as easy to grant you, my dear lady."

She stepped back, amazed in her turn.

"But I only have to certify personally by my eyes, not by lying with you."

And she completed her explanation, previously left incomplete. Her duty was simply to accompany me to the Patata in the Rue des Belles-Femmes—an establishment that I recommend to you, by the way—and there to buy me the most agreeable girl I the house and watch my frolics.

Well, I thought. *I was mistaken about the nature of the worthy lady's tastes. She really is an old lecher, as I suspected, but she's a specialist. Interesting! I've never encountered one of those—a female voyeur!*

At this point, Messieurs, I ask your permission to draw a veil momentarily. What I did obviously isn't entirely moral tale, and I'm somewhat ashamed of it. My excuse is that I was young, that the Patata is a famous establishment about which I'd heard marvelous things said, and entry to which was prohibited on my meager budget. Five louis a night, damn it! I couldn't afford that. I therefore accepted the good lady's offer. It's disgusting, I don't deny. But in the end, what do you ex-

---

[48] It is unclear who or what the "petit Florus" is to whom Richepin is referring. None of the hits scored by that phrase on Google seem relevant.

pect? And after all, the old woman was German, wasn't she? And it was a small restitution of five louis to set against our five billion.

In brief, the resident of the Patata was delightful, the examiner of Florus was sufficiently discreet not to be too much of an encumbrance, and your humble servant did his best to sustain the age-old renown of French gallantry. I might even say French galantine,[49] for the old lady, in arranging a rendezvous with me by the Perseus two days later, deigned to admit that I was indeed "very obscene."

Let us drink the shame to the lees! Two days later, at the appointed time, I was in front of the Perseus. It was infamous, I admit. I had got too much of a taste for the partial restitution of the five billion. I was playing the gigolo, I won't try to hide it. It's astonishing how the French lose their dignity when traveling!

At the appointed time, the good lady appeared. It was pitch dark. I followed her without saying a word, for after all, deep down, I wasn't proud of the role I was playing—but if you knew how pretty she was, the girl at the Patata! While walking, I was only thinking about her, and not paying any heed to the route we were following. I only woke up from that dreamy ambulation on hearing the old lady say to me: "Here we are. Try to be as obscene as the day before yesterday."

We were not in the Rue des Belles-Femmes, on the threshold of the Patata, but on a side-street running behind a large palace with high walls. A low door, pushed by the old lady, opened in front of us.

I recoiled slightly. Apparently, the female voyeur also had another passion. She had led me into a trap. Doubtless she

---

[49] The metaphorical significance of this wordplay is a trifle esoteric; although "galantine" is in Webster's, it is not widely used in modern cuisine outside France; in essence it is a kind of glorified sausage compounded out of some kind of meat, or even fish, and served cold, usually in aspic.

wanted to feast herself in her turn on my modest talents. Oh, but no—that wasn't the game.

"Come in, then, come in," she said. "What are you afraid of? My mistress is so pretty, so pretty, much prettier than the girl of the other night."

"Ah, so it was true then, that tale from the Thousand-and-One Nights? And why not? And what was I risking, in sum? That the poor old lady might still ravish me?

And I went in, although I squeezed my buttocks slightly

Oh, my friends, what an hour I spent then! The whole night at the Patata wasn't worth as much as that hour. An hour of paradise! Futile, impossible, to describe it to you. A princely chamber, and in the bed in that chamber, a fairy-tale princess, a fairy herself. A German woman, as exquisite as German women are when they set out to be exquisite. An undine out of Heinrich Heine, with hair like the Holy Virgin, utterly naïve periwinkle-blue eyes, a strawberries-and-cream complexion, and the Devil of a body, a rage of perverse curiosities, a mad desire to know everything, to submit to everything, to do everything!

"Above all," the old lady said to me, as she left me on the threshold of the room, "don't fail to remind her all the time that you love her, and that you're French. And say it loudly, very loudly."

And, without think about how ridiculous that instruction was, I fulfilled it, frantically, for I perceived immediately that the caresses became more ardent and more ecstatic, even savage, every time I uttered the commanded exclamations:

"I love you! I love you! I'm French!"

My lover swooned then, writhed in pleasure, and cried in a vibrant voice, with crazed intonations: "French! French! He's French! Vive la France!"

And it was as if I were mad myself, for, instead of that simply seeming grotesque—and it was—it threw me into a strange and insane paroxysm of lust.

Abruptly, the undine straightened up, her face now seemingly convulsed with fury and pride. Then, completely naked, she precipitated herself toward a curtain, behind which she disappeared and began to vociferate torrentially, in German, words that I didn't understand.

I remained there leaning on my elbow, utterly astounded.

At that moment the old woman came back in and said to me, muttering fearfully: "Quickly, quickly, get dressed and go, if you don't want to be killed."

I didn't ask any more. What point as there in seeing to understand? Besides, the old woman, increasingly terrified, could no longer find words in French and was stammering crazily. At top speed I leapt into my trousers and shoes, and then ran down the stairs and into the street, where I continued to dress myself as I ran.

I recovered my breath and my consciousness ten minutes later, without knowing where I'd been or where I'd come from. I went back to my hotel furtively, like a malefactor.

The next day, at coffee, there was talk of a crime committed during the night. A German Baron had killed his wife with revolver shots. He was liberated under caution, having been claimed by his consul, to whom he had furnished the following explanation, certified as true by the female companion of the Baroness.

The Baroness had been married virtually by force and detested her husband, against whom, it appeared, she had particular motives for hatred—no one said what they were. To avenge herself upon him she had had him bound and gagged by four bravi—who had, in fact, been found and who had confessed. Thus reduced to immobility and defenselessness, the Baron had been obliged to witness and orgy in which his wife had prostituted herself with a Frenchman, simultaneously outraging conjugal fidelity and German honor. Having regained his freedom of movement, the Baron had punished the criminal. He was now searching for the accomplice.

"And what did you do?" someone asked Pierre Dufaille.

Well, Dufaille replied, what I had to do. I put myself at the poor fellow's disposal. It was his right. We fought a duel—with sabers, alas. He ran me through with the point. That was also his right. But he had overstepped his right when he talked on the dueling-field, when he called me a pig.[50] Then I gave him his money back, and as I fell, I cried out with what remained of my strength: "French! French! Vive la France!"

---

[50] This is a pun, which does not translate, because on the previous occasions when the word *cochon* has been employed, transcribed in eye-dialect supposed reproducing a German accent as "*gogeon*" I have translated the intended metaphorical meaning of "obscenity" rather than the literal one of "pig," which is presumably intended here.

Immorality

The old Comte de Chamburlier lit his cigar slowly, sat astride his smoker, and began in these terms:

"Nephew, you will do me this justice, that I have never played the role of a comedy uncle with you, although I was as much an uncle by heritage as it is possible to be. That heritage you have not even the annoyance of waiting for, since I split my income with you. For my part, I ought to render you this justice, that for ten years you have spent that income as I desired, like a loyal nephew bravely having a ball. Thus, until last year, we only had reason to praise one another."

"Uncle," Raoul interjected, "I don't see why we should cease. Personally, I have the same sentiments toward you."

"Not me, sir," the Comte replied, "and I think you'll soon change your mind. Let me continue."

Raoul sat down sadly. He had a strong suspicion about what has discontented the Comte since the previous year. The matter had already been discussed between them twice. It was the matter of the great Constance, a woman of the world with whom Raoul had become involved. The Comte did not like that relationship, had tried to get Raoul to give it up, had not succeeded, and had then appeared to stop thinking about it, for he had not mentioned it again for six months. But Raoul knew his uncle too well not to have understood immediately, by the ceremonious tone of the conversation, that he was about to lay the matter on the table again. And the Comte's obstinacy saddened him, because he was no less obstinate himself in his involvement.

"My dear boy," the Comte resumed, "Six months ago, you gave me reasons to excuse your liaison with Constance that caused me to reflect at length. I concluded at first that you were not endowed, as I had believed, for the life to which I had destined you—too lightly, I admit. Playing the rake was not your forte. I was mistaken. You were born for marriage."

"Oh!" protested Raoul. "For marriage! Get away! You think that, Uncle?"

"As I told you, Nephew. Look at the situation, I beg you. You had mistresses. You changed them. You went from one whim to the next. You were exactly as I wished, what I had always been myself. In a word, you were worthy of me, and, as they say in commercial circles, you were following in the family business. I was delighted. Suddenly, you settled down. You no longer had more than one mistress. She trapped you. You found that regime comfortable. If that's the way it is, I ask you, why not a fit of marriage? For after all, you declared to me six months ago that you could not give Constance up, didn't you?"

"I admit that, Uncle—but admit, in return, that I explained to you very frankly why. If you aren't a comedy uncle, no more do I behave like a dramatic nephew. I didn't inflict any great tirade on you about the invincible force of passion or Constance's uncomprehended virtues. I made no claim to be rehabilitating her. I never once pronounced the word 'ideal.' I told you, quite simply, that Constance had rapidly become a habit for me. I even recall having made, in that respect, a comparison whose justice you found striking."

"Quite vividly, yes," the Comte put in. "You asked me whether I could easily give up a brand of cigar or liqueur to which I was accustomed."

"And you then replied…"

"I replied that it would, indeed, be difficult for me."

"You see!"

The Comte took a delightful puff on his cigar, drank a few sips of his old cognac, and said: "That too, my dear boy, led me to reflect at length. Personally, I'm not stubborn. I take good arguments into consideration. I therefore understood that you weren't entirely wrong."

Raoul's face lit up. This was going better than he had expected! His uncle was definitely still a good uncle, and the beginning of the discussion had only been ceremonious as a joke. The Comte doubtless wanted to give his nephew a pleasant surprise. Oh, what a dear uncle!

"Nevertheless," the Comte went on, "I wanted to know to what extent you weren't wrong. That I can't get rid of a habit without great difficulty—that I can't even give up my cigars and my cognac, that's what's understood. But it's also necessary to admit—and you'd be the first to admit it—that my cigars and my cognac merit that attachment. You appreciate them with me, as much as I do, isn't it so?"

Raoul's only response was to pour himself a small glass and light a *Colorado* in his turn, raising his eyes to the heavens ecstatically."

"Because," the Comte continued, "you have very nearly the same tastes as me, and we're generally in agreement in the choice of good things. It's even happened, occasionally—and good God, I'm not reproaching you for it—that you've even filched mistresses from me, so likely is it that what pleases me pleases you.

Raoul smiled, and said, negligently: "I understand, Uncle, and good God, I shan't reproach you for it! In brief, you want a...taste of Constance."

"Another taste, Nephew, another," riposted the Comte, no less cheerfully. "I've had her before, in fact—before you, and before many others, and afterwards too, you know."

"I know that, Uncle; and permit me to repeat to you what I've already told you, six months ago: that I'm not in any way jealous of Constance—no more, I insist, than you are of your cigars and your cognac, with which you delight I regaling your friends. So, if your experience has caused you the slightest scruple..."

"Not the slightest, my dear boy. Knowing your principles, which are mine, that's quite natural, isn't it?"

"Quite natural, Uncle. I would even dare to add that you're accomplishing a certain duty there. It was a matter of judging for yourself, in full impartiality and purposefully, whether I was or was not getting carried away falsely. That's what you thought, I'm sure, and that I understand it, you can't doubt."

"Put it there, my dear boy," said the Comte, extending his hand. "You're still to some extent worthy of being my nephew."

"And what," Raoul continued, "has been the result of your…sampling?"

"Good," the Comte replied. "Very good—much superior to what I expected; entirely conclusive in your favor, I confess. Constance has gained a great deal in growing older."

"Like your cognac, Uncle."

"You said it, Nephew."

"Then, since you share my opinion on that…"

"Absolutely, even more so than you think."

At the sarcastic fashion in which the Comte emphasized the last words, Raoul felt a slight frisson. He had suddenly remembered what the Comte had said a little while before: "You were born for marriage."

Is it, he wondered, *that he wants me to marry Constance? Damn! It's a charming immorality, no doubt—me too; but not to that extent.*

And it was with a constrained smile, poorly concealing his frightful secret, that Raoul stammered: "Oh, yes, I get it. Very funny, in truth, yes, very funny, my dear Uncle. You have a way of joking with a straight face, without laughing. Very humorous, of course, very humorous. And to think that I let myself be taken in. No, there I'm being stupid!"

"Rather stupid, in fact, I'm afraid," the Comte replied. "For you don't seem to me to have understood at all. Come on, my dear nephew, gather all the judgment you have, and let's recapitulate. I'll return to my departure-point."

"What's that, Uncle?"

"That you're the marrying kind."

"I admit it, in theory."

"So, I'm going to marry you off. I've put together a very nice dowry for you. You're a superb catch. I'm going to marry you off, I tell you."

"But I don't want to."

"What do you mean, you don't want to? You aren't being logical."

"Marry a woman who has been the mistress of all my friends, including you, Uncle? Oh, the joke's gone beyond the limit this time. Make fun of me as much as you want. You have the right to do so, undoubtedly. But in final analysis, my habituation to Constance doesn't extend as far as permitting you to suppose that I'd consent to..."

"Eh? Good God, who mentioned marrying Constance?"

"Well, it seems to me that the natural conclusion of what you were saying...that you'd clearly led me to understand..."

"But you don't get it at all, my poor nephew not at all. It's not to Constance that I want to marry you."

"Who, then?"

"I don't know. I'll go along with your choice. You'll marry whoever suits you—it doesn't matter who, except for Constance, since..."

"Since what, my excellent Uncle?"

"Since it's Constance, my excellent nephew, that I'm going to marry."

"You?"

"Me."

"Because?"

"Because you're right, my dear Raoul, because that bitch has a certain *je ne sais quoi* that makes you want to go back."

"Like your cigar and your cognac."

"Exactly. Then you understand know, that I can no longer rid myself of her either."

"But my dear Uncle, what's to prevent us...?"

"From sharing her?"

"Yes—like your cigars and you cognac."

"I've thought of that, my dear nephew—but she won't agree to it. She wants to reach an honorable conclusion. She demands it, you see. She demands it."

"And you'll accept?"

"Indeed!" The Comte took Raoul's hands, shook them affectionately, and said: "You'll have to forgive me, you see. At your age, one still has the strength to break such a habit. But at mine, my dear boy, at mine, is that possible?"

The Man With the Pale Eyes[51]

The examining magistrate Pierre-Agénot de Vargnes was the absolute opposite of a practical joker. He was dignity, seriousness and correctness personified. As a serious man, utterly incapable of committing, or even imagining in a dream, anything even remotely resembling a practical joke, I can scarcely compare him to anyone but the current President of the Republic.[52] There is, I think, no need to say more.

Given that, you will easily understand that I felt a distinct frisson when Pierre-Agénor de Vargnes did me the honor of telling me the following story.

One day last winter, t about eight o'clock in the morning, as he was about to leave home to go to the Palais, his valet de chambre handed him a visiting-card thus inscribed:

DR. JAMES FERDINAND
Member of the Académie de Medécine de Port-au-Prince
Chevalier de la Légion d'honneur

At the bottom of the card, written in pencil, was: "on behalf of Madame Frogère."

Monsieur de Vargnes knew that lady very well—a very amiable creole from Haiti, whom he had met in several salons. On the other hand, although the doctor's name did not awaken any memory in him, the quality of the individual and his titles alone, even without Madame Frogère's recommendation, would have demanded he politeness of a welcome, however brief it had to be. So, although he was in a hurry to leave, M.

[51] *Gil Blas*, 29 October 1889, reprinted in *Le Journal*, 16 August 1897 as "Le docteur Burpitt."

[52] Sadi Carnot, President of the Republic from 1887 until his assassination in 1894.

de Vargnes instructed the *valet de chambre* to show his early morning visitor in, while warning him that the judge, whose minutes were precious, was expected at the Palais.

When the doctor came in, M. de Vargnes, in spite of his habitual impassivity, could not suppress a start of surprise.

In fact, the doctor presented the strange anomaly of being a negro of the most beautiful black color, with the eyes of a white man from the far north: very pale, very cold, very bright blue eyes.

M. de Vargnes' surprise increased when the doctor, after a few words of apology got the undue time of his visit, added, while smiling enigmatically:

"My eyes astonish you, don't they, Monsieur? I was sure that they would astonish you. And to tell the truth, I've only come here so that you can get a good look at them, in order that you'll never be able to forget them."

The smile, and the assertion even more than the smile, seemed to be a lunatic's. It was moreover, said so very softly, in a child-like lisping voice particular to negroes, with the *r*s crushed under the tongue in a soft whistle. And in that chirping, the words with a mysterious, almost menacing, meaning gave an even greater impression of being proffered at hazard by an individual devoid of reason.

But the gaze itself, the very pale, very cold and very bright gaze, was certainly not that of a lunatic. In truth, it declared very clearly a threat—yes, a threat—and also an irony, and an implacable ferocity into the bargain. It was only a flash, but was flamboyant, in such a fashion that one could, indeed, never forget it.

"I've looked deep," said M. de Vargnes, in describing it, "into the eyes of many murderers. In none of them, however, have I plunged as far as in those, into such depths of crime and impudent security in crime."

The impression was so strong the M. de Vargnes thought at first that he was the victim of a hallucination—all the more so as the doctor, having finished his statement, continued, while smiling very broadly, and in his most child-like accent:

"You won't understand, Monsieur, what I just said. For that too, please excuse me. Tomorrow, you'll receive a letter that will explain everything—but it's necessary, first, that I allow you to see me, or at least that I let you see, really see, see fully and completely, my eyes—which are mine, my own and really mine, as you can judge."

After which, with a bow of supreme distinction, the doctor withdrew, leaving M. de Vargnes flabbergasted, prey to this suspicion:

Was that only a lunatic? Could the ferocious expression, the criminal depth of that gaze, have been caused solely by the bizarre contrast between that tenebrous face and such pale eyes?

Thus absorbed, M. de Vargnes unfortunately let a few minutes go by. Then, suddenly, he thought: *But no, I'm not the victim of any hallucination. It wasn't an optical illusion. That man is obviously a frightful scoundrel. I've utterly failed in my duty by not arresting him myself, on the spot, even illegally, at the risk of my life!*

And the judge hurtled downstairs in pursuit of the doctor—but too late! The other had disappeared.

That afternoon, M. de Vargnes went to the home of Madame Frogère, to ask her for information. She did not know anything about the negro doctor and was even able to certify that the individual was fictitious, for, being up to date with Haitian high society, she knew full well that the Académie de Médecine de Port-au-Prince did not have any doctor of that name among its members.

M. de Vargnes persisted and, when he gave a description of the doctor, with special mention of the extraordinary eyes, Madame Frogère burst out laughing and said: "You've certainly been dealing with a trickster, my dear Monsieur. The eyes you're describing are undoubtedly white eyes. The individual must have blacked up.

Recalling his memories then, M. de Vargnes realized that the doctor had indeed, had nothing of the negro about him except the black skin, the hair and the beard—adornments easy to counterfeit—not the physical type, or even the typical undulating gait. Perhaps, then, he really was nothing but a practical joker. All day, M. de Vargnes was satisfied with that idea, which was slightly wounding to his dignity as a serious man, but appeased his scruples as a magistrate.

The next day, he received the promised letter. It was inscribed, and addressed, in printed letters clipped out of newspapers. It said:

Monsieur.

Dr. James Ferdinand does not exist, but the man whose eyes you have seen exists, and you will surely recognize him by those eyes. That man has committed two crimes. He has no remorse in their regard. However, being a psychologist, that man is afraid of one day yielding to the imperious temptation to confess his crimes. You know better than anyone—for it is your most powerful aide—with what irresistible force criminals, especially intellectuals, experience that temptation. The great Edgar Poe has written masterpieces on that subject, which are an exact notation of the truth. Nevertheless, he has forgotten to note the ultimate phenomenon, of which I shall inform you, Monsieur examining magistrate. Yes, I, a criminal, had a terrible need to let someone know of my crimes— but once that need is satisfied, and my secret has been revealed to a confidant, I shall be tranquil forever, rid of 'the imp of the perverse,' which only tempts once. Well, this is what will happen. You shall know my secret, for the when the day comes that you recognize me by my eyes, you will seek to discover of what I am guilty and how I did it; and you will discover it, being a master of your profession—which, in parentheses, has won you the honor of being chosen by me to bar the weight of that secret, henceforth shared by the two of us, and the two of us alone. You could only obtain that secret in fact, and prove its reality to anyone, by my confession, which I defy you to obtain in the form of a public confession, since I have now found a means of making it to you alone, and without danger.

Three months later, at a soirée, M. de Vargnes encountered Monsieur X***, and at the first glance, without the slightest hesitation, he recognized in him the extraordinary eyes, very pale, very cold and very bright: the unforgettable eyes.

The man himself remained utterly impassive, to such an extent that M. de Vargnes was reduced to saying to himself: *It's probably that this time, I'm the victim of a hallucination—either that or there are two pairs of exactly similar eyes in the world. But what eyes, though! Is it really possible?*

Monsieur de Vargnes mounted an investigation of the life of Monsieur X***. What he learned removed all his doubts.

Five years before, Monsieur X*** had been a poor medical student, and a very brilliant one, who, without qualifying as a doctor, had already made a name for himself by curious microbiological endeavors. An extremely rich young widow had become smitten with him and had married him. She had a child by her first marriage. In the space of six months first the child and then the mother, had died of typhoid fever, and Monsieur X*** had thus inherited, duly and legally, with no possible dispute, the large fortune. It had been with one voice that people proclaimed that he had lavished his cares upon the two patients with admirable devotion.

Was it necessary to see those two deaths as the two crimes mentioned in the letter?

If so, Monsieur X*** must have poisoned his two victims with the microbes of typhoid fever, cleverly cultivated in such a fashion as to render the infection invincible even to the cares of the most admirable devotion.

Why not?

"Did you believe that?" I asked Monsieur de Vargnes.

"Absolutely," he replied. And what was most frightful of all was that the scoundrel had been right in defying me to compel a public confession. I could not, in fact, see any means of achieving one. Briefly, I thought about magnetism—but who could magnetize that man with the eyes that were so pale, so cold and so bright? With such eyes, he would be the one who would force the magnetizer to denounce himself as the guilty party."

Then, uttering a profound sigh, he said: "Oh, the justice of old had its merits!"

And as my gaze interrogated him, Monsieur de Vargnes added, in a firm and convinced tone: "The justice of old had torture at its disposal."

"My word," I replied, with the unconscious and naïve egotism of an artist, "it's certain that, without torture, that strange tale has no conclusion—and, for the story I want to make of it, that's very annoying."

Countess Satan

There was talk of dynamite, social revolution, nihilism. Everyone, even those least interested in politics, put a word in. Some were frightened. Others philosophized. A few tried to smile.

"Bah!" said N***. "We'll see whether we get blown up. Perhaps, after all, it will be amusing—provided that get blown a long way up!"

"But we won't get blown up at all," put in G***, the optimist. "All that's just fantasy."

"You're mistaken, my dear chap," said Jules de C***. "It resembles fantasy, but with that diabolical nihilism, everything takes on the appearance of fantasy, and it's necessary not to trust it. So, my friend, the manner in which I met Bakunin..."

He was known as a story-teller; no one was unaware that his life had been full of adventures. Everyone drew closer, and listened religiously. This is what he said.

It was in Naples that I met Countess Nirska W***, the strange woman nicknamed Countess Satan. I attached myself to her immediately out of curiosity and soon fell in love with her. Not that she was beautiful! She was a Russian, with all the worst aspects of the Russian type—thin and thickset at the same time; the fact white and puffy; the Cossack nose—but her conversation was bewitching: complicated, erudite, philosophical, scientifically depraved and satanic.

Perhaps the last word is pretentious, but it expresses my meaning perfectly. In other words, she loved evil for evil's sake. She enjoyed the vices of others. She loved to sow them in order to see them bloom—and that on a large, enormous scale. Corrupting individuals was not sufficient for her; she only did that to keep her hand in. What she wanted was to work on the masses. She could have taken Caligula's famous

160

saying as her motto in arranging things as she wished. She too would have liked the human species to have only one head—not to cut it off, but to cause the philosophy of nihilism to flourish there.

What a temptation it was to become the lord and master of such a monster! I allowed myself to be tempted and embarked on the adventure. The means was obvious; it was merely to show oneself to be more perverse, more satanic, than she was. I therefore played the little Satan.

"Yes," I said, "we writers are the best workers in the world. Our books can be phials of poison. So-called men of action only fire the machine-guns whose barrels we have loaded. It's with formulas that the world will be blown up, and it's us who invent formulas."

"That's true," she said, one day, "and that's what Bakunin lacks, alas."

That name often came to her lips. I asked her for details. She gave them to me, knowing the man intimately.

"Basically," she said, "with a scornful moue, he's merely a kind of Garibaldi."

And she related to me, mockingly, the odyssey from barricade to penitentiary that had created Bakunin's legend, but which is not strictly true: his role as the leader of the insurgents in Prague, and then in Dresden; his first condemnation to death; his internments at Olmutz, in the Fortress of Saint Peter and Paul and a dungeon at Schlusselburg; his exile in Siberia; his miraculous escape along the river Amor in a Japanese coaster, his journey via Yokohama and San Francisco, ultimately arriving in London, where he took on the direction of nihilism.

"You see," she said, "he was primarily an adventurer—and now the adventures are over. He's married in Tobolsk, become bourgeois. No personal idea, anyway. It's Herzen,[53] the pamphleteer of the *Kolokol* who found him the only fe-

---

[53] Alexander Herzen (1812-1870), the "father of Russian socialism."

cund phrase he ever pronounced: Land and Liberty! But that still doesn't constitute the definitive formula, the general formula—what I call the dynamite formula. At the very most, Bakunin might be a burner of cities—and what's that, I ask you? Pooh! Re-heated Rostopchin.[54] He needed a prompter; I wanted to play the role, but he didn't take me seriously."

There's no need to go into the psychological details marking the course of my passion for the countess. There's no need either to explain at greater length the attraction of curiosity that increased by the day. It became exasperating, all the more so because the perverse woman rejected me, in sum, as the craziest of innocents.

In spite of that, by the end of a month of frantic Satanism, I finally got a clear idea of what she was up to. Do you know what she had come to imagine? Making me the prompter of whom she dreamed for Bakunin. At least, that was what she told me—but she doubtless retained in secret, as I also understood, that role of prompter for herself. My passion, which she left unslaked by design, assured her of absolute power over me.

All that must seem to you to be folly, something out of Ponson du Terrail; it is, however, the truth.

In brief, one day, she offered me a straightforward bargain.

"Become Bakunin's soul," she said, "and your can have me."

I accepted. It was too fantastically strange to refuse, wasn't it? What an adventure! What a chance!

A series of letters between the countess and Bakunin prepared the way. My name was introduced to him. I was discussed. I became a sort of Occidental prophet, a mystical

---

[54] Feodor Rostopchin (1763-1826) was responsible for defending Moscow against Napoléon's 1812 invasion, and was probably responsible for ordering the burning of the city, although he never admitted it in so many words.

charmer ready to nihilize the Latin races: the Saint Paul of the new religion of nothingness.

A meeting was eventually fixed. It was in London that I saw him.[55] He was living in a small house in Pimlico: a simple, two-story house with a small front garden, nothing out of the ordinary.

The Countess and I were taken into the banal "parlor" that all English homes have, then taken up a staircase carpeted with a kind of leather-cum-rubber. The room where we were left was small, almost bare, with a square table in the middle, and writing materials on the table. One might have thought it an administrative vestibule.

It was the sanctuary. The god soon appeared there. I saw him in the flesh and bone—the flesh especially, for he was enormous. The broad face, with prominent cheekbones in spite of the fat, a nose like a double funnel, wrinkly eyes with a magnetic gaze, all advertised the Tartar: the old Turanian blood that has generated Attilas, Genghis Khans and Tamerlanes. The characteristic obesity of nomad races, always on horseback or in chariots, added to that Asiatic aspect. For sure, the man was not a European, a Slav, a son of deist Aryans. He really was the descendant of the atheist hordes that had almost destroyed our world several times already, and which, instead of the idea of progress, carry deep in their hearts the idea of nothingness.

I was astonished. I had not expected that majesty of an entire race revived in one man. My amazement increased after an hour of conversation. I understood why such a colossus had not wanted the Countess as an Egeria. She was only a child, a simpleton, for having dreamed of that role with regard to such a thinker. She had not sensed the profundity of the atrocious philosophy concealed beneath that material activity. She had not seen the prophet in the barricader—or perhaps he had not judged it wise to revealed himself to her in that fashion.

---

[55] Bakunin was in London for 14 months between 1861 and 1863, when this story is presumably set.

To me, he revealed himself, and he frightened me.

Prophet—oh yes! He believed himself to be an Attila, and foresaw the consequences of his revolution. It was not by instinct alone but by theory that he was driving a people to nihilism. The word was not his—it is, I believe, Turgenev's—but the idea, yes.

He had taken his program of agricultural communism from Herzen, and his destructive radicalism from Pugachev,[56] but without stopping there. In that, far greater than the other two, I heard evil for evil's sake. Herzen wanted the happiness of the peasant-slave. Pugatchev wanted to be elected emperor. Bakunin only wanted to annihilate, by any means whatsoever, the present order of things, and replace social concentration with an infinite scattering.

It is a Tartar dream. It is true nihilism pushed to extreme practical conclusions. It is, in a word, the applied philosophy of chance, of indeterminism, of universal dissolution without laws.

Monstrous, perhaps—but grandiose in its monstrousness!

And note that the man of action, so scorned by the Countess, was combined in Bakunin with the gigantic dreamer that I have just shown you. His dream had not remained in the state of a dream. He had begun to realize it. It is due to the cares of that organizer that the nihilist party has acquired a body—a party in which there is a little of everything, you know; but, in sum, a formidable party because of the avant-garde group directing it. And that group consists of the pure disciples of the master, those who know the secret of his thought. The dream of that group is the veritable nihilism, which intended nothing less than blowing up the Occidental world, in order to see blossoming in the ruins the infinite scattering, the ultimate conception of modern Tartarism.

---

[56] Yemelyan Pugachev (1742-1775) was a pretender to the Russian throne who led a Cossack revolt against Catherine the Great.

I never saw Bakunin again. Trying to play a comedy with the Old Man of the Mountain was paying too dear for the conquest of the Countess. In any case, after that visit she seemed to me to be absolutely inept, that poor Countess Satan. Her famous satanism was merely the flame of a punch-bowl, compared to the universal flame of which the other dreamed. Truly, she had shown herself to be quite stupid by not understanding that prodigious monster—and as she had seduced me with her intelligence and her perversity alone, once that mask had been lowered, I was instantaneously disgusted by her. I left her without warning. I never saw her again either.

Both of them must have taken me for a spy send by the third section of the Imperial Chancellery. If so, they thought me very clever, and I wouldn't be here if their affiliates had ever recognized me.

With that, he smiled and turned to the waiter who had just come in. "In the meantime," he said, "open us another bottle of champagne—and make the cork pop. That will accustom us a little, won't it, for the day when we all go pop ourselves?"

La Morillonne

They called her La Morillonne[57] because of her black hair, her complexion gilded like Autumn leaves, and her mouth with thick violet-tinted lips, which resembled a mulberry when they were pursed.

It was a mystery of atavism that she had been born with that Moorish appearance among a fair-haired people, engendered by a father and mother with flaxen hair and buttery skin. One of her ancestors must have sinned with one of those wandering coppersmiths who had been passing through the region since time immemorial, with swarthy and indigo faces, coiffed in spongy steel wool—and from that ancestor she had, not merely her dark face, but also her dark soul and her treacherous eyes, in which that troubled soul lurked: eyes in which the night lit up, at times, with flashes of all the vices; the eyes of a perverse and malevolent beast.

Beautiful? No—not even merely pretty. Ugly, absolutely ugly. Such a false gaze! A bulbous snub-nose. A mouth like an unhealthy, rotten fruit, always drooling with greed, from which evil words hissed. A hirsute and dirtily frizzy head, a nest of vermin. And the whole on a thin, feverish body, badly-molded in flesh, built askew, with a creeping gait.

In brief, a monster!

With that monster, however, all the lads of the locality had lain, and whoever tasted her wanted to do it again.

As soon as she began to learn the catechism she had become the commodity of the village. Children of her own age had been corrupted by her, taken into alleyways and behind barns, under the pretext of bird's-nesting or blind man's bluff, and came back home with love-bites. Young men too, at the risk of prison, and even serious men, old, notable and venera-

---

[57] A morillon is a kind of black grape.

166

ble, such as the farmer des Eclausiaux and the former mayor Monsieur Martin, and others, and better, were ensnared by her, by the slut's imperious petticoat. If the *garde-champêtre* had not hauled her up in court, in spite of his love of legal procedure, it was only because, it was said, he would have been hauled up in court himself.

And so she had grown up in impunity, the official mistress of each and everyone, as the local schoolmaster put it—who had been included therein himself.

The most curious part of the story is that no one was jealous of her. Everyone passed her around. When someone chanced to express astonishment on that score one day, she had replied to the unintelligent foreigner: "Isn't there enough for everyone?"

How in any case, would a jealous individual wanting to monopolize her have gone about it? There was nothing with which to hold her. She was not self-interested, Gifts and money she accepted gladly, but never asked for them. One might even have thought that she preferred not to ask for them, but to pay herself in her own fashion, by stealing. What she was allowed to steal, as the price of her skin, was all that she needed. An écu placed in her hand gave her less pleasure than a sou picked from someone's pocket.

To be dominated by a single male, like a proud cockerel, was unthinkable too Who, among the strongest and broad-shouldered, would have been capable of it? Some had tried, in vain. They had broken their backs without satisfying her. When their eyes were hollow, their nostrils pinched, their bones emptied of marrow, they had seen her still vigorous and frisky, still unslaked, all of her flesh screaming with desire.

"I can't do any more!" they had croaked. And she, sniggering, riposted: "But I need more." And it had been necessary to pass the shovel to someone else, in order to stoke the mouth of that furnace, which was never full. What right had anyone, then, to pose as her master? It was as if one had wanted to bake one's bread all alone in the common oven in which the entire village baked.

Thus, just as there was that common oven, the undivided property of the commune, to nourish the body, La Morillonne was also common property for the bread of love.

Only one man in the locality did not cook in the communal oven—and similarly, he did not share in La Morillonne. That was Ch'tiot-Bru, the shepherd.

He lived in his hut on wheels, in the open fields, on unleavened pancakes, which he kneaded on a stone and grilled under the embers, sometimes here and sometimes there, at the bottom of a hole hollowed out among the stones and embers of dead wood. That, potatoes, milk, a few hard cheeses, wild fruits and a small cask of gin that he distilled himself, made up his sustenance.

Of amorous sustenance, none at all—with regard to women, undoubtedly, it was said, but with regard to females, who could tell? No one hesitated to accuse him unthinkingly of bestial acquaintance with his ewes—but no one said it to his face, firstly because Ch'tiot-Bru had a muscular arm and iron, handling his crook like a drum-major's cane; secondly because of his three dogs with wolf-like teeth, who knew no one but their master; and finally, for fear of the evil eye. For Ch'tiot-Bru, it appeared, knew spells for inflicting the wheat with rust, sheep with scrapie, oxen with the staggers and making cows abort their calves, and could set fire to hayricks with his gaze.

But as Ch'tiot-Bru alone did not stick his tongue out at La Morillonne, naturally, one day, she set her cap at him—and she was also alone in declaring that she had no fear of spellcasters.

They told her to be careful. She went to him.

"What do you want?" he said.

And she replied, brazenly: "What do I want? You."

He replied: "All right—but then, you'll be mine alone."

She smiled and replied: "I don't say no—if you can."

He smiled in his turn, and then lay with her. And that night, she didn't come back to the village, but slept in the hut on wheels. And the next day, too, she didn't come back, nor the day after that, nor all week. The local commodity was now, well and truly, Ch'tiot-Bru's commodity.

The village got excited. They were not jealous of one another, but they were jealous of him. What! He had held out—*him*? Unlike the comrades, he did not have hollow eyes, pinched nostrils, bones devoid of marrow, a broken back? So he knew charms and magic words and spells for that too? They became enraged.

They grew bold. Someone watched for afar from the fork of a tree. The couple was seen. Oh joy! She was still robust and frisky, but he was a phantom. Ha ha! She had eaten him too, had drunk him dry, La Morillonne!

They became even bolder. She must have need of a substitute male. The most boastful of the band approached, rifle in hand.

"Tie up your dogs, Ch'tiot-Bru," he shouted, from a distance. "Tie up your dogs, or I'll put them down."

"Have no fear of the dogs," shouted La Morillonne. "They won't do anything, I'll answer for that."

She smiled. The lad with the rifle arrived.

"What do you want?" asked the shepherd.

"I'll tell you," La Morillonne put in. "He wants to do it with me—and I want it too. So there!"

Ch'tiot-Bru started weeping. She continued: "Since you can't anymore!"

And she left with the lad.

Ch'tiot-Bru leapt on his crook. The lad with raised his rifle, while moving backwards.

"Go! Go!" howled the shepherd, rousing his dogs.

The lad already had his finger on the trigger, ready to fire on them. La Morillonne pushed the gun-barrel down and sang: "Here, dogs, here, my pretties. Prr! Prr! My pretties."

And the three dogs ran to her, licked her hands, and followed her, gamboling, while she shouted at the shepherd from afar: "You see, Ch'tiot-Bru—they aren't jealous!" Then, with a shrill and bitter laugh, she added: "And as you know, they just have as much right to be as you do."

The Malay

Poor as I was, and so poorly dressed, but with my good twenty-five-year-old arms under my jacket, I'll be damned if I feared unfortunate encounters, even in that sinister quarter where I lived among the worst riff-raff in London. The most cunning and boldest rogues saw immediately, judging me at a glance, that there wasn't much to clip from me—might as well say nothing—and that the nothing in question would, in case of an attack, be vigorously defended. Thanks to which, and also to a certain knowledge of English slang, I could take a bath of poverty and rascality, in total security, whenever I wanted, in the mud of that underworld, reputedly so dangerous.

I was, therefore, if not anxious, at least a trifle astonished on the day when I noticed that I was being followed, positively followed, but the strange individual whose face, gait and costume had said to me the other night: "Hey! De Quincey's Malay!"

He did, in fact, resemble in a miraculous fashion the fantastic apparition described in the *Confessions of an Opium-Eater*: the same emaciated face, simultaneously pale and tenebrous; the same hallucinated gaze; the same exotic rags; the same spectral stride; and also something unspecifiable, almost inexpressibly dream-like and symbolic—as if within that wanderer all of Asia, ecstasized by opium, surged forth, and as if the individual, visible and tangible, and hence real, was nothing himself but one of the fugitive clouds taking on substance in that ecstasy.

Yes, thus he had appeared to me the other night, that strange individual—on the night when I had gone to pay a visit to one of the palaces of "just, powerful and subtle opium," as De Quincey the Visionary puts it.

A somewhat lamentable palace, however! A kind of cupboard above the back room of a shop, with a wooden divan for its only furniture. It reminded you of a sentry-box—and what a stink the ten or twelve unfortunates lying on the floor exhaled, from their greasy and damp rags, their sweaty bodies, in that close room with the low ceiling, overheated by the large flame of a gas-jet! But a palace all the same, inhabited by emperors and gods, a palace whose bare walls stirred incessantly in the most magical and paradisal décors.

"Hey! De Quincey's Malay!"

Yes, that was exactly what I had said—or, rather, thought—on seeing the strange individual enter, and then sit down facing me, and in following him, a few moments later— but a long, long time—through the course of interminable voyages in which he was my guide, silent and enigmatic, through all the floras and faunas, all the architectures and crowds, all the multicolored lights and tenebrous sensualities of the most marvelous and monstrous Orient.

To such an extent that on awakening, on returning from my magical pilgrimage, when I had found myself once again on the wooden divan, between two heaps of human flesh like two cadavers, a scarcely-resuscitated cadaver myself, observing that the strange individual was no longer there, I had doubted that I had ever seen him other than in a dream, through my memories of reading De Quincey, as an evocation of the opium.

But no! Here he was, alive, apparently solid, no longer an apparition of smoke—since, that morning, in the open air, walking through the swarming crowd, every last trace of smoke had evaporated from my brain. I was in full possession of my faculties, my perception clear and my senses sharp, my eye as bright as a basilisk's. And he was there, the Malay; it was really him!

Certainly, the first time I had turned around a little while before, obscurely troubled by a gaze drilling into the back of my neck, and I had seen the man following me, I could have believed it a reflorescence of my nocturnal dream—all the more so when, abruptly, the man disappeared into the crowd, vanishing like a furtive and fulgurant vision.

The second time, however, half an hour later, he presented himself to me face to face, in the manner of someone seeking to recognize and be recognized. It is true that then, again, when I mechanically closed my eyes to avoid the extraordinary glare of his, he had disappeared as if he had been swallowed up by the ground. Nevertheless, I was sure of not having been, this time, the victim of a persistent hallucination.

Furthermore, during the last half hour, it was neither once nor twice but a good ten times that I had been haunted by him. Sometimes, I sensed him at my heels, of which I made certain by turning my head. Sometimes, I almost bumped into him at a street corner. Sometimes, I rubbed shoulders with him in the eddies of the crowd, where I had him for a neighbor for a few strides, his arm brushing mine with a quasi-communicative pressure, and his eyes, his nostalgic eyes, burning with fever, trying o enter into a mute dialogue with my own fugitive eyes.

Finally, now, I could no longer maintain the slightest doubt as to the reality of his presence. The tailing, closer and closer, less and less concealed, had reached the point at which, in the bar into which I had gone to escape the pursuit, the man had come in behind me and, on the empty bench where I had at down, the man had come to sit down beside me.

Immediately, of course, I stopped avoiding his gaze and turned to face him squarely, frowning, my expression hostile, teeth clenched, nose to nose.

His face suddenly expressed a profound sadness. Two large tears ran down his cheeks. Then, gently, he placed a hand on my breast, and began to speak—or, rather, to whisper—in a language that I did not understand, but in an extremely musical and seductive voice. One might have thought him a child singing like a bird.

Not knowing how to respond, I asked the barmaid for two glasses of whisky, and offered one of them to the stranger. He wet his lips with it, then gave it back to me with a gesture telling me to finish it, and that he wanted to do the same with mine. That was a politeness customary in the low taverns of London, and I complied.

After which I said to the man in English: "Now that we're friends, tell me what you want ad why you've been following me as you have."

I saw in his large desolate eyes, however, that he did not understand what I had said. I was, therefore, obliged, like him, to resort to sign-language. This time, he understood.

From the folds of his belt he took a long silk ribbon, which he unrolled in front of my face, asking me, by means of gestures, to read the characters that were inscribed on it. At the same time he explained to me, still by gestures, but quite clearly, that the inscription represented an enormous and fabulous treasure of gold and precious stones. He expressed gold by pouring out, between his thumb and index-finger, imaginary coins that accumulated in cascades. He signified precious stones by making his fingernails shine, polished like onyx, and blinking his eyelids very rapidly, within the fissures of which his eyes flashed and sparkled like diamonds.

I demonstrated that I had missed nothing of his mute discourse, and he seemed delighted—so delighted that he flung his arms around my neck and embraced me, weeping, as if he had gone mad.

I had, however, paid close attention to the silken ribbon, and I had recognized that the characters were Sanskrit, of which I possessed a vague knowledge: not enough, certainly, to translate the exceedingly long inscription, but sufficient to decipher a few scattered words. I pointed them out to him with my finger and mimed their meanings. One meant "king," which I interpreted by the simulation of a crown on my head. Another signified "sky," and another "earth," which were easy for me to render. Finally, one word recurred frequently, which signified one of the mysterious names of the god Shiva. I happened to know that the word is represented in Hindu architecture by a certain hieratic design. I traced the outline of that design in the air, after having touched the word on the silken ribbon.

From these various identifications, the man must have imagined that I understood the entire inscription, and that undoubtedly struck him with terror. So, at least, I judged on seeing him suddenly throw himself at my knees, frightened, his hands trembling, like a criminal begging for mercy. At the same time, he resumed his bird-like twittering, but this time with extreme volubility, and in an exceedingly shrill tone, which was deafening.

Unfortunately, I was not the only one who was deafened. A drunkard who as sleeping in a corner was woken up by it, and rushed at the poor devil, who was still prostrate.

I tried to launch myself to the unfortunate fellow's aid, but he thought, on the contrary, that I was joining In with his aggressor and falling upon him. Admittedly, the three of us composed, on the ground, an incomprehensible amalgam. At any rate, by the time I found myself sitting astride the drunkard, the other had decamped.

With one bound I was in the street, searching for him— but in vain, as one might imagine. Agile, slippery and furtive as he was, how could I tell where that human eel had replunged into that human mud?

I was never to see the strange individual again.

In the opium den, to which I returned in an attempt to obtain some information, I got none. The man had only been there once, on the night when I was there myself.

Who was he? What did he want with me? What did the inscription on the silk ribbon represent? Why did he want to make me, in particular, party to it? And then, why that terror at the idea that I was able to translate it? Was that exile in possession of a fabulous treasure? Had he stolen it? So many questions without answers!

And how many hypotheses I formulated, with regard to that bizarre adventure, as marvelous and absurd as a dream!

That it was only a dream I have not believed for a long time, having had before me so much evidence that proved its visible and tangible reality during those few hours of my life. But today, through the distant mists of the past, when I find that admittedly-implausible story in my memory, I sometimes wonder whether the powerful and subtle opium is as just as De Quincey claims, and whether it is not instead a very mischievous demon, which amused itself with me by parading me for an entire morning through the mirages of a hallucination as consistent as life itself—for I forgot to mention that I never found the bar in which the scene had unfolded again either.

And yet, what a tableau it all makes, distinctly outlined in vigorous colors, in the museum of my memory!

The Old Fogey

"Oh no, not him!—it's futile to persist. He and his fellows can no longer be entertained, under any pretext. Doubtless they rendered services in their time, but that's no reason to eternalize them at the Prefecture."

"His great memory for physiognomies, though, his good advice..."

"Eh! It's precisely his so-called good advice of which I want to rid us. Yes, I know, traditions! That's our loss, the traditions. We need young men, active and inventive. The press criticizes our routines, and the press isn't mistaken. Well, your Lejars is the finest specimen of the old school, the repertoire of all the routines. He still believes in disguises, for instance. Why not Vidocq's methods, then? No, no, those fellows, so far as I'm concerned, are finished. Pension them off! I've had enough of them, the old fogeys."

And on these words from the new Prefect of Police—an advocate and a reformer—in spite of all the efforts off the head of the Sûreté, Brigadier Lejars was "out on his ear."

Certainly, that ear was a little hard of hearing now, and that was why, for two years, he had had scarcely been employed in anything but office work and minor court cases, but all the same, he wasn't useless. On the other hand, some consideration ought to have been given for his thirty years of loyal service, especially for some of his campaigns, still legendary: veritable models of patience, ingenuity and boldness. He asked for nothing more, in fact, than to do more of the same, and if he had not done so, it was because he was no longer given the opportunity, having been relegated to sedentary tasks.

Of what, then could anyone complain? That he liked to advise his younger colleagues? But they went to consult him of their own accord, and didn't find it bad. Besides which, that proved he had a passion for his profession. Yes—perhaps he had too much. A past master in the art of make-up—of *camouflaging* himself, as they say over there—he had been gripped in his old age by an innocent mania for "making faces" without any necessity, out of habit, for pleasure, in a way. But that was a mild ridiculousness that didn't trouble anyone and didn't prevent him from doing his duty. The worst result of it was that the agents made jokes about it, but not maliciously, without undermining the respect they had for him. And when he was teased about it he replied, very good-humoredly: "Yes, I make faces—just to keep my hand in."

So it was that Père Lejars was in despair when he was told that he would no longer be a member of the Sûreté Brigade. That struck him as an injustice and an outrage.

The loss of his position hardly affected him, from a pecuniary point of view. Sober, used to living on his meager salary, and even saving out of that poor budget, his savings and his retirement pension were more than sufficient for him. He had not the slightest chagrin in that regard.

What pained him, and revolted him, was that he had thrown in the rubbish-bin as if he were good for nothing. And in what terms! For the prefect's words had been repeated to him. The reformer, moreover, did not hide it. He loudly advertised his intentions, his motives, his hatred of routine, and his love of the new. That was the order of the day at the Prefecture. There was no question of anything but that new broom. Everyone knew that Père Lejars' retirement would be followed by several others, and that the boss did not want any more "old fogeys."

An old fogey, him, Lejars! The man who has tracked down and caught the famous Crusier, nicknamed le Rouge, alias the Comte de Montarley, alias the Abbé Rostaing, that real Rocambole of sorts! An old fogey, the man who had reeled in the Gendret gang single-handed, and who had been stabbed twice, and whose bloody hands had knocked down and tied up that terrible old lag, nicknamed, with good reason, Cop-Killer! An old fogey, the man who, disguised as a man of the world—yes, as a man of the world, which is the most difficult of all—had caught the former notary Heurteville, who had become the leader of a colossal blackmail agency, with his hand in the till! An old fogey, the man who, that very day, in the district court, had immediately recognized faces that had disappeared from circulation ten years ago! An old fogey, him, Lejars, Père Lejars! Oh, it was too much!

Accustomed to discipline and hierarchical respect, he dared not call his superior, the Prefect, the big chief, a fool. But in his soul and his conscience, that was what he thought. And he suffered from keeping silent, not only because of his wounded self-esteem, but also and above all because of his beloved police force, which he now saw as disorganized and going downhill, since it had fallen into the hands of a bumpkin for whom Père Lejars was an old fogey. All that he permitted himself to say, by way of recrimination, was: "The cut-throats will have a fine time from now on."

And as the head of the Sûreté, very amicably, did his best to console him by heaping praise on his fine career, he added, bitterly: "It's not over yet. I still have good feet and eyes, and I'll prove to the Prefect that I'm not an old fogey."

"How?"

"That's my business."

What he meant became clear a few days later, when a mysterious crime was committed. At the same time as the official report of the agent charged with the investigation, the Prefecture received a report from Père Lejars. He had acted on his own account and sent the results of his enquiries. They were found to be accurate, but unnecessary, for another agent, a newly-promoted young man, excited by the desire to distinguish himself at the outset, had had the guilty party arrested before anyone could make use of the reports. Père Lejars took this setback hard, albeit while rendering justice to the enterprise of his rival.

He had even less luck in another expedition. Reduced to his own resources, deprived of the information on file at the Prefecture, he went astray and wasted time in pointless research, and that resulted in the ground being cut from under his feet.

A third time completed his misfortune. The young agent, who was definitely first rate, spurred on by the competition, took a malign and dishonest pleasure in sending him on a false trail, with the result that the veteran was led up the garden path like a new recruit.

They laughed long and loud at the prefecture, where the new personnel were no longer sympathetic to him. The Prefect himself, who was amused by the fellow's obstinacy, did not have the generosity to hide the petty pleasure he took in seeing him discomfited. As for the newcomer, proud of his successes, which were masterstrokes, he was loudly triumphant, and, further raising the stakes on the boss's theories, he declared to anyone who would listen: "Well, the old ways are dead and buried! The old fogeys are dead and buried!"

Père Lejars, who had maintained his acquaintance with a few agents, heard about all that, and his resentment was violent. Thus, not only was he unable to take the revenge on the Prefect that he had promised himself, but in addition, in that ill-judged duel, he risked losing his former renown. A greenhorn was queening a pawn! And everyone was laughing at him! And the exploits of yore no longer counted for anything, humiliated pell-mell with his present failures! They had had every reason, then, to send him packing and call him an old fogey!

The injury to his self-esteem was further aggravated by reading the newspapers. The Prefect of Police had a few obliging reporters at his beck and call, and they did not fail to praise the brilliant start made by the new organization, not without smearing the old one. Even the papers that were not in fief to the Prefect's political party could not help doing justice to his efforts and his reforms, and the good results they were producing, especially the deference he had manifested to the unanimous press criticism of his predecessors' routines. All of that appeared to Père Lejars to be a campaign to his personal detriment. He was not far from thinking that all Paris was out to get him. One reporter who had got wind of his recent exploits made a funny story out of them; that was the *coup de grâce* for the poor pensioner, who thought that he had definitely become an object of universal ridicule, and who fell ill in consequence.

The head of the Sûreté still felt affection for him, and came to see him; he found him in bed, aged and jaundiced.

"Come on, Père Lejars," he said, "you're not being reasonable, damn it! What's the point of worrying yourself sick like this, instead of settling down quietly, with your little pension and your consciousness of always having done your duty? You ought to be happy."

"No, no," replied Père Lejars. "I won't be happy as long as I haven't proved..."

"Eh? What do you expect to prove, old chap, without help and without resources? You might well be Père Lejars, but you can't be stronger on your own than the entire Prefecture. That's childish. You're a sensible man—think about it."

"I'm only thinking about one thing—that I've been called an old fogey."

"They were wrong, that's certain. An unfortunate choice of words! But it shouldn't poison your old age. All the good people at the Prefecture, me first of all, and the Prefect himself, you can be sure, know perfectly well what you are, and that there's never been a better servant than you, more loyal, braver and more expert."

"That didn't stop them throwing me out on my ear."

"Well, it comes to us all. My turn will come too."

"But there's out on one's ear and out on one's ear. I know what they're saying in the bureaux, you know—and in the press too, damn it! It's not just the Prefect, it's everyone know who's calling me an old fogey."

"Come on—you're beating yourself up over a word, Père Lejars."

"Maybe. I'll put the record straight."

"By doing what? Continuing your private enquiries? You won't succeed. Once again, you don't have the necessary means for that. You're wasting time and effort. Would you permit me to tell you something, between ourselves, as a friend? Well, if you continue you'll compromise the good opinion that people have of you—that's all you'll get out of it. And at the same time, it'll rebound oñ us, all the policemen of the old school. Is that what you want, Père Lejars?"

"No, of course not. And if I thought any such thing..."

"Believe me, my friend, I'm telling you the truth. Alone against the Prefecture, you can only come unstuck, and it's all of us who'll bear the consequences—those whom you love, the old guard."

"That's true, I suppose," said Père Lejars, resignedly. "I didn't think of that. Forgive me. I'll keep quiet."

"Good! Now you're being reasonable. Come on, old chap, don't spill any more bile over these follies. Look after yourself and put on a brave face. That's what will annoy your enemies the most."

"I'll try," Père Lejars concluded. "I'll try. I only ask one thing in return, just one—a hope that will give me the courage to get back on my feet."

"Anything you wish, my friend, if it's possible."

"Well, this is it: if there's an affair that no one could fathom, a closed case with which no one is any longer concerned, I'd like you to entrust it to me, to give me a distraction."

"Oh—I'll talk to the Prefect about it; I don't think he'll raise any difficulty. It will give him a means of making up for is unfortunate phrase. You can consider it agreed."

And Père Lejars, give new heart by that promise, did indeed begin to revive.

A short while later, the head of the Sûreté saw him again, still jaundiced, very thin, like a man still consumed by an obsession, but not defeated and despairing. On the contrary, he seemed rejuvenated, sturdy, upright, confident and energetic.

"You see," he said, "I'm ready to go to work. I don't look much like an old fogey now, do I?" But he said that without any apparent bitterness, more in a humorous fashion, almost smiling.

Unfortunately, he and the head of the Sûreté had counted without the still-acute jealousy of the Prefet's young protégé and the hostility of the Prefect himself. Yes, the high functionary, who had initially been amused by Père Lejars' obstinacy, was now mean enough to hold it against the old pensioner. A few less fortunate operations had provoked reproaches in the press, in which it had been suggested that the famous reforms, so loudly advertised, were not producing the marvels that had been promised. The young policeman, going behind the Prefect's back, had insinuated that there had been an offensive reprisal by the party of routine. Père Lejars had been held responsible for that. His rancor was thus paid back in kind, and two or three closed cases, on which he already had designs, were not entrusted to him as he had hoped. He was definitely not wanted, even in an auxiliary role. There was, therefore no mans-none at all—of taking his revenge. An old fogey he had been judged to be, and he was condemned irrevocably to die an old fogey.

It is necessary to believe that at length he became resigned to it, for two months went by without him offering his services again—except that the head of the Sûreté knew that the silence in question did not conceal a renunciation. One day, he had run into Père Lejars, thinner and more jaundiced than ever, undermined by fever, but also more than ever determined to end his career with a bang.

"I'll bide my time," the old man had said. "An occasion will present itself, when the Prefecture can do nothing—absolutely nothing—without a trump card in its hand. Then I'll join in the came on equal terms. And we shall see."

"Ah!" said the head of the Sûreté, "I recognize you in that, Père Lejars. We men of the old school are all like that. Once on a track, with an idea, we don't let go."

"No," the old policeman replied, "we don't let go. And that's why I'll have the last word, you see. I belong to the bulldog breed, me."

But the old man was fooling himself, undoubtedly, or he was still waiting for a sufficiently good opportunity. At any rate, an entire year went by without anyone hearing any news of him. The Prefecture continued in its routines, sometimes hunting successfully, something coming back empty-handed, praised by the papers of the ministerial party, denigrated by the others—in sum, in spite of the reforms, giving neither more nor less satisfaction than before. As for Père Lejars, he was now forgotten, or very nearly so. There were too many other cats to skin to bother about someone who had dropped out of sight. People were primarily preoccupied with the next change of ministry, which would probably lead to the Prefect's dismissal, and bring in another new broom sweeping through the bureaus. There was only one chance of salvation for everyone, for the prefect as for his protégés, and that was some major affair that could be settled with drums beating, and which would demonstrate the necessity of keeping the present administration.

In the nick of time, two truly admirable affairs emerged.

A stroke of luck! thought the Prefect.

"Right!" said his protégé. "They might have been made to order—one couldn't ask for anything better."

The press, in fact, was seething with excitement; the public was impassioned—and the police were sure of rapidly finding the solution to the double mystery. They had exact descriptions of the two malefactors, and were only a few hours behind in setting out on their trails.

You will recall the two crimes in question, committed on the same night: an Undersecretary of State murdered on a train between Étampes and Orléans, and a prostitute whose throat was cut at her home in the Rue du Rocher. The latter murder, however, only caused a stir because of the coincidence; the reportage was primarily focused on the other. A thousand hypotheses were formulated. In the case of the prostitute, it was merely a matter of a vulgar murder followed by theft, but for the Undersecretary of State it was a whole other story. No theft there, except of documents. What documents? Family documents or political documents? No one knew.

The hypotheses followed their course, and the most absurd found credence. In any case, there was only one voice demanding from the police the key so impatiently awaited by universal curiosity. The rumor went around that the Prefect had said: "We'll solve the two puzzles at the same time." And imaginations were carried away, combining the two affairs into a strange medley, as if they were only one. The Prefecture allowed them to bark and invent, sure that its triumph would be all the more striking.

For that triumph was certain. How could they fail to find the two murderers with all the information they had? One, the killer of the Undersecretary of State, having returned to Paris after his crime, had been seen there again the following day. The other, the killer of the prostitute, was a regular at the Folies-Bergère. More than twenty women called as witnesses had recognized him immediately from his description: a short, thickset Brazilian with curly hair, an olive complexion, remarkable for a white scar on his right cheek. He had supped with Pauline Grédel, the victim, two days before the fatal night, and she had boasted, on the very eve of the crime, of having arranged a rendezvous with him for the following night. There was, therefore, no possible error in his regard.

The murderer of the Undersecretary of State was not so easy to track down. However, a railway employee had studied him carefully at the departure because of his anxious appearance, and a family of three persons who had boarded the train at Orléans, in the carriage that he left, remembered him very clearly. These four witnesses agree in describing him as quite tall, distinguished, well-dressed, dressed in a top hat, with red side-whiskers and slightly shady eyes. And it was definitely the same individual who had been seen the next day coming to book two seats in the orchestra stalls at the Vaudeville, which he had not taken that evening, the press having already reported the crime by then.

With so many precise details, could the guilty men possibly escape all the sleuths on their heels? Was the triumph not certain?

It was necessary to reduce that confidence, the Prefecture was obliged to admit, after a few days. They had found the Brazilian's domicile, but the man was no longer there. As for the other, there had been no further sighting. The trails had gone cold.

There was an outburst of anger in the press and among the public, all the greater because the Prefecture had already proclaimed victory. The head of the Sûreté was threatened with being forced to exercise his right of retirement before his term was up. The Prefect's protégé was sacrificed and, without any kind of trial, reintegrated into his brigade as a mere agent. The Prefect himself became the butt of gossip columnists and caricaturists, and if he did not hand in his resignation, it was only because his political party insisted that he remain in office until the change of ministry.

"Oh, Monsieur le Préfet," the head of the Sûreté said to him, "perhaps all this wouldn't have happened if we had our good agents of old!"

"Which agents, Monsieur, which?" replied the Prefect, bitterly. "Your Père Lejars, perhaps?"

"Well, Monsieur le Préfet, why not? He had his merits, Père Lejars. He unraveled, to his honor, affairs more mysterious than these. Our new personnel are zealous, undoubtedly, but at the end of the day, our men no longer possess..."

"Traditions, no? It's the traditions you mean? And you think that with these traditions, Père Lejars..."

"We could at least try, Monsieur le Préfet. He's a good and faithful servant, who would like nothing better, I'm sure, than to serve again, if only for the honor of the profession. Sometimes, you know, these old hands...! Not to mention that if Père Lejars found us a lead, well...that's would be in everyone's interests, Monsieur le Préfet—everyone's!"

"Perhaps you're right, in fact. Have him come in."

"He's in my office, Monsieur le Préfet. He asked to see you, but I didn't dare..."

"Does he know something?"

"He says he does, Monsieur le Préfet."

"Oh! Bring him in, quickly."

Père Lejars was introduced. He had a victorious expression that the functionary found offensive, but so what? The head of the Sûreté had summed up the situation: Père Lejars might save them all. The Prefect therefore straightened his face. That was already a revenge for the old man.

"Yes," said the Prefect, further emphasizing that revenge, "yes, we need you. The interests of the police come before anything else, Monsieur Lejars. It's your devotion to that to which I'm appealing. It appears that, for your part, you've been more fortunate than us."

"I believe so, Monsieur le Préfet," Père Lejars replied.

"You've picked up a trail?"

"I'm on both of them."

"What! You know where the two guilty men are?"

"There's only one of them, Monsieur le Préfet."

"What are you saying?"

"I'm saying that there's only one."

In spite of the old policeman's convinced and earnest tone, the Prefect could not help smiling.

"You haven't even read the newspapers, then?" he said, scornfully. "You don't know the descriptions."

"A thousand apologies, Monsieur le Préfet, I know them; but I'll remind you that I once arrested the famous Crusier, who had five of them—descriptions, that is."

"Agreed, Monsieur, agreed—but Crusier was a professional bandit. Here, we're dealing with a society criminal and a personal vengeance—I'm taking about the Undersecretary of State, of course. The other..."

"The other was committed to deflect attention from the first, Monsieur. It is, I repeat, the same man."

"How! The same night, at the same time!"

186

"Forgive me, but the return train from Orléans arrives in Paris at two thirty-one a. m. The murder of the prostitute Grédeal occurred at about four a.m. I will ask Monsieur le Chef de la Sûreté, who knows what he's talking about, whether a man like Crusier would not have had the time, in an hour and a half, to go from the Gare d'Orléans to the Rue du Rocher, while 'decamouflaging' and 'recamouflaging' himself on the way."

The "who knows what he's talking about" and the concluding argot terms had been pronounced in a deliberately wounding manner, demonstrating the small credit that Père Lejars was giving his interlocutor. The Prefect could not bear it any longer. Besides which, the old policeman's idea seemed to him to be so crazy, so stupid, that he did not see any need to humor him any longer. Evidently, the man was talking nonsense, gripped once again with his mania for make-up and disguises, more infatuated than ever with his Vidocqesque theories.

"Well I, Monsieur," the Prefect retorted, "who don't know what I'm talking about, claim that you're talking nonsense, and that I was wrong to waste my time listening to it, and that I was right, a thousand times over, on the day when I rid myself of your services."

The head of the Sûreté dragged Père Lejars outside, white with shame and anger. He tried to calm him down and console him, but deep down, he agreed with the Prefect, that the old man was talking nonsense. What evidence was there, I ask you, that the Undersecretary of State's murderer, that man of the world, was a bandit comparable to Crusier? And what an aberration to suggest that that man and the prostitute Grédel's murderer were one and the same! Yes, Père Lejars had lost his head. Poor old chap! And, while escorting him out, the head of the Sûreté tried to make him understand.

"Then you don't believe me either?" said Père Lejars.

"Come on! It's fantasy!"

"Then for you too, for the whole world now, I'm an old fogey!"

And Père Lejars went away.

Two weeks later, the ministry collapsed, and the Prefect of Police fell with it, and, at the same time, into ridicule, pursued by the gibes of the entire press, including that of his own party—for no one forgave him his celebrated reforms, so pitifully abortive, and his final fiasco became legendary.

On the very day of his discomfiture, he received as a thread of consolation the following letter:

Monsieur,

If ever, which seems doubtful, you are ever reappointed Prefect of Police, remember that traditions are traditions, that the old routine is still the best that has been found, and that make-up and disguises are the A-B-C of police work. Yes, Monsieur, it is one and the same man who committed the two murders that our young men left unpunished. That man knew the art of Crusier and Vidocq. That man is, at the present moment, in my hands. And since the police force, disorganized by you, is no longer capable of arresting such criminals, I shall rid society of him myself. His two costumes will be found, his two wigs and his cadaver, in my house, where I shall momentarily blow that old fogey's brains out.

Lejars.

In Less Time Than It Takes To Write...

Oh, the battle of Paris, against Paris, in the melee of interests, passions and ambition; the terrible battle, frenzied, merciless, but with a chance of victory! A superb dream—and a banal dream, too, for it's that of all young provincials: a dream with an awakening that is almost always lamentable. How many of those mad moths, flown from native lands where they could have been so happy, come here only to burn their fragile wings in the flame of the enormous lamp?

But try to reason in that fashion with a young lad of eighteen, strong in his pride, full of valor and hope! He will call you a discourager, a bird of ill-omen, and it's your reflections that he will find banal and lamentable.

That is what Félibien Lefeuve had thought when his old aunt had said to him: "You're wrong to go to Paris, my boy. The wise thing to do, you see, is simply to continue your mother's small business. Undoubtedly, it's not going very well. A bookshop in Varincourt, a land of five hundred souls, certainly isn't Peru, but after all, my poor sister got by on it anyway, and found the means to bring you up as well. You can get by in your turn..."

"Get by! It really was a matter of *getting by*. Félibien, though, wanted to live, to become rich—and since that wasn't possible in Varincourt, off to Paris!

All that his old aunt had obtained was that the bookshop would not be put on sale immediately, as Félibien wanted. There were some petty savings in the house: two thousand francs. Well, that would suffice to try to make his fortune. It was more than all the millionaires of whom Félibien spoke with so much enthusiasm had started out with—those famous millionaires who had arrived in Paris in clogs.

"But at least, my boy," the aunt had added, "if you don't succeed, there'll still be a safe refuge for you here. I'll keep the bookshop going while you're gone. That way, you'll have something to fall back on."

Félibien had consented to that arrangement, out of condescension, and also out of affection for his old aunt.

Worthy aunt, he had thought, *she's not well off. I'll leave her the shop. She'll handle the petty business very nicely.*

For he was not a bad fellow, Félibien Lefeuve. He did not even have a poor mind—one of those reckless minds in which the flower of adventure grows naturally. To tell the truth, it had required very particular circumstances to make the chimerical ideas germinate in his brain that were now blooming like artificial flowers.

To begin with, a burning desire for liberty had gripped him after the death of his mother, Madame Lefeuve, who, while loving him very much, had always kept him under a rather right rein, not only when he was a half-boarder at the Collège Municipal de Varincourt, but even when he had graduated from it. He had felt the bridle about his neck since then, ever-ready to break into a gallop like an escaped colt.

Even so, the gallop would doubtless have been limited to a few sprees in the next town if Félibien had only had to satisfy that desire for independence, perfectly explicable at his age. Unfortunately, his imagination was at that moment utterly intoxicated by the veritable orgy of novels in which he had indulged during the last six months. "Orgy" is not too strong a word, for he had rushed into the reading-room of which he was now the proprietor with the gluttony of a drunk inheriting a cellar.

Novels of manners and novels of adventure, in particular, he had swallowed them all in a rage of childlike curiosity and a fever of juvenile passion. From all those implausible stories, to which he had naively added his faith, he had formed an idea of life and of Paris akin to a catechism of conduct.

It is necessary to admit, although it is scarcely to the credit of writers of feuilletons, that that idea was as unhealthy as it was false, and that the catechism in question had nothing moral about it—on the contrary. In fact, Félibien imagined

Paris as populated entirely by rogues and imbeciles, and had concluded that it would be better to be among the former than the latter.

Let us add, however, that that conclusion did not fail to frighten him when he thought about the means of putting theory into practice. At that point, his deep-rooted honesty rebelled, and his natural timidity also came to the rescue. Damn! He had no desire to end up, like some of the heroes of his acquaintance, in the penitentiary or on the scaffold.

Furthermore, if he had made some effort to believe that he was fully committed, he would have found it very difficult, in sum, even to decide how he was going to make a start, for he felt none of the irresistible vocations that indicate an objective to attain or a route to follow. He was neither a writer, nor an artist, nor an inventor, nor a tradesman, nor anything whatsoever, in reality. Precisely because he had no special aptitudes, however, he judged himself to be ready for anything.

Then again, he said to himself, *so many things happen in Paris; the essential thing is to be there. One can profit from a chance, a complicity.*

And he dreamed then, while wide awake, of one of the thousand and one turns of events about which he had read. There was a runaway horse that he stopped, thus saving the life of a rich heiress of whom he would become the happy spouse. There was a secret to which, miraculously, he found the key. There was a supposedly-lost child whose family he discovered—an all-powerful family, it goes without saying. There was a mysterious association into which he entered under a false name. He was recognized himself by certain signs as the descendant of a prince of finance—and many other clichés, the most absurd of which seemed to him, not merely possible and probable, but the most ordinary reality.

As you can imagine, he avoided confiding these fine plans to his aunt.

What's the point? he thought. *She wouldn't understand. Perhaps she'd be afraid. Poor old woman! She knows nothing at all about life. She's never come out of her hole.*

And when she said to him, not without anxiety: "But after all, what are you going to do in Paris?" he replied: "I don't know. I'll see what comes. I'll look around. Who knows what game one will come across when one goes out hunting?"

And he departed for the great Parisian forest, where so many men think themselves hunters when they are only game—sometimes, alas, gallows-birds.

Voyagers with too vivid an imagination almost always have the cruel disappointment of finding the reality inferior to their dream. Félibien, however, was all imagination, and he lived so fully in his dream that he continued it even in confrontation with the reality. He was like a man whose rose-tinted spectacles have taken root on his nose, and who can no longer see anything other than through their lenses.

Paris, therefore, did not appear to him as it is, but as he had conceived it, absolutely in conformity with the memory of his reading. All the passers-by seemed to him to be characters in a novel, whose stories he attempted to reconstitute. Some had the effect on him of old acquaintances, so strong was his impression of having met them before. It would not have taken much for him to put names to their faces. Having only arrived in the morning, he felt entirely at home, and as if in a country conquered in advance.

He wandered at hazard, vaguely expecting something, without knowing exactly what.

Suddenly, a hand tapped him on the shoulder, and a voice exclaimed in a familiar accent: "Bonjour, Lefeuve."

He turned round and looked at his interlocutor, but could not put a name to the face.

It was a man of about twenty-five, perhaps less, but in that case very weary and careworn, who looked much older than he was: a pale face in a red bead; red and feverish eyes; in sum, a rather unpleasant appearance.

Doubtless poverty had caused that precocious dilapidation, for the poor devil displayed its livery in his dirty and crumpled costume: his doubtful linen, his jacket with white patches, his threadbare trousers, his worn boots and a hat almost as unkempt as his beard.

"I don't have the honor of knowing you, Monsieur," Félibien said. "You've probably made a mistake."

"Come on, don't play the joker," the other replied, with a mocking smile. "What! Monsieur doesn't have the honor of knowing me? You mean recognizing me. Bah! After all, it's possible that the beard and partying have changed me in seven years—but you'll doubtless recall my name. Larbel! Jules Larbel! Eh? Is it coming back to you now?"

"Yes, indeed," Félibien replied. "Then it's you who..."

"Say *tu*, not *vous*!" cried the other, extending his hands to the young man.

Félibien, however, was in no hurry to respond to that mark of cordiality—for he remembered Jules Larbel, perhaps a little too well. They had once been schoolfellows for two years, Larbel being one of the older boys while he was one of the younger ones, and he was not a very commendable schoolfellow, having been expelled after a murky affair of theft.

Thinking about that expulsion, and finding the bad lot in poverty, perhaps in shame, Félibien scarcely wanted to renew a relationship with him. But Larbel was not about to be beaten because of a handshake that seemed to be on the point of being refused. He suddenly linked arms in a familiar fashion with Félibien, and resumed by force, so to speak, the camaraderie of old.

"Come to sample the vice-dens of Paris, then, have you?" he said, sniggering.

"That's a funny way of speaking—are you a sailor?" Félibien replied, gently trying to disengage his arm but without being able to do so.

"What a prude you are!" Laberl riposted. "Don't be afraid—I'm not going to eat you raw. Why are you trying to get away? Because I'm badly dressed. That doesn't prove anything. I can be useful to you all the same. Come on, what are you doing in Paris?"

"What are you?" asked Félibien.

"Oh, cunning!" Larbel replied. "You want me to tell you my story before you tell yours. All right! I understand your mistrust. You're not stupid. We understand one another."

In a way, Félibien regretted having solicited that confidence, but there was no longer time to step back.

"What I'm doing, my dear chap," Larbel continued, "is rather difficult to describe clearly. I'm what they call a businessman. My trade depends on the kind of business I find. I've been a bailiff's clerk, a bank employee, a café manager, a schoolteacher, a salesman, a journalist. I have connections in all parts of society and profit from them. That's what I do."

"You profit from them," Félibien put in. "That's a manner of speaking, isn't it? You don't appear..."

Larbel burst out laughing. "Oh, you really are a provincial," he said. "You always judge people by appearances. I'm not elegant, that's all—but that doesn't prevent me from occasionally doing well, you know. So, at this moment, for example..."

And, plunging his hand into the pocket of his wretched trousers, he pulled out a fistful of coins, copper and silver mingled pell-mell with about twenty louis. "Well," he added, enjoying Félibien's astonishment, "you don't find me so despicable now? In fact, I can help you earn some cash too, once I know what you're good at. But if you don't want to tell me, bonsoir!"

"I've got nothing to tell," Félibien replied, piteously. "I've come to Paris to seek my fortune, that's all."

"Just like that, on the off chance?"

"My God! Yes."

Again Label burst out laughing. Félibien was annoyed. Evidently, he was being taken for a simpleton. But no! After all, he wasn't as stupid as all that!

And in a single breath, enthusiastically and proudly, he recounted his dreams, his plans, how he intended to make his way, taking as his departure point the first god opportunity he happened upon, and that he knew full well what it took to get along in Paris, and that he was ready to do anything to succeeded—yes, anything."

"Damn!" said Label, affecting a serious expression. "You're a soldier of fortune, then?"

"I believe so," Félibien replied, proudly.

Larbel's imperceptible smile was concealed beneath his beard. "And you have some capital with which to make a start?" he said, abruptly.

Félibien was on the point of displaying his two thousand francs, which would have put Larbel's fistful of louis in the shade, but he remembered just in time the last recommendation that he aunt had made to him when she saw him off at the station.

"Above all," she had said to him, "don't let the Parisians see your money. It's said that they have glue, not merely on their fingers, but in their eyes."

He therefore contented himself with saying to Larbel: "Oh, not much. Enough to stay for three weeks or a month."

Larbel, however, had clearly discerned the truth beneath the slightly belated and hesitantly-voiced lie. Aha! The kid had a money-bag. Look out!

"Look at me for a moment," Larebel said, suddenly, stopping and planting himself directly in front of Félibien. "Or rather, let me look at you. Don't be scared. I've just had an idea. A great idea!"

Félibien blushed, not without a vague anxiety, under Larbel's gaze, which examined him, squinting, with clicks of the tongue, like a horse-dealer weighing up a stallion.

"What? What's got into you?" said the young man.

"Yes, yes," muttered Larbel. "Very nearly. We'll see. You're not a bad-looking fellow, you know. Tall, thin, rather elegant. Distinguished face. Gray eyes—which is an indication of domination. With a certain *je ne sais quoi* to find, something might be made of you. A name on top—a fine name— and the affair's almost in the bag."

"But what are you talking about?" stammered the young man. "Explain yourself. I don't understand."

"By Christ!" Larvel exclaimed. "You can count yourself very lucky that you ran into me. It's staggering, all the same, the coincidence!"

"Tell me, tell me quickly," said Félibien, almost with anguish. And he did, indeed, bless the stroke of good fortune that had thrown him into the path of his adventurer, and was already imagining a prodigious romance, as implausible and as believable for him as for all those with which his head was crammed. Yes, to be sure, a novel of which he was about to become the hero, thanks to a resemblance that he doubtless had to some great and mysterious individual! Larbel had mentioned a fine name, and had thought his faced distinguished.

"Quickly, quickly, tell me," the impatient young man repeated.

"Oh, you're in too much of a hurry," said Larbel. "It's necessary not to go faster than the violins. I have an idea, it's true—but from there to the execution there's a way to go. You understand that what I'm doing isn't just for your lovely eyes. I have an interest in it too. Because, you see, I'll be honest. If I take an interest in you, it's because there's something in it for me. You understand that, eh?"

"It goes without saying," Félibien replied. Suddenly, however, his enthusiasm evaporated, and, gripped once again by suspicion, he put his hand on his jacked mechanically, to fell his wallet there.

"Oh, have no fear for your four sous," said Larbin, whom the movement had not escaped. "That's certainly in play, but I only ask for honoraria after success. So, you understand!"

"Success at what?" Félibien asked, again.

"You'll know in time, curious fellow," Larbel replied. "For example, suppose it were a marriage. Well, it seems to me that I'd have the right to a little fee, eh? In short, I'm not working for the King of Prussia. Then again, it's quite natural that, before engineered the thing, I want to take out a few guarantees. That's all I ask, nothing more."

"But that's understood," said Félibien. "As many guarantees as you want. I repeat that I'm ready for anything. A marriage, you said?"

"I said *suppose*. A marriage...or something else. Anyway one doesn't talk about such things in the street. Look, I'll invite you to dinner. We'll chat over dessert. Let's go get an aperitif in the meantime. It's only five o'clock."

This slowness irritated Félibien, who wanted to know right away on what strange adventure he was about to embark.

"Come to my hotel instead," he said, "and let's chat now. What's the point of putting it off?"

"What's the point?" said Larbel. "The point is that I'm not alone, old chap. I need to consult my..."

"Oh! You have an associate?" Félibien interjected.

"A boss, rather."

"A boss? Really?"

"Shh!" said Larbel, putting his finger over his lips in a mysterious manner.

And that mystery, and the idea of the association, of the boss, made Félibien open wonderstruck eyes wide, giving him a delightful frisson of both hope and fear. "And when will you see him, this boss?"

"Not until tomorrow."

"What! Not before tomorrow?"

"No—but this evening, at my restaurant, I can say something to his second-in-command, and find out right away whether I ought to make overtures."

They sat down in a café and Larbel ordered two absinthes. Félibien drank his very rapidly, without paying attention to what he was drinking, and immediately, a warmth rose to his brain, causing the crazy ideas that were already beginning a saraband there to whirl even more madly.

He talked abundantly, returning to the memory of his reading, explaining his romantic theories, and Larbel only interrupted him from time to time to say: "All these things happen! People think that it's only in books, but not at all! They happen! You'll see."

"Oh," Félibien exclaimed, "it's astonishing, Paris!"

"Don't tell me!" said the other. And he topped the stories imagined by the young man; he told others more extraordinary still, with which he cited dates and names.

It was merely a matter of having the luck. Now he, Félibien, had the luck. As soon as he had disembarked in Paris, he had found the bird on the nest. An affair worth millions!

"Millions!" Félibien repeated, ecstatically.

"Oh, but I was wrong to talk," Larbel replied. "What is the boss doesn't want to do it? It might not suit him, the boss. Let's talk about something else—that would be better."

But the conversation always returned to romances of Paris, and the adventurers those mysterious novels brought to life. That was the only topic until dinner time, and even during the dinner that Larbel provided in a little restaurant in Montmartre. And Félibien got drunk on that nonsense, as much as on the wine that Larbel poured out in large draughts.

As they were on the liqueurs, a man who looked like a bookmaker came to talk to Larbel in English.

"That's the lieutenant," Larbel said to Félibien, when the man had gone.

By that time, Félibien had almost lost his composure, to the point that he was no longer thinking about demanding the famous explanations that he had earlier anticipated with so much impatience. He retained just enough reason to sense that he was about to lose the little that he still had, conclusively.

"I've drunk too much," he said. "What will he think of me, the lieutenant?"

"Oh, don't worry—nothing bad," Larbel replied. "On the contrary, it's good to unwind a little, between future accomplices. Wine loosens the tongue. So, I've told you things. You recall, a little while ago, that story about the India Company? All those millions? Well, that's it, our business. You'll know the details tomorrow."

"Isn't it a matter of a young woman?" Félibien asked, his voice slurred.

"Exactly."

"The marriage, then…?"

His head was heavy, his tongue thick. His eyes fluttered. He got up, his legs unsteady. Larbel came to hold him up and took him to a little room at the back, where there was a large bench. As there was no one there, the gaslight was turned down.

"Go to bye-byes, my boy," said Larbel. And he let Félibien fall on to the bench, who immediately fell into a troubled and feverish sleep, muttering inarticulately.

By virtue of what sequence of events Félibien, after having gone to sleep on that bench, did Félibien find himself lying in a hotel room? He had no idea.

His last precise memory was that of the small room at the back, where the gas was turned down, and where he had said to Larbel before falling asleep: "ready for anything, you understand, ready for anything."

After that, a medley of confused images: swarming streets, full of people he seemed to recognize, by virtue of having seen them in feuilletons; then cafés, all similar to the one in which he had drunk absinthe; then little glasses of various liqueurs, drunk while telling and listening to strange stories. From all that, pell-mell, nothing stood out but the face of the man who had come to speak to Larbel in English—and that face took on enormous almost fantastic proportions.

Besides which, it seemed to Félibien that the man had reappeared during the evening, and that on that occasion, he had expressed himself in French, displaying papers covered in vertiginous figures and stamped with the emblem of the India Company.

And one word, one magic word, came back like a refrain at the end of all these vague memories. That word, Félibien now repeated aloud: "Millions!" he said. "Yes, millions!"

He looked around. The room was unfamiliar. It was broad daylight.

His clothes lay on the floor, all crumpled, with two large rips in one of the tails of his frock-coat. His top hat was flattened on the chest of drawers, squashed like an accordion, the silk bristling.

Abruptly, Félibien was gripped by fear. He had just perceived a bloodstain on the sleeve of his shirt.

He leapt to his feet, but he nearly fell over on finding himself suddenly upright. His head was spinning. He collapsed on the edge of the bed.

Oh! he thought. *What's happened to me? Yes, that's it. They must have made me drink more. I must have been dead drunk. I'm hammered. Perhaps I've been robbed?*

Abruptly sobered up by that idea, he ran to his frockcoat, looked in his pocket for his wallet, and was thunderstruck to find that it was no longer there.

"Oh, the wretch!" he cried. And he started shouting for Larbel in a thunderous voice. At the same time, without knowing why, he went out on to the landing and collided violently with the next door.

A little hole at head height, blocked by a wad of paper, was suddenly unstopped. Then Félibien heard a loud burst of laughter and the door opened.

"Oh, it's you?" said Larbel "Good—I was afraid it was a creditor. That's why..."

He had not finished the sentence when Félibien leapt at his throat, howling: "Thief! Thief! My wallet!"

Félibien, still unsteady on his feet, was knocked to the ground by a fist.

"No funny business," said Larbel. "Paws down, my lad. Come on, you're still drunk."

Félibien got to his feet, somewhat dazed, but increasingly furious.

"Try to keep calm, eh!" said Larvel, brandishing a short cane with a lead pommel. Don't move, or you'll make the acquaintance of Zozo. You know Zozo, it's this little toy. It will sit a man down without him having the time to say *oof.* Come on, calm, down—that's better than getting yourself dusted down by Zozo."

"Coward! Villain!" growled Félibien, dully.

"Oh, insults, as many as you want!" Larbel replied, unemotionally. "Insults are fine by me, but no fisticuffs. Now, what is it? Let's explain ourselves. It's your money that you're demanding?"

"Yes, my money, which you stole from me."

"Stole! Rather say saved! It would be far away, your money, if I'd left you, in the state you were in. I put it in a safe place, that's all. Look, here it is..."

And Larbel threw him his wallet. "Oh, you can count it," he added. "Nothing's missing. And I hope that after this proof of honesty, you won't doubt me any longer."

"That's true," Félibien replied, with tears in his eyes.

"Then let's go to breakfast," said Larbel. "The time has come to make the serious overtures I mentioned yesterday. But before then, let me warn you—what I'm about to confide to you is a terrible secret. Once you're our confidant you'll also be, by the same token, our accomplice. Are you in?"

Félibien trembled, and stammered as he asked: "Is it a matter of a crime?"

"Perhaps," Larbel replied, with a sinister expression.

Félibien could not help shivering. At the same time, he suffered a hesitation. Was he, then, about to engage in one of those black adventures in which one risks one's honor and one's life? Was he ready even to commit a crime in order to make his fortune? On the other hand, if he refused the offered confidence now, would that not provoke the vengeance of the dangerous rogues who had, in a way, put themselves in his hands by the proposition alone? All things considered, would it not be better to become their ally than their enemy?

"Well?" Larbel asked. "Is it agreed? Do you accept our secret?"

"Yes," Félibien replied, in a firm voice. "But why don't you tell me here, right away?"

"Because hotel rooms have ears. At my restaurant, soon! We'll be at home. Anyway, that's where he'll come to fetch us, to take us to the boss."

"Who?"

"The lieutenant, of course."

Félibien got dressed quickly, replacing his torn frock-coat and crushed silk hat with a jacket and felt hat that he borrowed from Larbel. The jacket and hat resembled the lieutenant's, and Félibien remarked on it.

"That's true," said Label, laughing. "And that's even better for your introduction to the boss. It gives you a English appearance that will please him."

They returned to the little restaurant where they had dined the night before, and installed themselves in the back room.

"Closed session, all right?" said Larbel to the waiter who served them.

The waiter winked, understanding what this mysterious instruction signified, and brought them breakfast in the English style—which is to say, with all the dishes on the table at once, in order not to have to come back—after which he left, leaving them alone in the carefully closed room.

As soon as his initial appetite had been appeased, Label lit a cigarette. It was, he said, his habit to have a smoking break in the middle of the meal. Then, placing his elbows on the table, he said: "And now to our little story. It's time to show off my abilities as a narrator. A veritable fairy tale, what you're about to hear. Pay attention!"

He wiped his nose, coughed and spat in a comical fashion that made Félibien smile, in spite of his impatience and the gravity that the imminence of the terrible confidence inspired in him.

"Here goes," said Larbel. "Once upon a time there was a poor English working man who lived in London with his wife and daughter. Honest folk! The cream of honest folk! So, they weren't well off, for virtue is never rewarded. And so they tugged the devil violently by the *tail*." He used the English word, and explained its meaning.

"You're taking a long time," said Félibien.

"I'm teaching you an English word *en passant*," Larbel replied. "It's not a waste of time—you'll see. I'll go on. They were, as we said, unfortunate. The husband worked on the docks. The mother and daughter made rag dolls."

"As in Dickens," Félibien couldn't help remarking.

"Absolutely," Larbel continued. "Now, with the fruits of that labor, they had just enough not to die of starvation. Except that the father was, as they say, not in the best of health, and the other shared that deplorable habit. A month of illness here, a month of unemployment there, the doctor and the medicines to pay for, the debts—all that resulted in a deep poverty that would have had a great success in an exhibition of misery. I won't elaborate. You get the picture."

"Yes, yes," Félibien put in, exasperated by the slowness. "Go faster."

"Take it easy," said Larbel. "I'm telling the story wittily. Besides, it'll get exciting, don't be impatient. Here comes the first twist. Get ready. A real *coup-de-théâtre*. Are you ready?"

"Get on with it, slowcoach. Let's see your *coup-de-théâtre*."

"Bang! Change of scene. But don't jib, at least. Don't cry implausibility, or cheat. Everything I'm telling you is the strictest truth."

"Oh, how annoying you are, with your preambles!"

"Well, that English worker had a brother, who had gone to India a long time ago."

"And that brother," Félibien put in, "had died, leaving him heir to an immense fortune. That's it, isn't it? I've guessed your story. It's as old as the hills."

"No matter!" replied Larbel. "I'm not responsible for the tiresome repetition of chance. I'm not inventing; I'm relating. Yes, the brother left him an immense fortune, something like a hundred thousand pounds sterling, which represents, in good French money, two and a half million bullets. Virtue was finally rewarded."

Félibien smiled again at that reflection, made in a comical tone—and, at the same time, his eyes lit up at the word "million."

"Yes," Larbel went on, "but would you believe it? Vice was lying in wait, vice full of cunning, excellent vice, which cuts the ground from under the feet of virtue. Vice was represented here, and admirably, by the brother's clerk, a trusted clerk—who, incidentally, was punished later as if he had been virtuous...but let's not get ahead of ourselves."

Félibien uttered a deep sight. His patience was running out.

"Enough joking!" said Larbel, abruptly. "I'll abandon the witty tone now to become entirely serious. What remains for me to tell you is rather confused. Listen carefully."

Félibien was breathless.

"That clerk," Larbel continued, "possessed all the documents necessary for the liquidation of the business. Without those papers, no inheritance possible! The fortune, by virtue of certain contracts too complicated to explain here, passed into the custody of the India Company. On the other hand, our scoundrel couldn't make use of those papers himself, not being a relative of the deceased. So this is the situation: the documents without the poor heir remained valueless; but the poor man without the documents remained a poor man. Do you understand?"

"Of course!" said Félibien. "Nothing could be clearer!"

"Well, that's what the poor man didn't understand himself, although the clerk explained it quite clearly. As soon as he arrived in London he explained the situation to the potential heir, to whom he read a copy of the papers, which he had put in a safe place, and then he made him the following polite arrangement: equal shares!"

"But the other refused."

"Naturally. These poor folk are all the same. As stupid as geese! This one could get his hands on more than a million, which fell from the skies like a ready-roasted skylark—and what a skylark! But he couldn't bear the idea of losing as much, of being iniquitously and cynically robed. He counted on human justice. What cretins these honest men are!"

"Enough reflections!" Félibien put in. "Stick to the facts! How did it all end?"

"Oh, quite simply. Our scoundrel wasn't half a scoundrel. He dug up another rogue, an alienist physician, who thought it was a good deal, and asked for nothing better than to enter into it body and soul. And one day, the imbecile of a poor man was locked up as a lunatic. You know that that can happen unceremoniously in England—a delightful country for that!"

"But what did they hope for, in doing that?"

"To get the poor man to sign over half the inheritance by means of torture, of course, and to make him understand, by all possible means—all, you understand—the necessity of that transaction."

"That was well played, in fact."

"Yes, but not for our scoundrel."

"Why's that?"

"He'd found his master in his associate. The doctor, not content with the percentage promised in case of success, told himself that it would be better to eat the entire cake. For that, it was necessary to get rid of the clerk and take possession on the papers."

"And he did that? How?"

"Again, the details would take too long to explain. You can see that I'm abridging the story. It's you who are asking me to extend it now. But no—let's cut it short. So, the doctor achieved his objective—and to be sure that the shorn sheep wouldn't squeal, he made him disappear. The clerk…"

"Was locked up as a lunatic?"

"Better than that, my dear chap. Account settled. Disappeared, I tell you."

"Murdered."

"Shh! No words of that sort. Let's say that he was punished as he deserved, and pass on!"

Félibien shuddered.

"The situation," Larbel continued, "wasn't getting any better for the heir. On the contrary! The doctor was, in fact, more demanding. He demanded two million for himself, only offering five hundred thousand francs to the poor devil. Refused more forcefully than ever, as you can imagine."

"So there was no means of getting round him!"

"Not with that fellow—but there's no means of settling the accounts without him. His life is indispensable, and he knows it, the animal! That's why he's holding firm."

"And then?"

"Then one approaches the problem from another direction. To marry the daughter—that's the whole thing. And this is where it gets spicy, for the mother and daughter have got wind of the coup in time. Unfortunately, they've been allowed to see the father, and they've made a plan together, that the mother and daughter will disappear in order to escape ambushes. And one morning, *pft!* no longer anyone there. No one but the father, still locked up, unbreakable."

Larbel rubbed his hand together joyfully as he recounted this new twist—which, however, seemed to have ruined the doctor's plan completely.

"But all was lost," said Félibien.

"No," Larbel relplied. "For we've found the fugitives."

"And now?"

"Now? Why, it's merely a matter of getting the daughter to fall in love, of marrying her."

"And I'm the one who…?"

"Yes, you're the one who! Can you believe the stroke of luck you had, running into me?"

"And my share will be?"

"Two million."

Félibien was petrified.

"Yes, two million," Larbel repeated. "At present, it's two million that the doctor will let go—and you'll understand why. It's now five years since the heir's brother died. During that time, the Calcutta business has been run, on behalf of the potential heirs, by the India Company, while awaiting its legal reversion to the State. Now, the business has prospered in an astonishing fashion during those five years. The money has gained interest. At present, the inheritance has increased to seven million."

Félibien started, and suddenly exclaimed: "What! Seven million! And I'm only being offered two!"

"Come on," said Larbel. "Now you're getting disgusted too, like the poor man. Be careful my dear chap! Don't try to haggle with the boss. Remember the clerk. If you're not satisfied, it must be said, you can still withdraw from the affair. No one's forcing you."

"Me, withdraw from the affair!" exclaimed Félibien. "Are you mad? I accept, I accept. Let's go find the boss right away—let's go!"

At precisely that moment, the waiter opened the door to let in the man from the previous day—the man who looked like a bookmaker.

"I've come to fetch you," the man said, with a strong English accent. "The boss is waiting for you."

Félibien was slightly astonished by this sudden appearance, which seemed to him to have been arranged in advance. One might have thought that the man had been posted outside the door, and that he had made his entrance just at the psychological moment—but Félibien no longer had time to reflect. He felt that he was in the action, and that it was time to get going.

He leapt into the lieutenant's carriage—a private carriage parked outside the restaurant. The other two got in with him, and ply the whip, coachman!

Not a word was exchanged during the nearly ten minutes that the journey lasted. Each of the three men remained absorbed. Furthermore, the carriage's blinds—wooden blinds—were lowered, and it was as if they were traveling at night.

They came to a halt in the inner courtyard of a small detached house in a new quarter that Félibien imagined to be somewhere near the Parc Monceau, although he could not be completely sure.

A footman introduced the three men into a reception room whose shutters were closed and curtains drawn, illuminated by a chandelier of gas jets.

The mystery of that journey in a private carriage closed like a prison van, the even greater mystery of that reception room, which resembled a dungeon, and the silence of the house surrounded by gardens, could not fail to frighten Félibien a little, in spite of the inner enthusiasm inspired in him by the thought of millions.

His enthusiasm abandoned him completely, to give way to real fear, when he finally saw the boss, the terrible English doctor.

He was an old man of glacial appearance.

Tall and enormous, he seemed to be frozen in his fat. He evoked the idea of a monstrous sleeping hippopotamus. What rendered him particularly sinister was that obesity, for one generally imagines fat men as jolly individuals, and this one by contrast, was a sad and bleak fat man who oozed spleen.

His broad face was not at all rubicund, like those ruddy and plethoric English faces bursting with health, in which the blood of roast beef and the gilded sun of strong beer flourishes. It was flattened over a chin with several stages, puffy and wan in its frame of russet beard mingled with white hairs, beneath his bald head, as pale and shiny as a pat of butter. But it was as if that unhealthy pallor were set alight by two small eyes, very small and very dark, whose gaze was as piercing as a drill—and those two sparks were strangely alive in that flaccid and almost dead skin.

Félibien had great difficulty sustaining the glare of that gaze, by which he seemed penetrated, traversed, as if excavated—for at that moment, the doctor was examining him, running that gaze over him like a scalpel cutting into the depths of his soul.

"Yes, indeed," he said, finally, in a clear and cutting voice, almost devoid of an accent. "Indeed, this gentleman is what we need. Thank you, Monsieur Larbel. I'm content with you." Then, addressing Félibien, he added: "Do you speak English?"

"Badly, Monsieur," Félibien replied, trying to suppress his disturbance. "I only know the English one learns in school."

"Which is to say that you don't know any," the doctor put in. "Have you a good memory, at least?"

"Yes, Monsieur."

"You will learn English, then," the doctor said. "It's necessary that you speak it quite adequately in a month."

"So be it, Monsieur," replied Félibien, with naïve confidence.

The doctor turned to Larbel and the lieutenant and said to them in English: "It would even be as well to find him a professor who can teach him a little Gaelic, for Lucy often talks to her mother, who is from Dublin, in that language."

Félibien had understood a little of that, and was not sorry to be able to show that he was not as ignorant of English as the doctor seemed to think. "I'll also learn Gaelic," he said. "But who is this Lucy? I'm still awaiting more elaborate details of the role that's been allotted to me in this story."

The doctor looked at him loftily and replied: "Less haste, young man, I beg you. You're not here to command but to obey. Before anything else, will you please pick up that pen, and write what I shall dictate to you, which you will sign."

Félibien was not disconcerted. In sum, they needed him. In consequence, he had the upper hand over the bandit, who really was talking a little too arrogantly.

"I'm ready to write," he replied. "As for my signature, that depends on the nature of the undertaking."

"Write, then," said the doctor, without seeming to have noticed the insolence of the final remark. "Write on this piece of headed notepaper, previously notarized.

And he slowly dictated the following lines:

"I, the undersigned Félibien Lefeuve, today, the..." He paused here to say: "Leave the date blank." Then he continued: "engage myself as the secretary of Doctor Harry

Hutchinson, in return for a sum of fifty thousand francs, duly paid, which I shall return to him at the first requisition if I cease my service before the expiration of ten years, to run from the present contract."

Félibien had written it down, quite astonished, not understanding what this singular engagement implied.

"Sign it now," said the doctor.

"But what does the document mean?" Félibien objected. "I'd like to know..."

"Nothing simpler," Label put in. "I'm bound in the same fashion. In the improbable event that we were to betray the doctor, as he is English and we could only damage him in England, and in England one can still go to prison for debt, the doctor would have a rapid and sure recourse against us there."

"Not if we possessed the fifty thousand francs," Félibien retorted.

"If you had it," said the doctor, "You wouldn't be here at my orders."

"That's true," Félibien replied. "But later?"

"Later, if you have them, it will be because the affair has been successful. Then my part will be finished and I'll no longer have any need of you. Anyway, what's the point of so many explanations? Do you want to come in on the affair, yes or no? If yes, sign this first."

The tone brooked no reply. Félibien understood that, and signed.

"Now," said the doctor, "let's pass on to entirely serious matters. Larbel has told you what it's about, hasn't he? I'll shortly give you, as well as my lieutenant, all the details you lack and which are necessary to you. Let's get to the shares. The father's—which is to say, yours, when you've married Lucy, is two million. You know that."

"I know that," Félibien replied—and had the audacity to add: "It's not much."

The doctor did not react to the remark and contented himself with saying: "Please examine the latest set of accounts, and assure yourself that the assets have indeed risen to seven million." And he set before Félibien's eyes two letters, one in English, the other in French, stamped and certified by the Consulates and Chambers of Commerce of Calcutta, London and Paris, established that the Gripshall Company, temporarily administered by the India Company, did represent, in colonial properties, fields, houses, shops and duly ensured merchandise, a disposable capital of two hundred and twenty-four thousand pounds sterling, the equivalent of seven million in French francs.

"You're very trusting, Monsieur," Félibien put in, adopting a slight tone of superiority.

"Why, Monsieur?" relied the doctor, slowly.

"Because I know the name of the heiress now."

"So what?"

"Well, what if I pushed rascality to the point of seeking her out and making her fall in love with me without your help?"

"Don't say such stupid things," the doctor replied, "or you'll make me think that you're too young for the mission that I want to give you."

"Stupid things?"

"Yes, Monsieur. First of all, let's suppose that you could find the heiress. A letter would suffice to let her know that you're my agent, and then, farewell any hope of marriage! Secondly, even if you married her, how could she inherit without the documents that are in my possession?"

"I'd buy them from you for less than five million," Félibien retorted, bravely. "In theory, I could also try to take them from you."

"That," said the doctor, very coldly, "I advise you to try on the day that you're tired of life. Come on, enough badinage, Monsieur. Let's get it over with. Sign these donations for me."

While speaking, he had gone to open a safe, and had taken out a stack of papers and parchments bearing seals appended to colored ribbons.

"What's that?" Félibien asked, his eyes sparkling.

"Oh, don't get excited," said the doctor, with a pitying smile. "These aren't the famous papers. It's simply a series of deeds of sale representing all that will remain of the inheritance once your two million has been removed. The date of the contracts is blank, and will be inserted the day after your marriage. Do you understand?"

"Perfectly," said Félibien. "But forgive me if I ask for all the *i*s to be dotted. Once married, if the father inherits and my wife were to die, how would things work out?"

The smile that Doctor Hutchinson had had a little while before was angelic by comparison with the one that suddenly pulled at his thin lips and revealed his white gums. That smile sent a chill into the marrow of Félibien's bones.

"Don't worry about things that aren't within your competence," said the doctor. "My business is by business. This is your role: to take lodgings on the same landing as Mrs. And Miss Gripshall. The room is already rented. Learn English. You'll pass yourself of as a poor schoolteacher. Make the acquaintance of the two women. Seduce Lucy. Become her lover. Set everything to rights by becoming her husband. And for that, you get two million. Is that clear? Sign the deeds of sale, then."

Félibien still hesitated. "I repeat, Monsieur, he said, "even though it seems to you to be outside my competence, that I find these arrangements imperfect."

"You're becoming annoying," said Larbel. "What more do you need?"

"I need," Félibien replied, "the certainty that my future father-in-law won't be the only one to profit from these papers. I put the following problem to you: he has the papers; he inherits; his daughter dies; we lose everything."

"Child!" said the doctor. Then, articulating all the words more slowly than ever, he added: "Don't worry; the father will die on the very day of your marriage."

Félibien could not suppress an exclamation of horror—but he suddenly saw a farandole of banknotes whirling around him. He picked up the pen precipitately, closed his eyes as one does when jumping into water, opened them wide again, and signed.

That same day, Félibien was installed in the mansard next door to the one where Mrs. Gripshall lived with her daughter. It was on the top floor of a rooming-house for working folk situated in the Rue de Tourtille in Belleville.

"Why," Félibien had said on learning his new address, "the Rue de Tourtille—I've seen that already."

"Where?" Larbel had asked him.

"Oh," Félibien had elide, "in half a dozen novels. I no longer recall the titles."

And in the same way, he seemed to recognize his mansard, whose description he had read so many times: a square room, a small iron-framed bed, a few items of battered furniture, a skylight looking out on a forest of chimney-stacks.

Nothing, moreover, was to be unexpected for him for some time, until the day he made the acquaintance of the Gripshalls. In the meantime, his life was regulated in advance, like a musical score, and he observed the instructions strictly, exactly as they had been imposed on him by the doctor.

Early every morning he went out to take his lessons in English and Gaelic, with an excellent teacher obtained by Hutchinson. On the other hand, he pretended to be busy teaching himself during that time, for it was as a teacher that he had taken up residence.

At about noon he went home when the entire house was out and about for the midday meal. In that fashion, there was no old gossip who missed seeing him, with his meager lunch from the charcuterie, wrapped up in paper, and his piece of bread inexpertly hidden under his frock-coat. That poverty was supposed to attract the sympathy of all his poor neighbors.

The concierge had been conquered in advance by a generous handout, and it only required a few further tips to nourish that precious affection. Besides, Félibien did not fail to chat with her occasionally, pouring out confidences about his difficulty, modest and settled life. So she said, to anyone who cared to listen: "Oh, the young man on the fifth—a pearl! And doesn't put on airs, you know."

And Félibien found that he was a real little Machiavelli, playing his role so well and thus deceiving the old woman and the entire house. He laughed wholeheartedly when, in the evening, having been working on his English all afternoon in his room, he went to meet Larbel in Montmartre. That was where he was going when he said to the concierge: "Alas, yes, my good Madame Carbonnet, I have to go out again to give lessons until midnight. It's for shop-workers, who aren't free until then, and it pays very badly—but what can one do? People have to render small services to one another other among poor folk, don't they?"

"Oh, how good you are!" exclaimed the concierge. And she didn't hold it against him that she had to wake up, sometimes well after midnight, to pull the cod and let him in.

Poor boy, she thought, *he'll make himself ill.*

On the evenings when he was a little later than usual, it was because he was running around the brasseries of Montmartre with Larbel—always at the doctor's expense naturally. And to tell the truth, that devil of a boss was as generous as a great lord. Larbel had pockets full of gold. It was a delightful life.

Nevertheless, amid those delights, Félibien did not forget the serious task in hand. To be sure, having a god time was not disagreeable, but to arrived at his goal—which is to say, the millions—he had to sacrifice everything else. Thus clutched in the claws of ambition, Félibien had gone about things full tilt.

The doctor had given him a month to learn English passably. When the month had gone by, Félibien not only spoke English, more than passably, but a little Gaelic too.

What was slightly less easy was to enter into a relationship with Mrs. and Miss Gripshall—and when Larbel interrogated him about that, Félibien was always obliged to reply: "Ah, that's the snag! The neighbors are diabolical savages. Everyone else in the house talks to me and likes me—the concierge idolizes me—but the two Englishwomen, walled up like prisoners, are as mute as carps."

"You know them by sight, at least?" Larbel asked.

"Yes, of course," Félibien said, "but only by sight. I've crossed paths with them more than once on the stairs and the landing—especially on the landing, when I arrange things so as to be going to fetch water when one or other of them is at the tap—but whatever I do, they don't even look at me."

"Perhaps you look at them too much," Larbel suggested.

"Honestly, no," Félibien retorted. "I weighed them up at the first glance. I'm a physiognomist, you know. Then too, I seem to have seen them somewhere before."

"Get away!"

"But yes. Take the mother, for example. She's like all Englishwomen of her age, at least as they're depicted in books. A tall, stiff woman with straight hair, cheeks both pink and jaundiced, a blotchy nose and teeth like piano-keys."

"And does she seem nasty?"

"Not in the least. She doesn't seem nasty or sly. A good workhorse brutalized by poverty."

"And Lucy?"

"Not pretty, my future wife. Her mother's daughter, for sure! But much fresher, less aged, without blue veins at the end of her nose. No malice either, but surliness to spare. And I believed that young Englishwomen were, on the contrary, quite open in their manner."

"The rich ones, yes," Larbel observed.

"Well, not the poor ones," said Félibien, "I can assure you of that. I'm not a fool, am I? In spite of that, I'm still at square one. No means of exchanging two words with those bitches. All the more so, you'll understand, because I'm afraid of exciting suspicion by a false move."

The difficulty, however, only stimulated Félibien's self-esteem—and the next day, he finally found his chance.

It's a good thing that I've read so many novels, he said to himself. *How instructive they are!*

He had suddenly remembered, in fact, a feature of mores that had struck him in all the novels he had read in which England figured. It was observed therein that there is scarcely a single English family, no matter how poor, that does not possess a hymn book and a Bible. And that was what Félibien counted on.

The concierge handed Mrs. Gripshall a letter from Félibien—in English, naturally—in which he asked his neighbor to lend him a Bible, which he needed for an urgent task, and which his poverty rendered too costly for him to purchase. Félibien hoped to receive a reply via the concierge, and thus take a first step, which would later enable him gradually to enter into conversation with Mrs. Gripshall.

The result of the letter surpassed all his hopes. It was Mrs. Gripshall in person who came to knock on the young man's door, bringing him the requested Bible.

"People have to render small services to one another other among poor folk, don't they?" she said, repeating a remark of his own, which the concierge had trumpeted to everyone in the house. She said it in bad French, painfully articulated, with an English accent that nearly made Félibien burst out laughing, all the more so as the good woman emphasized the comical aspect by attempting to adopt a sympathetic expression.

Fébilien was, however, able to maintain his gravity. It was no time to be amused, damn it! Was not this introduction, in reality, a first step toward the famous millions? He recovered all his self-composure on that thought, and set about the commencement of his maneuvers right away.

When he had replied, very correctly, in English to Mrs. Gripshall's amiable remark, she asked him whether he was English; he replied in the negative, and immediately concocted a story that ought to render him interesting in the poor woman's eyes.

"No, Madame!" he said. "I'm not English and have never even been to England. If I speak your language as fluently as you imply, I owe it to my mother, who was originally from Ireland."

"Really?" exclaimed Mrs. Gripshall, increasingly drawn toward her neighbor.

"Yes, Madame," Félibien went on. "My poor mother was a teacher, like me. Alas, her lessons were our sole resource. With that, she was able to bring me up and care for my unfortunate father, whom a reversal of fortune had deprived of his reason."

"Deprived of his reason!" Mrs. Gripshall sighed, dolorously, thinking about her husband, locked up in a madhouse.

That parallel caused all her usual reserve to depart. Touched by a misfortune that resembled her own so strongly, she immediately extended her hand to the young man, and gave him a vigorous English handshake. Then, without further ceremony, she sat down, as if soliciting further confidences.

Félibien did not need to be asked twice, and continued. "My poor saintly mother," he said, pretending to suppress a sob, "died of grief, alas! For long years, Madame she suffered incessantly before dying, and her slow agony was rendered even more cruel by the thought that I alone had to answer the needs of her illness and my father's. I have no need to tell you with what piety I devoted myself in my turn to the woman who had sacrificed so much for me, but misfortune pursued us relentlessly. I could only find poorly-paid work, and was scarcely able to afford all the necessities, even by devoting all of my days and a part of my nights to the wearying tasks I accepted. So, when my mother died, I fell ill in my turn."

"Oh, you poor, poor boy," Mrs. Gripshall put in, with an entirely maternal generosity.

"And yet, it was still necessary to pay for my father's accommodation. I didn't want him to go into a communal hospital. I thought it would cause my courageous mother's soul to suffer if I stopped the work that she had, after all, done so well—if I took my unfortunate father away from the house where he at least found all the care that his sad condition required."

"And what did you do, unfortunate young man?"

Again Félibien had a secret desire to laugh at that exclamation, whose outdated for, reeked of English preaching—but he contained himself, and continued his tissue of lies without embarrassment.

"I got into debt, Madame," he replied. "I knew a teachers' agent who, confident in my honesty and my knowledge, advanced me what I needed to continue paying for my father's board and look after myself—but the man, alas, was nothing but a wretched usurer. He lent me the money on exorbitant terms. I couldn't refuse them. And today, Madame, I'm still obliged to give numerous lessons on behalf of my creditor, which bring me nothing by the honor of gradually paying off me debt."

"And you father?" asked Mrs. Gripshall.

"I'm happy, at least, in thinking that he has everything he needs," Félibien replied. "Outside of my work for my creditor, I still give other lessons, which enable me to pay for my father's accommodation and to live as best I can."

Félibien admired himself, secretly, for being so easily able to improvise that whole story and play the comedy to the full. Decidedly, he had a genius for intrigue!

And how much prouder he was, the next day, on finally setting foot inside the Gripshall's abode. He seemed to be entering a conquered Eldorado, even though his neighbors' mansard was no palace. It was not a hovel either, however.

A meticulous neatness offset and ornamented that poverty. The cast iron stove, not much bigger than a saucepan, was shiny with black lead, and the metal flue was gleaming like a brand new silk hat. The uneven tiles were washed like a baby's cheeks, and as rosy. On the sideboard, a pewter teapot dazzled you with its glare.

Furthermore, Félibien was not surprised by that neatness, which he had expected, for it is traditional in English homes, and more than one novel with a tomato-red cover had edified him in that regard.

What we was less prepared for was the real bareness that his beneath that varnish of marvelous neatness. A sad Eldorado, that home into which he had penetrated as into a gold mine! And yet, it really was one! There were millions to be gained by pleasing the fairy of that humble abode!

For the moment, of course, the millions were a distant prospect. Oh, the wretched furniture! Not even in walnut, like that of the poorest workers. The chest of drawers-cum-sideboard and the table were in white wood, as were the two chairs, save for the seats of common straw. The camp bed only bore a thin single mattress. The whitewashed walls, devoid of paper, were like prison walls, their only ornament being a small round mirror with a pewter frame, and a colored engraving representing Queen Victoria and her family.

In spite of everything, the room was not funereal, thanks to Miss Lucy's endeavors—endeavors that Félibien also recognized, by virtue of having read descriptions thereof. On the table there was a heap of multicolored fabrics, bits of ribbons, velvets, silks and satins, with which Miss Lucy was fabricating tiny dolls, which caught the light joyfully.

As on the first occasion when Larbel had told him about the young woman's profession, Félibien could not help observing that it was, first and foremost, classic Dickens. At the same time, he examined Miss Lucy, his future, with a rapid glance, finding that she was really prettier than she had earlier seemed on the staircase. Her face was a trifle long, but delicate. Her eyes, extremely soft, were the tender color of forget-me-nots. Her pale blonde hair resembled the silk of a cocoon. In sum, even without the bait of the monstrous inheritance, she was a very desirable young woman.

If only I can make the first impression on her that she has made on me, Félibien thought, *I'll answer for the rest. She must be loving, that's obvious. Everything depends on making a good start.*

And he started with a masterstroke.

"I've brought back your Bible, Madame," he said, as he came in, "And I thank you very much for your kindness. But, as it is written in the Holy Book, gratitude in words is merely sown on the wind, and I thought that you might permit me to prove mine in a less chimerical fashion."

At the same time as the Bible, he held another book out to Mrs. Gripshall.

"You will doubtless find this pleasant to leaf through," he added, "And you will give me great pleasure by allowing me to lend you the book, which my mother gave to me. It's a collection of Irish ballads."

Lucy stood up, clapping her hands, and her expression, full of gratitude, demonstrated to Félibien that he had immediately found the way to that poor heart.

And that is why, that evening, in rendering an account of his day to Larbel, Félibien was able to say, proudly: "My dear chap, I'm sure now that the thing is in the bag. The first step is the most difficult to take. It's taken—and a giant stride, eh? I'm Mama's friend, and it won't be long before I become the daughter's good friend. And the millions will be mine!"

"Oh, you're good!" Larbel exclaimed, with sincere enthusiasm. "It has to be said—you're good."

"Even better than you think," Félibien replied.

Sure, in fact, of success in respect of Lucy, the young man was now thinking of nothing less than going into battle against the redoubtable Harry Hutchinson. And the proof that Félibien really was good, and entirely equipped to undertake that duel, is that he only required a week's reflection to come up with a plan of campaign against his terrible adversary.

It was such a simple plan of campaign, however, that Félibien dared not settle upon it immediately.

Come on, he said to himself, *it isn't possible that the doctor hasn't thought of the means I have to counter his plan. Or else the man before whom Larbel trembles, and who even gives me the shivers, who seems to us to be a monster accomplished in crime, this so-called evil genius, is nothing but a vulgar imbecile.*

And this, in fact, is what Félibien had conceived in order to triumph over the doctor.

Once Lucy was seduced, and seduced from every viewpoint—which is to say that she had become Félibien's loving and submissive slave; an imminent result, of which he was certain in advance—he had only to confide everything to the young woman and make an alliance with her against Hutchinson. Through her, he would influence Mr. Gripshall, whom she would convince finally to sign an abandonment of the millions demanded by the doctor. With the signature given, and the Gripshalls in possession of the famous papers, they would bring a lawsuit against the doctor for capitation, and it would be easy to have Mr. Gripshall's signature annulled, he being interned as a lunatic and, in consequence, legally incapable of thus disposing of his inheritance.

There was nothing astonishing in the fact that that the Gripshalls, poor working folk, had not thought of that means of cheating the cheat—but the fact that the cunning Hutchinson had not been fearful of the intervention of someone able to suggest that advice to them did surprise Félibien.

For in the end, he thought, *all these cessions signed in advance are worthless in case of a subsequent lawsuit—and if the law sticks its nose into it, I'll be damned it if doesn't find it shady. Not to mention that, once it's on the track, with a word in the ear, one could suggest investigations regarding the late accounts clerk. Hasn't the famous doctor foreseen all that, then? And I bowed down before him as before a master? Get away! It's him who'll be humiliated. It's him who'll accept the conditions I dictate to him.*

And Félibien drew himself upright up proudly, in the consciousness of his genius and his power.

In fact, everything progressed according to his desires, and with an ease and a rapidity that surpassed his wildest hopes, to the point that the young man was frightened by the very insolence of his good fortune.

Seducing Lucy, making her a devoted instrument, ready for anything, and also conquering the mind, heart and will of Mrs. Gripshall, did not require more than a fortnight. To be sure, Félibien knew that he was a charmer and did not doubt

221

what his intelligence, his youth and his brilliant faculties, aided by so much reading, could accomplish. He had been convinced that, with all of that, he could make the two women love and admire him, but he had not dared to count on a victory so rapidly won and so complete. In truth, it seemed to him that he had a magic wand.

It's just like the novels, he said to himself.

And in the same way, in entire plan that he had conceived, nothing went awry, nothing even suffered the shadow of a difficulty. Circumstances and hazard brought no change to the scenario he had imagined..

Larbel did not suspect for a moment that he was helping to deceive the boss, thanks to the false reports that Félibien dictated to him. The redoubtable doctor himself did not suspect for an instant the war-machine that was being set up in the shadows against him. He allowed himself to be fooled, gave Félibien all the time necessary for his maneuvers, and believed that, in the meantime, the young man was continuing to pay court to Lucy.

The most difficult thing was to obtain Mr. Gripshall's consent to sign the documents that would frustrate him of so many millions. It was not easy to make that dense mind understand that it was a temporary renunciation, in sum, and that the entire fortune would be recovered subsequently by the legal challenge to the signature. Lucy required a great deal of time and patience to explain all that to the unfortunate man.

The two women had returned to England for that purpose. Naturally, Félibien had gone with them, still on the pretext of courting Lucy, who, he told the doctor via Larbel, was only just beginning to become a little more tractable.

London had not astonished Félibien any more than Paris. There again, thanks to his memory of his reading, he seemed to be returning to a familiar country—all the more so because he was there with Lucy and her mother, who guided him there as Larbel had guided him in Paris.

In any case, there was scarcely time to be astonished by anything whatsoever. Business before all! And God knew how serious it was! It was no longer, in fact, seven million that was at stake, but an almost incalculable fortune.

Yes, among the possessions of the Gripshall Company, a diamond mine had just been discovered; Félibien had learned that two days before, and not through the intermediary of the doctor or a letter from Larbel, nor even from the newspapers, but from Lucy herself, who had got the information from her father. In spite of being interned, Mr. Gripshall had, in fact, received that official communication from the India Company, as the potential heir to the Gripshall Company. The matter was, moreover, to be kept secret until further instructions, and Hutchinson himself ought not to have been informed, for the senior employee of the company who had come to announce the news to poor Gripshall had told him verbally and had recommended him not to let anything leak out.

Why? Félibien could not guess and tried in vain to understand. What was certain, however, was that it was necessary, at all costs, to prevent the doctor catching wind of it, for he might then increase his pretentions. Thus, it was urgent to take action.

Who was amazed? It was Doctor Hutchinson, when, in the middle of reading a letter informing him of Félibien's engagement to Lucy, he received a telegram from Mr. Gripshall that read: *Come. Will sign.*

Understandably, however, that moment of comprehension swiftly turned to joy. Since the fellow had finally given in, doubtless out of weariness, Félibien's marriage became unnecessary to the doctor. That was one share less to be deducted from the millions.

With the insolence of his triumphant crime, Hurchinson did not hesitate to inform his young accomplice, on the very evening of the day when Mr. Gripshall had signed.

"My dear Monsieur," said the doctor, looking at Félibien scornfully, "I have no further need of your services. You can go back to France. I'd even advise you to embark as soon as possible. If not, you know that there are debtor's prisons in England, and you're my debtor. If the cap fits, wear it!"

Félibien had let him speak, responding to the scornful gaze with a stare that was even more scornful. When the doctor had finished, the young mean contented himself with shrugging his shoulders and adding: "Poor imbecile!"

"What did you say?" said Hutcinson.

Félibien repeated it, and, as the other stood here open-mouthed, doubtless thinking that he was mad, the young man began to laugh. Then, in a singly breath, with the eloquence of an assured victory, enthusiasm and fever, he told the doctor everything that he had done and everything that he was going to do: Lucy's seduction, the absolute conquest of Gripshall, the lawsuit that would be brought the following day and, final-ly, the prodigious news of the diamond mine.

"For it's ours now—Lucy's and mine!" he cried. "Yes, mine, since Lucy's father now has the papers establishing him as the heir to the Gripshall Company."

It was the doctor's turn to laugh, but in his case, with a frightening, sarcastic laugh that caused Félibien to shiver to the marrow of his bones.

"At the present moment," said the doctor, in a voice that had become very calm again, "the sole heir of the Gripshall Company is me."

"You!" exclaimed Félibien.

"Yes, Monsieur," the doctor replied. "I have simply ced-ed twenty thousand pounds sterling to Mr. Gripshall, and that's all. The rest, including the diamond mine, belongs to me by virtue of documents duly signed."

"The signature of a man interned as a madman!" Félibien interjected. "That's not a valid signature, as you're not una-ware."

"Monsieur," the doctor replied, "I'll take the trouble to educate you, because your audacity interests me. Know then that the contracts in question, signed this morning, are, in fact, dated at an era when Mr. Gripshall was at liberty and capable of signing."

"But he'll protest, Monsieur. He'll prove that the con-tracts were antedated, and that his signature was extorted by you. The law will shine light into the darkness. That's why we've brought the lawsuit against you." And he added, triumphantly: "At the same time, perhaps they'll become anxious about the late accounts clerk."

"Oh," said the doctor, negligently. "Well then, they'll learn that the clerk was murdered by one of your friends, Monsieur—a man named Larbel."

"Larbel!" exclaimed Félibien, alarmed.

"Yes, Monsieur," the doctor went on. "And at the same time, they'll learn that this Larbel has been your accomplice in a further crime, which he will confess while accusing you himself."

"Me? Accuse me! Me, Larbel's accomplice!" cried Félibien. "In a further crime, you say! What crime?"

"A crime from which you were to take all the profit."

"I don't understand."

"What, you don't understand? But the judge, Monsieur, will understand—don't worry. Who, if not you, Miss Lucy's lover and future husband, had an interest in killing Mr. Gripshall this very day, in order to inherit his twenty thousand pounds sterling?"

"What!" stammered Félibien. "Mr. Gripshall is dead?"

"Yes, Monsieur," the doctor replied, coldly. "And—see how Providence takes responsibility for punishing criminals—do you know what the police will find in the clenched hands of the victim, if you judge it appropriate to call the police? Do you know what the police will see, immediately, in the unfortunate man's hand?"

"What?" croaked Félibien, terrified. "What?"

"Well, Monsieur," said the doctor, "in the clenched hands of the victim, they will find a piece of cloth—and that piece of cloth, Monsieur, is missing from the flap of the frock-coat that you are wearing at this moment."

Félibien observed that his frock-coat was indeed torn on the right side. How had that happened? By what infernal conjuring trick had the doctor engineered all that? Félibien could not imagine, and had, in any case, neither the time nor the calmness of mind that he would have needed to try to figure it out. He could only see one thing: that he was defeated, in the power of the terrible master that he had dared to take on.

"Mercy! Mercy, Monsieur!" he said, throwing himself to his knees.

And Doctor Hutchinson appeared to him as a sort of diabolical incarnation, as a monstrous idol of evil, before whom one had to prostrate oneself. Was he, in truth, the Devil, or was terror disturbing the crazed imagination of the young man? At any rate, he suddenly saw, or believed that he could see, the doctor growing in size and undergoing a transfiguration, and he heard him cry out in a thunderous voice:

"No, no! No mercy! You shall go on to the end of the fatal path that you have taken. You wanted to be the accomplice of criminals. You shall know prison, the anguish of interrogation, the terrors of trial, the horror of condemnation, and finally, this. Look! Look!"

And, as the doctor was speaking, Félibien had seen himself, first tracked by the gendarmes, then arrested, then submitted to the torturing questions of the examining magistrate, and then in the dock at the court of assizes. He had heard the foreman of the jury say, in a slow voice: "On my honor and on my conscience, before God and before men," etc...

And now he felt himself marching, supported by two men, accompanied by a priest who was weeping and saying: "Courage! Courage!"

And in front of him, there, beneath a lamentable sky in which the dawn twilight was beginning to whiten, the guillotine loomed up, brandishing aloft in its two long arms the blade with the sinister lightning gleam. And he was about to put his foot on that infamous plank, be laid upon that bascule, set his neck within that semicircle, whose other half would immediately close upon his neck.

And then, abruptly, like a thunderbolt, the triangular blade would fall.

It fell! He could already feel the wind in his hair. Horror! He uttered a loud scream.

He uttered a loud scream, and awoke from that hideous nightmare.

The guillotine, the tribunal and the doctor had disappeared—and also London, the Gripshalls, the mansard in the Rue de Tourtille and even Larbel.

Yes, including Larbel.

Félibien rubbed his eyes and looked around. What! Where was he? What did it all mean? So all that had only been a dream, one of those interminable dreams in which one lives weeks, months, or even years, in a few seconds.

Yes, all that—everything, the Gripshalls, and Doctor Hutchinson, and the pact, and the signatures, and the mysterious little house in the Monceau quarter, and the awakening in the hotel room whose door had had a hole blocked with a piece of paper...

Yes, all of that was nothing but a nightmare.

Félibien found himself back on the bench were Larbel had laid him down a little while ago, in the back room of the restaurant where they had both dined.

"Waiter!" called Félibien, in a strangled voice.

The waiter appeared and answered his questions.

"Monsieur has been asleep for about ten minutes. Your friend told me not to disturb you."

"What time is it?"

"Seven minutes to midnight."

Félibien was still bewildered. Suddenly, the idea of his wallet came to mind. Quickly, he dug into his pocket. The wallet was there. He opened it. A hundred-franc bill was missing.

Only one, he said to himself. *I've been lucky. He could have taken them all.*

Then he turned to the waiter. "Do you know where my friend lives?"

"I don't know," the waiter replied. "It's the first time he's come here."

Félibien remembered, however, that Larbel and the man had seemed to know one another a little while ago.

At that memory, fear gripped him. Abruptly, the final fumes of his drunkenness flew away. He reviewed, with an extraordinary clarity of judgment, everything that had happened to him during that one day in Paris: his stupid confidences to Larbel, the fashion in which that rogue had manipulated him by exploiting his romantic disposition, and how he had become intoxicated by his dreams while getting drunk on wine, and how his entire nightmare was based on scraps of their conversation and the memories of his reading.

And that was why, the following morning, by the first train, Félibien Lefeuve arrived in Varincourt, to the great amazement of his worthy aunt, to whom he said: "I'd definitely prefer to live here. It's safer. You were right."

And since then, when anyone mentions Paris to him, the bookseller Lefeuve takes on a mysterious expression, winks and then rubs his hands—after which he adds, raising his arms to the heavens:

"Oh, if I told you everything that happened to me there..."

"What?" you ask.

"Can you imagine," he says, "that I nearly had my head cut off. Fortunately, it was only a nightmare."

And he tells you, very nearly, what I've just told you.

Correspondences

Sadly, he went along the Rue des Martyrs.
Sadly, she went along the Rue des Martyrs.

He was already old, pushing sixty, with a bald head beneath his brown top hat, his beard grey in his worn detachable collar, his eyes dim, his mouth bitter, and the taste of bile in his mouth.

She was no longer young, having passed forty-five, thinning hair beneath her occasional curls and plaits, wearing dubious underwear, and outmoded costume and a bonnet bought second-hand.

He was thin.

She was rather plump.

He had been handsome, proud, ardent, full of self-confidence, sure of his future, holding all the trump cards necessary to win the game on the Parisian green baize.

She had been pretty, spirited, sought-after, reputed to have a house and a carriage and to be highly prized on the turf of gallantry among the favorites destined for fortune.

He sometimes remembered, in his darkest hours, the time when he had arrived from the provinces, with a volume of verses, dramas in progress, a scorn for the glories then in vogue and the desire and the certainty of supplanting them.

She often remembered, in bleak awakenings, the joyous epoch when she had been "launched," when she already saw herself as cleverer than such and such, companions in low dives who had found their niche and whose lovers she stole,

He had had a superb start—not as a poet and dramatist, as he had originally hoped, but thanks to a campaign of scandalous newspaper articles that had made an impact on the boulevard. A lawsuit, a few duels, and he had been "our witty and brilliant colleague who..."

She had had her moment of insolent luck. Not to the extent, certainly, of eclipsing La X*** or La Z***, in respect of whom Aspasia and Ninon were cited, but sufficiently, even so, to be talked about in the newspapers, and to revolutionize certain Montmartrean *tables d'hôte*.

One day, the scandal-sheet for which "our witty and brilliant colleague who..." wrote had died, killed by an even more cynical competitor, thanks to the even more venomous pen of a much wittier and more brilliant colleague who... Then, the outrage of the former becoming pure and simple mud-slinging, the genre itself had rapidly burned out, in total public disgust—and the celebrated columnist Someone had had great difficulty finding a place at some weekly, where he had transformed himself into the obscure journalist Hack.

One evening, the quasi-rival of La X*** and La Z*** had fallen ill, and then from illness into poverty, and had woken up as the common prostitute Anybody, in search of her dinner, only too glad to catch an eye among the Montmartrean *tables d'hôte*.

Hack had been ambitious to make a comeback, with his verses and dramas. But what! His old verses had lost their florescence, and the dramas of his youth now seemed infantile. He would have to write new ones. Of course! He felt capable of doing that. He had the ideas and plots for them in his head: the wherewithal to demolish him or him, who had been successful for some unknown reason. To be sure, if he buckled down to it, he would sink them right away! Except that, there's the rub—the difficulty was buckling down to it. How could he find the necessary leisure and concentration? He had his daily bread to earn—bread and dessert! For he also had vices to nourish now: the café, gambling, the need for well-being! For all that, the bitter slog of one article after another was just sufficient.

And the days, the days had gone by, and the months, and the years, and Hack had remained Hack.

She too had been avid for the initial stroke of luck. Finding a lover ready to launch her wasn't a matter of finding the

Devil. Come on! Such and such, comrades not worth as much as her, had managed to unearth one. Why not her? But would you believe it? She was no longer young. The chance had gone. Then again, lovers of the heart were devouring all she had. She was obliged to turn tricks for them, day after day, at a reduced price. From gallantry, she had descended into making do.

The days, the days had gone by, and the months, and the years, and the common prostitute Anybody had remained the common prostitute Anybody.

He often said to himself, in his darkest hours, in thinking about such and such, who had "made it": *But I'm better than that bastard!*

She invariably said, on bleak awakenings, in thinking about such and such, now set up: *What does that slut have that I don't?*

And Hack, already old, pushing sixty, his bald head beneath his brown top hat, his beard grey in his worn detachable collar, his eyes dim, his mouth bitter, and the taste of bile in his mouth, was eaten away by envy.

And the common prostitute Anybody, soon to be fifty, thinning hair beneath her occasional curls and plaits, wearing dubious underwear, and outmoded costume and a bonnet bought second-hand, blamed it on society.

Oh, the sad dark hours!

Oh, the bleak awakenings!

And that evening, he was in one of those sad hours, having lost at dice his meager next month's wages, the wages so hard-won at the filthy rag he practically filled from cover to cover for three francs a month.

And that evening she was in one of those bleak awakenings, having drunk too many beers offered by a charitable friend, and then having nursed that heavy drunkenness on a publican's bench in Les Halles, and going back to her fleapit, on which she owed a fortnight's rent, the landlord of which had said to her that morning: "From now on I want to be paid the arrears, at least twenty sous a day, or you're out, and I'll keep your clothes."

Sadly, she went along the Rue des Martyrs.

Sadly, he went along the Rue des Martyrs.

No one on the sidewalks. Darkness, dirt, the rain starting. The mouths of the drains stinking.

He overtook her.

In a mechanical voice, she murmured: "Aren't you coming home with me, handsome?"

He replied, hurrying on: "I don't have the cash."

She ran to catch up with him, grabbed his arm and said: "Just one franc—that's nothing."

He turned round, looked at her, saw that she must once have been pretty, that she was still plump—and he liked plump women.

"Where do you live?" he asked. "is it far?"

"Rue Lepic."

"Why, me too!"

"How about it, then, my dear?"

He rummaged in his pocket and pulled out what remained: six two-sou coins and a half-sou.

"That's all I have," he said, "word of honor!"

"That'll do," she replied.

And sadly, they continued along the Rue des Martyrs, together now, without saying any more, and doubtless with no suspicion that their two corresponding lives were in such perfect accord, and that in coupling shortly, they would be accomplishing so precisely the incest of two twin destinies.

The Murder at the Pitcher that Pitches

Oh, it's not something that happened recently—it goes back a long way, a very long way, thirty-some years, believe me!

And yet, I recall all the details with extraordinary precision. They were so profoundly engraved, those details, on my childish imagination. They made the first impression of horror there, and every time I retrace the course my memory, I find in the distance, way back, that first impression, just as horrible.

I was a child; I lived in the Rue de Paris in Belleville; and every morning, I went to a little school, from which our house was only separated by four shops: a pharmacy, a ceramics shop, a butcher's and a wine-seller's.

The wine-sellers had a sign over the door representing a jug with a hole in the side, from which a red jet spurted. Curving around the lower rim of the painting this inscription was legible, which filled me with joy: *The Pitcher that Pitches*.

I always stopped briefly in front of the wine-sellers to admire the sign and to play with the shopkeeper's dog, a kind of Pug/Pomeranian mongrel with yellow hair called Poussot, which was my friend.

At length, and through the intermediary of Poussot, the wine-seller also became my friend. He was a handsome fellow with a cheerful expression, soft eyes, a luminous face, with very long legs. He was known as Big Louis. He seemed to me to be an extremely remarkable man, because of his height, his sign and his dog, and the cherries in brandy that he sometimes fed me.

One morning, I was amazed not to see Poussot coming to meet me, as usual, wagging his yellow tail, and my astonishment increased on finding the shop shut. I'd never seen it like that before, with its display-window bleakly shuttered and barred. It was, however, still almost dark, for it was mid-

233

winter. There was a bitter north wind blowing. The metal sign was swinging as if it were about to come unhooked, uttering seemingly plaintive squeaks.

I had a distinct feeling that something bad had happened to someone, but I remember very clearly that it was not Big Louis who occupied the most important place in my fears. I was much more anxious about the poor sign, which I heard positively groaning—and most of all, most of all, I was thinking about my friend Poussot.

It was his name that I pronounced as I approached the shop-front, searching for a crack through which to call out.

There was only one, low down. A half-door, opening to the inside, was ajar, forming a fissure in the wall of shutters. I stuck my mouth to it and murmured the dog's name. There was no response. I was then gripped by a deep despair, and started to scream and weep as if I were lost.

Workmen and old women stopped. One of the butcher's boys came out, then the manager of the ceramics shop. They exchanged expressions of astonishment and questions behind me. I made out:

"How is it that he hasn't opened up?"

"Is this kid a relative of his?"

"Big Louis is an hour late—that's not natural."

"Oh—a crime! Impossible! Poussot would have barked."

"Go fetch a policeman."

Meanwhile. I felt myself pushed against the shop-front. The half-door yielded to the pressure, and as I was small enough, I suddenly found myself, almost involuntarily, inside the shop. At the same time, I heard the butcher's boy, who had stuck his curly head through the gap, shouting: "Hey! Big Louis! Is something wrong, old chap?"

For myself, I continued calling for Poussot, sobbing.

But there was still no response, either from Poussot or Big Louis.

I could no longer see anything. The butcher's boy's head blocked the little light that the pale dawn had begun to spread; I was in total darkness. Moreover, in order not to see that

234

darkness, which frightened me, I had automatically put my school satchel in front of my eyes.

Suddenly, I heard the bolt of the shutter-door grating. The butcher boy, having finally got in, unbolted it with a hasty and doubtless tremulous hand, for the iron hiccupped as it scraped the wood.

A stifled cry uttered by my companion caused me to drop the satchel and open my eyes. With both battens of the shutter-door open, the light from the street had filled the shop. At the back, on a couchette placed on two long wooden tables, lay Big Louis, no longer with his cheerful expression, his soft eyes, his luminous face, but pale—frightfully pale—and his gaze fixed, fearful and vitreous.

The butcher's boy repeated, in a hoarse voice: "Hey, Big Louis! Is something up?"

I then perceived, in a corner, and pointed out with my finger, poor Poussot, whose tongue was hanging out and feet were in the air, utterly rigid. At the same glance, I saw that there was something like spilled wine on the floor—thick, black wine. It looked like a pool in the process of drying out, and sticky.

At that moment, one of the old biddies outside said: "Perhaps he's drunk."

Another added; "Try shaking him a bit, then."

The manager of the ceramics shop had come in and the other butcher's boy with him. All three of them went to the couchette. The first butcher's boy repeated again, more loudly this time: "Hey! Big Louis!" And he emphasized the appeal by pushing his head rudely, to "shake him a bit."

The head fell to the floor.

There was a violent backward movement. I was bustled out, thrown on to the pavement by the three men, into the midst of a crowd that was already forming, amid cries of horror.

A neighbor took me home. For a week, prey to the most frightful nightmares, I was under the threat of a cerebral fever. I was taken to my grandfather's house in the country, to spend a month convalescing. When I came back to Paris, we were no longer living in the same neighborhood. When I tried to ask my parents whether they knew anything about the story of the crime, they replied evasively. All that I could get out of them as that the murderer had not been identified.

But nothing—neither their silence nor the time that had gone by—weakened my curiosity in that regard. When I became a young man, as soon as I found out what a newspaper was, I set out in quest of judiciary periodicals in which I might discover, narrated at length, the murder at *The Pitcher that Pitches*, and thus tried to reconstitute what I didn't know.

What I learned in that fashion, far from calming my curiosity, only irritated it further. The murder had, indeed, never been identified, and the case, still mysterious, had, as they say, been closed.

For sure; the perpetrator or the crime had been an intimate of Big Louis'. That followed from the following reasoning: Poussot was an excellent guard-dog, and when he barked, the butcher's two bulldogs never failed to respond to him. Now, on the night of the crime, no barking had been heard; and yet Poussot, according to the veterinarian's report, had only been killed after the murder had been committed. On the other hand, the murderer must have been introduced, during the day, to the cellar of the shop's back room, where he had remained hidden, and it was in the dead of night that he had cut the shopkeeper's throat, without needing any light to find the place to strike.

Was it a woman, then? Big Louis had several mistresses—but the strength and skill necessary to section the neck like that could not be a woman's.

Was it one of the butcher's boys, then? It had been thought so, because the butchery implied an expert hand—but the two boys had established their perfect innocence without any possible doubt.

What, in any case, had been the motive for the crime? An unanswerable enigma. Nothing had been stolen from Big Louis; he was not known to have any serious enemy—rivals in love, at the most; and he disarmed them by the scant importance that he attached to his conquests, all temporary and not long-lasting.

I too was forced to close the case, to tell myself that I would never know the truth about the murder at *The Pitcher that Pitches*.

Nevertheless, you can imagine that I could not forget the hideous vision so profoundly engraved in my juvenile memory, and which I still see again, from time to time, at moments of distant recurrence, of the pale and haggard face of Big Louis, his head falling to the floor among the clots of the sticky pool, and poor Poussot in his corner, with his tongue hanging out and his feet in the air, utterly rigid.

So, imagine the shock I received the other day, full in the chest, when I suddenly heard a girl's voice behind me shouting: "Poussot! Poussot!"

I turn round. I nearly fall over. It is, indeed, Poussot that I'm looking at—a Poussot almost identical to the old one. A kind of Pug/Pomeranian mongrel with yellow fur.

The little girl, very elegantly dressed, is walking in the Bois de Boulogne, in the company of a governess. At the risk of being taken for a lunatic, I run to her and ask her: "How is it that your dog is called Poussot?"

She's frightened, and ran away to her governess, while Poussot barks frantically at my legs. I don't get excited, and address myself to the governess, very politely this time, with my hat in my hand. She replies in German, which I don't understand. I start to follow them, in spite of the alarm this causes them—all the way to a house in Neuilly.

I ask for information in the vicinity and this is what I learn:

The girl lives with her mother, who is a widow, and her maternal grandfather, an old man of seventy who has been senile for eighteen months. They came to lodge there three years ago. They arrived from Algeria, where the father died of consumption. Before the paralysis that nailed the old man to his armchair, the old man was a very gentle, very amiable, much loved grandpapa. Today, his dog Poussot is the only creature he recognizes. In the era when the fellow still had his head and his tongue, when he was asked where the name had come from, he smiled and replied: "That's my business."

One day, someone had persisted more forcefully, and the old man had murmured, with a kind of bliss: "It brings back memories."

I wanted to see the old man. I lay in wait on hot sunny afternoons, when invalids are taken for walks. I saw him, with a face still amiable, in spite of its stupidity. That face must have been one of those of which people say that they radiate honesty.

Am I, then the victim of a haunting?

Undoubtedly, I can, with a clear conscience, tame the frightened girl, get to know her mother through her, interrogate her discreetly, and then...

And then, what?

Dead Drunk

My friend Ledantec and I were then about twenty-five. Ledantec was a Breton. We were in London for the first time, one Saturday evening in December. There was a lugubrious and glacial fog. And those, I think, are more reasons than are necessary to explain why, that night, my friend Ledantec and I were abominably drunk.

To tell the truth, we didn't feel ill at all. On the contrary, we were floating in an exceedingly soft bliss. Soft and gloomy. We weren't talking, in fact, no longer having the energy, but without feeling the need. What was the point? We could read all our thoughts easily enough in one another's eyes. And all our thoughts consisted in the unique and sweet consciousness of thinking absolutely nothing.

It was not, however, in order to arrive at that state of delightful intellectual annihilation that we had set out on campaign through mysterious Whitechapel. We had gone into the first tavern with the firm intention of "studying the local customs" there, as curiosity-seekers, artists and philosophers. But from the second one on, we had become specimens for our study ourselves—which is to say, sponges steeped in alcohol. Between one tavern and the next, the external chill seemed to squeeze those sponges, increasing their thirst proportionately. And so, from tavern to tavern we had rolled, and the sponges were henceforth incapable of anything but further swelling.

So, some time before, we had said goodnight to studies of local customs. They were now reduced to only two impressions: zigzags in the external darkness and punches of light at the counters of taverns. As for the ingurgitation of brandies, whiskies and gins, it happened mechanically, even the stomach scarcely being aware of it.

A few bizarre beings had, however, rubbed shoulders with us during those long stations. So many faces to register, accoutrements, attitudes, remarks and outfits!

And to begin with, in fact, we had tried to record them precisely in memory. But there had been so many, and our brains had been so rapidly reduced to pulp, that now we no longer had a clear impression of what had been done or who had done it. Even the things that were immediately present appeared to us in a vague fuliginous phantasmagoria, confused with anterior images, blurring them and blending with them. The world became, for us, a kind of kaleidoscope seen in a dream through the half-light of an aquarium.

We were abruptly snatched from the somnolent limbo, reawakened as if by a punch in the gut, and imperiously forced to focus our attention. In that saraband of strange visions, one, stranger than all the rest, loomed up before our eyes, looked at us and seemed to say:

"Look at me."

There was an open tavern. In the midst of the opaque fog, a beam of brightness flooded from that door into the street, and the brutal illumination fell full upon the specter that had just surged forth, mute and motionless.

A specter, in truth: a lamentable and frightful specter, and one that could not be confused with the others, so much more lamentable and more frightful was it—and, above all, more real, thus standing out vigorously against the black background of the street, which was rendered even blacker behind it.

Young—yes, for sure, the woman was young. How could one doubt it, before that skin free of wrinkles, that smiling mouth displaying child-like teeth, that form bosom so easily divined beneath the thin tartan cloth?

But then, how to explain that entirely white hair—not gray or graying, but absolutely white; an octogenarian whiteness?

And those eyes too, those eyes beneath a wrinkle-free forehead, those eyes in close proximity with that mouth with

240

the child-like teeth—were they not the eyes of a old woman? Oh, certainly, certainly—and how aged an old woman! For it must have taken years, dolorous years, and tears, and sleepless nights, and the whole of a very long existence, to tarnish them in that way, to efface them, to take the shine off those vitreous irises.

Vitreous? Not even that—for unpolished glass still retains a troubling and milky gleam, like a memory of transparency. But *her* eyes seemed rather to have been made of metal, a metal now rusted. Positively, if tin could rust, I would willingly compare them to rusty tin. They had the deathly pallor of tin, and, at the same time, they emitted a gaze the color of brown water.

It was, in any case, by an effort of retrospective analysis that I attempted subsequently to define them in this approximate fashion. At the time, utterly incapable of such an effort, I was only able to establish the idea of extreme decrepitude, of frightful old age, that they evoked in my imagination.

Have I mentioned that they were encased in exceedingly leathery eyelids completely devoid of lashes? Have I also mentioned that there was also no trace of eyebrows on her wrinkle-free forehead? Given that, and with their extinct gaze, and beneath those octogenarian white tresses, there is no need to be astonished by the fact that Ledantec and I, confronted by that evidently young woman, began murmuring: "Oh, the poor, poor old woman!"

Her great age, moreover, was further accentuated by the atrocious poverty revealed by her costume. Had she been better-dressed, perhaps her youthful aspects would have made more impact upon us, but her thin tartan, draped over her chemise, her only skirt, full of holes, hanging down in rags and threads over her bare feet, her straw hat with barb-less feathers and ribbons of no determinable color, all seemed so ancient, so prodigiously Methuselah-esque.

From what distant, outdated, abolished epoch did those rags come? One dare not calculate it. And by virtue of an entirely natural association of ideas, one attributed the decrepitude of her clothes to the unfortunate woman. By "one" I mean Ledantec and me—which is to say, men who were abominable drunk, and reasoning with the special logic of drunkenness.

It was also in the compassion of the alcohol that we considered the vague smile of that mouth with the child-like teeth, without pausing to reflect on the youthfulness of those teeth, seeing only the sadness of that fixed, almost idiotic smile. Contemplating it thus, it no longer made a contrast with the dead expression of the gaze, but, on the contrary, corroborated it. In spite of the child-like teeth, it was itself a smile of old age for our imaginations turned in that direction. For myself, I took a real delight in the thought of being very perspicacious, in supposing that that grandmother with the pale lips had the teeth of a little girl.

Still thanks to alcoholic compassion, I did not hold that artifice against her. I even found it singularly laudable, since, in sum, the miserable creature was, in full consciousness of that, exercising her profession, which was to seduce us. For, there was not the possible slightest doubt about it, that grandmother was definitely a prostitute.

Oh, drunk, of course! Sinisterly drunk. Even more drunk than we were ourselves, Ledantec and me. We two, in fact, had able to murmur to one another: "Oh, the poor, poor old woman!"—whereas it was impossible for her to articulate a single syllable, or even to sketch a gesture, or even to ignite a gleam of promise or a furtive glimmer of provocation in her cadaverous eyes. With her hands folded across her abdomen, her shoulder leaning against the window of the tavern, her entire body rigid in a seemingly cataleptic immobility, she conserved nothing alluring and appealing but her sad smile.

And that inspired in us even more pity, tender and absolute pity—the fact she was even deeper in drunkenness than we were. Without conferring, with an identical movement spontaneous in both of us, we each took one of her arms, in order to take her into the tavern with us.

To our great astonishment, she resisted, threw herself backwards, and was suddenly back in the shadows, outside the beam of light that flooded through the door. At the same time, she started walking into that shadow, drawing us with her, for she was clinging to our arms.

We went with her, without saying anything, not knowing where we were going or being in the least anxious about it. Except that when, as she walked, she suddenly burst out sobbing, Ledantec and I sobbed in chorus.

The chill of the fog, moreover, had suddenly congested us again, and again we had lost any precise consciousness of our actions, thoughts and sensations. There was nothing dolorous about our sobbing. As before, we were floating in an exceedingly soft bliss, soft and gloomy.

All I can remember is that at that moment, it was no longer the external world that seemed to me to be viewed in a dream through the half-light of an aquarium, but myself—a self composed of the three of us, who had changed into something floating adrift in an I don't know what made of palpable fog or intangible water.

And it was deliciously exquisite.

Apart from that, nothing else subsists in my memory, until this, which produced the effect of a thunderbolt in dragging me up, drowning, from the depths of an abyss into which I had gradually sunk:

Ledantec is standing in front of me, his face convulsed with horror, his hair standing on end, his eyes open very wide, and he is shouting: "Run! Run!"

I open my eyes in my turn, equally wide. I find myself lying on the ground, in a room illuminated by daylight. With a glance, I see ragged clothes hanging on the walls around me, two chairs, a chipped water-jug that is my neighbor on the floor, and in a corner, a wretched bed in which the woman is doubtless dead, for her head is hanging down, and her long white hair is trailing as far as me.

With one bound, I'm standing up, like Ledantec.

"What!" I say to him, my teeth chattering. "You've killed her? Is she dead?"

"No, no," he replied, "but that doesn't matter. Run."

I feel completely sobered up, and I think that he must still be drunk. Otherwise, why this urgency? A residue of pity for the unfortunate woman therefore obliges me to say: "What's up? Is she ill? Let's look after her."

And I go to the bed in order to put her head back on the bolster. I observe then that she's neither dead nor ill, but profoundly asleep. I observe, too, that in reality, in spite of her octogenarian tresses, she is very young. Her idiotic smile persists, but her teeth really are hers, and those of a little girl. Her wrinkle-free skin, her firm bosom, are certainly no more than sixteen, perhaps even less.

"You see, you see," Ledantec goes on. "Run."

He tries to drag me outside. He's surely still drunk. I deduce that from his feverish gestures, his trembling hands, his fearful expression. Now he's begging me, stammering: "I slept with the old woman. She isn't old. Look, Look. And yet, how old she is!"

And he lifts up a handful of the long tresses, like a tangle of white silk, and he adds, evidently in a sort of delirium that causes me to fear alcoholic dementia: "When I think that I have given her children—three, four children…who knows how many children? Yes, a heap in one night! And who were born right away, and have grown up already! Run!"

It's definitely an attack of dementia. Poor Ledantec! What can be done to snap him out of it? I put my arms around him and try to calm him down, but he thinks I'm trying to make him lie down again, and he shoves me away, stumbling and shouting at me with tears in his eyes: "If you don't believe me, look under the bed. They're there, the children. They're there, I tell you. Look, look, just look!"

He lies down on his belly, and does indeed pull toward him one, two, three, four children who were hiding under the bed: boys, girls, I don't really know, but all similar to the sleeping woman, all with white hair, the tresses of an octogenarian.

Am I still drunk, like Ledantec, or mad? What does his strange hallucination signify? Momentarily, I hesitate. I pat myself, and I shake myself in order to take stock of myself.

No, no, I'm fully in possession of my reason. I really can see that monstrous brood. They all have their faces in their hands. They're weeping; they're wailing.

Suddenly, one of them leaps on to the bed. The others do likewise. The woman wakes up.

And there we are, contemplated by the stares of five pairs of eyes devoid of lashes or eyebrows, by those eyes whose irises have the dead pallor of tin and whose gazes have a mysterious tint of brown water.

"Run! Run!" repeats Ledantec, abandoning me.

And this time, I listen, and, after having thrown a few coins on the floor, I catch up with him, in order to make him understand, when he sobers up, that he has slept with a poor albino prostitute who has brothers and sisters.

Mademoiselle

He was registered at the Mairie under the name Jean-Marie-Mathieu Valot, but no one ever called him anything but "Mademoiselle."

He was the local idiot.

Not, however, one of those lamentable idiots in rags who live on public charity. He lived in a little house rented by his mother and honesty administered by his guardian, so he was more to be envied than pitied.

Nor was he one of those idiots with a glowering expression and a bestial appearance who disgust or frighten people. He was a joy to behold, with his lips always parted and his eyes always smiling, especially with the perpetual masquerade of his feminine garments.

For he dressed as a girl, thus demonstrating how scarcely disagreeable he found the nickname of Mademoiselle.

And how could he not love it, that nickname, of which his mother had once made a gentle term of endearment, when he was a child, so delicate, so weak, with a wan and wretched complexion, a poor little failed boy, punier than many girls his age? It was as an entirely affectionate caress, from his earliest infancy, that his mother murmured to him that tender "Mademoiselle", while his old grandmother repeated cheerfully: "The fact is, I must say, that even though he's got a stick, there's not much of it to speak of, by Christ—without meaning any offence to the good Lord."

To which his grandfather usually added, no less cheerfully: "Just as long as it doesn't fall off as he grows, like a tadpole's tail!"

And he was treated as a true daughter, and coddled, inasmuch as the household was prosperous and had no need of a male to get it back on its feet.

The grandparents and the mother having died, Mademoiselle had scarcely less good fortune with his paternal uncle, who cared for the idiot as best he could, becoming increasingly attached to him as he did so. For that gentleman too, Jean-Marie-Mathieu Valot had continued to call himself Mademoiselle—and similarly for the entirely neighborhood, still without anyone having slightest malevolent intention, but, on the contrary, everyone finding it an opportunity to give pleasure to the poor gentle creature who never did any harm to anyone.

Even the street-urchins meant no harm by it, habituated as they were to greet in that fashion the overgrown innocent in a dress and bonnet. What would have appeared extraordinary to them and driven them to mockery, would have been seeing him dressed as a boy.

But Mademoiselle never did that. Like his nickname, his costume was dear to him. He delighted in wearing it, and only delighted in that, with the particular refinement that he was perfectly conscious of not being a girl and of living in disguise.

People understood that, moreover, by virtue of the exaggeratedly feminine appearance he adopted, as if to demonstrate that the appearance was not natural to him. His enormous bonnet, scrupulously frilly, was lavishly decorated with monstrous multicolored ribbons. His skirts were gathered in countless layers, ballooning behind on a great excess of hoops. He walked with a mincing gait, with extravagant wriggles and swaying of the hips, his arms remaining stuck to his sides and his hands like a fan, fluttering in the pretentious gestures of a comical coquetry.

It was necessary then, in order to be his friend, to say to him seriously: "Oh, Mademoiselle, what a fine girl you are!"

That put him in a good mood, and he replied, quite joyfully: "Aren't I? But you can see that it's humorous."

Nevertheless, at local festivals, when there was dancing in the square, he wanted to be asked to dance in the quality of Mademoiselle, and never asked a girl himself.

One evening, when someone asked him why, he opened his eyes wide, guffawed as if at a lewd joke, and said: "But I can't ask girls because I'm not a boy. Look at my dress, imbecile."

His interlocutor, being a judicious man, riposted: "Dress as a boy, then, Mademoiselle."

He reflected momentarily, and then said, sly: "But if I dressed as a boy, I'd no longer be Mademoiselle. And since I am Mademoiselle..."

And he shrugged his shoulders.

The observation did give him pause for thought however, for some time thereafter, on encountering the judicious man, he said to him, abruptly: "If I dress as a boy, will people call me Mademoiselle anyway?"

"Of course," the other replied. "People will always call you that."

The idiot seemed delighted. Undoubtedly, he was fonder of his nickname than of his costume. The next day, he was seen arriving in the square without his skirts, dressed as a man. He had taken trousers, a frock-coat and a hat from his guardian's wardrobe.

It was a revolution for the neighborhood.

The people who had been accustomed to smiling at him amicably when he was dressed as a woman looked at him with alarm, with astonished expressions that seemed peevish. The most indulgent could not help laughing, visibly mocking.

The involuntary hostility of some, the over-apparent mockery of the others and the disagreeable amazement of everyone disturbed in an old habit, the idiot perceived in full, and suffered in consequence

What was worse still was the first street-urchin who started shouting in a jeering tone, while gamboling around him: "Ahoy! Mademoiselle's wearing trousers! Ahoy Mademoiselle!" And it became even more frightful when an entire gang of scamps was on his heels, yapping and mocking, as if at a grotesque carnival mask.

It was certain that now, even more than before, the unfortunate seemed to be in disguise. By virtue of living as a girl, further exaggerating the feminine appearance, he had completely lost any boyish physiognomy. His hairless face and his long fine hair, demanded the beribboned bonnet, and became a caricature beneath the old doctor's top hat. In that old-fashioned frock-coat, and those excessively large trousers, Mademoiselle's upper body, and even more so, the mobile rump danced hectically—and nothing was as funny as the contrast between that earnest garb and the mincing gait, the flirtatious carriage of the head and the pretentious gestures of the madly-waving hands.

Soon, the young men, the young women, the old women and even the mature men, including the judicious adviser, joined in with the kids in hooting at Mademoiselle.

The bewildered idiot broke into a run and went home terrified.

There he put his poor head in his hands and tried to understand. What did everyone have against him? For they evidently had something against him. What harm had he done, and who had he hurt, by dressing as a boy? Wasn't he a boy, after all?

And for the first time in his life, he conceived a horror of his nickname. For was it not with that nickname that he had been insulted?

Then, a horrible doubt occurred to him.

"What if I really were a mademoiselle?"

He would have liked to consult his guardian about that, but he did not dare. He sensed, besides, albeit obscurely, that the gentleman might not tell him the truth, in order to be kind. Furthermore, he preferred to work it out by himself, to find out without asking anyone anything.

All his idiotic cunning, latent until then because he had never had occasion to employ it, came into play out then and drove him to a solitary and tenebrous action.

He dressed as a girl again the next day and reappeared in the locality pretending to have completely forgotten the previous day's escapade. But the people, and especially the children, had not forgotten. They looked at him obliquely, and the best of them did not hide their ironic smiles. The urchins began to follow him again, shouting: "Ahoy, Mademoiselle! Where's your trousers?"

Be pretended not to understand, or even to suspect that they were referring to him. As before, he appeared cheerful, a joy to behold, with his lips always parted and his eyes always smiling. As before, he sported enormous and multicolored bonnets and ballooning skirts. As before, he walked with a mincing gait, swinging his hips wriggling, gesticulating coquettishly and licking his lips with an appreciative tongue when anyone called him Mademoiselle, although deep down, he now wanted to leap at the throat of the people who called him by that name.

Days and months went by, and the people around him ended up no longer remembering the strange episode that seemed so completely abolished in his memory. But he had never stopped thinking about it, nor of watching, perpetually on the lookout, to discover by what means he might recognize his quality as a boy and by what means he might prove it victoriously. Innocent in reality, he ha arrived at the age of twenty without knowing that, without it ever having entered his head to think about it.

Tenacious, curious and secretive, he never asked any questions, but observed. Often, during dances, he heard the boys glorifying about girls seduced, and girls boasting about some boy or other. Often, too, after the ball, he saw couples leave entwined. No one had any suspicion of him. He listened. He spied.

Finally, he saw the thing at close range, and several times—for he wanted to be absolutely sure; he had the joy of knowing.

And one night, as the dances were coming to an end and couples were going away, with their arms around one another's waists, a loud scream was heard from the corner of the woods through which the path to the next village ran. It was

Josephine, the beautiful Josephine, who uttered it, calling for help: a good girl, who was going home alone, also being brave. People ran to answer her appeal.

They arrived to tear her, choking, from the grip of Mademoiselle, who was raping her after having strangled her.

The idiot had lain in wait, and had rushed her in order to do to her what the other boys did to girls. She had resisted valiantly. Then he had grabbed her by the neck and squeezed with all his might. She had lost her breath. She was dying. And quickly, quickly, he had hastened to prove to himself that he was a boy.

And as, in liberating Josephine, he had been rudely knocked down, half-stunned, he suddenly leapt to his feet, foaming and drooling, crying: "I'm no longer Mademoiselle. I'm a boy—I'm a boy, I tell you."

And with his skirts lifted, he proudly shook in the moonlight a poor little stick of macaroni, flaccid and tremulous.

Violated

Exactly, repeated the burly Paul. Exactly! Yes, me, as you see me, I've been violated. And violated by...but if I told you right away, it wouldn't make a story, would it? And since it's a story that you want, I'll tell it like threading a needle and starting at the beginning.

I'd been hunting for a week in the heart of the Breton region, on the heaths in the vicinity of the Black Mountain. Desolate, wild and full of game! You can walk for hours without encountering a human being, and when you do meet one, it's just the same as of you hadn't met one, because the local people absolutely ignore the French. In the evening, in the inns, I had to indulge in pantomimes to get something to eat and a bed.

Being in a melancholy mood at the time, however, that solitude delighted me. The company of my dog was mostly sufficient for me. So, you can imagine my aggravation when, one morning, I perceived that I was being followed, positively followed, by a hunter who seemed to want to strike up a conversation with me. I'd noticed his presence already, the day before, obstructing my horizon on several occasions. Then, I'd attributed it to the hazards of the chase, which were bringing us both to the same game-trails. But today, there was no possible illusion about it. The chap was ostentatiously dogging my footsteps, trotting along as best he could with his little legs in order to match my long stride, taking short cuts in order to catch up with me obliquely.

As he was being to obstinate, it goes without saying that I did likewise, and our entire day's hunting was spent, for him, in trying to catch up with me, and for me, in running away. It was as if we were playing tag.

Conclusion: when dusk fell, I was completely lost in the lost deserted part of the heath. Not a hovel in sight, not even a bell-tower in the distance. The only reference-point I had for half a kilometer around was the ironic silhouette of my blessed man.

No two ways about it—he'd won the game. There was nothing left to do but face fortune with a stout heart, let him catch me up—or, rather, go to meet him, meekly—if I didn't want to sleep under the stars on an empty stomach. So that was what I did, going up to him, moreover, with a scowl, to ask him for directions.

He replied to me in a very affable tone that there was no inn in the vicinity, that the nearest hamlet was five leagues away, but that, to reach his house, it only required an hour's walk, and that he was only too happy to be able to offer me hospitality.

I was worn out. How could I say no? And we set off together through the gorse and the heather, me slowing down out of tiredness, him still trotting lightly on his basset-hound legs, which seemed indefatigable. He was an old man, though, and puny, not at all strongly-built, whom I could have knocked down by blowing n him. But how he could walk, the animal!

Not a very inconvenient companion, however, the opposite of what I'd imagined. He didn't seem to have the slightest desire to strike up a conversation with me, as I'd feared. His invitation made, and my brief thanks accepted, he didn't open his mouth again. We went silently. Except that his gaze continued to annoy me slightly. I felt it weighing upon me, as if he wanted to force the intimacy that my sealed lips refused. All in all, though, that tenacious gaze, which I observed with covert glances, seemed to me to be sympathetic, even admiring. Yes, in truth—admiring!

Oh, I couldn't pay him back in the same coin. He wasn't pretty, the pilgrim! Short in the legs and rather knock-kneed. Narrow, thin torso. Weather-beaten face, furrowed and wrinkled, with prominent cheekbones, without a hair of beard to hide the leathery creases. The hair of an old mendicant friar, with gray wisps hanging down over a greasy collar. The nose of a ferret, the eyes of a rat.

In sum, though, he was offering me a bite to eat and a nest, wasn't he? There was no need, for that, to be handsome.

A serious bite too, and a comfortable nest. A manor house, in fact—a genuine manor-house of the olden days, very chic, and in the dining-room, in front of the big blazing fireplace, a dinner that I can't describe. A hotchpotch in the fashion of long ago, doubtless cooking since morning. Ragouts of woodcock for which angels would have taken up arms! Buckwheat tartlets in cream scented with aniseed! A cheese, rare and hard to find in Brittany, to devour with a four-pound loaf merely by sniffing the rind. And all washed down with authentic old Chambertin, then a cider brandy to make you believe that you were drinking the good Lord in velvet trousers. Not forgetting the cigars: pure Havanas imported as contraband, enormous, strong, not in the least dry, but on the contrary, quite fresh, with a dense and intoxicating smoke.

And how he guzzled, the little old man, how he swilled and puffed! Like an ogre, a cantor, a chimney!

Me too, it's necessary to confess.

But of everything that we might have said while playing Gargantua, I no longer remember anything at all. We did chat, of course, certainly—but about what? Doubtless about hunting. Women too, probably. Well—between men, after drinking! Yes, yes, about women, I'm sure of it. And he let his hair down, the little old man. Notably with regard to a portrait, perched above the big fireplace, which represented his ancestor, a Marquise of the *ancien régime*. And there's one who had had a good time—at seventy, it appears, she still had busy thighs!

"It's extraordinary," I said, "how much you resemble that portrait."

"Yes," the little old man replied, smiling.

And in his quavering, shrill voice, he added: "I resemble my grandmother in everything. I'm sixty, but I feel fire in my loins good for another ten years." Then, suddenly softening, considering me with the same admiring gaze as before, he said to the portrait: "Hey, Marquise—what a pity you didn't know this fine fellow!"

That shred of our conversation, that remark, that gaze—I remembered that very well when, an hour later, fairly drunk, I went to bed in the white and gold room to which a big broad-shouldered valet guided me, and wished me goodnight in Breton.

Good night, fine! But it was necessary to be able to go to sleep, and I couldn't. The Chambertin, the cider brandy and the cigars had got me drunk, but not to the point at which one collapses like a pole-axed ox. On the contrary, I was agitated, my skin prickling, my blood beating the charge, in a semi-sleep in which I felt very much alive, my entire being in vibration and expansion, as if I'd taken hashish.

All right! Good! Evidently, that's it, I'm dreaming while awake. This is what I see. I see the door open and the Marquise appear, having got down from her frame. She's taken off her dress and trimmings. She's in a night-dress. Her fancy hair-do has given way to a single knotted ribbon, which holds her powdered heir in a pony-tail. But by the flickering light of the candle she's carrying, I recognize her clearly. It's her face with the piercing eyes, the pointed nose, the sensual and smiling mouth. She seems less young than in her portrait. Bah! Perhaps. Maybe that's due to the weak, dancing light! Then again, I don't have time to take account of it, or to reflect n the strangeness of the vision, or even to debate with myself and say: *Am I dead drunk or is this really a ghost?*

No, I don't have the time—it's true!—for the candle has been abruptly snuffed out, and the Marquise is in bed with me, wrapping her arms around me.

One fixed idea, the only one I have, haunts me—that at seventy, the Marquise still had busy thighs. And I say to myself, in jest, that she's still seventy, whether she's a phantom or not! My only thought is this: *Does she really have busy thighs?*

Well, damn it yes! More than busy! Crazy! Enraged! Diabolical! She doesn't say a word. She acts. Oh, Marquise, Marquise!

And suddenly, involuntarily, to convince myself that I'm not in the heart of the fantastic, I exclaim: "Good God! But I'm not dreaming."

"No, no, you're not dreaming," replies a mouth that is trying to press itself to mine.

Horror! That mouth reeks of cigars and brandy! That voice is the little old man's!

With one thrust, I hurl him to the floor, and I leap out of bed, bawling: "Pig! Filthy pig!"

I hear the door close, and behind it, on the stairs, the sound of bare feet running away.

I get dressed in the dark, and then I go downstairs, still shouting.

Down below, in the vestibule where first light is showing, stands the big broad-shouldered valet. He has an enormous cudgel in his hand. He's shouting too, in Breton, and he points with his finger at the open door, outside which my dog is waiting.

What could I say to that savage, who didn't speak French? Should I have taken on his cudgel? Why? Then again, I was more ashamed than furious. Swiftly, I picked up my rifle and game-bag, which were set outside on the steps, and I took flight without looking back.

Disgusted by the hunting in that region, I went back to Brest the same day, where I tried, timidly, with infinite precautions, to obtain some information about the individual who...

"Oh yes, I know," one of the people I questioned said to me, "you're talking about the Manoir de Kervénidozec, where the old Comtesse lives who dresses as a man and sleeps with her coachman."

And it was with a profound sigh of relief that I replied, to the great bewilderment of my interlocutor: "Oh! Thank God!"

Jeroboam

It would have required a very malicious tongue to claim, or even to insinuate, that the Reverend William Greenfield, vicar of St. Sampson's, Tottenham, did not make Mrs. Anna Greenfield, his wife, perfectly happy. In twelve years of marriage he had honored her with twelve children. Could anyone decently demand more of a saintly man?

Saintly to the point of heroism, in truth—for Anna, who was endowed with invaluable qualities and incomparable virtues, a model wife and a paragon of motherhood from the moral viewpoint, had not been as well served physically. To put it bluntly, she was hideous.

Her hair, stiff though scarcely abundant, displayed the national color of "half-and-half,"[58] but a troubled half-and-half, as if drunk several times already.

Her complexion, simultaneously earthen and blotchy, seemed to have been kneaded out of sand mingled with brick dust.

Her teeth, long and angled forwards, gave the impression of wanting to be torn out of their sockets in order to escape that lipless mouth, whose sulfurous breath turned them yellow. It was understandable that the unfortunate objects did not like it therein.

Her enameled eyed gazed vaguely, one considerably to the right, the other to the left, in a divergent and alarmed squint, doubtless in order not to perceive her nose, of which they were ashamed.

---

[58] This phrase is rendered in English, and presumably refers to the now-obsolete popular habit of drinking pints compounded out of mild and bitter ale.

And with good reason! This, soft, long, slack and pale, terminated by a violet-tinted ball, it evoked irresistibly the idea of a member unnamable except in a medical textbook.

As for poor Anna's body, it contrived to be, by an inconceivable irony of nature, both thin and flabby, ligneous and chubby, without having either the elegance of rigidity or the flexible grace of healthy flesh. One might have thought it a once-adipose body now devoid of fat and deflated, the enveloped of which had remained loose, suspended over the articulations of the frame.

She was evidently no more than skin and bone, but at the same time she had too much skin and too much bone.

It was obvious that the reverend had done his duty, all his duty and more than his duty, in sacrificing himself a dozen times at that altar. Yes, a dozen times, bravely and loyally! A dozen times—Anna could not say any different, nor quibble over the number, since the children were an impartial counter. Twelve times, not one less!

But not one more, alas!

And that is why, in spite of appearances, Mrs. Anna Greenfield dared to think, in the utmost depths of her heart, that the Reverend William Greenfield, vicar of St. Sampson's, Tottenham, had not rendered her perfectly happy.

She thought that all the more because, for four years already, she had even had to renounce the hope of that annual sacrifice, once so slight and so fleeting, now fallen into desuetude. After the twelfth child, in fact, the reverend had made a formal declaration:

"God has blessed our union, my dear Anna. We have attained the sacred figure of the twelve tribes of Israel. To persevere further in the work of the flesh would be debauchery. You would not want, I suppose, the Reverend William Greenfield, vicar of St. Sampson's, Tottenham, to complete his exemplary life, thanks to you, in the practices of lust."

The blushing Anna had bowed her head; the saintly man, with the legitimate pride of virtue finally satisfied, had uttered in the Lord's direction an *oof!* like that of the Hebrews emerging from Egypt.

A model wife and paragon of motherhood Anna had remained, without complaining to anyone, pickled in her desolation, for four years. She contented herself with asking the Lord, in eloquent prayers, whether he would care to inspire the reverend with the desire to commence a further series of twelve tribes.

In the meantime, to render her prayers more efficacious, she strove to foment that desire by culinary means. She spared no effort, and gorged the saintly man on the spiciest nourishment: soups of hare, ox-tail marinated in Madeira; green turtle; purées of mushrooms, artichoke hearts, celery and horse-radish; sauces enliven with peppers, pimentos, truffles and pickled cabbage-palm; dark meat in ragouts sprinkled with cayenne; lobsters accommodated in the most diabolical curry; hot pies baked with the kidneys, crests and roe of chickens; cakes into which raw vanilla was mashed; buttered ginger tarts; all washed down with strong beers and generous wines: Scotch ales, clarets and extra dry champagnes, not to mention the brandy, whisky and gin—in sum, the innumerable army of spirits with which English alcoholism loves to whip up the blood.

And the reverend's blood was, in fact, whipped up: blood that exploded in his ears, his cheeks, his nose, making them into two pairs of blooming poppies and a formidable trumpeting tomato.

But the Lord remained inflexible nevertheless, and the revered remained uninflammable to Anna—who continued to mope, dreamily, before the futile magnificence of that turgid nasal appendage, still alone, alas, in manifesting itself thus in trumpeting fashion.

She became more and more rigid in consequence, and at the same time, flabbier and flabbier, and had almost reached the point of losing confidence in God when, a fortnight ago, the Lord sent her an inspiration.

Was it really the Lord? Was it not rather the Devil? She did not want to think about that too deeply, finding the inspiration good.

Now, this is what the Most High or the Evil One had whispered to her:

"Go visit the Exposition Universelle. Perhaps you'll bring back the secret of making yourself loved."

And it is necessary to believe that fate definitely favored her, for the reverend immediately granted her the desired permission, and immediately on arriving at the Esplanade des Invalides, Anna fell upon the Algerian dancers—and as soon as she saw them, she exclaimed: "That's what will infuse William's heart with the imperious need to give flight to a thirteenth tribe!"

But how could she make him witness to that abominable orgy of flesh? For the honest Anna could not conceal from herself that it was an infernal exhibition, and how scandalized the reverend would be by the Babylonian luxury of those lustful bellies and delirious buttocks.

Now the vicar's wife had no doubt about the Spirit that had guided her to that Pandemonium. It was surely the Devil! But she could no longer retreat. A new inspiration had come to her, and she would follow it even so—so much the worse!

And for twelve days you could have seen the tall wife with the yellow teeth ready to escape her sulfurous mouth, the poor woman with the spare hair the color of beer vomit, the pale squinting eyes, the earthen and blotchy complexion and the sad nose unnamable outside a medical textbook, attentive, curious and ecstatic before the rotating hips of the Algerian women.

Mrs. Anna Greenfield was learning.

And the other evening, scarcely disembarked in London, she raced to the reverend's bedroom, undressed in a trice, and appeared to him, for the first time in her life, in all the horror of her nudity.

"Come, come!" stammered the saintly man. "Have you gone mad, Anna? What demon's got into you? Why inflict the shame of such a spectacle upon me?"

But she did not hear a word, nor reply with any, and suddenly began to rotate her hips, like an Alma.

The reverend could not believe his eyes. He did not even think, in his stupefaction, of covering them with his hands, or even of closing them. He watched, dazed and bewildered, prey to the hypnotism of ugliness.

He watched those waves of skin coming and going, rising and falling, fluttering and writhing, rippling in extraordinary ebbs and flows, splashing around those beanpoles. He watched that rump twirling, like the pleats of an overly large pair of trousers—oh, much too large! He watched the turbulence of that belly, like a deflated gourd in which walnuts were being shakes. He watched the flag-like flapping, like collapsing old socks, the flatulent zigzags of those slack mammary purses, which beat time with slapping sounds, sometimes against the ribs, sometimes in the hollow of the naval and sometimes behind the back.

He watched, and remained motionless for a long time, without having the strength to articulate a sentence. He merely murmured, in a low voice: "Twelve times, Lord! Twelve times! Twelve! Twelve! Twelve!"

Meanwhile, Ana collapsed, exhausted and breathless, saying to herself: *Praise the Lord! William has the distraught expression he used to have, in the days when he honored me. Praise the Lord! There'll be a thirteenth tribe, and then a further series of tribes, for William is methodical.*

But William took a blanket and threw it over Anna, crushing her with these harsh words:

"You're no longer called Anna, Mrs. Greenfield. Henceforth, your name is Jezebel. I regret having mingled my blood twelve times with your impure blood." Then, gripped by pity, he added: "If only you were in a state of inebriation, of intoxication, I could excuse..."

"Well, yes, yes!" she cried, repentantly. "Yes, I'm in that state. Forgive me, William. Forgive an unfortunate intoxicated woman!"

"I forgive you, Anna," he said. And he brought her a bowl, saying: "This will relieve you, Ana. And when your head is clear, remember the lesson that it's necessary to take from this adventure."

"What lesson?" she asked, humbly.

"It is," he replied, "that one should never break one's habits."

"But what about you, William?" she suggested, timidly. "Why, then, have you lost the...?"

"Shut up!" he cried. "Shut up, Jezebel! Is your intoxication getting hold of you again? I had, indeed, for twelve years, the habit of multiplication once a year—but for four years, I've had another habit, which I don't want to break."

And the Reverend William Greenfield, vicar of St. Sampson's, Tottenham, the saintly man whose blood was whipped up with spices, with ears like poppies in bloom, and a nose like a trumpeting tomato, left Anna there in order to go— as had been his habit for four years, in fact—to sleep with Polly, the maid.

"Listen, Polly," he said, as he came in, "you're an intelligent girl. I shall therefore try with you the latest Parisian invention."

And to refine his pleasure, as he was jocular, he called her his little Jezebel, and said to her with an unctuous smile:

"Call me Jeroboam. You don't understand why?[59] Me neither—but that doesn't matter. Take off all your underwear, Polly, and call me Jeroboam."

---

[59] It is not obvious that Richepin readers would have readily understood why either. The Biblical Jeroboam battled for the succession after Solomon's death in the first Book of Kings, taking the Hebrews back temporarily to paganism—a reversion continued by his son Ahab, the husband of the infamous Jezebel. It might or might not be relevant that the first objects

TALES WITHOUT MORALS

Behemoth

The little old man had been there when we got out of the Staouëli rattletrap to spread out into the Sidi-Ferruch countryside, and he had examined our dozen faces before settling on mine. Then he had started to follow me, prowling to the right and the left, passing I front of me, darting oblique glances at me. Finally, on the sea shore, when I was alone with him, he had decided to murmur to me, in a high-pitched voice: "A nice view, isn't it, Monsieur, for an artist? Nice sky, nice sea—for an artist!"

As I had responded with a simple nod of the head, he had hesitated at least five minutes before recommencing, and his timidity had found nothing better, in order to resume the attack, than to repeat: "Oh, very nice, very nice, for an artist! Monsieur is an artist, I think?"

"Indeed, yes, I admit it."

"And Monsieur must find it lonely, in this land of Barbarians!"

"But..."

"Oh, yes, Barbarians. A true exile, I may say. Oh, if Monsieur wished! Perhaps Monsieur would be agreeable, even so, to make the acquaintance of one, an artiste, who is *di primo cartello*."

---

of ungodly worship set up by Jeroboam for worship are a pair of golden calves.

Very short, almost a dwarf, with the infatuated expression of dwarfs, a nose like a skunk's muzzle and the gaze of a drill-bit, he was sweating malice from every pore of his hairless face, shaved raw, which irresistibly evoked the idea of a curé for apes.

He was old, but his white hair seemed to be made of mold, and I couldn't help imagining that that mold as like the flower of his soul, a poisonous mushroom.

Why the devil, with such a face, was he lacking in boldness? And why, first of all, was he plying his trade here, in this almost deserted wilderness, where he could only find clients among the rare winter caravans of hurried travelers? And finally, why, among the dozens of us that there were today, had I had the honor of being picked out?

Because all these reasons were piquing my curiosity, and also out of pity for the poor wretch, I replied to his final question that it would, in fact, not be disagreeable for me to meet the artiste *di primo cartello* that he had mentioned. His mouse-like eyes sparkled with joy, and he exclaimed, clicking his tongue: "Oh, how content she will be, *la povera*! And Monsieur too, of course!"

He leapt in front of me, almost running, and I lengthened my stride to follow him as far as a kind of small country house, all white, amid the dark verdure. A small garden preceded the house, every fresh, intercut with wooden irrigation channels full of running water, literally overflowing with flowers.

"Tee hee!" he said. "Nothing is more agreeable than flowers, to the diva, a flower herself."

And so saying, he pivoted on his heel, with a move so graceful that the heel gave me the impression of being rounded. He ran to a little shed and came back rapidly with a pair of secateurs, with which he swiftly cut roses. Having made an enormous bouquet, almost as big as him, he put them in my arms.

"Monsieur will offer them to her; she'll be delighted, *la povera*, since Monsieur is an artist. But come, come! *La cara* is expecting us and I expect, myself, that my pochette[60] is being prepared in accordance."

The sounds of a pochette were, in fact, audible: an antique pochette as shrill and buzzing as a flying insect. We went into the house and I saw her then, *la cara*. She was a huge and monstrous woman, very fat, sallow and swollen, with a face like a full moon and the body of a bloated blister, at least fifty years old, dressed as a dancer. I stood there nailed to the threshold, open-mouthed, stupefied. Yes, dressed as a dancer, her torso and legs in a leotard—that torso of lard, those elephantine legs!—and beneath the seething pleats of the skirt, which she lifted up at the front, one could see the pillars of her thighs in a tutu.

The little old man bowed deeply and said: "Rina, Monsieur is a visiting artist, who has come to offer you a bouquet as admiration."

The hippopotamus replied, smiling: "Yes, Rino, I can see, and I'm proud." Then, extending her hand to me with a queenly gesture, she said: "La Rina authorizes you, Monsieur, to kiss your hand, doesn't she, Rino?"

"Yes, Rina," said the old man, "and I'm not jealous." He nudged me with his elbow and whispered in my ear: "Say something, Monsieur—tell her how beautiful you find her!"

His gaze was so charged with supplication that I was obliged to obey. I therefore stammered a few vague compliments, which the old man repeated and amplified.

"What a connoisseur Monsieur is, Rina, as you see! A true artist, no? He says that you're the most beautiful, the most exquisite, the diva Rina, the illustrious *cara* Rina, and that these roses are no more roses, no more flowers, than you."

That was said gaily, volubly, with pirouettes on his imaginary rounded heel and bows all the way to the ground, with circular movements of the arms and legs, while the mastodon swelled up as if to burst all the seams of her leotard. The

---

[60] A small violin

dwarf leapt upon his pochette, stuck it under his chin and started to play a quaint and garish tune.

"Dance a little, Rina, dance for the Monsieur, that he may know your glory; dance your famous dance for him, your triumphant dance of the Siren. Go on, Rina, my *cara*."

And the mountain seemed to be shaken by an earthquake, and the pillars seemed to come apart under the pressure of some invisible Samson, and I was gripped by fear, expecting a collapse. But no! The mountain danced. The pillar exulted. The swarming mass did not crumble. And in her famous dance of triumph, the siren changed into a whale tried to charm me. Behemoth smiled.

The little old man wriggled and writhed, scraping his pochette frantically, beating time with his foot, playing with his entire hectic body, and only stopped crying *bravas* to murmur surreptitiously: "Shout too, Monsieur, shout," in such an imploring fashion that, mechanically, unable to refuse, I stammered as best I could: "Yes, yes! *Brava! Brava!*" until the moment when it finally arrived—the collapse that I had feared. Abruptly, like a punctured, deflating aerostat, the unfortunate woman fell to the floor. She was choking, fuming, croaking, still smiling.

"Ah, *la povera*!" moaned the old man. "Come on, come on, it's nothing. Keep going. It's for Monsieur, who is an artist. He knows what an artist is. Isn't it true, Monsieur, that you know! *Brava! Brava!* Listen to how genteel he is, also crying *Brava, Brava!* Isn't it so, Monsieur that you're taking account of it?"

I was already putting my hand in my pocket, but he leapt forward, grabbed my hand and glared at my furiously. I let myself go, no longer understanding. He dragged me outside briskly, almost brutally.

"Go away, quickly, quickly," he said to me. "I'll look after her, *povera*. Go away."

I was in the garden. He picked a rose.

"Throw that through the window," he said, "and cry *Brava!* again. I implore you!"

266

I obeyed, and fled.

"Monsieur! Monsieur!"

It was the little old man, completely out of breath, who was running after me.

"*La Rina* sends you a souvenir, as an artist."

He ran away after putting a piece of paper into my hand. I unfolded it. It contained a lock of hair, gray and greasy.

The coachman's horn was calling us back to the rattle-trap. I arrived there, dazed and harassed. What the devil could that ridiculous adventure signify? I tried to ask the coachman for information.

"Oh yes," he replied. "Rino and Rina, the mad couple of Sidi-Ferruch. You've had the session, then, this time? It's very good! Well worth the trip, no?"

And he burst out laughing in my face, while I looked down my nose at him.

The Korrigan

"Yes certainly," said the Comtesse Diane, with a firmly convinced expression. "That, I affirm. I'd put my hand in the fire to swear it; I'd give me head to be cut off. Korrigans definitely still exist today. Or, at least, they still existed forty years ago, when I was young and married to my first husband. Of that, personally, I don't have any doubt. I don't believe in God or the Devil, obviously, but in Korrigans I believe. I'd be an ingrate not to."

"You're obliged to them, then?" asked someone.

"Oh, not to all of them, unfortunately," sighed the Comtesse, "but certainly to one of them, it's true, and obliged in a fashion that's quite unforgettable. Just think that after forty years, I can't think about it without a sigh of regret. That tells you a lot."

Again, Comtesse Diane sighed, rolling wrinkled eyes and pouting voluptuously, expressing in the most cynical possible fashion an amorous regret, perhaps even more sensuous than amorous. What she seemed to be regretting thus was something like a good wine on which one has got drunk, a succulent dish that has given one indigestion. Immediately, we thought, feasting on it in advance: *We're going to get our teeth into a tasty morsel. The Comtesse is in a mood for lewd remembrance.*

It's necessary to know that Comtesse Diane was not at all a woman of our era, but of the last century. Not in terms of her age—she was barely a sexagenarian—but in terms of manners, a free, almost libertine spirit, a taste for dirty anecdotes, impudent gossip, sometimes extending to indecency, the outrageous boldness of confessions always ready to strip bare in public, and finally, and above all, by virtue of her absolute lack of moral sensibility in anything relating, as she put it so politely, to "matters of gallantry."

This was to such an extent that, if someone had told her, in the form of a contemporary adventure, the story of Lot or that of Oedipus, she would gladly have cried, irresponsibly, without further persistence: "Did they enjoy themselves?"

It is also necessary to say, by way of excuse, that Comtesse Diane was what she was quite naturally, naively, without seeking any malice therein, without even perceiving that one might seek malice therein. In that too she was not of our era, but that of the century before last, of which she had the childishly mischievous eyes, the head held high, the insolently uncovered cleavage, the white-powdered wig and the heavily made-up face with the corner of the mouth punctuated by an ingenuously overblown beauty-spot.

Comtesse Diane had been married four times. To any curious individual who enquired whether that had been for love, she replied point-blank: "Yes, for love of adultery." And if the simpleton seemed offended, she added: "You find my character a trifle lively, don't you? It's not yet as lively as my thighs, though."

Introduced thus, summarily and in haste, one might take Comtesse Diane for a debauchee. Not at all, however. Debauchery is dirty and unhealthy. Now, Comtesse Diane exhaled good health, and in spite of all the follies she had committed, her soul retained, as she did, clean underwear, fresh linen dazzling in its candor. And it's necessary never to lose sight of that, if you want to appreciate her tale of the Korrigan, with the good humor, devoid of any obscene subtext, that she set out to tell, with an utter simplicity that truly innocent, by virtue of unconscious jollity.

"So, Comtesse," asked the friend who held the dice of the conversation and knew how to throw the cast of Venus in the game of lewd stories, "You've had an affair with a Korrigan?"

"Yes, darling," she replied, "And a serious affair, I beg you to believe."

"As serious as that?"

269

"I dare say so. For it's with that Korrigan that I made my first husband a cuckold for the first time. You want the story of the adventure; I can see it in your eyes, all aimed at my mouth, peppering it with curiosity. You shall have it, then. But I warn you, the prudes had better leave. It's a little bit racy. You'll all have red tips to your ears, even the gourmands of *haulte gresse.*"[61]

For the Comtesse to take such preambulatory precautions, the story really had to be enough to make an ape blush. And you can imagine that I, a fourteen-year-old scamp—who came to be there as a result of a freak of chance impossible to explain here in a few words—sensed my sensually-alert schoolboy imagination lighting up already.

What a disappointment it was, the, when the Comtesse turned to me and said: "I won't insult you, my little friend, by thinking you a prude. At your age, that would be too soon. But in return, you won't insult me by thinking that I'm a perverter of schoolchildren. At my age, that would be too late. You will, therefore, be so extremely polite as to go smoke a cigarette in the billiard-room. My story will last just as long as a cigarette—swallowing the smoke, of course, as I'm sure you know how to do."

Whether I liked it or not, with a crestfallen expression, I was obliged to retire to the next room, the door of which was carefully closed by the Comtesse herself—much less vicious, as you can see, than her reputation made her out to be.

But a schoolboy is only a schoolboy, isn't he?—which is to say, a vicious little swine, utterly avid to know exactly what people want to conceal from him. I shall not astonish anyone, nor render anyone indignant, I think, by confessing that as

---

[61] The term *"livres de haulte gresse"* [literally, "highly-greased books"] was adapted from a phrase originally applied to fattened sheep for specific euphemistic reference to the works of Rabelais, and was generalized thereafter to refer to all racy books.

soon as I was in the billiard-room I stuck my ear to the key-hole.

Alas, there was a thick curtain covering the door, and besides, the Comtesse, doubtless rendered suspicious of me by my gaze, full of concupiscent curiosity, lowered her voice just at the most thrilling point in her story. Because of that, I was, to begin with, only able to catch uninteresting fragments of it.

It concerned a manor-house in Finistère, near a forest where clog-makers lived who only spoke Low Breton. It also involved a company of gypsies lodged at the château, who had animals with them, including a bear and a huge orangutan. There was also mention of the forest being haunted by Korrigans, malevolent and lubricious spirits of a sort. After that, though, I couldn't make out anything at all except *Ohs!* and *Ahs!* and bursts of laughter.

It was at this point that the Comtesse spoke in the lowest tone, and I lost the thread of the story entirely, not knowing any longer whether it concerned the cog-makers, the beasts or the Korrigans, and what had happened between Comtesse Diane and any of them—and I was enraged by not being able to understand, not even being able to guess.

Since then, on reflection, I think I have understood and guessed. That is, above all, by virtue of recalling a snatch of dialogue that I heard on going back into the room, exchanged between the Comtesse and her friend.

"And why the devil," said the latter, "Are you absolutely convinced, Comtesse, that he was a Korrigan?"

"Because," she replied, "if I hadn't been absolutely convinced of that, disgust would have put me off men forever—and I would have been very upset, for I've loved many of them and been loved by many of them since, while I knew full well that a Korrigan is unique, and never to be encountered again in a lifetime."

And once again, Comtesse Diane uttered a great and profound sigh of regret.

An Honest Man[62]

All things considered, he thought, *I'm a perfectly honest man. My entire life gives me the right to shake my own hand—and that without any hypocritical pretention to virtue. Oh no—it's doing myself justice, that's all.*

A psychologist, perhaps, might have been able to find fault with that honesty, so blissfully self-satisfied. For example, it's certain that our man had no scruples about seeing to profit from his neighbor's misfortune or vice, provided that he was not its original author, bearing the sole responsibility in his own estimation. In the final analysis, though, it was only a way of looking at things, nothing more. There was material there for casuistic debate. Now, that kind of debate is particularly displeasing to simple minds like that worthy fellow's. He would have been content to reply to the psychologist: "What's the point of splitting hairs? So far as I'm concerned, I'm simply honest, and that's that."

Furthermore, don't think that that simplistic straightforwardness condemned him to an ignoble down-to-earthness. Far from it! He prided himself on having a certain *je ne sais quoi*, a weakness for whimsy, for the unexpected. And if he would have been offended to be deemed a dishonest man, he would probably have been even more annoyed if anyone had attributed bourgeois tastes to him. Thus, with regard to what love is, he professed an utterly virtuous horror of adultery, the consummation of which would have prevented him from rendering himself he testimony, soothing to his conscience, that never—oh no, never, never ever—had he ever wronged anyone!

---

[62] This is a slightly abridged but otherwise unaltered version of a story previously published in *Cauchemars* as "Une Bonne affaire" [A Good Deal].

On the other hand, he could not be content with voluptuousness on a tariff, which "reduces the noblest instinct of the heart to the vulgar satisfaction of a physical need." He needed something, so he had, raising his eyes to the heavens "a little more ideal than that!"

To tell the truth, that search for the ideal did not cost him any great effort. It was pure and simply limited to not entering houses with frosted glass windows unceremoniously, and not approaching *belles-de-nuit* with a curt "How much?" It consisted above all, of wanting to be gallant, no matter what the cost, with "the ladies," of persuading himself that they liked him for himself, and in preferring those whose appearance, costumes and faces permitted adventurous hypotheses and romantic illusions—such as, for instance: "One might think that she were a little seamstress, still virtuous," or: "No, she's just a young widow who's had bad luck," or even: "After all, she might be a woman of the world, in disguise?" and other old saws, which he knew to be false as soon as he imagined them, but whose imaginary savor was nevertheless delectable.

Given such tastes, it goes without saying that the pilgrim was a great lover of crowds, and most especially of all, a great window-shopper, nothing exciting him quite as much as half-closed shutters behind which a barely-glimpsed face appeared, from which emerged a furtive appeal. Is she young, pretty? Is she an old woman who no longer dares to show herself—yes, but horribly knowledgeable? Is she, on the contrary, a debutante, still poorly provided with audacity? So many alluring mysteries. In any case, it's the unknown!

And every time he said to himself: "Who knows? The ideal, perhaps?" The ideal, for sure, at last during the time it takes to climb the stairway in that unfamiliar shadow. And every time, in making that ascent, his heart was palpitating, as if at a first rendezvous with a first mistress.

But never, never ever, had he experienced a frisson like the one that seized him on the day when he went into that old, old house on the Rue des Petits-Haudriettes. Why? He would have been incapable of explaining—for he had often sought fortune in stranger places. That day, abruptly, without a reason, he had the presentiment that he was entering into an adventure—and that was a delight to him, and a long, long tickle of pleasure.

The window-haunter who had signaled to him lodged on the third floor. From the first step to the fifty-sixth—he counted them—his emotion only increased, and when he arrived on the landing, his heart was beating at a hectic pace. At the same time, the further up he went, he had breathed in a very particular odor, becoming stronger and stronger. While enumerating the steps, he had tried to analyze that odor, without being able to determine anything but its species.

"It reeks of the hospital. That's curious! I've smelled it before somewhere."

The door on the left at the end of the third-floor corridor opened slightly as he set foot on the landing, and the woman said to him in a soft voice: "Come in, my little man."

A gust of the reek leapt to his nostrils through the door, opened wide to let him in, and suddenly he cried:" Ah! I've got it now! How stupid I am! It's easily recognizable—it's phenol, of course!"

"Of course," the woman replied. "Don't you like it, my dear? It's very hygienic, you know!"

She was by no means ugly, the woman, although a trifle mature. She had particularly beautiful eyes, careworn and sad—and that gave a special piquancy of strangeness to the vague smile that she tried to sketch in order to appear more welcoming.

Under the influence of the presentiment that he had had a little while before, and gripped once again by the most beautiful of his romantic imaginations, the man began to think, delighted by the idea: *I see! She's a widow forced by poverty to sell herself.*

The lodgings were small, very neatly kept—not without a hint of coquetry, even—which confirmed his supposition. He visited the three rooms one after another, in sequence. The bedroom was the first; then came a sort of small drawing room; then a dining room that must also have served as a kitchen, for the middle was occupied by a Flemish stove on which a thin soup was simmering. The soup smelled very good, in truth, and yet, it was in that room that the smell of phenol was strongest. He remarked on that, and added cheerfully: "Aha! Do you put it in the grub, then?"

While laughing he had put his hand on the brass handle of a glazed door. He wanted to see everything, including that corner, which, according to appearances, must be some kind of lumber-room."

"Oh! No, no, my dear! Not there! Not there! You can't!"

The woman had grabbed him, and was pulling him back violently.

"What, I can't?" he replied, his desire to go in becoming stronger—and, with an abrupt gesture, he opened the glazed door. The odor of phenol lashed him in the face. He recoiled.

On a little iron-framed bed, he had just seen a corpse—a child's corpse—fantastically illuminated by a candle. Frightened, he turned to flee.

"Stay, stay, I beg you, my little man!"

And, in a deluge of tears, she told him that it was the child of a friend of hers, who had died six months ago, and that he had been there for two days, and that there was no money in the house for burial expenses. Ten francs! Only another ten francs was needed!"

"Ten francs! That's all. Don't go, my dear. Stay. You'll see how nice I can be."

"Oh, no," he said. "I'll give you the ten francs—but stay, no, never in this life."

On the threshold, however, he reflected. He was about to lose ten francs. The woman, in sum, was plying her trade bravely. What harm was there, after all, in taking advantage of her kind disposition? And then again, it certainly wasn't bourgeois! Whimsy, the unexpected...

"Listen," he said, turning round, in a tremulous voice. "What if, instead of ten francs, I gave you...twenty. Then you'd be able to buy flowers, wouldn't you?"

"That's true! That's true!" said the unfortunate woman, her face lighting up with joy. "You'll really give me twenty francs?"

"Oh yes," he replied, in a light tone. "That depends on you, my dear." And, while rubbing his hands, he added, as an aside, while swelling with pride internally: "That's all right; as I've always said, I'm an honest man!"

A Monster[63]

The tent, lamentable, as if ashamed of its poverty, was situated at the very end of the fairground, in the unfrequented place where the cheapest pitch is. Its only lighting was two meager oil-lamps with smoky flames, tremulous and reeking. In their ruddy light, as well as a fog, figures whose covers had faded to a phantasmal gray were dancing on a canvas sign. One could make out there—or, rather, divine—a kind of Quasimodo with amputated forearms, sitting with short frogs' legs folded over his torso, and, fanned out around him, with admiring faces, a worker, a peasant, a nurse with a babe in arms, a lady in evening dress with her neckline plunging to the navel, a gentleman, stiff in his frock-coat, and a marshal of France with a huge sash. Almost as vague and faded as the individuals in the painting, in threadbare costumes and darned leotards beneath smocks with no determinable color, four specters of female appearance were performing a semblance of a parade in front of the poor entrance, their feet in the mud, their melancholy gazes searching the shadows in which no passers-by paused in temptation.

And who the Devil, in fact, except for some curiosity-seeker of poverty and lover of the wretched, could have been attracted by the promises of such a calamitous sign, by the sad lamps like the dim candles of a funeral crypt, and especially, most of all, by the four wretched women shivering in masculine overcoats and ugly, with an ugliness not conducive to laughter but to tears? For in truth, tears came to the eyes in contemplating their attempted parade, the oldest one drumming muffled sobs on a crate, another shaking a sniffling hand-bell, the third drawing croaking hiccups from the death-

---

[63] *Gil Blas*, 5 November 1889.

throes of a wheezy accordion, while the youngest sketched dance-steps with the slowness of a ghost stretching its limbs.

And every evening for a week, it was the same thing. Every evening I found myself there again, alone, or very nearly, in front of the lamentable tent, into which I penetrated as tumultuously as possible, trying to draw in by my example the two baldies and a boy that my tenacious halt sometimes caused to halt. Yes, two baldies and a boy, no more! For we had never had five spectators in total, in spite of the hoarse cries of the woman who shouted: "Roll up, Mesdames et Messieurs, roll up! Follow the crowd!"

And yet, he was worth the trouble of being seen, the Quasimodo advertised by the calamitous sign. He was a brave monster, who did his best to please the public, and who gave us—the four of us—more than our money's worth, for sure, and every bit as much as if each of had been the very marshal of France painted on the calamitous sign.

With his two stubs without forearms, the elbows of which had been replaced by a single finger without phalanges, he poured a drink and drank, sliced bread and ate, threaded a needle and sowed, loaded a rifle and shot an apple set on the head of one of his children, like William Tell. With his frogs' legs, folded over his torso, which were only flexible between the knee and the ankle, he leapt on to a table-top, where he steadied himself with a thrust of his stumps. To finish off, the ghost and he danced a pantomime ballet of Beauty and the Beast, during which he sometimes made swimming motions, sometimes hopped on his limp legs like a lame insect, and sometimes balanced upside-down on his head and his two fingers, and then righted himself with a carp-like somersault that smashed his backside on the floor with a brutal and crushing shock, making one think that he was about to be entirely flattened, his hips broken, his head staved into his breast, his muscles and entrails collapsing.

And all that, the poor monster, with his poor old man's body, with the beard and hair of an apostle, white and venerable.

Needless to say—isn't it?—instead of the four sous requested, two for the first performance and two for the second, I gave the monster a silver coin every evening, and gave another silver coin to the plaintive ghost who mumbled afterwards, so lugubriously, while sticking a battered iron cup under your nose: "Don't forget my little tip"—so often and so handsomely that one day the honest monster felt the need to demonstrate his gratitude, and, no longer contenting himself with the habitual *thank you*, added, with an emotional expression: "You, Monsieur, are indeed a connoisseur."

I replied to the compliment, that being what it was, with another. A conversation began. Sympathy grew. I could do no less than water it with a good liter. One liter led to another. After the third, the monster confided his troubles to me.

"No, I've had bad luck. Bad luck, more bad luck and more bad luck, that's been my life—and yet, in the name of God, I've had everything necessary for success." So saying, he pointed to his stumps and legs. "Damn it, yes—everything necessary! Weedy legs such as are scarcely ever seen, and wings that one can't see at all. Only, you see, I've been a gourmand. Ambitious, see! I imagined that with a wife of my sort, we'd have kids like I don't know what—choice phenomena, that could make hundreds or thousands. So I set up house with Naïde. Perhaps you saw her once, Naïde, the big Zénaïde, whom they called the Venus-trunk. A cripple, but a perfect cripple, with neither arms nor legs?"

"No, I only knew Césarine, the broad-backed Venus."

"Oh yes, a silly thing. She had arms—but Naïde had nothing by way of arms: two little fins at the shoulders, nothing more. And as for anything behind, no deal! A behind, but no tail. Buttocks, a point, that that's all."

The monster's eyes misted over with affectionate memory; then he continued, his face suddenly changing expression, and becoming bitter: "The bitch, all the same. Built like that, who could have told me that she'd deceive me?"

I adopted the compassionate expression that a cuckold's confidence required. He understood, and cried excitedly: "No,

279

no, she didn't deceive me the way you think. She was a virtuous woman, you know, Naïde. She loved me as much as I loved her. We never cheated on one another, either of us, I can assure you of that. Where she let me down was with regard to the kids, you see. Six we had, in six years and all six undamaged, like everybody in the world. Isn't that bad luck? No, but, in God's name, isn't it, though, bad luck?"

He thought he could read some sort of reproach in my gaze, criticizing the stubbornness of his attempts.

"I can see," he said, "that you want to know why I persisted. I'll tell you. Between the first and the second, there was a stillbirth of an abortion—you know, of a kid with her mother's fundament. That's why I persisted. We always had the hope of another kid like that one, who might have lived. Oh, he would have been a gift, that one! He would have consoled us somewhat for all the others."

I suggested that the others seemed to me to be behaving as good children for their father, and that therefore...

"Good, good!" he cried. "You think so! Yes, for sure, they're not bad girls. You've seen them at work; they do what they can—but wait a minute. You'll judge in time. Let me finish the story of Naïde. In spite of everything, she and I couldn't get by. We were a fine couple, unmatched, and when people had looked at us, they didn't regret their entrance money. Well, come the seventh childbirth, she left me. Kicked the bucket! Died! Goodnight Venus-Trunk. And I was left alone, all alone with six good-for-nothings on my hands."

And he raised his crippled arms to the heavens, his courageous stumps—and I swear that the baroque image had nothing ridiculous about it at that moment.

"But that wasn't my last stroke of bad luck," he went on. "Here's the kicker. I'm obstinate, I don't deny it. One can't remake oneself, can one? So, when my eldest daughter was eighteen—you know, the one who beats the drum at the door,[64] I recovered my confidence. It seems, so I've been told, that hunchbacks skip a generation. So I thought that my daughter might have kids like my wife and Bibi, and to be surer that she might, or at least something approaching, I married her to a chap who'd been born with one leg. She didn't love him, but she consented all the same. She isn't stupid. She understood that it was necessary, to pick us up of the floor."

"Well," I said, "if you don't find that obliging, you're very difficult to please. It seems to me that that's a daughter such as one rarely sees."

"Her!" he cried, furious. "Her! Oh, the cow! But wait, I tell you, wait! Or rather, come and judge with your own eyes—you'll see whether she's obliging, the mare! Come see the rotten children that it amuses her to make—and two at a time, you hear, in twos! Yes, twins every time, Monsieur! Two a year ago and two a fortnight ago! Come and see, it's worth the trouble!"

He was drunk, and angry, and the wine he'd drunk had brought back all his misfortunes as he related them to me.

He had grabbed my hand with his solitary finger, and, hanging from the end of my arm, supporting himself with his free stump on the ground, he dragged me out of the wine-tent with convulsive bounds.

In a few bounds we had crossed the causeway and climbed the five steps of his tent.

Underneath it, sheltered from the wind as well as possible by a raged tarpaulin, lying pell-mell in the straw, his six daughters were snoring. Inside the caravan there was a bed on which I saw by the light of a burning candle, four children asleep, two at the foot and two at the head.

He lifted up the blanket gently, and said to me, in a soft whisper, so as not to wake them; "Hey? These piglets—do you thinks that's funny? Not a single cripple, damn it—not one!

---

[64] This phrase, which I have translated literally, contains an untranslatable double meaning referring metaphorically to solicitation by prostitutes.

All complete! And they've taken my bed, too! Yes, I sleep on the floor, there, in a corner, in order to give my place to those muffs!"

At that moment the two smallest ones stirred and began to mewl, reaching out their arms as if toward their nurse.

"There, there!" said the monster. "You'll be served, lazybones! Yes, Monsieur, I have to be their servant too. The mother has no milk, the sacred cow! So I'm the one who..."

He placed in each of their mouths, with infinite precaution, a bottle with a teat made of a piece of rubber—a bottle he had probably made himself, with his two stumps!"

"And real good milk," he said. "Expensive milk! Milk that costs me four sous for half a liter. Milk for rich folk! And you ought to see them lying on their stomachs, the little sluts!"

Gently, coaxingly, maternally, he lifted up the bottles with his two charitable stumps, and his face lit up in the ecstasy of a doting grandpapa, and he turned toward me, his eyes moist and affectionate, and added with a tender smile:

"Damn! What can you do? One can't let them starve, poor mites, just because they have all their limbs, ruined like angels."

The Two Gwaz

When one asks the honest folk of Ploubaznaëc where the finest lobsters in the world are to be found, the honest folk of Ploubaznaëc are in accord in replying to you immediately, without the slightest hesitation: "The finest lobsters in the world are to be found in Ploubaznaëc.

And when one asks the good folk of Ploubaznaëc were the finest lobsters in Ploubaznaëc are to be found, the good folk of Ploubaznaëc are similarly in accord in answering, just as immediately, and without the slightest hesitation, exactly as before: "The finest lobsters in Ploubaznaëc are to be found between the rocks known as the Hatchets of Ploubaznaëc, at the exact spot where the eddies in the narrows form the whirlpool known as the Funnel of Ploubaznaëc.

It is exactly as if the good folk of Ploubaznaëc were in accord in declaring to you that the finest lobsters in Ploubaznaëc only exist in their imagination, and in the state of legendary lobsters, because the Devil knows that it is humanly impossible to set lobster-pots in the Funnel of Ploubaznaëc. Does not one have to maintain, within sight of the Hatchets, a distance of at least two hundred fathoms, in order to avoid the furious currents that drag you into it; is it not the case that on seeing the furious foam of the whirlpool from afar, and hearing its formidable roaring from a respectable distance, one is convinced that no one in the world has ever gone to fish there, not even thought of fishing there, for the finest lobsters in Ploubaznaëc?

And yet, when anyone says that to the good folk of Ploubaznaëc, the good folk of Ploubaznaëc are still in accord in immediately replying, still without the slightest hesitation, of course: "No one in the world, it's true, always excepting the two Gwaz."

And, as the good folk of Ploubaznaëc are all very proud of possessing the two Gwaz, and very jealous of the two Gwaz, they will leave you flat in that regard, enjoying your admiration for Ploubaznaëc, its funnel, its lobsters and its two Gwaz, but without wanting to give you the slightest hint of further information about the two Gwaz, no matter how much desire you manifest to known more, in order to admire even more the two Gwaz, and especially the lobsters—the finest lobsters in Ploubaznaëc, and, in consequence, the finest lobsters in the entire world.

By virtue of patient cunning, nevertheless, and by means of numerous cups of ingeniously-offered eau-de-vie, I ended up obtaining certain circumstantial details about the two Gwaz—these, for example, which seem to me to be rather precious, although contradictory.

"The two Gwaz are fine seamen, first-rate sailors."

"The two Gwaz are idiots, who know nothing, twice over."

"The two Gwaz have a boat that has the Devil at the tiller."

"The two Gwaz have a clapped-out boat that doesn't like the water."

"The two Gwaz go out in all weathers, no matter what."

"The two Gwaz only go out on moonless nights."

And finally, I was given one final item of information, summarizing all the others very well, it seemed to me, put providing very little enlightenment.

"The two Gwaz, in sum, are the two Gwaz."

That was all well and good, undoubtedly, but I would have much preferred to see for myself, with my own eyes, the two Gwaz in the flesh and blood, and question them about the famous lobsters. But to see them, the two extraordinary Gwaz, no one wanted to furnish me the opportunity, in spite of all my cunning and all my cups of eau-de-vie. When I mentioned that to the good folk of Ploubaznaëc, the good folk of Ploubaznaëc were, more than ever, in accord in giving me no answer at all, and putting on a semblance of not even understanding what I was asking.

I was reduced to trying to recognize the two Gwaz in the harbor, by means of the very vague description I had. Imagining them to be young fellows, bold and adventurous, I searched among men of that sort, of which there was no lack in Ploubaznaëc, but I searched in vain. There were too many of them!

For want of the fellows themselves, perhaps, at least, I would be lucky enough to recognize their boat, which had to be a marvelous boat in order to brave the interval between the Hatches and the terrors of the Funnel—but all the boats on Ploubaznaëc are, as everyone knows, marvelous boats. And in that direction too, my investigation drew a blank.

Despairing of the cause, I had given up on seeing the two Gwaz when, one evening, on the quay, I heard a nearby urchin saying: "Look! The two Gwaz' boat no longer has its boom."

There was only one single boat in the harbor whose boom had, in fact, been broken off at the stem. I stood there, amazed that that was the two Gwaz' boat, for it was an antique carcass, patched up with summary caulkings, and of which there certainly remained less wood than oakum filling up the holes. To go out to sea in that was no longer audacity but folly, for sure!

Suddenly, my desire to make the acquaintance of the two Gwaz was transformed, quite simply, into a frenzy.

"Ah!" I said to the urchin. "So they have boat as old as Methuselah, the two Gwaz!"

"Well," he replied, "they might well have, since they are."

I fell off my perch. What! The two Gwaz weren't young men, then? At hazard, playing it false in order to discover the truth, and pretending that I knew the two Gwaz, I said, negligently; "Bah! They're not as old as that, the two Gwaz, not so very old!"

"Oh," the urchin retorted, "the two Gwaz are certainly in the hundred and eighties at least, if not more, between them."

"Continuing the pretence, I insinuated that I didn't believe it."

"Come on!" said the child. "But the wife alone is over ninety-five."

The wife! He really had said "the wife!" The two Gwaz were, therefore, the couple Gwaz—there was a female Gwaz! And they were two nonagenarians, one of whom went out on that piece of rotten wood to plant lobster-pots in the interval between the Hatchets, in the monstrous whirlpool of the Funnel of Ploubaznaëc!

I was alone on the quay with the child. I put a handful of silver coins into his hand and I said, combining persuasion and threat: "Show me the two Gwaz and all that is yours. If you don't show them to me I'll take it back and clip you round the ear, hard enough to make your bones smoke."

It was cowardly, I agree. Too bad! I wanted to know the two Gwaz. Put yourself in my place!

"Look," said the urchin. "There they are, the two Gwaz. They're coming along the jetty—and they have a real one today: a lobster! Just look at that lobster!"

Two individuals were, indeed, coming along the jetty, carrying a big basket in which an enormous lobster was tied up, which appeared to me to be nearly a meter long. But fantastic as the animal was, the fishers were more fantastic still, similarly dressed in yellow waxed jackets, with sou-wester hoods, dungarees, shod in sabot-boots, all worn-out, tanned, patched, wrinkled and curled up—but not as much as their faces, however, which also resembled one another, the color of smoked herring marinated in tobacco-juice, absolutely hairless, no longer having anything alive but very bright small eyes and a little pipe smoking between the nose and the chin.

"They're still drunk, the two Gwaz," said the urchin. "Damn! Every time they go out there they both come back with their liter of eau-de-vie inside them. And to think that they've been doing it for seventy years!"

But I was no longer listening. I only had need of one single item of information about the two Gwaz—one alone, which I demanded almost with rage.

"Which of the two is the woman?"

The urchin had leapt away from me. From afar he looked at me, winked at me, and replied: "Come on—you know very well!"

And as the good folk of Ploubaznaëc are malicious, with their foolish expressions, and as the child was the fine flower of the good folk of Ploubaznaëc, he added, with a burst of laughter:

"It's the other one!"

A Confession

"Oh, my poor dear child, you don't know what you're giving up in not being Catholic—what profound, original, complex joys, what an ever-renewed spice seasoning this exceedingly insipid life, what strange pepper for the passions, and, while awaiting the angelic paradise possible of attainment in the other world, what diabolical paradises in this one!"

In the era when the Comte de Myers said that to me, in the manner of an old Thiérachian aristocrat, who was then sixty years old, I was too young a man myself to understand. Freshly molded by my philosophical studies, very proud of my independent atheism, I baulked at any attempt to lead me to religious faith. And that, and no more, is what I saw in the *ad hominem* argument with which the cunning old man—I thought, suspiciously—was trying to indoctrinate me.

I only realized much later what he meant at that time; and perhaps I would still be unaware of it if I hadn't subsequently learned, thanks to a hazard of posthumous indiscretion, the extraordinary history of that singular Catholic.

At that time, moreover, I confess—having not yet acquired the habit of reading people between the lines—I could scarcely imagine that the gentleman in question, a simply country landowner with a banal, regular, narrowly devoted appearance, could have been the hero of a novel by Barbey d'Aurevilly.

Such was the truth, however. Who would have suspected it?

"Me, my lad! And from the first day when our master came back to settle here, without his wife and alone with his son."

But it's necessary to say that the man replied to me thus, twenty years later, was not a fugitive from college; it was my

288

old friend the Borgnot,[65] a fine Thiérachian rogue, a mole-catcher, poacher, smuggler and bone-setter, whose one little eye was able to drill into hearts merely by looking at your sideways, and whose two big hairy ears stored away all the gossip in the region—including, he claimed, to the secrets of the confessional.

That that pretention was justified, in truth, I couldn't doubt, given the revelations he made to me, and which must have been made to him. By whom, if not the confessor *in extremis* of the Comte de Myers? But how did he, the Borgnot, come to be acquainted, and so closely, with the Capuchin missionary who had assisted the Comte de Myers on his death-bed? That's what the Borgnot did not tell me.

"All good-for-nothings are friends with one another."

I could get no more out of him. Make of that what you will. Anyway, what does it matter? The essential thing is that the story should be a good one—and I think it is.

When the monk, who came to preach the Lenten fast at Vervins, arrived at the beside of the dying man, after five hours rising a cart through back-roads, his first words were: "Why did you sent to fetch me the very man who was the original cause of all the misfortunes that have fallen on your house?"

To which the Comte de Myers replied, with the curt tranquility of someone who still had a soul securely wedged in his moribund body: "Because I was sure that he alone, the Borgnot, could convince you to come here with him, because I knew that you would recognize him, without having seen him, by virtue of what my son has told you about him."

He pronounced the words "my son" in an ironic tone, and then added: "My son, or rather, as you're not unaware, that man's son."

The monk could not help shuddering at those words, and said: "How do you know about my relationship as priest to penitent with the Vicomte de Myers, and especially what I

---

[65] The nickname signifies "the One-eyed."

learned from him in confession? Have you called me here, in sum, to confess me in my turn, or to confess yourself?"

The monk's tone was harsh, almost malevolent, but the old man did not appear to notice it, and continued in a perfectly calm voice: "I called you here, Reverend Father, to hear my own confession before dying, and to receive from your own hands the absolution that I believe I have deserved. You alone, in fact, can give me that in full knowledge of the case. You have heard the Vicomte de Myers, I know, at the tribunal of penitence. You shall hear me there likewise, and in my final hour. You will then have the competence required to judge me. I am relying on your warrant to appear pure before God,"

To this appeal, made with all desirable unction and humility, the monk could only respond in the affirmative, as his holy ministry obliged him to do, and the dying man began his confession.

"When I acquired the certainty," he said, "of the abominable crime committed by my wife; when I had the proof in my hands of that adultery, perpetrated in such base and atrocious circumstances, I thought I would die of dolor or go mad. So she had profited from my illness to deceive me! And with whom? With that servant, that apprentice gamekeeper, that petty farm-hand, whom she must have debauched. And she was pregnant as a result! And the child she was bearing, who was going to inherit my name, was the fruit of that filthy and crapulous treason! Oh, I confess, the first thought that occurred to me was to take my revenge, to punish her, to obliterate that infamous past and that ignoble future with a legitimate murder. Tell me, Reverend Father, according to human law, did I not have the right?"

"According to divine law," the monk replied, "you had only the duty to forgive."

"That is what I did," the old man continued, insistently. "I did not, in fact, kill. I did not even make anything manifest—neither my torments not my righteous indignation. No one in the world could have suspected that I knew anything at all. That was more than forgiveness, it seems to me. It was more like absolute forgetfulness."

"You have not forgotten, though," the monk put in.

"I admit it," said the Comte de Myers, with a bitter smile and a pale gleam in the depths of his bleak eyes. "No, I have not forgotten. I have not yet forgotten—but I have avenged myself, in my fashion, by respecting divine law and simply letting things follow their fatal course according to human law."

"You have aided them in that," said the monk, violently.

"That," the dying man replied, "is undoubtedly the Vicomte's opinion. Permit me to enlighten yours. If I had not been the fervent Catholic that I am, what would I have done, I pray you, to avenge myself on the worthy mother through her son? I would have devoted all my efforts to developing in that son the perverse instincts of his bad blood. I have, on the contrary, applied myself to their inhibition. I have provided that son with a perfect Christian education. I have wanted him not only to be an honest man, but almost a saint. And I have succeeded in that. He is one. Is that true?"

"It's true," said the monk. "He is that. But what about her?"

"Her," the old man said ferociously, "I have abandoned to her vices, allowing her to seek the opportunities to do so. Of that, yes, I accuse myself. Certainly, there was some fault of mine in her progressive fall. I sinned by tolerance toward the filthiest needs of her nature. I closed my eyes to her excesses, more monstrous from day to day. I have, besides, submitted to punishment, in allowing her to drag my name into the ultimate mire of ignominy into which she has fallen. Ought my sin, in that regard, not be remitted, since I have done penitence so bitterly, by virtue of the shame of accepting that my wife, the Comtesse de Myers, first became an adulteress publicly known as such, then a veritable courtesan, then a member of the old guard of Parisian gallantry, and finally what she is today: a horrible and repulsive prostitute of the lowest kind?"

"Let God judge what you have done there!" the monk replied. "Only he can know whether the penitence was cruel enough to redeem your crime. To me, it seems obvious that you are still delighting in that crime. At least you enjoyed it with the most implacable cruelty on the day when you told the Vicomte de Myers that he was not your son, and that he was the adulterous bastard of the Borgnot, and that he had for a mother that hideous corruption whose abomination you have tenaciously and cleverly desired, prepared and intended."

The Comte de Myers propped himself up on his elbow. His gaze was fiery. His bitter smile had constructed into a bestial rictus. His hoarse voice, between bouts of coughing, articulated these words: "Things have followed and are following their fatal course. Let the saint, now, come to terms with the corruption! Let him extract what he ought to extract from that impact between the son and the mother! Let them find their hell there, in this world and the next! It no longer has anything to do with me. For myself, if I have sinned, I repent of it. For myself, I have confessed. For myself, I request, I demand, absolution."

In a rude fashion, the monk shouted full into his face: "Since you want someone to forgive you, say that you have forgiven. No, no, I can see that even at this moment, even with the certainty, if you do not forgive, of being eternally damned, you still do not forgive."

"Well, no," retorted the dying man. "No, I don't forgive. I can't forgive. If I said that I forgive, I'd be lying, and for that lie, I'd be damned anyway. But what does damnation matter to me? In eternal torment, the idea that I do not forgive will be an eternal relief to me."

And the Comte de Myers died, murmuring with an ecstatic blissfulness: "Be blessed, my God, for having maintained that consoling faith in my heart!"

Thus was related to me, by the Borgnot, who laughed at it, the demise of the Comte de Myers. Thus was the extraordinary history of that singular Catholic made known to me. And only then did I take account of the Barbey d'Aurevilly hero that that simple country landowner, apparently banal, conventional and strictly devoted, had really been. And then, too, I was able to understand what he had once tried to tell me, in his own manner, of an old gentleman of Thiérache.

And although I have remained a very hardened miscreant, I sometimes feel envious of that happy believer, whose life must have tasted such diabolical paradises, as he put it, and whose death had been that minute of intense life, at the paroxysm of passion, in the absolute certainty and real sensation of an eternal paradisal Hell.

CHIMERICAL THEATER

The Monster
Academic Session for the Thirty-Somethingth Century

DRAMATIS PERSONAE

The President of the Academy
Doctor Subtil
Sanus
Members of the Academy
A Peevish Member

THE PRESIDENT: Messieurs, the Modern Academy of Physiopsychosociobiological Sciences has convened today to witness the examination and pronouncement on the nature of a curious phenomenon, which our celebrated correspondent member, Doctor Subtil, has discovered in the course of one of his extraordinary voyages, and which he has the honor of presenting to your study. Our eminent colleague has the floor.

SUBTIL: Messieurs, I shall not offer any preliminary theory regarding the teratological case that I have the honor of submitting to you today. The explanation, it seems to me, can only be sought in the most ancient sedimentary alluvia of the most distant atavism. But I have a certain scruple even about suggesting that, and I prefer to refer myself fully to your impartial enlightenment, limiting myself to a methodical interrogation of the subject, whose responses will tell you more than all my commentaries. It goes without saying Messieurs, that each of you is free to ask questions. There is, I pray you to believe, no charlatanism in this.

THE PRESIDENT:
Everyone, my dear colleague, is convinced of that.

THE PEEVISH MEMBER (*aside*): We'll see about that.

SUBTIL: Messieurs, here is the subject. Firstly, with your permission, I shall summarize the information furnished in his regard by the anthropometric bureau. The subject is thirty years old. His height is one meter sixty-five centimeters.

THE PEEVISH MEMBER: Exactly?

SUBTIL: A few millimeters more.

THE PEEVISH MEMBER: It's necessary to measure with a Vernier.

THE PRESIDENT: These details really have no importance.

THE PEEVISH MEMBER: Everything has importance. Anyway, let's get on!

SUBTIL: In addition, Messieurs, I'm in haste to proceed to the interrogation, the gravity of which, I believe, will silence all malevolence. I shall begin with nourishment. *(To Sanus)* Tell these Messieurs on what you nourish yourself.

SANUS: On bread, meat, eggs, dairy products, vegetables, fish and fruits.

SUBTIL: You heard, Messieurs.

THE PRESIDENT: We did, indeed hear, but I think I am serving as an interpreter for the entire Academy in saying that we heard without understanding.

THE MEMBERS: That's true, that's true.

THE PEEVISH MEMBER: Personally, I understood—but I think that we're the victims of a hoax.

SUBTIL: Explain yourself.

THE PEEVISH MEMBER: I mean that this is simply an employment of obsolete words, in order to throw dust in our eyes. Can the subject really take these aliments in these barbaric forms, and through the mouth, or is he simply indicating his alimentary bolus, and does he not assimilate it, like everyone else, by means of an enema, through the only nutritive orifice today in use, which is the anus? That is the whole question.

SUBTIL: He eats these things, Monsieur, through the mouth, nothing but the mouth.

THE PEEVISH MEMBER: Get away! That's impossible.

SUBTIL (*to Sanus*): How do you eat? Through the mouth or the anus?

SANUS: Through the mouth, of course!

SUBTIL: Messieurs, that's all I can get him to say.

THE PEEVISH MEMBER (*aside*): There's some confusion here.

SUBTIL (*to Sanus*): Show us how you take it.

SANUS: Oh, that's no trouble. *(He eats.)*

THE MEMBERS: Astonishing! Prodigious!

THE PEEVISH MEMBER *(aside)*: What a conjuring trick!

SUBTIL: Messieurs, he drinks the same way.

THE MEMBERS: What? What?

SUBTIL *(to Sanus)*: What do you drink?

SANUS: Wine; water when I have no wine—but I prefer wine.

THE MEMBERS: Wine? Water? What is he saying?

THE PEEVISH MEMBER *(violently)*: And also by mouth? Not by hypodermic injection?

SANUS: Hypodermic yourself! How do you expect me to drink, idiot?

SUBTIL: Excuse the subject, Messieurs, I pray you. He's often irritable. You can imagine that such anomalies are not unaccompanied by profound mental disturbance. If you want the interrogation to proceed fruitfully, permit me to conduct it gently, as is appropriate with a sick person.

THE PEEVISH MEMBER: Ah! It's obvious now that it's rehearsed!

SUBTIL: Nothing has been rehearsed, my dear colleague, I swear to you. Interrogate him yourself if that offers you more confidence—but again, I pray you, gently. Personally, Messieurs, I have only succeeded in obtaining replies by employing an extreme forbearance, to the point of allowing the subject to treat me as an imbecile and a fool.

THE PEEVISH MEMBER (*aside*): He certainly wasn't wrong!

SANUS: For sure, Doctor, you're a fool and a madman. And all these Messieurs seem to me to be no better than you.

SUBTIL: You see, Messieurs. But the interests of science before all, no? Let that not prevent us from pursuing our studied. *(To Sanus.)* Would you like to tell us, my dear friend, how you understand the genesic function?

SANUS: What?

SUBTIL: In other words, would you be kind enough to explain to these Messieurs that you find the act of copulation with a person of the sex opposite to yours quite natural?

SANUS: Eh? What?

THE PEEVISH MEMBER: Our eminent colleague does not intend, I suppose, to have us believe that his subject practices sexual union in the manner of animals?"

SUBTIL: I do have that intention.

THE MEMBERS: Oh! That's a bit too much!

THE PRESIDENT: I beg our honorable colleague's pardon, but I think I translate the thinking of the entire Academy in affirming that that seems absolutely unworthy of belief. Our honorable colleagues know full well that artificial fertilization alone is natural, today and since time immemorial. He also knows that so-called sensual delights are only admitted, by definitive morality, between individuals of the same sex. The laws of modern society do not tolerate or accommodate any others.

SUBTIL: I'm not unaware of any of that, my dear and illustrious president.

THE PEEVISH MEMBER: But you persist in maintaining that your subject is aberrant to the point of...?

SUBTIL: If not, Messieurs and eminent colleagues, would I have had the audacity to disturb you by promising you the study of an altogether exceptional case? No, no; if I thought that I ought to call your attention to this phenomenon, it's because it really is phenomenally and absolutely abnormal.

THE PEEVISH MEMBER: And he puts this extraordinary theory of bisexualism into practice?

SUBTIL: So he says.

THE PEEVISH MEMBER: Would you like to ask him in what fashion he goes about it?

SUBTIL (*to Sanus*): You heard! Reply, I beg you.

SANUS: Load of imbeciles!

SUBTIL: No, don't get carried away, my friend. There, there—calm down, and have the kindness to reply to us. We're men of science here. We're seeking the truth. We want to learn. We're working for progress. With regard to your means of reproduction, give us a few explanations...

SANUS: Of what? Of how to make love?

SUBTIL: Of how you do it, yes, my friend, of your way, which seems strange to us.

SANUS: How can it be strange? It's the only natural way, that of all animals!

SUBTIL: You see, Messieurs—that's all I can get him to say.

THE MEMBERS: Oh! Oh! Miraculous! Astounding! Amazing!

THE PEEVISH MEMBER: One last question. Does the subject, perhaps, compose verses?

THE MEMBERS: Eh? What did he say? Verses? What's that?

SUBTIL: Indeed, Messieurs, the subject does compose verses.

THE PEEVISH MEMBER: And with what, if you please, does he compose verses?

SUBTIL (*to Sanus*): Yes, with what, my friend, do you compose verses?

SANUS: But with ideas, sentiments, sensations, words, images, rhymes and genius.

THE MEMBERS: Ha ha ha! That's too funny! Ha ha ha ha! Images! Words! Rhymes! Genius! Ha ha ha!

THE PRESIDENT: Messieurs, this general and legitimate hilarity seems to me to resolve the question. Our eminent colleague has done well to consult us as to the nature of the subject he has presented to us. I believe that I am the spokesman for the entire Academy in saying that our religion is now duly enlightened. There can only be one possible opinion on the subject, and I think it is unanimous. This singular product of atavism is...

THE PEEVISH MEMBER: I demand the priority of the observation, and that I be accorded the honor of discovering that it's a...

THE MEMBERS: A monster! A monster! It's a monster!

SUBTIL: Messieurs, I have no more to say.

SF & FANTASY

Henri Allorge. *The Great Cataclysm*
Guy d'Armen. *Doc Ardan: The City of Gold and Lepers*
G.-J. Arnaud. *The Ice Company*
Charles Asselineau. *The Double Life*
Cyprien Bérard. *The Vampire Lord Ruthwen*
Aloysius Bertrand. *Gaspard de la Nuit*
Richard Bessière. *The Gardens of the Apocalypse*
Albert Bleunard. *Ever Smaller*
Félix Bodin. *The Novel of the Future*
Alphonse Brown. *City of Glass*
André Caroff. *The Terror of Madame Atomos; Miss Atomos; The
Return of Madame Atomos; The Mistake of Madame Atomos; The
Monsters of Madame Atomos; The Revenge of Madame Atomos*
Félicien Champsaur. *The Human Arrow; Ouha*
Didier de Chousy. *Ignis*
Captain Danrit. *Undersea Odyssey*
C. I. Defontenay. *Star (Psi Cassiopeia)*
Charles Derennes. *The People of the Pole*
Georges Dodds (anthologist). *The Missing Link*
Harry Dickson. *The Heir of Dracula*
Jules Dornay. *Lord Ruthven Begins*
Alfred Driou. *The Adventures of a Parisian Aeronaut*
Sâr Dubnotal *vs. Jack the Ripper*
Alexandre Dumas. *The Return of Lord Ruthven*
Renée Dunan. *Baal*
J.-C. Dunyach. *The Night Orchid; The Thieves of Silence*
Henri Duvernois. *The Man Who Found Himself*
Achille Eyraud. *Voyage to Venus*
Henri Falk. *The Age of Lead*
Paul Féval. *Anne of the Isles; Knightshade; Revenants; Vampire City;
The Vampire Countess; The Wandering Jew's Daughter*
Paul Féval, *fils. Felifax, the Tiger-Man*
Charles de Fieux. *Lamékis*
Arnould Galopin. *Doctor Omega; Doctor Omega & The Shadowmen*
Léon Gozlan. *The Vampire of the Val-de-Grâce*
G.L. Gick. *Harry Dickson and the Werewolf of Rutherford Grange*
Edmond Haraucourt. *Illusions of Immortality*
Nathalie Henneberg. *The Green Gods*

V. Hugo, P. Foucher & P. Meurice. *The Hunchback of Notre-Dame*
Michel Jeury. *Chronolysis*
Gustave Kahn. *The Tale of Gold and Silence*
Gérard Klein. *The Mote in Time's Eye*
Louis-Guillaume de La Follie. *The Unpretentious Philosopher*
Jean de La Hire. *Enter the Nyctalope; The Nyctalope on Mars; The Nyctalope vs. Lucifer; The Nyctalope Steps In; Night of the Nyctalope*
Etienne-Léon de Lamothe-Langon. *The Virgin Vampire*
André Laurie. *Spiridon*
Gabriel de Lautrec. *The Vengeance of the Oval Portrait*
Alain le Drimeur. *The Future City*
Georges Le Faure & Henri de Graffigny. *The Extraordinary Adventures of a Russian Scientist Across the Solar System* (2 vols.)
Gustave Le Rouge. *The Vampires of Mars The Dominion of the World* (w/Gustave Guitton) (4 vols.)
Jules Lermina. *Mysteryville; Panic in Paris; To-Ho and the Gold Destroyers; The Secret of Zippelius*
Jean-Marc & Randy Lofficier. *Edgar Allan Poe on Mars; The Katrina Protocol; Pacifica; Robonocchio; Tales of the Shadowmen 1-9*
Xavier Mauméjean. *The League of Heroes*
Joseph Méry. *The Tower of Destiny*
Hippolyte Mettais. *The Year 5865*
Louise Michel. *The Human Microbes; The New World*
José Moselli. *Illa's End*
John-Antoine Nau. *Enemy Force*
Marie Nizet. *Captain Vampire*
C. Nodier, A. Beraud & Toussaint-Merle. *Frankenstein*
Henri de Parville. *An Inhabitant of the Planet Mars*
Gaston de Pawlowski. *Journey to the Land of the 4th Dimension*
Georges Pellerin. *The World in 2000 Years*
Ernest Pérochon. *The Frenetic People*
Pierre Pelot. *The Child Who Walked on the Sky*
J. Polidori, C. Nodier, E. Scribe. *Lord Ruthven the Vampire*
P.-A. Ponson du Terrail. *The Vampire and the Devil's Son*
Henri de Régnier. *A Surfeit of Mirrors*
Maurice Renard. *The Blue Peril; Doctor Lerne; The Doctored Man; A Man Among the Microbes; The Master of Light*
Jean Richepin. *The Wing; The Crazy Corner*
Albert Robida. *The Adventures of Saturnin Farandoul; The Clock of the Centuries; Chalet in the Sky*

J.-H. Rosny Aîné. *Helgvor of the Blue River; The Givreuse Enigma; The Mysterious Force; The Navigators of Space; Vamireh; The World of the Variants; The Young Vampire*
Marcel Rouff. *Journey to the Inverted World*
Han Ryner. *The Superhumans*
Brian Stableford. *The New Faust at the Tragicomique;The Empire of the Necromancers (The Shadow of Frankenstein; Frankenstein and the Vampire Countess; Frankenstein in London); Sherlock Holmes & The Vampires of Eternity; The Stones of Camelot; The Wayward Muse.* (anthologist) *The Germans on Venus; News from the Moon; The Supreme Progress; The World Above the World; Nemoville; Investigations of the Future*
Jacques Spitz. *The Eye of Purgatory*
Kurt Steiner. *Ortog*
Eugène Thébault. *Radio-Terror*
C.-F. Tiphaigne de La Roche. *Amilec*
Théo Varlet. *The Golden Rock. The Xenobiotic Invasion; Timeslip Troopers* (w/André Blandin); *The Martian Epic* (w/Octave Joncquel)
Paul Vibert. *The Mysterious Fluid*
Villiers de l'Isle-Adam. *The Scaffold; The Vampire Soul*
Philippe Ward. *Artahe*
Philippe Ward & Sylvie Miller. *The Song of Montségur*

MYSTERIES & THRILLERS

M. Allain & P. Souvestre. *The Daughter of Fantômas*
A. Anicet-Bourgeois, Lucien Dabril. *Rocambole*
A. Bernède. *Belphegor*; *Judex* (w/Louis Feuillade)
A. Bisson & G. Livet. *Nick Carter vs. Fantômas*
V. Darlay & H. de Gorsse. *Lupin vs. Holmes: The Stage Play*
Paul Féval. *Gentlemen of the Night; John Devil; The Black Coats ('Salem Street; The Invisible Weapon; The Parisian Jungle; The Companions of the Treasure; Heart of Steel; The Cadet Gang; The Sword-Swallower)*
Emile Gaboriau. *Monsieur Lecoq*
Goron & Emile Gautier. *Spawn of the Penitentiary*
Steve Leadley. *Sherlock Holmes: The Circle of Blood*
Maurice Leblanc. *Arsène Lupin vs. Countess Cagliostro; Lupin vs. Holmes (The Blonde Phantom; The Hollow Needle); The Many Faces of Arsène Lupin*

Gaston Leroux. *Chéri-Bibi; The Phantom of the Opera; Rouletabille & the Mystery of the Yellow Room Rouletabille at Krupp's*
Richard Marsh. *The Complete Adventures of Judith Lee*
William Patrick Maynard. *The Terror of Fu Manchu; The Destiny of Fu Manchu*
Frank J. Morlock. *Sherlock Holmes: The Grand Horizontals; Sherlock Holmes vs Jack the Ripper*
Antonin Reschal. *The Adventures of Miss Boston*
P. de Wattyne & Y. Walter. *Sherlock Holmes vs. Fantômas*
David White. *Fantômas in America*

SCREENPLAYS

Mike Baron. *The Iron Triangle*
Emma Bull & Will Shetterly. *Nightspeeder; War for the Oaks*
Gerry Conway & Roy Thomas. *Doc Dynamo*
Steve Englehart. *Majorca*
James Hudnall. *The Devastator*
Jean-Marc & Randy Lofficier. *Royal Flush*
J.-M. & R. Lofficier & Marc Agapit. *Despair*
J.-M. & R. Lofficier & Joël Houssin. *City*
Andrew Paquette. *Peripheral Vision*
Robert L. Robinson, Jr. *Judex*
R. Thomas, J. Hendler & L. Sprague de Camp. *Rivers of Time*

NON-FICTION

Stephen R. Bissette. *Blur 1-5. Green Mountain Cinema 1; Teen Angels*
Win Scott Eckert. *Crossovers* (2 vols.)
Jean-Marc & Randy Lofficier. *Shadowmen* (2 vols.)
Randy Lofficier. *Over Here*

HEXAGON COMICS

Franco Frescura & Luciano Bernasconi. *Wampus*
Franco Frescura & Giorgio Trevisan. *CLASH*
L. Bernasconi, J.-M. Lofficier & Juan Roncagliolo Berger. *Phenix*
Claude Legrand, J.-M. Lofficier & L. Bernasconi. *Kabur*

Franco Oneta. *Zembla*
L. Buffolente, Lofficier & J.-J. Dzialowski. *Strangers: Homicron*
Danilo Grossi. *Strangers: Jaydee*
Claude Legrand & Luciano Bernasconi. *Strangers: Starlock*

ART BOOKS

Jean-Pierre Normand. *Science Fiction Illustrations*
Raven Okeefe. *Raven's L'il Critters; Rave's Faves*
Randy Lofficier & Raven Okeefe. *If Your Possum Go Daylight...*
Daniele Serra. *Illusions*